THE LAST WORD

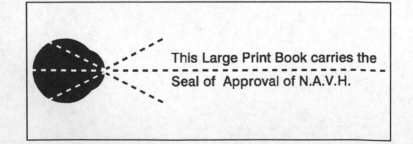

THE LAST WORD

A SPELLMAN NOVEL

LISA LUTZ

THORNDIKE PRESS
A part of Gale, Cengage Learning

GALE
CENGAGE Learning·

Detroit • New York • San Francisco • New Haven, Conn • Waterville, Maine • London

GALE
CENGAGE Learning®

Copyright © 2013 by Spellman Enterprises, Inc.
Thorndike Press, a part of Gale, Cengage Learning.

Thorndike Press® Large Print Core.
The text of this Large Print edition is unabridged.
Other aspects of the book may vary from the original edition.
Set in 16 pt. Plantin.

LIBRARY OF CONGRESS CATALOGING-IN-PUBLICATION DATA

Lutz, Lisa.
    The last word : a Spellman novel / by Lisa Lutz. — Large print edition.
        pages ; cm. — (Thorndike Press large print core)
    ISBN 978-1-4104-6335-7 (hardcover) — ISBN 1-4104-6335-4 (hardcover) 1.
Spellman, Isabel (Fictitious character)—Fiction. 2. Women private
investigators—Fiction. 3. Large type books. I. Title.
PS3612.U897L38 2013b
813'.6—dc23   2013029754

Published in 2013 by arrangement with Simon & Schuster, Inc.

Printed in Mexico
1 2 3 4 5 6 7 17 16 15 14 13

For Ellen Clair Lamb

VOICE MEMO

12:38 A.M.

Can't sleep. Again. The final notice for the electricity bill came today. I shredded it, paid the bill out of pocket, and then shook down a delinquent client by reminding him that company policy is to tell a cheating spouse about an investigation when payment is past due three months. It's never been policy before, but I'm warming up to it.

A fed came to visit today. Bledsoe is his name. Agent Bledsoe. B-l-e-d-s-o-e. He knows about the money. If he has the evidence, I think we could lose the business. Thirty years down the drain because somebody wasn't paying attention. Embezzlement. Of all the stupid things that could take us down. It isn't even enough money to save us.

Some days I wish I weren't the only one doing the fixing. I feel like I'm playing a solo game of toy soldiers with just a few pieces out of my control. Some days I really believe there might be something left to salvage if we know when to call it quits.

Some days I think that this just might be the end.

■ ■ ■ ■

PART I
OPENING
STATEMENTS

SIX WEEKS EARLIER

■ ■ ■ ■

"Boss"

MEMO

```
To All Spellman Employees:
Pants are mandatory.
Footwear is encouraged.
                    Signed,
            The Management
```

Three lazy knocks landed on the door.

"It's open!" I said as I'd been saying for the past three months. I leaned back in my new leather swivel chair. It was less comfortable than you'd expect, but I wasn't letting on.

My father entered the Spellman offices carrying a bowl of oatmeal, topped with a few raisins, walnuts, and honey. I don't have a problem with people eating at work, but I did take issue with his attire — boxer shorts, a wife-beater (the likes of which he hadn't owned until he started wearing his skivvies into the office), and a cardigan that had been feasted on by a hungry moth. I foolishly thought that lowering the thermostat would encourage my father to put on slacks. Live and learn.

The Spellman offices are located on the first floor of my parents' house at 1799 Clay Street in San Francisco, California, a three-story Victorian sitting on the outskirts of Nob Hill. A Realtor would tell you that the house has "good bones" — three floors, four bedrooms, three baths — but everything needs to be updated and the exterior demands a paint job so badly that some of the neighbors have taken to writing *paint me* on our dusty windows. Even a few "anonymous" handwritten letters have arrived from a *concerned neighbor,* but since Dr. Alexander has sent other handwritten missives in the past, his anonymity was lost. Point is, my parents have a nice house in a nice neighborhood that looks like crap from the outside and is not so hot from the inside, and not enough money to do anything about it. I remember the blue trim on the window frames from when I was a child, but I'm not entirely certain that I'd know it was blue now since it's almost gone and the thirty-year-old lead-loaded green paint beneath it is what ultimately shines through.

Those now-retired painters must have been really good.

The office itself is a fourteen-by-twenty-foot room with an ancient steel desk marking each of the four corners. The fifth desk is parked between the two desks with a window view. Perhaps "view" is an overstatement. We look out onto our neighbor's concrete wall and have a slight glimpse into Mr. Peabody's living room, where he sits most of the day, watching television. There's nothing to recommend the décor of the office. The white walls are covered with bulletin boards so tacked over with postcards, notes, memos, cartoons, they resemble the layering of a bird's feathers. The collage of paperwork hasn't been stripped in years. In fact, I wouldn't be surprised if an archeological dig produced data from as far back as 1986. It's not pretty, but you get used to it after a while. The only thing that begs for change is the beige shag carpet, which is so worn down you can slip on it in footwear without treads.

As for my father's extreme casual wear, it would have made sense that my parents might find the home/workspace divide difficult to navigate, but they'd been navigating it just fine for more than twenty years. These wardrobe shenanigans were purely for my benefit.

"What's on the agenda today?" Dad said through a mouthful of steel-cut oats. He shook his computer mouse, rousing his monitor from slumber, and commenced his workday with his new morning ritual: a two-hour game of Plants vs. Zombies.

"Mr. Slayter will be here in an hour, Dad."

"Should I have made extra oatmeal for him?" Dad asked as he planted a row of flowers and a peashooter. I would have used the spud bomb and taken the extra sunlight. But Dad seemed to be doing fine on his own.[1]

"I think Slayter would prefer pants over oatmeal."

"You can't eat pants," Dad said.

The pants conversation would have continued indefinitely if my mother hadn't dipped her head into the doorway and said, "Everybody decent?"

"No, Mom, everybody is not decent," I said.

Then Mom entered, indecently. While less skin was exposed, her sartorial choice was

1 I've probably clocked in a full workweek of Plants vs. Zombies hours, I'm ashamed to say. But Dad played as if he were an employee of Pop-Cap Games.

perhaps even more perplexing. Her hair, coiled in plastic curlers, was imprisoned in a net that she must have stolen from Grammy Spellman. She wore a housecoat pockmarked with daisies and pink fluffy slippers on her feet. I had not seen this outfit before, and were we at a Halloween party, I might have found it mildly amusing. My mother, at sixty, is one of those classic beauties, all neck and cheekbones, sharp lines that hide her wrinkles from a distance. She still gets whistles from construction workers from three stories up. With her long bottled auburn hair flowing behind her, a carnival guesser wouldn't come within a decade of her birth date. Although today, in curlers, she was looking more like her true age.

"Mom, those curlers must have taken you hours."

"You have no idea," she said, easing into her chair, spent from the chore. I would bet my entire share of the company that Mom hadn't used curlers since her senior prom.

We'd never had a dress code before all the trouble began[2] and it was foolish of me to think that a memo posted on bulletin boards scattered throughout the house

2 I'll explain all that later.

would have any impact. But I think it's important to note that the dress code was perhaps one of the least ambitious dress codes that ever existed in an office setting.

And to further illustrate my laissez-faire management protocol, I even instituted pajama Fridays (so long as a client meeting was not on the books). The next Friday Mom showed up in a muumuu and a turban, resembling Gloria Swanson in *Sunset Boulevard,* and Dad slipped on his swim trunks and a wool scarf (I was still keeping the thermostat low, stupidly certain of an auspicious result).

For more than three months I had been president and primary owner of Spellman Investigations, and I can say with complete certainty that I had more power in this office as an underling. My title, it seemed, was purely decorative. I was captain of an unfashionable and sinking ship.

Edward Slayter, the man responsible for my position at my family's firm — and for close to 20 percent of Spellman Investigations' income — was coming in for a ten o'clock meeting. I had to get my parents either out of the office or into suitable clothing in less than twenty minutes.

Just then Demetrius entered in a tweed coat and a bow tie. While I appreciated the effort he put into his attire, I had to wonder whether this was his own form of self-expression or an act of mild derision.

"Demetrius, you look great. I guess you saw the memo."

"It was hard to miss," D said.

"That was the point," I said, glaring at my parents. Twenty-five posters on the interior and exterior of the house. If they opened the refrigerator, used the restroom, opened their desk drawers, or took a nap,[3] they couldn't have missed it. "Why are you rocking the bow tie, D? This is new."

"I'm going to San Quentin this afternoon to interview an inmate for Maggie on a potential wrongful-conviction case."

Maggie is my sister-in-law, married to my brother David. She is a defense attorney who devotes 25 percent of her practice to pro bono wrongful-incarceration cases. Demetrius, having once benefited from Maggie's pro bono work, regularly assists her with those cases. Because we believe in the work that Maggie is doing, we help out when time allows, and even when time doesn't allow. I'd like to think that if I were in prison for a crime I didn't commit,

3 Put one in large print on the ceiling of my parents' bedroom.

someone would be trying to get me the hell out of there.

"That's great. Still doesn't explain the bow tie."

"I'm not wearing a slipknot in a maximum-security prison."

"Excellent point. Speaking of nooses," I said, turning to my parents. The clock was ticking. "What will it take to get you to change into real clothes and lose the hair accessories?"

"These curlers took *three* hours," Mom said.

I really couldn't have my first Slayter/unit meeting under these circumstances.

"I have an idea," I said. "Why don't you go back to bed?"

"I'm hungry," Dad said.

I turned to D, the de facto chef, for assistance.

"I'll make some pancakes and bring them up," he said.

Mom and Dad filed out of the office.

"See you tomorrow," Mom said.

I wish I could say that this was an unusual workday, but that was not the case. I wish I could say this sort of negotiation was uncommon; also not true. The worst part: I had to consider this a win.

Not-So-Hostile Takeover

It happens all the time. One company is struggling and another company buys that company, and it thrives. Or one company puts itself up for sale and accepts the best offer. Or in a smaller, family-run company, it can go like this: One member of the family-owned company buys (through a wealthy proxy) the shares of her two siblings and becomes the primary shareholder of the company, in essence the owner, blindsiding the previous owners, who happen to be her parents. This isn't the first time in the history of family-owned businesses that there has been conflict among the filial ranks. Although one could argue that our conflict was strangely unique.

But I'm already getting ahead of myself, so please indulge me briefly for a quick refresher on all things Spellman.[4]

I'll start with a name. Mine. Isabel Spellman. I'm thirty-five, single, and I live in my brother's basement apartment. If I were a man, you'd assume there was something wrong with me, like a porn or video game addiction or some kind of maladaptive social disorder. But I'm a woman, and so

4 For brief dossiers on family members and a few other relevant parties, see appendix.

automatically the response is pity. Let's remember something here: I am the president, CEO, and probably CFO[5] of Spellman Investigations Inc., a relatively successful private investigative firm in the great metropolis of San Francisco. I am the middle child of Albert and Olivia Spellman, the ill-dressed people you met three and four pages ago. There are other things that you'll need to know eventually, like I have an older brother, David (an occasional lawyer and full-time father to his daughter, Sydney); a sister-in-law, Maggie, the defense attorney I just mentioned; and a much younger sister, Rae, twenty-two, a recent graduate from UC Berkeley, which makes me the only Spellman spawn without a college degree. But, hey, who owns this sinking ship? As for Rae, it would be difficult to reduce her essence to a few sentences, so I'll save her for later and leave the essence-reducing to you. I also have a grandmother who lives within walking distance. You'll meet her soon enough. There's no point in rushing that introduction.

There are two other Spellman Investigations employees worth mentioning. Foremost, Demetrius Merriweather, the bow-

5 Why not?

tied fellow you just met. D, as we call him, is a complex, multifaceted human being, but if you had to describe him in an elevator ride, this is what you'd say: 1) He spent fifteen years in prison for a crime he didn't commit. 2) He's a freaking unbelievably great chef and shares his gift with anyone in the vicinity. 3) He doesn't take sides. 4) He really doesn't like snitching, but he understands the value of the subtle dissemination of information under a specific set of circumstances. He's also been employee of the month for the past twelve months.

If you were to find yourself alone in a parking garage with him, you wouldn't automatically assume ex-con. He doesn't possess any identifying prison tattoos; he doesn't have the hardened look of a man who spent fifteen years behind bars, although he's not a small man — six-two, softer in the middle than when he first got out, because he has other pastimes besides going to the prison gym, and his favorite hobby is cooking, and there are more ingredients on the outside than the inside. He's black. Did I mention that? He has a few freckles, like Morgan Freeman, but the resemblance ends there. Unfortunately. He shaves his head, not because he's going bald, but because the look works on him.

He can look intimidating sometimes, but when he smiles he has these ridiculous dimples. They're adorable. But you never want to call an ex-con "adorable" no matter how harmless he is. And the truth is, I doubt D is all that harmless. He was in prison for fifteen years. You're going to tell me he never got in a fight? I've asked (repeatedly); he just doesn't answer.

And, finally, our part-time employee, Vivien Blake. A college coed who used to be the subject of an investigation, but we've never been good with boundaries, so now she works for us. Something about Vivien reminds me of the old me: a recklessness, a history of inappropriate behavior, a penchant for vandalism. Some years back Vivien managed to steal an entire fleet of golf carts from Sharp Park Golf Course in Pacifica and relocate them to a cow pasture ten miles away. I've asked her at least twenty times how she managed to do it, and she refuses to reveal her professional secrets. The seventeen-year-old delinquent who still resides somewhere deep in my core has profound respect for that.

Vivien has only just returned from one month abroad in Ireland. She was supposedly taking a four-week intensive summer course on James Joyce's *Ulysses* at Trinity

College, but I noticed that when my sister pressed her on the details Vivien only mentioned castles and pubs and a walking tour of Joycean Dublin, which Rae said was totally open to the public.

Viv has taken some time settling back into San Francisco life. The last time I saw her she was in the midst of a heated phone call that might have suggested she was working in the drug trade (and completely unconcerned with wiretaps): "Where is my stuff? The delivery was supposed to happen five days ago. I've called you every day since then and you say it will be the next day and every day I wait around like some patsy and it never shows. I should charge you for my time. My rate is twenty-five dollars an hour. I've now waited over twenty hours. So, let's see, you owe me at least a thousand dollars.[6] You will not get away with this. I know people. I know terrifying people, people who have done time,[7] the kind of people who make weapons out of soap. Why do they make weapons out of soap? Isn't it obvious? What are you, an idiot? Because if you murder someone with a sharpened

6 Her math gets iffy when she's angry.
7 Demetrius, at that point, walked over to the chalkboard and wrote, *I will not get involved.*

23

blade of soap, then the rain and the blood will . . . change the form of the weapon and you lose fingerprints and the blade won't match. That's irrelevant. I really hope it doesn't come to that. Listen to me carefully. Every hour of my life that you destroy, I'm going to take an hour from your life. Hello? Hello?"

Vivien put her phone in her pocket.

D said, "Honey, not vinegar."

"I want to pour a vat of boiling vinegar on that bastard's head," Viv said.

"Assault with a deadly weapon. Two to four years. Or attempted murder, five to nine," D said as he strolled over to the pantry. He pulled out a bar of Ivory soap and then collected a paring knife from the kitchen and placed them in front of Vivien. "You might want to get a jump start on these soap weapons you've heard about. Or you can take a walk and chill out."

Vivien took the soap and paring knife and stepped outside.

"Is she okay?" I asked after Viv left.

"She'll be fine. Customer service just isn't what it used to be."

I would like to say I delved deeper into her hostile phone conversation, but I had more pressing matters to contend with. If any of the information I've provided thus far is confusing or you need a refresher, I suggest consulting previous documents.[8]

Now is probably as good a time as any to explain how I became boss and why my two most seasoned employees were wearing undergarments to work.

I began working for the family business when I was twelve. I won't pretend that I was a model employee, and I'll come straight out and say that I was an even worse teenager. Some might have called me a delinquent. A more generous sort would suggest I was finding myself. I would probably tell the generous sort where to stick their new-age bullshit and own the delinquent part. So, I admit I was trouble, but I grew out of that phase at least five, six years ago and now I'm a relatively upstanding citizen. As you know, your average citizen probably commits between one and five misdemeanors a day.[9]

About nine months ago our firm took on a series of cases that turned out to be interconnected. A man hired us to follow

8 All available in paperback!
9 "Crime and No Punishment: Misdemeanor Rates Skyrocket as Criminals Realize Prison Time Is Shorter for Nonfelonies" (2011). See appendix.

his sister. His sister hired us to follow her husband. Two of the three people involved were not who they said they were. When I noticed their stories didn't match, I began investigating the client. Generally, a private investigator investigates the subject, not the client, but I believe that if the client is hiring us under false pretenses, it is our job to set things right. My father, however, believes we should serve the client, lest we develop a reputation for being the private investigators with a de-emphasis on the *private*. During our company standoff, my father enacted a Chinese wall and only allowed the assigned investigator to work on his or her respective case. I tried to climb the wall a few times, only to be met by an escalating series of warnings from my father, which culminated in a direct threat: If I continued to defy company policy, I would be fired. I disregarded his warning, took a sledgehammer to the Chinese wall, and uncovered our clients' true and malevolent motives. While I considered my investigation a success, my father considered it a breach of the basic tenets of our livelihood. My dad's threat to fire me was, in fact, not a bluff.

I politely and then impolitely asked for my job back. I even pretended that bygones were bygones and simply showed up for work day after day. If we were a major conglomerate, a security team would have promptly surfaced and escorted me out of the building with my one sad box of belongings. Instead, each day of each week, I was shown the door and then invited back for family dinner on Sunday.

After a great deal of soul-searching and scheming, I did the only thing I could do. I warned the person whom our clients were surveilling, one Edward Slayter, of the potential danger posed by his scheming wife (now ex). Mr. Slayter, a wealthy businessman, became my benefactor in a way. When he heard that I was fired because of my work on his behalf, he offered to intervene, in this case negotiating a buyout with my siblings, who, for the record, took my side.[10] At the time, the parental unit had a 40 percent share of the company, Rae had 15 percent, David had 15 percent, and I had 30 percent. After Slayter bought out my siblings' shares, I owned 60 percent, which, according to the company bylaws, gave me the authority to hire and fire employees and veto power over all major company decisions. My first order of business was giving

10 Or they really needed money. But I prefer my first theory.

me my old job back.

But power comes at a cost. The coup made me enemy number one to my father and rendered me permanently beholden to Edward Slayter. So, even though I'm technically the boss of Spellman Investigations, Edward Slayter is kind of the boss of me. Our deal is quite simple. I do jobs for him at a discounted rate and when he asks me to do something, I generally do it.

That's just so you understand why I'll be jogging in seven pages.

MEMO

To All Spellman Employees:
At 10:00 on Tuesday morning,
Mr. Slayter will be joining us
for a meeting about a potential assignment. Please dress
appropriately for the occasion.[1]

> Signed,
> The Management

Edward Slayter arrived at 10:00 A.M. sharp, which meant that he arrived five minutes early and waited in his car. I learned in the young days of my serfdom that when Slayter said 8:15, he didn't mean 8:10 or 8:20 or 8:16. He meant 8:15. So, you'd allow for traffic, often arrive early and loiter outside

1 I realize this is open to interpretation.

his office, and occasionally argue with a security guard over the NO LOITERING sign.

As I traversed the twelve-foot expanse of the office to meet Mr. Slayter at the door, I caught a half-clad woman on my father's computer screen. I clicked off the monitor just as Slayter's eyes clocked the image. Since I haven't yet gone into great length about my father, let me briefly defend his honor. The Playboy.com website was my father's way of illustrating to Slayter that I had no control over my employees. For the record, Dad doesn't make a habit of ogling naked women or perusing porn sites.[2]

"Missing-persons investigation," I said, explaining away the naked woman.

Edward raised his eyebrow and gave me a kiss on both cheeks. Let me be clear: Everything was strictly professional between me and my new boss, but Spellman Investigations was kind of his pet project and, as far as I could tell, so was I.

Professor Merriweather got to his feet when Slayter entered the room.

I made introductions.

"Edward, this is Demetrius, our best employee."

2 Not that this isn't perfectly normal male behavior, as I've been told repeatedly.

"From the looks of it," Edward said, "he's your only employee."

"We had a last-minute surveillance job. Couldn't find anyone else. I'm afraid I had to send the unit into the field."

Just then the theme from *Sanford and Son* blasted from the television in the upstairs bedroom.

Slayter turned to me and squinted with his right eye, his nonverbal manner of communicating that he doesn't believe me. I was rather familiar with that look.

"Neighbors," I said, completing the lie.

"I see," Slayter said. He turned to Demetrius. "Nice to see you again, um — oh, I'm terrible with names."

"Demetrius," I repeated.

"Nice to see you again, sir," Demetrius said, playing along.

They had never met. Slayter compensated by always assuming he'd met a person and always claiming to be bad with names. He had Alzheimer's. Maybe I should have led with that. It wasn't that advanced, but names and nouns and locations could be a problem. The disease was early onset and the diagnosis was grim, but for now the symptoms were minimal and Slayter insisted on business as usual. The only people who knew so far were me, Mr. Slayter, his doctors, and Charlie Black, his navigational consultant. I'll get to him later. The web of secrecy was to protect a business that my boss had slaved over for twenty-five years. He had been the CEO of Slayter Industries since the beginning and owned 25 percent of the company. He was the only shareholder on the board of directors and there'd never been a vote that hadn't fallen on his side. He was the boss, is my point. Kinda like what I had going on at Spellman Investigations. Slayter had made it clear that he would continue to run his company, a venture capital firm, until he and his doctor decided it was time to quit. At least that was the plan. For now, we did his bidding.

"I was really hoping to meet your parents today," Slayter said.

"I'm sorry that didn't work out. Next time," I said, sliding a chair next to my desk.

Slayter waited until I was seated behind my desk before he took a seat. This dance used to take an unusually long time until I figured it out. Women sit first. Once I told him that was stupid and it didn't go over very well. I just sit down now. What's the big deal? It's not like I can't vote.

"Does anyone want coffee?" Demetrius asked.

"No, thank you," Slayter said pleasantly.

"Can I interest you in a freshly baked blueberry muffin?" D asked.

"Yes!" I said.

The glorious smell had been wafting into the office for the last twenty minutes.

"I was talking to Mr. Slayter."

"He doesn't eat things that taste good," I said.

Slayter smirked, Demetrius departed, and I sat up straight, gathered my notebook, and poised my pen, awaiting further instructions.

"We're looking at a company called Divine Strategies Inc. They specialize in niche financial software for religious organizations. They got their start with HolyBooks, an accounting program for churches, but they're branching out into other areas. My people have already done the financials and checked for any legal issues and they're clean. I just want a few background checks on the partners and some of the support staff."

"Are you looking for anything in particular?" I asked.

"I just want fresh eyes on it," Slayter said.

"Anything else?"

"My younger brother is coming to visit."

"When?"

"Any day now. He likes to surprise me."

"I didn't know you had a brother."

"I haven't seen him in five years."

"Does he know about . . . ?"

"No."

"Are you going to tell him?"

"Why would I do that?"

"Because he's family. You have to tell him."

"I'm afraid we don't have that close bond you Spellmans share," Slayter said.

On cue Dad blew his nose so loudly it reverberated throughout the house.

"No need to brag," I said. "Still, I think you should consider telling him. At least he won't be offended if you forget his name. What is it, by the way?"

"Ethan Jones."

"Half brother, actor, or took his wife's name?"

"Changed it. He had some trouble a while back."

"Interesting choice. What kind of trouble?"

"The kind involving prison."

"Now you've got my attention," I said.

"I should have had it when I walked in the door."

"Wow. You having a brother who did time is kind of exciting. I don't have a brother who did time."

"That must be very difficult for you."

"What did he do?" I asked.

"What difference does it make?"

"You can tell me or I'll waste two hours of my day running a background check."

"Ponzi scheme," Slayter said, studying his shoes.

"What happened?"

"A lot of people lost their retirement. He paid back what he could. Did time. Seven years in a federal prison."

"The good kind," I said. "I think I'd do okay in a federal prison."

Slayter stared out the window, either lost in thought, trying to decipher the argument between Sanford and his son, or spacing out, which does sometimes happen.

"When he got out," Slayter said, "he used whatever money he had stashed away and opened a bar in Los Angeles. He's good with people. He's thinking about opening a bar here. Or so he says."

"That would be great. Because I've been looking for a new place to drink."

"We need to keep an eye on him."

"Which eye? Left? Right?"

In my entire relationship with Slayter, I've never made him laugh, not even when I showed up at his office wearing a dress inside out.[3]

3 I had an overnight surveillance and got only a

"Do you have a safe in your office?"

"We do."

Slayter reached into his breast pocket and pulled out an envelope filled with cash.

"Can you put this in your safe?"

I took the envelope and peeked at the stack of Benjamins inside.

"How much is this?"

"Five grand."

"Why do you want me to keep five grand in my office?"

"You might need it sometime. Or we'll get lucky, and you won't."

Mr. Slayter got to his feet, which meant that our business here was done. I walked him to the door.

"See you tomorrow. Our usual time."

"Tomorrow?" I spun my calendar around so that Slayter could see the entry. "My apologies, but I can't make it tomorrow. I have a new-client meeting at eight. I don't know how long it will last."

"Mr. Hofstetler shouldn't take up more than forty-five minutes of your time."

---

half hour of sleep. The inside of the dress had obvious stitching and seams exposed. I have no idea how I managed to drive to his office, take an elevator, and walk down a hallway without noticing.

It would have been impossible for Slayter to have read that name over my shoulder.

"How did you —"

"I had my secretary make the appointment yesterday. I'm on to you, Isabel."

I took up running exactly eight weeks ago, when Mr. Slayter phoned me one morning requesting my presence in Golden Gate Park. He told me to wear sneakers and something comfortable. How was I to know he had exercise on his mind? I wore a pair of jeans, a JUSTICE 4-MERRI-WEATHER T-shirt, and pair of Jack Purcells.

Mr. Slayter, in shorts and a T-shirt in state-of-the-art moisture-wicking fabric, waited for me on a bench outside the de Young Museum. I'd never seen my new boss so casual, but I figured he couldn't wear pressed suits twenty-four/seven. It seemed indecent looking at his exposed legs, maybe because he had the legs of a man half his age — a healthy man half his age. Edward was one of those people who did everything in his power to stay young, which made his disease particularly cruel. To avoid gawking at Slayter's well-toned calf muscles, I turned to Charlie Black, Slayter's navigational consultant, who was circling on his bicycle.

"Hey, Charlie. What's going on?"

"We're running," Charlie said.

"I've never seen anyone run on a bicycle before," I said. Then I made direct eye contact with Mr. Slayter, demanding an explanation.

"Isabel," he said, giving me a once-over. "You might want to invest in more appropriate attire."

"Have you been talking to my mother?"

"Let's get started. Have you stretched?"

"Yes."

"When?"

"Nineteen ninety-eight. August, I think."

"We'll warm up first."

"Charlie, what's going on?" I asked Charlie because I figured he'd understand my confusion.

"Mr. Slayter likes to multitask. Sometimes he likes to do business while he runs."

"I see. Edward, I hate to break it to you, but I'm not a runner."

"Do you do any cardiovascular activity?"

"I'm alive, aren't I?"

Mr. Slayter looked at his watch and started running without further comment.

"He's pretty fast, so I'd get a move on if I were you," Charlie said as he circled me on his bicycle.

I chased my new boss down John F. Kennedy Drive past the pond, where a gang of

38

pigeons blocked the sidewalk, and caught up before he reached the underpass at Crossover Drive.

"Hold up," I said, gasping for air and doubling over with a side cramp.

I wish I could cite heat exhaustion for my weak showing, but if you've ever been in San Francisco during summer, you know that's not the case. While the rest of you clowns are cramped in air-conditioned cubicles or sweating it out on porches, fanning yourselves in the shade and drinking lemonade, waiting for the sun to set, we're pulling on cardigans, hoping that the fog will break. At least in some parts of the city. There is no "San Francisco summer." Golden Gate Park is often socked in with a heavy layer of fog until afternoon. Then again, the sun can hit the Mission in the morning and start burning off the pools of urine from the night before by mid-afternoon. The Van Ness corridor at times is a wind tunnel that can send the most modest outfit adrift. You should never speak about weather in San Francisco except in the immediate moment.

That morning, in the park, it was chilly and the fog was like a gauzy filter on a camera for an aging movie star. The moist air had a moldy scent with a hint of pine.

Slayter slowed to a walk while Charlie pedaled beside us. He took my arm and said, "Walk it off."

"I really don't think this jogging is for me," I said. "Maybe I could ride the bike."

"My last running partner retired and moved to Florida. You'll have to do for now."

Most people can't make me exercise against my will, but as I've explained, Slayter kind of owns me, and if he wants to have meetings while simultaneously trying to kill me, there's not much I can do about it. Slayter and I parted ways after he suggested I stretch against one of the park benches. I made a feeble show of it until I saw his car disappear in the distance. Then I collapsed on the park bench and watched a gang of fake hippies and their pit bull puppy take over the bike path and get in an argument with a pair of well-equipped cyclists who were itching for a brawl. The cops showed up and ruined what was gearing up to be an excellent show. I limped back to my car and returned to the office.

The next morning, Mr. Slayter's secretary phoned me and scheduled regular jogging meetings on Monday, Wednesday, and Friday. My protest was met with a gift certificate to a sports apparel shop and a note that somehow managed to convey in the most subtle manner that I should buy not only running shoes but a sports bra. I believe the note read: *You might also want to consider any long-term gravitational side effects and purchase any items that might offset that particular issue.*

After the torture of one week's exercise, I decided that it was my body and I should be able to do what I wanted with it, even if that meant absolutely nothing. The next time Evelyn called to confirm our running appointment, and the time after that, I said I was unavailable. Edward would promptly get on the line for the specifics of my unavailability. Our conversations usually went something like this:

ISABEL: My grandmother died.[4]
SLAYTER: My condolences. But I have never heard of a seven A.M. funeral.
ISABEL: I have a doctor's appointment.
SLAYTER: Why would you schedule a doctor's appointment for a time when you already had an appointment on your calendar?

4 I have been using this excuse for years and it's always worked. And no, I don't feel bad about it. And you won't either once you meet her.

ISABEL: I don't feel well.

SLAYTER: Exercise will improve your hangover.[5]

ISABEL: I really don't want to do this anymore.

SLAYTER: Sometimes it's good to do things we don't want to do.

Eight weeks later, I'd mostly given up the fight. The morning after my unusual conversation about Slayter's alias-sporting brother, I was back at the park. It was a crisp Wednesday morning in July, with fog as thick as smoke from a wildfire. Edward and I ran in unison around the soccer field. Four loops, four miles is our usual on Wednesday. I always let him do most of the talking, so I can do most of the breathing, but I have finally grown accustomed to these bouts of exercise and will reluctantly admit that it was doing me some good. For instance, after a four-mile run with Slayter, returning home to find my parents wearing their ugly-American costumes at work (matching Hawaiian shirts, Bermuda shorts, and Ray-Ban sunglasses on nylon straps) didn't get my hackles up like it used to.

On this run, the day after the foiled meeting with my parents, Edward decided to

5 Depends on how bad the hangover.

impart some advice.

"It must be difficult running a business when you don't have the respect of your employees," he said.

I could have launched into an extensive defense, explaining family history and my parents' predilection for gamesmanship, but breathing took priority.

"It is."

"Did you read the book I gave you?"

"I skimmed it."

When the trouble began after my coup, Mr. Slayter gave me several books that had influenced his management style.

"Have you completed step one?"

"Working on it," I said, slowing my pace to cut back on the chitchat and because I didn't want to lie any further. The book Slayter was referring to, called *How to Undo a Fiasco,* included exercises. Chapter 1 encouraged you to make a list of all of your transgressions over the last ten years. For me that could have taken upwards of a year.

"Have you tried listening to them — opening a dialogue to discuss what happened and how they feel? Maybe they just need to be heard, and then you can move on."

That was from one of the other books he gave me. I can't remember which one. Or maybe it's just common sense.

"I'll try that," I said. "Again." Because I was pretty sure I'd tried that before.

"Please do. And report back to me. I think it's important that I meet your parents before the fissure in communication becomes as deep as a canyon."

When we reached the end of the third loop, I slowed to a walk.

"Good run," I said.

"We only did three loops, Isabel."

"No, we did four," I said.

"Are you sure?"

"Positive."

Edward turned to Charlie and said, "Charlie, how many miles have we covered?"

I ducked behind Slayter and made the universal sign that means *Don't rat me out.*

"Three, sir," Charlie, the rat, said.

"Isabel, I can't believe you would exploit my condition for your own benefit."

"I swear, I thought we did four laps."[6]

"Two more," Slayter said, as punishment.

"Only one more."

"Two. I forgot about the third. It happens."

Slayter picked up the pace. I trudged in his wake, drafting off of him. It helps a little

6 Don't judge me. Running is hard.

and Slayter finds it annoying, which also improves my mood.

After the final loop, I came to a complete stop and lay down on the grass.

Charlie was across the field, riding in our direction. Slayter extended his hand, meaning for me to get up. He pulled me to my feet. For an old guy, he sure was strong.

"Albino, gingivitis, and . . ." Slayter trailed off, staring at the white sky.

In case you were wondering, my boss hadn't contracted some rare language virus. At the beginning of every jogging session or other meeting, if I remember, I try to give Slayter three words to remember at the end of the meeting. Sometimes I forget the three words, which makes the whole thing a disaster, but now we make sure Charlie hears the words.

"Three-card monte," Slayter said, snapping his fingers. "Let's stick to single words only in the future."

"No," I said flatly. "You tell me what to do all the time. Some things are entirely in my purview."

Slayter pretended like he hadn't heard me and moved on to the next subject.

"I bought Charlie that sweater," Edward said, nodding in Charlie's general direction.

It was a nice sweater. It had that soft

cashmere look and was a blue-gray with a slim red trim around the collar. It might have been the priciest thing Charlie owned.

"I like it."

"I believe he was wearing it yesterday as well. And the day before that," Slayter said.

"It's his favorite sweater," I said. "He wears it at least three times a week."

"Next time you get a chance," Slayter said, "I'd like you to discuss rotating his wardrobe with him. And maybe you can take him shopping so that he has a few more items to rotate. And then maybe you could discuss dry cleaning with him."

"I'm not sure that I understand dry cleaning. I mean, can you really get something clean without getting it wet?"

"He smells, Isabel. You need to have a hygiene talk with him."

"Do you really think I'm the best person for this job? Some nights I go to bed without —"

"Isabel, I realize this isn't part of your job description, but it's either you or me and I think it would be better coming from you."

"Okay, I'll take care of it," I said.

"I want his new sweaters to be tasteful," Slayter warned me. "Not like the last time."

The previous holiday season, Slayter had asked me to buy Charlie a Christmas sweater. He meant a sweater for Christmas. I interpreted it more literally and purchased a red knit number with snowflakes and snowmen stitched over the fabric, creating a terrain not unlike a relief map. I thought it was fun; Charlie loved it and wore it for a week straight until Slayter made me make it disappear. Seriously, I had to steal it from Charlie and pretend it was lost in an over-heated cab ride. Charlie spent half the afternoon phoning cab companies while it was at the bottom of my parents' trash bin. We called it Sweatergate. Charlie still talks about it.

Maybe now would be a good time to tell you about Charlie Black, navigational consultant.

I met Charlie on the steps outside of 101 Market Street maybe eight months ago while I was surveilling Edward Slayter. To kill time, I was studying a chess book that my ex-boyfriend Henry Stone was making me read. Charlie asked if he could interest me in a game, swiftly pulling a chessboard out of his backpack. I agreed; he won in about three minutes flat. As I continued my surveillance of Mr. Slayter, I kept running into Charlie, since my surveillance took me to his haunts. I discovered that Charlie was intelligent in a very particular way, unemployed, lonely, and trustworthy. When I discovered that Mr. Slayter had Alzheimer's we embarked on our unusual partnership; I suggested Slayter hire Charlie as an assistant to discreetly make sure Edward was at the right place at the right time.

As it turned out, Charlie and Slayter got along swimmingly despite their epic differences. Edward is wealthy, handsome, charismatic, prone to suit-wearing, and quite powerful; Black was a public servant made redundant who passed as a homeless person who played chess on the streets until his latest gig, and has been known to wear the same outfit five days in a row. The only thing they have in common now is their driver and chess. Charlie is a good companion for Slayter; he doesn't have a problem with nervous chatter, a habit Slayter has no patience for, and he can navigate the streets of San Francisco with the best of them. His feel for social terrain is far murkier.

Because of this fact, Slayter will often leave the more delicate conversations to me, which is silly, if you've met me. I'm not exactly famous for mincing words, although I've made a marked improvement.

Slayter and I parted in our usual fashion. "I'll see you Friday," Slayter said.

"Friday doesn't work for me," I said to deaf ears.

Edward's driver pulled up and attached Charlie's bike to the rack that had been recently added, and the three men got into the Town Car and drove away. Charlie waved a cheery good-bye as I staggered over to my beat-up Buick, crawled into the backseat, and took a short nap.

So far, all I've mentioned are hostile take-overs, jogging, and wardrobe disturbances, which serve up only an appetizer in the world of Spellman Investigations. Let me be clear: Before we're a dysfunctional company and family, we are investigators, and no matter what personal or professional conflicts simmer, our work does indeed take priority.

SUBORDINATES

MEMO

To All Spellman Employees:
Albert and Olivia will be out
of the office until Thursday
afternoon. We will arrive when
our other business is taken
care of.

Signed,
the Subordinates

No matter what my ragtag group of investigators is wearing, Spellman Investigations tries to have a weekly summit in which we debrief each other on our current caseload. This routine was intact for close to two years before I took the reins, and it will remain intact as long as my parents don't become nudists. It is policy to have the meetings in the morning, since we don't run the tightest ship and people like to skip out early on Friday. I'm the kind of boss who doesn't mind that sort of thing, so long as the work is getting done and my employees aren't in the other room eating pancakes.

At the very least they could have been sneaky about it, but the unit was openly flaunting their pancake consumption during the weekly summit.

I entered the kitchen to see whether I could wrangle my parents/underlings.

"Would you care to join us for the meeting?" I asked.

"Didn't you get the memo?" Dad said.

"I did. Thank you for laminating it and Krazy Gluing it to the top of my desk. However, since you're only twenty feet from where the meeting is taking place, I don't see why you can't make that short trek into the office."

"Can't you see we're eating?" Mom said.

"You can bring your pancakes," I said.

"They taste better in here," Mom said, devouring half the stack in a mouthful.

"Well, we can wait ten, twenty minutes, until you're done," I said, being accommodating. For a hundred-and-ten-pound woman my mother eats like a longshoreman. You'd think she has a tapeworm.

"Nah, we don't want to rush our digestions. We'll see you later," Dad said. Dad, alas, most definitely does not have a tapeworm. I didn't want to say anything. But Dad has no business eating pancakes. It must have been his cheat day, but yesterday was his cheat day.

There was no point in pushing the matter further. My current strategy for coping with renegade employees was failing, and I needed to come up with another plan. I returned to the office to find Demetrius (bow tie–free) and Vivien whispering conspiratorially. I could only gather that they were discussing the dissension among the ranks. My lack of leadership was becoming not only a professional problem but also a personal embarrassment.

My presence halted the sotto voce conversation. Vivien, looking worse for wear even for a college coed, returned to her desk. I'm not one to judge; from age twelve to twenty-five you could generally rely on my being the least-polished-looking person in the vicinity, unless you dropped me by helicopter against my will at a Grateful Dead concert.[1] But Viv, that day, didn't just appear ungroomed — she had clearly given up on a knotty tangle in her long dark hair, and her clothes had the imprint of repeated wear

1 And it would have had to be against my will.

— but unhinged as well. Her bloodshot eyes darted around, like overcaffeinated scopes attached to trigger-happy rifles.

"Have you eaten anything today, Viv?"

"Yes," she said.

"No," D said. "She raided Rae's junk food stash."

I returned to the kitchen, plucked a stack of leftover pancakes from the stove, squeezed some fake maple syrup on top, and grabbed a fork. I responded to the unit's protest by explaining that the hotcakes were for Viv and returned to the office, putting the plate on her desk.

"Since my parents are up to speed on the cases,[2] let's have a quick meeting without them. D, can you do some background checks on any employee who has been with Divine Strategies longer than five years?"

"I'll get started today," D said, shuffling papers distractedly.

"How did your interview with the inmate go?"

"Fine. Why do you ask?" D said. He said it defensively, if I was not mistaken.

"Because I usually ask about these cases. Is there a reason you don't want to talk about the interview?"

2 Never admit defeat.

"No," D said, pulling the file from his desk. "His name is Louis Myron Washburn. He was convicted twelve years ago of armed robbery and second-degree murder. The witness ID seems shaky. During the first interview she said it was the wrong man and then changed her mind. Looks like a case of an unreliable cross-racial witness ID and maybe some unhealthy influence from the cops. Washburn has a rap sheet — assault, possession with intent to sell. The police probably were itching to take him down."

"If you need any help, let me know," I said. "Vivien, I need you to serve papers next week. One looks cut-and-dried. He knows it's coming. The other is a divorce situation. The wife has filed and the husband has made himself scarce. I tried to serve him two days ago at the golf course and he took off in his golf cart. Since he got a look at me, I figured you could have a go at it. Considering your history with golf carts, I'd rather you try to serve him at home. Other than that, I don't have much. Hope you have some papers due next week."

"I can handle being at a golf course," Vivien said.

"I don't want to risk it."

Just then my sister Rae entered the office, eating a lone pancake folded like a taco.

54

"Have you tried these pancakes?" Rae said. "I think Mom stole your secret recipe, D."

"I don't believe in secret recipes," D said.

"Colonel Sanders would disagree with you, and that is why Colonel Sanders is rich and you have enough money to put a down payment on a one-bedroom apartment in the East Bay."

Quick explanation for the mildly hostile exchange: When D was exonerated, Rae relentlessly encouraged him to file a lawsuit for malicious prosecution. After almost a year of debating his options, Demetrius finally agreed. He had a solid case, but both parties wanted to avoid the public scrutiny of a lengthy and costly civil trial. D was given a fair offer but never disclosed the sum to my sister, since she's got a habit of offering unsolicited financial advice. Rae merely assumed that it was a paltry settlement and has been on D's case ever since. It was not a paltry settlement. But D has managed to be conservative with his investments and unless my sister opened his bank statements, she'd be none the wiser. I can always see a veiled smirk of satisfaction on D's face when Rae trips over the subject.

"Is there something we can do for you, Rae?" I asked.

There was a time it seemed that my sister and I, together, were the future of Spellman Investigations. As a child she was far more interested in the family business than I ever pretended to be. But people change, I've discovered. Their goals and motivations make invisible seismic shifts over time. My sister learned that you can't get rich being a PI; since she readily admits that money is her first love, the job eventually lost its luster. Nowadays, Rae always manages to find lucrative part-time employment and will only take a Spellman job under extreme duress. She comes to the house for the obligatory Sunday-night dinners and is rarely heard from in between.

"I've got a case," Rae said. "A friend of mine hired a moving and storage company when she moved out of her apartment over summer and took a short holiday. She signed a contract for the full service and paid fifty percent up front, which was twelve hundred dollars. The services they were to provide included packing up her belongings from her old apartment, keeping them in storage for four to six weeks, and then moving them to the new location within a twenty-five-mile radius. When my client arranged for the delivery of her stored items, the movers held her belongings ransom, claiming that they exceeded the weight limit in the contract of two thousand pounds, and they added a surplus charge for the single flight of stairs into her building. Not only that, her television was cracked, her mattress was infected with bedbugs, and she thinks some of her underwear is missing.

"When she tried to get reimbursed for the damages, the guy she dealt with, Owen Lukas, said that she was entitled to twenty-five dollars since the insurance only covered one dollar per pound of the property. After her stuff was in her house, she went to the owner of the company and questioned the extortion money for damaged property. Lukas simply repeated again and again, 'I suggest you review the contract.' "

"What does she want to get out of this?"

"Justice," said Rae. "And maybe her money back."

"The cost of investigating and filing a claim could be a wash," I said. "And that's if she wins."

"She doesn't care. This Lukas guy lied to her and cheated her and they knew they could get away with it. I looked into it," Rae said. "Moving companies aren't properly regulated. If you ask me, it's the new mob."

"Can she pay?" I asked.

"No," Rae said.

"Then why would we take the case?"

"Because he's Satan," Vivien said through a mouthful of pancakes.

"Meet our client," Rae said, nodding in Vivien's direction. "Lightning Fast Moving Company, they're called. I don't think she's their only victim, based on my preliminary research. I'll check their corporate status and bankruptcy filings and see if there are any lawsuits on record, which seems likely. You wouldn't believe their reviews on Yelp."

"What does this have to do with you?" I asked.

"She came to me for help," Rae said.

"I take it these are what the phone calls have been about, and your bad hair days?"

"This man is the worst person I've ever met," Vivien said.

"Then why didn't you come to me? I'm pretty good at dealing with assholes."

"You were really busy jogging and other stuff for the old guy, and when you were here you were trying to pay the bills, which seemed more important."

I'll admit the last part hurt, since the "trying to pay the bills" was so on-the-nose. I had resorted to handwriting on check forms meant for laser printers, which meant that 50 percent of our payments got calls from

58

the bank to be sure they weren't stolen checks.

"I'd like to do the legwork," Rae said.

"Why?" I asked.

"Because I feel like keeping the blade sharp," said Rae.

"What blade?"

"Until I decide about graduate school, I have some free time. I'll take this case for free, see if I can drum up some other business on my own. Do you have a problem with me bringing more money in?"

"Of course not."

"I might want to do a little surveillance on this Lukas character. Is that cool?"

"If you're taking the case, that means you're keeping watch on Viv. Her involvement should be minimal."

"I can hear you," said Viv.

"Understood," Rae said. She extended her hand. "Good to be on board again."

I reluctantly shook her hand but could not help but have an uneasy sensation. My sister's sudden interest in returning to the business was like a car that drove just fine but made a loud clanking noise that let you know something was amiss. Still, I was two employees down. Adding one who made no financial demands was a plus.

"Walk me out," Rae said, stepping into

the hallway. But the hallway wasn't exactly private, since it was within earshot of the kitchen. My parents were now doing the crossword puzzle together.

"Nine letters. French martyr. Starts with a *J*," said Mom.

"Pepe Le Pew," Dad said.

"It fits."

"Nice," Dad said.

"Oh my God," Rae said in horror. She leaned into the kitchen. "Martyr. French *martyr.*"

I can only assume my parents were staring blankly at Rae. Crossword puzzles aren't really their thing.

"Joan of Arc," Rae snapped.

"That works too," Dad said.

My sister and I walked to the foyer.

"Any jobs I get on my own, I want a seventy-five percent cut after expenses," Rae said.

"Then why don't you just take the jobs on your own?"

"Because it's more professional to work under the shingle of a PI firm."

"You're old enough to get your own license," I said.

"I don't have time for that," Rae said.

"Something about this isn't right," I said.

"I'm looking to make some extra money.

60

Do you want to take a twenty-five percent cut, or should I go to RH³ Investigations?"

"I will take your money, thank you. Please don't do anything to embarrass the company," I said, walking down the stairs.

"I think you've got that part covered," Rae replied.

My parents arrived at work without making a wardrobe change.

"So, let me see if I understand this," I said. "You sleep in your pajamas; you work in your pajamas, or a swimsuit if the mood strikes you; and then you sleep in your pajamas again."

"Is there a question in there?" Dad asked.

"I'm curious about the hygiene in all this."

"We shower and dress for dinner. We actually make an extra effort now," Mom said.

"Like the rich British people do, or used to do, in the movies," Dad said.

"And when does this happen?" I asked.

"After you've left for the day," Mom said.

3 Rick Harkey, PI, was a retired cop whose reputation was smeared (by me!) a few years ago when I found a collection of his old cases that involved serious police misconduct and witness tampering. He managed to pawn off his PI practice on some slob before he took off to Florida.

The phone rang and she answered with, "Isabel Spellman Investigations."

I shot her eye-daggers that landed on the wall.

"One moment, please," Mom said, transferring the call to my desk.

I picked up.

"What are you wearing?" Mr. Slayter asked.

"Clothes," I replied.

"Presentable clothes?"

"I look better than seventy-five percent of the people around me."

"I'm interviewing new lawyers right now. Ritz has been threatening to retire for the last twenty years and he's already in his eighties. We're tempting fate at this point. I have a candidate in my office who is the front-runner. I'd like to get your opinion. Are you free?"

"I'll be right over."

"Run a brush through your hair. Remember, how you look reflects upon me."

"That makes no sense at all."

I brushed my hair in the parking lot of Slayter's office building on Market Street. I even applied some lipstick, eyeliner, and cover-up. I've only recently discovered that when people tell you that you look tired, they're suggesting you use cover-up, not get more sleep.

I approached Edward's reception desk. His secretary, Evelyn Glade, pretended that she didn't notice me. I cleared my throat. When she raised her head she looked me over like someone studying questionable produce at the supermarket.

Speaking of produce, Evelyn's the kind of woman who thinks of her breasts as accessories, like a really nice bracelet or earrings. I've never seen them *not* on display. To her credit, her outfits are always otherwise tasteful. Her uniform is a pencil skirt, four-inch pumps, and a silk blouse, always with two more buttons undone than I would undo. Men seem to find her attractive, but you have to wonder whether they're merely distracted. Her eye makeup is always spare, but her lips have never been anything but a deep crimson red. She must reapply her war paint at least four times a day. She's in her midforties but still wears her hair long, curled in light, flowing waves that probably kill an hour every morning. *That's* dedication.

Evelyn offered up her usual tight, fake smile and buzzed Edward's office.

"Ms. Spellman is here to see you," she said.

Edward sat behind his behemoth desk,

which did not provide the empowering effect he intended. It simply dwarfed the man sitting behind it and everything else in the room. Across from Mr. Slayter was another man in a suit. Early forties, with thick eyebrows, a flat nose that looked like it might have been broken once or twice, and unruly black hair. His suit was nice, but it lacked a tailored fit. The overall effect was *unlawyerly.*

"Damien, I'd like you to meet my niece, Isabel," said Edward Slayter. "Isabel, Damien Thorp. He's interviewing for chief counsel at Slayter Industries."

"Damien Thorp, that sounds so familiar. Have we met?" I asked.

"No. I'm sure I'd remember."

"Not if you were drunk," I said.

Slayter cleared his throat. It was a warning, not an actual throat clearing. He's the least phlegmy person I know. If this particular sound could be translated into words, they would be *Don't be yourself today.* A phrase he has in fact used with me at least half a dozen times.

"It's a pleasure meeting you, Isabel," Damien said, extending his hand.

"Yes, a pleasure," I said.

The handshake was perfect, like he practiced it on different subjects and adjusted accordingly.

"Isabel also works for my company in many capacities, mostly charitable," Edward said.

"Yesss," I said, checking to see if Uncle Ed was looking confused the way he does sometimes when navigating the city. "Uncle Ed really likes to give his money away, and I'm happy to help him any way I can."

"Which charitable organizations do you work with most closely?" Damien asked.

I had no idea, and Uncle Ed wasn't leaping to my aid.

"We really like the zoo. In fact, we helped rebuild the lion cage so they can't escape anymore."[4]

"We have many organizations we work with," Edward said.

"But mostly the zoo," I added.

"It's been a pleasure," Edward said. To Damien, not me.

"Thank you for your time," said Thorp.

"Isabel, why don't you walk Mr. Thorp to the elevators and validate his parking?"

"You never validate my parking."

4 Seriously, one escaped once. The first thing Grammy Spellman said when she heard was: "What do you think they'll do with his coat? I bet it's *gorgeous*."

"Good-bye," Edward said.

Damien and I strolled up to Evelyn's desk and asked for a parking validation. Once I made it clear it was not for me, she ponied up the stamper and gave Damien a toothy but vaguely seductive grin. I pressed the down button at the elevator bank and stared at my feet as one is supposed to do in the vicinity of elevators.

Damien said, "You have quite an uncle."

"Indeed," I replied, thinking about my uncle Ray, who was the definition of *quite an uncle.*

The elevator doors parted and Damien entered.

"I hope to see you again," he said.

As the doors closed I shot out my hand and the sensors parted the slabs of steel.

"Oh my God," I said. "You're one letter off from Damien Thorn. The antichrist from *The Omen.*"

I had a feeling Damien had heard that before. But maybe thirty years ago at summer camp.

"In my parents' defense, the film came out seven years after I was born."

The elevator tried to clamp shut again, but I swatted it open again.

"You could have changed your name."

"I'm not changing my name because of a

66

goddamn horror film."

"What do you think of him?" Slayter asked
when I returned to his office.

"I think his suit was a little big, Uncle Ed."

"What is your gut telling you?" Edward
asked.

"Pancakes."

"Certainly he made some impression."

"All lawyers seem the same to me.[5] Let
me run a background check on him and
verify his references, then we'll talk again.
Why did you tell him I was your niece?"

"If he learns I have a PI on retainer, his
guard will be up; he'll be extra cautious. It's
hard to know who to trust anymore. Good
thing I have you," Slayter said sweetly. Then
he ruined the moment by tugging at my collar and saying, "Do you own an iron?"

"I've done more ironing since I've known
you than I have my entire life to date."

"Fascinating bit of personal trivia."

Next Morning, 8:10 A.M.
"Banana, mononucleosis, and wombat," I
said as Slayter and I jogged through the
thick morning haze.

"My doctor always chooses perfectly

5 That's not true. Fifty percent seem the same.

ordinary words," Edward said.

"Well, he went to medical school," I said. Five minutes into the run and I was already out of breath. Charlie swooped up on his bicycle, looking so relaxed and carefree.

"Did you get that, Charlie?" Edward asked.

"Banana, mononucleosis, and wombat," Charlie repeated.

Edward looked out scornfully on the landscape, which you couldn't see much of. There was a dense-fog advisory out that morning. We passed the rose garden, but you couldn't see any roses, only joggers in the mist. Like Warren Beatty in *Heaven Can Wait,* only without Warren Beatty.

"This weather is atrocious," Slayter said.

"A San Franciscan complaining about the fog is like a Seattleite whining about rain, which is like a person from Los Angeles complaining about plastic surgery," I said.

"I wish you'd let us meet at the Marina Green," Slayter said.

It was quite possible the Marina might have had a bit of sun right now, but it came at a cost.

"Never!" I said. "Jogging is one thing. Jogging among Satan's spawn is another."[6]

"I don't want to hear the Marina rant again," Edward said. Then he started repeating the three words, which goes against the whole point of the exercise.

"Stop that," I said. "We're supposed to talk about business."

Out of the corner of my eye, I could see Edward mouth *wombat, mononucleosis, banana*. When he saw me catch him, he spoke.

"I met with Damien last night over drinks."

"Can he hold his liquor?" I asked.

"I offered him the job."

"Can *you* hold your liquor?" I stopped in my tracks, not because I was alarmed, but because I wanted to stop running. "I told you to let me run a background on him," I said as Slayter jogged in a loop around me.

I kept my feet firmly on the ground.

"Did you find anything?" he asked.

"No," I said.

"So what's the problem? Keep moving, Isabel, you want to keep your heart rate up."

Slayter loped off; I hobbled after.

"This decision seems hasty," I said. Some days it seemed Edward was in a rush to get

6 This is what I have to say about Marina people: Why don't you just move to L.A.?

his affairs in order, as if there were an imaginary ticking clock on his lucidity. I suppose there was, and maybe he was right in being overly cautious and prepared. The disease was deceptive. I knew that. Now he was fine. But he could have a moment where'd he forget my name, or a street he'd walked down for the past twenty years would look utterly unfamiliar. But then the moment would pass. And since he'd started the race faster than the rest of us, it was difficult to notice that he was slowing down.

"Isabel, his CV is impeccable and he was highly recommended by William Slavinsky."

"You mean Willard." Willard Slavinsky is one of Edward's oldest friends and one of the major shareholders in Slater Industries.

"I said Willard."

"You said William, which is a preferable name."

"I lost my train of thought," Edward said, slightly agitated.

"Happens to many people in my company," I said.

"Anyway, you don't know whether it's going to work out until you give the person a shot," Edward said.

"Point taken, but I think you could have waited for a brief surveillance and a Platinum Level[7] background check."

"He's new to the area. I've hired a Realtor to help him find an apartment, but I gave him your number, in case he wants someone to show him around the city. Places to go at night, that sort of thing."

"You want me to play tour guide?"

"Yes, only I don't want you to give him the Isabel Spellman dive bar tour."

"Sorry, that's all I've got."

"When are you going to talk to Charlie about his sweater situation?"

"I'm waiting for the right moment."

"There's never a good moment to tell a man he has an unpleasant odor."

"Sure there is. After he's won the Super Bowl."

"Invite him to lunch and have a casual chat."

"I'm a private investigator, Edward, not a tour guide or a hygiene coach."

"You're so many things to me, Isabel. Banana. Mononucleosis. Wombat," Edward said as he jogged off with even more energy than when we'd begun.

While Edward was at the office, Charlie

7 Working on marketing terms to bring in higher-end investigative work.

71

took the Geary bus to Polk Street and met me at a corner café across the street from Edinburgh Castle. The Polk/Geary corner, still in the clutches of the Tenderloin, always feels like typical San Francisco. Homeless people mark every corner and working stiffs loiter at bus stops, while just a short stroll away, you can dine at a fine restaurant or go to a strip club. Just one block away is a luxury apartment building, the swanky foyer on an unlit side street. Their doorman is a homeless guy who lives in the alley. At least that's how many of the tenants see him; he's apparently quite good at hailing cabs.

I used the ruse of wanting to keep my chess skills sharp when I made the invitation; Charlie was kind enough to play along, not once mentioning that my chess skills were as dull as the sheen on the twenty-year-old board we were playing with.

Charlie opened with his knight to c3. Don't worry, I'm not going to describe the entire game in chess notations, or even Isabel notations.[8] Charlie won in twenty-four moves. You're probably not surprised. Our meeting wasn't about chess. It was about

8 I moved my pawn, the one in front of the thing that moves sideways, two places, because it's the only time you can move it two places.

his sweater/sweater smell, so in between strategizing about chess, I had some other things to strategize.

Charlie Black isn't like other people. I don't know who he's like, but I got the feeling a flat/direct approach might be the way to go.

ME: Charlie, how often do you wash that sweater?

CHARLIE: It says "dry-clean only."

ME: How often do you dry-clean-only that sweater?

CHARLIE: You have to leave the sweater with a stranger to dry-clean it.

ME: Those strangers are usually quite reputable.[9] You only pay them when you get the sweater back. So they have no incentive to steal it.

CHARLIE: But if I don't have the sweater, then I can't wear it.

ME: You can wear another sweater.

CHARLIE: But Mr. Slayter bought me this sweater, so I think he wants me to wear it.

ME: I see.

Later that afternoon, I got a follow-up e-mail from Slayter.

9 Unlike moving companies.

Dear Isabel,[10]
Did you handle that business we discussed earlier?

Regards,
Edward

Dear Edward,
We discussed all sorts of business. What business are you referring to?

Yours truly,
Isabel

The sweater situation.

Edward

Charlie's not reading your e-mails. Why didn't you just say that to begin with?

Isabel

Did you talk to Charlie?

Yes.

And?[11]

Problem: Charlie's sweater smells be-

10 I think it's charming that some people pretend these are letters.
11 He eventually loses steam on the niceties.

cause it's the only sweater he has.
Solution: Buy him more sweaters.

Edward loathes long, inefficient e-mail exchanges, which I tend to inadvertently embrace. The phone rang shortly after I dispatched my last missive.

ISABEL: Hello?

EDWARD: Isabel. Edward.

ISABEL: Edward. Isabel.

EDWARD: Would you mind taking Charlie shopping for sweaters tomorrow?

ISABEL: I'm a PI, Edward. Not a fashion consultant.

EDWARD: That's obvious, dear. Also, would you verify that he's washing his undershirts? And maybe have a deodorant talk with him.

ISABEL: Where do you stand on the whole debate between natural deodorants and the aluminum-containing products that actually stop your sweat? Personally, I think it just makes you sweat in other places. I wonder what would happen if you put that stuff all over your body.

EDWARD: This conversation should have ended after I asked you to take Charlie sweater shopping. You should have said, "Of course," and we'd have ended the call.

ISABEL: Can't you find someone more suited for this?

EDWARD: His mother is dead. You're his closest friend.

ISABEL: I think now you're his closest friend.

EDWARD: I run a company worth fifty million dollars and I have over seventy employees. A good manager knows how to delegate. Will you *please* handle this for me?

ISABEL: Consider it done.

EDWARD: I'll consider it done when it's done. Anything else we need to discuss?

ISABEL: Well, your secretary is a bit overzealous with her perfume. Do you want me to have a chat with her about it?

EDWARD: Good-bye, Isabel.

The moment I hung up the phone with Slayter, it rang again. The caller ID said Henry Stone. I debated whether to pick up, because most conversations with my ex-boyfriend don't really go the way I'd like them to.[12] But he generally calls for a reason and then calls again if the call is not returned, so I answered.

"Hello, Henry."

"It's nice to hear your voice."

"Really? Many, many people disagree with you on that point."

"Have you gotten a grip on your dictator complex?"[13]

"It's much improved."

"Excellent. And has it had a salubrious effect on your workplace environment?"

"Maybe. If that means that my employees are in a constant state of mutiny."

"You don't know what *salubrious* means, do you?"

"Nope. Henry, you never call without a reason."

"I'd like to have lunch."

"I do not enjoy eating lunch with you."

"Why not?"

"In the past it was because you'd give me a dirty look if I ordered anything but salad. And now, you still give me a dirty look if I don't order salad, and then you usually tell

12 For more information on H. Stone, see appendix or previous document.

13 This question is more loaded than it might seem.

me about a new woman you're seeing. So I take it things didn't work out with Lola Leggert, and how could you expect they would with a name like that? And now you're dating someone new. Let me save you the twenty dollars in food and fifteen in beer and say, mazel tov, I hope it works out with you and Blank Blank."

"If lunch doesn't work, let's have drinks."

"You don't like drinking with me. I always have more than one."

"I'll make an exception."

"Ah, so things are going well with Blank Blank."

"Yes. Things are getting serious."

"I wish you and Blank Blank the best."

"She's pregnant, Isabel."

"Blank Blank is pregnant?"

"Her name is Annie Bloom."

"Well, that's better than Lola Leggert or Blank Blank."

"Did you hear me?"

"Yes. I take it you're the father."

"Yes."

"Wow. That was kind of fast."[14]

14 We broke up six months ago. He dated Lola Leggert for at least a month, some other Blank Blank for another few weeks, and this Annie character for four months tops.

"I know."

"They have these things called condoms now."

"It's serious."

It felt like that time I stole my brother's LSAT prep book and he sat on my chest until I gave it back. Actually, it felt worse than that. I don't go in for dignity all that often, but some occasions demand it. It's not just for you but the other person.

"Congratulations," I said, and I wanted to mean it, which is good enough. "We'll have lunch soon."

While I was truly happy for Henry,[15] I'm always surprised how quickly men manage to move on. I'm sure you've met the three-month widower already on his third girl-friend. I had wrongly assumed this particular heartache of mine had formed a tough scab. Apparently not. I hung up the phone, stepped into the walk-in closet in the foyer, and had a good cry. This type of behavior I considered to be the height of dignity. Until, of course, D knocked on the door.

"You in there, Isabel?" D asked.

I wiped away the tears and opened the door.

15 If you say it enough, eventually it becomes true. Right?

es. I was looking for this coat. I lost it a
; time ago."

"It's very hard to look for coats in a dark closet."

"You are a very wise man, D. Anyway, it's not there."

"There are other coats in other closets," D said.

"Indeed," I said, thinking we were both talking about the same thing.

Then he said, "There are some great summer sales going on now."

I spent the next three hours entering the staff's time sheets into a database and generating client bills; then I paid office bills in my usual slapdash fashion. Still unable to crack the computer accounting program, I handwrote the bills on the laser printer paper; jotted down a list with the check number, payee, and amount; added up the total; and then went online and made sure we were flush enough to cover the amount. As it turned out, for once, Spellman Investigations was in the black. I guess my mother had finally caught up on some collection calls, because we had more than enough money to cover all of our bills, payroll, and then some. I decided to count my blessings and call it a night. As I headed out, I heard my parents cooking dinner as they watched *Jeopardy!*.

> **ALEX TREBEK:** He was a playwright and president of the Czech Republic.
> **DAD:** Milan Kundera.
> **ALEX TREBEK:** Category: Famous Georges. She was the author of *Middlemarch*.
> **DAD:** Jane Austen.[16]
> **MOM:** I think she has to have George in her name.

I leaned into the kitchen, said good-bye to the unit, and casually mentioned that I'd gotten all of the bills and payroll taken care of. My dad looked surprised and said, "Huh. Good job."

"Have you reconciled the bank statements?" Mom asked.

"Not yet. I'll get to that tomorrow."[17]

It took ten minutes to find parking when I got home (David gets the one-car garage and Maggie the driveway). I traversed the narrow alley to the back of my brother's house and entered my apartment through

16 I never had a fighting chance with these two as parents.

17 Note to self: Learn how to reconcile bank statements.

the door adjacent to the garage. I walked through the narrow hallway that ended in the four-by-four-foot kitchen with a hot plate and minifridge and opened the refrigerator to be met by wilted spinach,[18] a jar of mustard, a stick of butter, and half a bag of Mallomars left over from my sister's last visit. I checked the liquor cabinet, which is just a cabinet where I put booze, if I have any. There was a pricey bottle of bourbon that was a Christmas gift from Slayter. Rarely is booze left untouched, but when my brother told me what it was worth, I thought I might need to pawn it someday, if things got really bad.

I didn't feel like walking to the corner shop and buying a bottle of wine and a bar of chocolate and having the clerk say, "That time of the month again?" so I circled the house and knocked on my brother's front door.

David answered the door in what had become his uniform in the last month — sweats with holes and a ratty T-shirt. This was not the clothing of an overworked stay-at-home dad but a calculated Oscar Madison slovenly wardrobe choice. I will explain it all shortly.

18 I never eat the stuff; why do I buy it?

"Isabel, what a pleasant surprise," he said.

"It's a ten-second commute. How much of a surprise could it be?" I said.

"Well, after last time," he said. "Come in."

I planted my feet firmly in the foyer, making sure to be no more than three steps from the door. "I'm in," I said. "Care to offer me a drink?"

David went to his far more impressive bar and poured me a shot of some midlevel bourbon. "Ice?"

"Yes, please."

He dropped two ice cubes into an old-fashioned glass and extended his arm. The distance between us was approximately ten feet. I stayed put and held out my hand. My brother brought the glass to me.

"You're being ridiculous."

"Can't be too safe."

Maggie, who was also dressed like she was auditioning for a midwestern couch potato competition, brought me a bowl of Goldfish (the snack food) and kissed me on the cheek.

"How are you doing?" I asked.

"I want to kill myself," Maggie said, referring to the thirty-pound dictator responsible for the tsunami of aggravation.

Sydney, my three-and-a-half-year-old niece, sat primly at her miniature dining set in the corner of the living room, wearing a pink crinoline dress, a tiara, and ballet slippers, sipping imaginary tea from an imaginary teacup.

She gave me a quick glance and said, "No Izzy!"

"Do not speak to Aunty like that," Maggie snapped, "or I'll give you a time-out."

Sydney resumed sipping air.

"Relax, Princess Banana, I'm staying right here," I said, planting my ass in the foyer.

"That's good," David said, "sitting on the floor. We should sit on the floor more often."

"We could eat on the floor sometimes too," Maggie suggested.

My brother then took a slug of beer and forced an unremarkable burp.

"Manners, Daddy."

"No manners, Sydney. We don't have those manners here," David said.

"Motherfucker," Maggie mumbled under her breath, but apparently Sydney heard her.

"Bad language!" Sydney said, parroting no one in this room.

Maggie turned to her husband mournfully and said, "What if she's always like this?"

"We'll send her to boarding school."

"Isabel, would you please come all the way inside?"

"I'm not really comfortable with that."

"I promise. No funny business."

"Put it in writing," I said.

Maggie drafted a document on a Post-it[19] and delivered it to me in the doorway.

"Thank you," I said as I relocated to the couch. Sadly, the document was binding only for the next twenty-four hours.

Maggie stretched out on an easy chair (the kind with a reclining lever) that she'd fought violently against as a newlywed and then became its primary occupant. My brother, dethroned, shot her a smug glance and sat next to me.

"Claire and Max are coming over tomorrow," David said to Maggie.

"Good-bye, Izzy," Sydney said.

She says that sometimes, thinking it will precipitate my departure. Sometimes it works.

"That's rude," Maggie said.

Then David muttered under his breath, "Remember, we don't use the R word."

"Don't be rude," Sydney said.

"Okay, it's time for bed," Maggie said. Instead of waiting for her daughter to get to her feet, she scooped her up en route and

19 Toilet paper, Post-it, back of a T-shirt — all can contain binding contracts.

held her under her arm like a football as they trudged up the stairs.

"You found someone to play with her?" I asked.

"Max is my buddy. He's a single dad. He's kind of doing me a favor. Also he wants his daughter to be more assertive, so he figures eventually Sydney will annoy her enough that she'll snap."

David finished his beer and grabbed another from the refrigerator. He attempted to uncap it with his teeth.

"What are you doing?" I said. "Sydney's not here to witness your bad behavior."

"I'm a method actor."

"I don't think your method is working," I said.

"It's just like a cult," David said. "Deprogramming takes time. Enough about my troubles. Let's hear about yours. Has employee morale improved at all?"

"Can't say that it has."

"That, too, will take time."

I suppose I have a little more explaining to do. Please allow me one final digression.[20]

20 Er, there will likely be more digressions than this.

THE IDES OF MARCH[1]

MEMO

```
To All Spellman Employees:
Please take note that Isabel
Spellman is now the primary
owner of Spellman Investiga-
tions. That means that she is
now your boss, no matter what
anyone else might tell you.
                     Signed,
             Management 2.0
```

There were about two weeks of relative calm as my parents were stunned into silence at the change in regime. I suppose we all expected to have some kind of succession plan and I made a few political promises, like making our filing system electronic.[2]

1 Coincidentally I took and lost power in March.
2 A great idea, but to keep even recent files up to date would involve a great deal of scanning.

Once my parents adjusted to the initial shock and were willing to accept my new role in the company, a personal shift happened that I must admit I'm not proud of. After the dust settled and your typical workplace malaise set in, I realized that I had an opportunity here that I was squandering. As the president/vice president[3]/CEO or whatever, wasn't it my job to shake things up a bit? Isn't that what happens in giant corporations when there's a massive personnel shift?

I'd never had power before. You know, like warehouse foreman, chain restaurant manager, camp counselor, gun owner, benevolent dictator kind of power. So, when I finally realized I had the right to call the shots, I will admit that it went to my head. I'll also admit that after thirty-five years[4] of being at the mercy of my parents' shenanigans and power plays and manipulations, I wanted a bit of payback.

The imperative memos were my first order of business.

3 Didn't yet trust anyone to be my right arm . . . or my left.
4 I count my infancy.

MEMO

To All Spellman Employees:
Tomorrow everyone must wear
something in a shade of orange.

Signed,
Management 2.0

MEMO

To All Spellman Employees:
Isabel Spellman should be addressed as Madame President
henceforth.

Signed,
Management 2.0

MEMO

To All Spellman Employees:
Isabel Spellman no longer
wishes to be addressed as
Madame President.[5]

Signed,
Management 2.0

5 It ended up being incredibly annoying and a
directive that was quite difficult to shake.

MEMO

To All Spellman Employees:
Tomorrow is Black-tie Tuesday.
Dress appropriately.

Signed,
Management 2.0

MEMO

To All Spellman Employees:
Filing must be completed every
morning before any office work
begins. The shifts are as follows.

Monday: Albert Spellman
Tuesday: Olivia Spellman
Wednesday: Demetrius Merri-
  weather
Thursday: Isabel Spellman
Friday: Filing-Free Day!

Signed,
Management 2.0

If it's not patently obvious, there was some
recreational malevolence to my filing protocol. Aside from ignoring my campaign
promise of making Spellman Investigations
a paper cut–free office, I was reigniting a fil-

90

ing war we'd had since the beginning of time. Since Friday was designated a *Filing-Free Day!* my father was left the bulk of the filing work (an activity he loathes more than jogging or getting the flu shot, and which he has, in the past, pawned off on any human who gets within spitting distance of the filing cabinet). I knew my mother wouldn't abide my father's leaving the filing to her. And that my mother, with her undying devotion to Demetrius, wouldn't insult him by leaving her day's filing for him. Since I was directly involved in getting Demetrius out of prison, I knew Demetrius wouldn't stiff me either. On Thursday morning, I'd arrive early, stash the stack of papers in my desk, and slowly slip them back into the filing pile on Friday afternoon. Perhaps not the wisest play for company morale, but I really do loathe filing and after years of being a grunt, I didn't see why there shouldn't be a slight shift in the power structure and some new benefits to being the boss.

Before anyone got wind of my filing scam, I stepped up my game and sent out what would ultimately be my last recreational memo.

MEMO

To All Spellman Employees:
As the company structure has changed, the Management has decided to reinterview all Spellman employees. Please schedule an interview with Vivien at your earliest convenience, but no later than one week from today.

Signed,
Management 2.0

Upon seeing the note, my father quickly attacked the sign-up sheet and got the first slot: the next morning at eight A.M.[6]

My father showed up in a seersucker suit (ah, the good old days when he wore outside clothes) and pulled a pastrami sandwich out of his briefcase, which he bit into only after I posed a question.

INTERVIEWER: What do you think are your primary strengths?
INTERVIEWEE: [under or over the sound of chewing] I'm loyal, reasonable, a human lie detector, have twenty years'

[6] What was I thinking allowing for such an early time slot?

92

experience as a cop, another twenty-two as a private investigator, and I know a good sandwich when I see one.

INTERVIEWER: What are your weaknesses?

INTERVIEWEE: [lettuce and bits of mustard have now migrated down to his tie] I could lose a few pounds, get some exercise. I'm no genius.

INTERVIEWER: Are you questioning your own intelligence?

INTERVIEWEE: That's all I've been doing these last few weeks.

INTERVIEWER: Care to elaborate?

INTERVIEWEE: I lost my business to someone thirty years my junior, who lives in a basement, has a rap sheet, and still doesn't know how to separate whites and bright reds when doing the wash.[7]

INTERVIEWER: Do you even want this job?

INTERVIEWEE: I don't know anymore. But you sure can't beat the commute.

Not the best interview ever, but shockingly, not the worst. My mother scheduled hers for the following day. At the appointed

7 Probably shouldn't have put my feet up on my desk.

time, there was a knock at the door and my sister entered in attire so professional I barely recognized her. She wore a pair of brown leather pumps, a houndstooth pencil skirt, a blue button-up shirt with a complementary navy blue cardigan. Her hair was strangled in a bun, and topping it all off were reading glasses dangling from her neck. My sister is petite, like my mother, with an even flatter chest. In jeans and a baseball cap, she is often mistaken for a thirteen-year-old boy. She favors my mother in many ways but is sandy-haired and doesn't possess Mom's striking good looks.[8] That morning my sister looked like something between an eye-catching young professional and a little girl playing dress-up.

"What are you doing here?" I asked.

"I'm here on behalf of Olivia Spellman," Rae said.

"You mean Mom?"

"Let's keep this professional," Rae said, donning reading glasses and looking over a sheaf of papers in a manila folder.

"You won't need those glasses for twenty years."

"I'm here," Rae said, clicking her pen to

---

[8] If I went to church, I think this is one of the things I would thank God for.

attention, "to negotiate the terms of Mrs. Spellman's employment at your agency."

"I am not looking to negotiate," I said. "This is simply a job interview."

"Mrs. Spellman would like to cut her hours and receive a ten percent raise."

"Why would I agree to that?"

"Do you know how to do her job?"

"Yes," I said, "I've been doing it for almost twenty years."

"Have you managed the payroll and bills, and liaised with our outside contractors and accountant?"

"No. But those have always been her responsibilities."

"And she would like to be appropriately compensated."

"I don't know that we have the money for that. Anything else?"

"Yes. Since Mr. and Mrs. Spellman own the property in which you do business, they would like a rental agreement in place. I've looked at comparable spaces, with access to a kitchen, bathroom, television, and a view."

"What view are you talking about?"

"There's a window. We think fifteen hundred dollars a month is fair."

"That would mean everyone would have to take a pay cut," I said, the error of my ways not just sinking in but drowning me.

"Not everyone," Rae said, removing her glasses, snapping shut her file folder. "You have forty-eight hours to negotiate the terms."

By the time Demetrius was up, the game was over. D arrived promptly for the interview wearing a tweed coat and tie. He sat down across from me and said, "Thank you, Ms. Spellman, for this opportunity." Then he placed a piece of paper on my desk.

DEMETRIUS MERRIWEATHER
CV
1994–1996: Merriweather Communications

Owner
- Procured inexpensive televisions and accessories (i.e., VCRs, stereo speakers) for the budget-conscious.

1996–2011: San Quentin Penitentiary

Inmate
- Worked in the kitchen, laundry room, and library. Familiar with the Dewey Decimal System.
- Specialized in dispute management and kitchen fork retrieval.
- Had only one disciplinary citation in fifteen years.

2011 to present: Spellman Investigations

Assistant Investigator
- Research assistant; specializes in database research and background checks; in-office catering; types 35 words a minute.
- Specializes in dispute management and food preparation.
- Employee of the month 12 months running.
- **Other interests:** Getting innocent people out of prison, origami, cooking, television, *Judge Judy,* Zumba.

"What's Zumba?" I asked.

"I don't know," D said. "But everyone lies on their résumé."

I looked over D's résumé and said, "You're hired."

"Thank you, Ms. Spellman. I promise you, you won't be disappointed."

"This was a dumb idea, wasn't it?"

"Girl, what were you thinking?" D said, finally out of interview character.

"I was drunk," I said. That's not a figure of speech. I really was drunk.

"Were you drunk when you wrote *all* the memos?"

"Not the filing one. That was a stone-cold-

97

sober calculation. The interview was just payback. When I was eighteen or something my dad made me interview for a job I already had."

"What did you do?" D asked.

"I wore a ridiculous outfit, ate a sandwich, and called him Mr. Mellman repeatedly."[9]

"You didn't think he'd remember that?"

"Now what do I do?"

"Watch your back," D said.

"It's not that bad, is it?"

"It's worse than you think."

"What are they going to do?" I asked.

"There's something you need to put in your mind. Spellman Investigations, to most clients, is Albert and Olivia and the relationships they've maintained for twenty years. The office is in their house. They're entitled to thirty percent of the equipment if they decide to go their own way."

"You don't think they'd branch off and start their own business, do you?"

"How hard would it be? Same location, switch the name a bit — you don't have a copyright on *Spellman.* They could downsize, take only the cases they want. It could be perfect for two people thinking about retiring," D said.

9 See document #4.

"What would be the advantage of that?"

"They'd be their own bosses and wouldn't work under the dictatorship of Madame President Isabel anymore."

"Is that what it looks like to you?"

"I'm Switzerland, remember?"

"So you're telling me they have all the power."

"They have most of it."

"If that happened and they offered you a job, where would you go?"

"Depends."

"On what?"

"Who gives me the better offer."

After the interviews, my parents took a disappearance to Big Sur. I left a series of increasingly apologetic messages on their cell phones. None were returned.

Three days later, when I pulled up to 1799 Clay Street, I was elated to discover Dad's Audi in the driveway. I raced out for bagels and lox from some bagel shop[10] and pastries from *none of your business;* picked up flowers, champagne, and orange juice from *a store;* and attempted to improve morale

10 We're not known for bagels, so I'm not going to provide free advertising for a meh bagel distributor.

with a sleep-inducing feast for all. My parents partook of the buffet, filled their bellies with baked goods and cured fish and drank at least a bottle of champagne on their own. They appeared rested and restored from their holiday, and I thought this might be the time to say a few words.

"I think I owe you all an apology, especially Mom and Dad. When the company structure changed, I didn't fully consider the ramifications of my actions, nor was I sensitive to my parents' feelings about the manner in which I handled the transaction. While I still do not regret my decision to buy out the company shares from my siblings, I must admit that all of my actions since then have been immature, lacking in leadership, and utterly pointless. Please accept my apologies. I hope we can restore the office to its previous state of mutual respect."[11]

"Anyone need a nap?" my dad said, tossing his napkin on his plate and stretching his arms in a long, leisurely yawn.

"I'm in," Mom said, not even considering clearing the table. "Thanks, Isabel. That was

11 Yes, I did write the speech out ahead of time, and the part about the "previous state of mutual respect" was baloney.

an excellent spread."

After my parents ambled up the stairs, Vivien said, "Maybe the champagne was a mistake."

Viv carried a stack of dishes into the kitchen; I turned to D, hoping for an explanation, guidance, anything.

"People forgive at their own pace," D said.

"Maybe you could take them to church with you sometime and speed it up. I hear forgiveness is really big in those places."

"So is humility," D said.

"Point taken," I humbly said. Right now D was my only real ally (otherwise known as not-an-enemy) and I couldn't afford to lose him.

In the days that followed, my parents came to work sporadically and rarely did any actual work. Mom collected office supplies for a decoupage project she'd decided to embark on; Dad made long-distance calls on the company line; Mom filed her nails (she apparently kept her nail file in her desk drawer); Dad played marathon games of Plants vs. Zombies; Mom handled her online shopping. Occasionally one or the other would answer the phone, always with the same line: "Isabel Spellman Investigations. How can we help you today?" If the client was an old friend, my parents would lead with the ugly truth.

"Our daughter participated in a hostile takeover. Yeah. She's now the boss. You think you can trust family, but you can't. What do you need, Bob/Jim/Tony/Sally? Olivia and I are always here to help. You have our cell numbers, right?"

Since direct communication was fraught with conflict and I had no idea what work my parents were doing for the clients who were in their purview, I would occasionally phone their clients, pretend I had misdialed, make small talk, and ask if I needed to relay any messages to the unit. That's how I learned that my folks were indeed handling the bare bones of their casework. That's also how the unit learned I was checking up on them, when I accidentally "misdialed" a client twice.

While the memo business got off to a bad start, I had to keep it in operation because when I spoke to my parents they would often not even register that I was in the room. Some days it felt like being a ghost. My attempts to draw my parents into conversation covered a range from banal to sensational.

"Some weather we're having."

"Did you see the 49ers game last night?"[12]

"Did you read about the triple-murder cannibalism case in the Netherlands? All connected to bath salts, I hear."

Sometimes I'd snow them just to see if they were listening.

"Did you hear Princess Banana has measles, mumps, and rubella?"

Mom would promptly call my brother's house, learn otherwise, engage in a chatty conversation with D, and then take an early lunch or leave the house and not come back until the end of the workday.

As far as I was concerned, the worst had passed. My parents were accomplishing some work after hours. I'd find database research and background reports for the major clients on my desk in the morning. I assumed this was all a phase that would pass, and since we were getting by, I chose to ride it out.

Then a slew of past-due bills began sliding through the door, and notices from the IRS and EDD (who the hell are they?). Apparently the payroll taxes were not being paid. Other than me, all the employees were receiving their checks as usual. I simply

12 Not the best conversation starter, since football season was long over.

handwrote my usual check and figured that refusing to write my paycheck was my mother's only form of fiscal dissension. I was foolish enough to believe that even in our hostile work environment we could maintain the status quo.

I had always put the bills on top of my mother's desk. She had always put them in her top right-hand drawer until she paid them. The first part had remained the same; the second part had not. One morning when I questioned Mom about whether the bills were being paid, she opened her desk drawer to reveal a bountiful stash of unopened envelopes and said, "Is that what those are?"

"Mom, why aren't you paying the bills?" I asked, trying to remain calm.

"I thought you were," Mom said.

I was lucky to get an answer.

"That was always your job."

"Maybe in the old days, when your father and I had a say in how the company was run."

"You still have a say," I said.

"Well then, I think — and your father agrees — that you should take over all the fiscal duties. You should certainly understand the financial responsibilities of running a company. Wouldn't you agree?"

I didn't disagree. However, I didn't actually know how the payroll was handled, nor was I educated on our accounting software. I asked my mother if she could train me on the financial protocol.

"Of course, dear," she said. "How does June of next year work for you?"

So that's when I officially took over all of the fiscal responsibilities for Spellman Investigations. If I didn't understand something, I looked it up on the Internet. If I wasn't sure if there was enough money in the account to pay a bill, I checked the balance and calculated how many checks hadn't cleared. Every night I read the manual for the accounting software and it put me right to sleep.

Between the "bookkeeping" and the client billing, this added another fifteen hours to my workweek. With my parents' hours trimmed at least 50 percent and the limitations of delegation to Demetrius (refuses to do surveillance)[13] and Vivien (too green for most jobs), I was working seventy hours a week and getting paid the same as before. Given the rampant disrespect and the fact that I was being held hostage by my em-

13 "Why is it so hard for you to understand why I don't want to follow white people around?"

ployees, you must understand that I was itching to fire someone. When my father's computer caught a virus from what was obviously a dodgy online game, and it spread throughout the office, I phoned Robbie Gruber, our disagreeable computer consultant, to repair the problem.

He arrived two hours late, soaked in an obscene body spray, which was only camouflaging an odor so rank you didn't mind the body spray. Every computer has access to the server, but Robbie sat down at my desk, pulled out a bag of Cheetos, and while annihilating our computer virus, chomped on his snack nuggets, licked his fingers, and finger-painted my keyboard with his DNA and yellow dye #4.

"How much?" I asked when he was done.

"One fifty."

"Your rates have gone up by fifty percent?"

"You no longer get the friend-and-family rate."

"Why is that?"

"You know why."[14]

"I'm deducting thirty bucks for a new keyboard."

"I might not be available the next time

14 I blackmailed Gruber a year ago. I kind of had it coming.

you call."

"I won't call. You're fired."

"Al, Olivia. Good luck with your new ar-rangement," Robbie said as he wadded up his dead bag of Cheetos and headed out the door. He twisted his beefy torso to throw the junk food carcass into the trash bin and missed, sending a cascade of orange dust onto the carpet.

There were times when I thought that every move I'd made in the last three months, year, decade, maybe, had been a mistake. I had thought the business might thrive under my new leadership. Now I wasn't sure if we could survive. Apparently, the worst had not passed. But before it gets worse, and I tell you all about it, how about a bedtime story?

Princess Banana and Her Wicked Great-Grandmother

Once upon a time a modest defense attorney and a slick corporate lawyer fell in love. Maggie Mason and David Spellman were their names. At first their differences made the match seem improbable. Maggie stashed baked goods in her pocket and wore old dresses with the hems coming undone at the seams; David went to a personal trainer a couple times a week and would hide sweets in his house, hoping to forget where he put them. But somehow they made it work, though not by meeting each other in the middle; David bent purely in Maggie's direction.

After the unlikely couple married, Maggie had a baby, a little girl named Sydney, and it was Sydney who turned David into a shadow of his former self.

After the child was born, David decided to give up his old life and become a full-time father. No one remembers exactly when David stopped looking in the mirror and only at his beloved wife and daughter, but it was probably right around the time they brought Sydney home from the hospital. The next thing everyone knew, David's custom-made suits had found their way to the back of the closet. Jeans, old T-shirts, sweatshirts, pajamas, and bathrobes became his daily uniform. He lost his hairstylist's phone number and eventually the barbershop around the corner was just fine. He shaved a couple times a week and he went to the gym as often as your average family man.[1]

Sydney grew up with a doting father as her primary caretaker, a working mother who managed as much quality time as she could, two adoring grandparents, and two aunties. Sydney's Aunt Isabel tried her best but had never taken a shine to babies or toddlers or people at eye level with one's kneecaps. Sydney's Aunty Rae, however — shorter in stature, which perhaps marks more of a commonality with her niece — generously offered to babysit. David and Maggie, sleep-deprived and housebound, like most new parents, greedily accepted the free babysitting whenever the opportu-

1 Three times a month.

nity arose.

All would agree that the first year of Sydney's life went quite smoothly. She learned to say *Mama* and *Dada;* she learned to walk; she learned to eat creamed carrots and applesauce. She learned to pick up Cheerios and throw Cheerios. And then there was this incident, mentioned in the previous document,[2] when she was about eighteen months old: Sydney learned how to say *banana.*

That is when the trouble began for David and Maggie and Sydney and a few other Spellmans.

Sydney began calling many things *banana.* If you held up an orange, she said *banana.* A carton of milk, *banana.* Cheerios, *banana.* Oddly enough, if you showed Sydney a banana she would shout, "No apple."

David discovered that his favorite babysitter and sister (Rae) was conducting linguistic experiments on his daughter. He never told anyone because when Rae was a child David wrote a children's book called *How to Negotiate Everything,*[3] which he read to Rae repeatedly as a toddler. This book

2 Now available in paperback!
3 Now available from Simon & Schuster Books for Young Readers. I'm not joking.

has informed Rae's character in more ways than any of her family wishes to consider. So, in a way, David performed his own experiment on a family member.

It wasn't that babysitters were in short supply. David and Maggie lived just a few short miles from Albert and Olivia Spellman's home. But he had seen what female product had come from the parental unit — Isabel and Rae — and he wanted none of that.

And that was a mistake David would pay for dearly.

Ruth Spellman — Grammy Spellman, great-grandmother to Sydney — like all grandmothers, lives to babysit. It was a win-win situation for David and Maggie. Or so they thought. No one likes Grammy very much, or at all. But she certainly would know how to keep a child alive and put her to bed at a decent hour and until Sydney complained, they would avail themselves of her services whenever they needed a night out.

This almost brings us up to date. Remember Isabel,[4] the impoverished younger sister of

4 This is the only time I will ever refer to myself in the third person.

David, who lives in her brother's basement apartment? One night, Izzy decided to forage for food upstairs. She entered quietly through the back door to avoid disturbing any sleeping children or awake adults. As Isabel perused the pantry and gathered bags of Goldfish, string cheese, and a bottle of cheap wine that she knew her brother would save for family dinners or unwelcome guests, she overheard a conversation in the living room that alarmed her working-class sensibilities. She placed her reserves on the dryer and tiptoed down the galley kitchen to the mouth of the dining area, where the acoustics were more eavesdropping-friendly. Two familiar voices were having the most disturbing conversation.

GRAMMY: Young lady, elbows off the table.

SYDNEY: I want fish.

GRAMMY: What do you say?

SYDNEY: Fish please.

GRAMMY: Those are empty calories, young lady. That's the kind of food your aunt Izzy eats. It's not good for you.

SYDNEY: Cookie please.

GRAMMY: Sit up straight. A young lady crosses her legs. You have to be very careful when you're wearing a dress, Sydney. Here's your cookie.

SYDNEY: Thank you.

GRAMMY: In the future you should say thank you before you start eating the cookie. And for every cookie you eat, you have to walk around the block at least twice or play in the park for twenty minutes. If you get hungry later, we'll have carrot sticks.

SYDNEY: I don't like this.

GRAMMY: It is a cookie for young ladies.[5]

SYDNEY: But I don't like it, Grammy.

GRAMMY: I don't like them either, but they're low in calories. So, Sydney, what do you want to be when you grow up?

SYDNEY: A princess. I want a cookie.

GRAMMY: How about I make you a deal.

SYDNEY: I want a cookie.

GRAMMY: Wouldn't you like a pretty pink princess dress?

SYDNEY: Yes. I want a princess dress.

GRAMMY: I will get you the prettiest princess dress you've ever seen if you promise Grammy that you will eat

5. Further investigation determined that it was Melba toast.

young-lady cookies and stay away from bad food.

SYDNEY: Izzy food?

GRAMMY: Right. Stay away from Izzy food.

SYDNEY: Where is the dress?

GRAMMY: Do you know what else a princess has to have?

SYDNEY: A crown.

GRAMMY: A princess has to have impeccable manners. Do you know what manners are?

And that is when the brainwashing began. Every Thursday night — movie night for David and Maggie; Emily Post night for Sydney and Grammy — Grammy would arrive, help Sydney into a pink crinoline dress and tiara that she purchased as a bribe for the occasion, and let loose with a series of manners tutorials fit for a 1950s cotillion.

David and Maggie, heady from the rush of freedom that movie (and sometimes dinner-and-a-movie) night provided them, were blind to the tiny shifts in their daughter's personality. Being a good sister and the sworn enemy of Grammy Spellman, Isabel warned her brother and sister immediately after she overheard the first disturbing conversation. Maggie and David promised to look into the matter, but a babysitter you could call at a moment's notice who didn't charge was hard to come by, and who could argue against teaching your daughter manners? It wasn't until Sydney's playdates started dropping out as fast as Grandpa Albert's hair in the eighties that David and Maggie began heeding Isabel's warning.

Maggie and David immediately installed a Grammy Cam and invited Grammy Spellman over for what would be her last unsupervised visit with her great-granddaughter. After witnessing the programming firsthand, Maggie and David decided to deprogram their daughter by example. Good manners went out the window. Anyone famously ill-mannered was welcomed into their home with open arms.

For the next several weeks Isabel found herself to be the guest of honor virtually every day in the Mason/Spellman household. She was treated like a queen, waited upon hand and foot, offered Goldfish, beer, bourbon, whatever food they were serving that night. Extra coffee and porridge were always made in the morning. If she accidentally swore or put her shoes on the coffee table, nary a comment was made. Isabel discovered that the less presentable she appeared, the more compliments she received.

Isabel had never known a more peaceful living situation, if you put aside the pink tyrant sipping air tea in the corner. Everything was perfect until one night when Isabel came home from a brutal day at the office. She dropped her coat and bag at her apartment and quickly climbed the stairs to the Mason/Spellman hearth to see what was for dinner. Maggie had ordered pizza that night, with mushrooms and olives. An interesting choice, Isabel thought. Her favorite toppings, but neither David's nor Maggie's. That wasn't the only thing that was out of the ordinary. Maggie was wearing a pretty blouse and a not-too-wrinkled skirt. Clothes she wore outside, not inside.

Maggie pulled a beer from the refrigerator for Isabel and opened the pizza box.

"Hungry?" Maggie asked.

"Starving," Isabel said, taking a plate from the cupboard as she sat down at the table. "Where's Princess Banana?"

"David's putting her to bed."

A few minutes later, David came down the stairs.

"She's out," he said.

David, too, had cleaned up. Isabel had an uneasy feeling in the pit of her stomach.

"Did you see the pizza?" David asked.

"Yes," Isabel said.

It was an unusual question since some of the pizza was in her mouth.

"Do you need anything else?" Maggie asked.

David and Maggie began inching toward the door. It was only then that Isabel knew something was terribly, terribly wrong.

"Are you going somewhere?"

"An eight o'clock movie. Sydney's asleep. She won't be a problem," Maggie said.

"We owe you," David said.

Before Isabel could say another word, David and Maggie ran out the front door and down the driveway as if the house was on fire. They jumped into Maggie's car and burned rubber, pulling onto the street. They were gone before Isabel could utter a single word in protest.

Isabel locked the door and calmly accepted her fate. As long as Princess Banana stayed asleep, there was no place she'd rather be and she had everything she needed — pizza, beer, and a large-screen TV.

But Princess Banana didn't stay put. Thirty minutes later, footsteps padded along the staircase and she heard the all-too-familiar words.

"No Izzy!"

"Banana, if you go back to sleep, when

you wake up I won't be here."

"No Izzy," the princess said again.

"You can keep saying that all you want, but it won't make me magically disappear."

"Where are Mommy and Daddy?"

"At a movie," Isabel said.

"Mommy and Daddy," the princess demanded, stomping her foot.

"They will return when the movie is over."

"Now."

"No. Come on, let's go back to bed," Isabel said, climbing the stairs.

Princess Banana sat down on the top landing and wouldn't budge.

"Sydney, go to bed," Isabel repeated.

Princess Banana said, "You have bad manners."

"You have bad manners," was Isabel's clever retort.

There was nothing to be said after that. Princess Banana remained stubbornly seated and trained her eyes wistfully on the front door.

"You're not a lady," Banana said.

"You got that right," Isabel said, taking a seat a few steps down from her niece.

That is where David and Maggie found them exactly one hour and forty-five minutes later, when they returned home. Sydney rushed into her father's arms. Isabel slowly got to her feet and worked out the kinks in her back.

Isabel looked at the couple with cold, dead eyes and said, "I could waste a few hours thinking about payback, but you know what you did was wrong. I had two unpleasant hours with your child. You have the rest of your lives. Sleep tight. Don't let the bedbugs bite."

WHERE WAS I?

MEMO

To All Spellman Employees:
Case meeting tomorrow, 10:15
A.M. ~~Attendance is Mandatory~~
Please attend, everyone. Your
input is invaluable.
                    ~~Signed,~~ Respectfully,
                    ~~The Management~~ Isabel

In case you've lost track of time, we're now
back to the beginning of the story, approximately four months after I took over
as chief operating officer of Spellman Investigations. Approximately a week after Rae
took Vivien's case, I first met Damien
Thorp, was enlisted to defragrance Charlie's
sweaters, and Henry told me his girlfriend
was pregnant. And, once more, I was trying
to wrangle the crew together for a meeting
and failing, as usual.

Even with D's blueberry muffins as incentive, the unit refused to turn out for the ten fifteen meeting. I phoned the home line to see if they'd pick up. No answer. Although I could hear them watching a morning program in their bedroom. There's that saying about the mountain and Muhammad and I'm not saying it, but as you can see I've been reduced to thinking in clichés. D grabbed the basket of muffins, Viv collected mugs from the kitchen, and I took the carafe of coffee and the case files up to my parents' bedroom.

I knocked twice, asked if everyone was decent, and we entered.

"I guess we'll have the meeting here," I said as I hunted for the on/off switch on the television. Once I clicked it off, Dad clicked it on again with the remote. We continued the on/off rally for a few more strokes until I pulled the power cord.

I politely poured my parents each a cup of coffee, which they accepted in silence. D's muffins, on the other hand, they snatched up with warm gratitude. Vivien took a seat on the floor by the window; I removed a pile of clothes from a captain's chair in the corner and offered it to D; I sat on the end of the bed like I did when I was a little girl.

"Who would like to begin?" I asked.

Silence.

"Anybody working any cases?"

More silence. I turned to Vivien.

"Any updates on your moving-company case?"

"I couldn't find anyone named Owen Lukas connected to Lightning Fast Moving, so Rae made a pretext call. She claimed that she'd had a really great experience with her moving consultant and described him to the secretary. The secretary said he sounded like Marcus. Cross-checking owner names on the corporate records, Marcus Lorre was his full name. There are three Marcus Lorres in a probable radius, so we're going to run a quick surveillance on known addresses and see if it's the same guy."

"Under no circumstances, Vivien, are you to speak to him again."

"Got it," she said.

"See if you can locate any of the other people who have claims against the company and if they were dealing with a Marcus Lorre or Owen Lukas."

"I think Rae is already on it," Viv said.

"Any theories on why the guy is using a fake name?" I asked.

"Rae thinks that if the owner is using an alias it provides another layer of protection. It's hard to file a complaint against a man who doesn't exist."

"How's your soap sculpture going?" D asked.

"They must use a different brand of soap in prison," Vivien said.

Mom and Dad managed to remain completely oblivious to the business meeting happening right in front of them. Dad reached for another blueberry muffin and Mom smacked his hand away.

"One is more than enough," she said.

"Is there anything you guys want to talk about?" I asked.

"The muffins are excellent, D," Dad said.

"Delicious as always," Mom said.

"I meant about work," I said.

"No, dear," one of them said.

"D, what do you have on Divine Strategies?"

"On paper everything looks great. I looked over the D & B that Mr. Slayter provided and the financials are solid. No UCC filings or even civil cases on record."

"That all sounds good. Any problems?"

"More executives have departed in the last ten years than support staff. In the last two years, they've given five percent bonuses across the board. Usually in a company with this kind of revenue the executives could expect more."

"Is it possible that a company exists without following the tenets of traditional corporate American greed?"

"It's possible," Mom said, interrupting.

"I asked Olivia to look over the report," D said.

"Mom, do you have something to add?"

Through a mouthful of blueberry muffin, Mom said, "Something isn't right there. I just can't say what. It's too perfect. Usually there's more turnover in the support staff than on the executive level, but with Divine Strategies it's turned upside down. Also, human resources could be remiss in their records, but even for a company that size, there's been only one disciplinary report and one firing in the last eight years."

"That sounds like a good thing to me."

"Companies are motivated by greed. You have firms that smartened up after the financial crisis, but Divine Strategies has been like this for years, it seems. It's possible they're a corporation with a conscience, but the cynic in me says it's something else."

"Any ideas?" I asked.

"Track down some of their previous employees and interview them," Mom said.

"Would that be something you'd consider doing?" I asked with a polite and even tone.

"I might be able to work it into my schedule," Mom said.

"Thank you. That would be wonderful," I said.

Viv looked at her watch and said, "I have a paper due in an hour and I haven't started it. Mind if I go?"

"No problem."

D's cell phone rang. He looked at the caller ID and said, "It's Maggie. I better take it."

After he departed, I looked at my parents, who hadn't moved from their state of repose.

"Anyone planning on getting out of bed?"

"Maybe later," said Mom.

"This can't go on forever," I said.

"Of course not," Dad replied. "We'll die eventually."

I returned to the office and caught D at the tail end of his phone call.

"Maggie, I would strongly encourage you to read his file in full before we invest any more time in this case."

Then he did a lot of listening and saying *uh-huh, uh-huh, I do understand, but — yes, okay. I remember.* Then he hung up the phone and stared out the window for an unusually long time. There is no view, no

125

matter what anybody tries to tell you.

"Everything okay, D?" I asked.

"Can't complain."

"How's the pro bono case going?" I asked.

"We, I mean I, interviewed Washburn at San Quentin State Prison the other day."

"How was it being back at the Big Q?" I said.

"Excuse me?" D said.

"San Quentin State Prison. The Big Q. We should use the right lingo, don't you think?"

D ignored my suggestion and said, "I need to do some follow-up interviews after I finish transcribing the tapes."

"Do you want me to help?" I asked.

"With what?"

"With the typing," I said. "No offense, you're still using two fingers."

"Won't get any faster if you do it for me, right?"

"Right," I said. Only there was something I was missing. "He's innocent, right?"

"His alibi was another convict but seems legit. And the witness identification was certainly suspect."

"Then what's the problem?"

"I don't like the guy," D said as he donned his headphones and put his index fingers to work.

After one of the better workdays I'd had in weeks,[1] which was subpar for any other workday in the last year, I decided to celebrate by going to my usual watering hole, which is also below its former standards. I blame the proprietor, Bernie Peterson. He's a retired cop who was friendly with my uncle, if *friendly* to you means having an intimate knowledge of a person's most gluttonous, avaricious, or salacious self. In the "good old days," as Bernie would call them, I had to extract the men from the grimiest establishments. At times it seemed they were hell-bent on shrugging off the usual habits of retirees. I think they played golf together once, more as a drinking game than any other kind of pastime. One beer per hole.[2] They lasted eight holes, until it took Bernie fourteen shots to sink a ball already on the green, causing a traffic jam on the links. Security finally removed them after they climbed into a golf cart and tried

1 We had a meeting with all employees in attendance.
2 It was more of a reward system, which I'm not sure they stuck to stringently. Let me put it this way: Bernie can drink eight beers easily.

to engage the other players in a game of chicken.

Uncle Ray has been gone for years, but I always forgave him because I knew his debauchery masked his pain. With Bernie I always got the feeling he was having a good time and couldn't have cared less if it screwed up anybody else's good time. Even if their idea of a good time was playing *golf*.

Now that I've mentioned Bernie, you might as well meet him.

I entered the Philosopher's Club and Bernie shot out from behind the bar and tried to pin me into a bear hug. This dance usually involves a minor contortion act as I dodge his embrace. Bernie had to settle for a solid pat on the back. He thinks we're like family; I don't even think we're like friends.

"Ain't you a sight for sore eyes," he said. He said it because it had been a while since he'd seen me and that's the way he talks. Work and all has cut into my drinking.

I sat down on a bar stool.

"What'll it be?"

"Whiskey and a beer back and not too much chitchat," I said.

"That kind of day," Bernie said, not taking the request personally. It was personal.

I picked up a leftover newspaper and held it in front of my face, reading attentively.

Bernie served my drink and started reading the other side of the paper, commenting aloud.

"It looks like we got some rain coming. Tuesday. Maybe a little drizzle on Friday. It's blazing in Arizona. Fifty percent off at Macy's on Saturday."

I put the paper down to get him to stop reading.

"There's that pretty face," Bernie said.

"How's Gerty?" I asked since Bernie wasn't going anywhere. Gerty is[3] Bernie's girlfriend. She also happens to be the mother of my ex-boyfriend Henry Stone. When I came to the bar, I had half-hoped to see Gerty. But this wasn't my day. Neither was yesterday, come to think of it, or the day before.

I managed snippets of peace and quiet while Bernie tended to the other patrons. I finished my drink and Bernie served up another beer without my asking.

"On the house," he said.

Just when I was done with the on-the-house beer, Henry Stone arrived. This was no coincidence.

Henry took the seat next to mine.

"I thought I might find you here," he said.

3 Oh how I wish I could say "was."

129

"Why? Because some buffoon told you I was here?"

"I prefer *gentleman* to *buffoon*," Bernie said.

"So do I," I said. "I didn't see you make a phone call."

Bernie pulled his smart phone out of his breast pocket and flashed it in front of me. "I text now. And sometimes I sext."

Henry cleared his throat.

"Sorry," Bernie said, and then he poured me a whiskey and Henry a light beer.

"I'm not paying for that," I said to Bernie.

"We're all family here," Bernie said, this time more to Henry than me.

Henry swiveled around on the bar stool, leaned over, and gave me a kiss on the cheek. He smelled like soap. In a good way. I tried to breathe through my mouth.

"How have you been?" he asked.

"Great," I said. "I think being the boss really suits me. It probably would suit me more if my employees showed up for work."

"It'll get better," he said.

"When? I'd like an exact date."

"About our phone call the other day."

"Hang on," I said, downing the shot of whiskey and smacking my hand on the bar for Bernie to pour another.

This time I paid.

"Haven't slowed down," Henry said, "have you?"

"Nope."

"Are you okay?"

"I broke up with *you,* remember?" I said.

"It was unplanned," he said.

"I'm happy for you. I know that's what you wanted. I hope she's nice and can handle nine months without a drink. God, that sounds unbearable."

"Maybe you can meet her sometime."

"Sometime," I said. "Been busy working and I'm seeing someone."

"Who?"

"You don't know him."

"I didn't think I did. Who is he?"

"He's, um, the new chief counsel for Edward."

"A lawyer? Your mother must be so proud."

"Yes."

"We should double-date."

When a telephone rings at such an opportune moment, it is certainly hard to believe. But, really, my cell phone rang just then. It was Edward.

"Isabel. Edward."

"Hello, Edward. What's up?"

"We have a problem."

"What kind of problem?"

"My brother just lost five grand at an illegal poker game in Oakland."

"Sounds like your brother has a problem."

"I need you to take care of it."

"How?"

"Take the five grand from the safe, drive to Oakland, pay his debt, and bring him back to my house."

"I don't think driving is recommended in my current condition."

"And that is?"

"Drunk."

"Then I'll call my driver and have him pick you up."

"Wouldn't it make more sense for your driver to pick you up?"

"It would."

"Then why don't you get your brother from the game?"

"Because if news gets out that Ethan is related to me, he'll be invited to every game in town."

Henry offered to drive me. And since Slayter wasn't sure when or from where he might rouse his driver, it seemed the most expedient solution. First we drove to the Spellman offices, where I could extract the money from the safe. It was all making sense now. I saw the flickering light of the television in the living room, and I wanted to avoid engaging in a lengthy explanation of my evening's plans and fielding questions such as:

We had five thousand dollars in our safe?

Are you driving drunk?

Henry's in the car outside? Invite him in; it's been ages.

I realize, for you grammar-conscious readers, that last part wasn't a question. My point is, entering the house through the front door would have caused more hassle than necessary. I used the slim jim I keep in my purse to pry open the window, hoisted myself inside, extracted the money from the safe, and was back in Henry's car in five minutes.

"Still door-averse, I see," he said.

"More parent-averse, these days."

For the record, I've made a drastic reduction in my window entries and exits in the past year. I'd like to say it was a result of maturity, but really, I'm just too old for it.

At eleven P.M. on a weeknight, the drive to the East Bay was blessedly brief.[4] Henry tried to talk about things, like feelings, closure, the passage of time, and all that

4 During rush hour, however, you are a fool if you don't take public transportation.

bullshit. I interrupted him and told him a story about when I was in the fifth grade and sent to sleepaway camp, more for my parents' benefit than mine. I used to break into the camp director's office at night and make crank calls and rearrange his office supplies. I'd study him each day to see how well my gaslight games were working.

"I used to follow him around with a notebook," I said. "Kind of like the way anthropologists study gorillas. If things had gone differently, maybe I would have been an anthropologist."

"I'm sorry," Henry said. "I think I'm missing the point."

"No point. I just wanted you to stop talking."[5]

We arrived at the address provided, which was a house on stilts embedded deep in the Oakland hills up a narrow canyon road. One had to wonder about men filled with drink traversing this terrain. The two-story rustic home was dim, but I could see lights beyond the driveway in what appeared to be a guesthouse.

Henry parked.

"Wait here," I said.

"I'm going in," he said.

5 The Avoidance Method™ at its best.

"You can't. If you see things you shouldn't see you might be inclined to arrest people, which could make matters worse for my boss's brother."

Henry picked up his phone and pressed number three on speed dial. My phone rang.

"Hello?" I said.

"Leave your phone on," he said.

I rang the doorbell to the guest bungalow in back. A middle-aged man — and when I say *middle-aged* I always mean at least fifteen years older than I am,[6] which would make him about fifty — with dark circles under his eyes and matching sweat stains opened the door. His work shirt, probably once a nicely pressed pinstripe, was as wrinkled as his brow and untucked, draping lightly over his protruding belly. There were five other men in the room, all approximately the same age, some dressed more casually than others, some booze soaked, and two aerating the room with dueling cigar smoke.

Then there was the guy wearing an ascot. While his clothing had endured the same twenty-hour marathon as his cohorts, he still tried to strike the pose of a man in control. He was beefier and shorter than

6 In ten years, the same math will apply.

Edward but had the same icy blue eyes and deep parenthetical creases around his mouth. I'd expected a man on his last legs, barely able to sit upright and perhaps groveling for another loan to play another hand. That was not the case.

"Darling, what took you so long?" Ethan said with a crisp British accent as he got to his feet, circled the table, and pulled me into an embrace.

"Tell me you have the money," he whispered in my ear.

"Tell me why you have an English accent," I whispered back.

"I will never hear the end of this when I get home," Ethan said to the group. I'm not sure anyone was believing that a) Ethan and I were an item and b) I held the purse strings in the relationship. Then again, I had arrived with five grand in cash.

"How much does he owe you?" I asked the room.

"Forty-five hundred," said one man. That one had eyes like a ferret and the jowls of a turkey. His look of amusement sparked in me a deep sense of discomfort. Guys like that like to help people become their worst selves. I got the feeling these games were his idea and he encouraged the players who were short on cash to return, because when a man owes you money, you have him on the ropes. I'd have bet the five grand that Ferret Eyes had had a lot of men on the ropes in his day.

I turned to Ethan. "How much did you come in with?"

The guy who answered the door, Pit Stains, responded for him. "Three grand."

I took the five grand from my purse and put it on the table.

"Here's a little extra. You don't let him back here again."

"Anyone who's paid up is welcome back."

I reached for the stack of bills on the table. Ferret Eyes gripped my hand over the cash, gluing me to the table.

"I don't believe we've been introduced," I said. "I'm Isabel. And you are?"

"Bob."

"What an unusual name," I said. "How do you spell that?"

My free hand reached into my pocket and pulled out my phone.

"Bob, I have a friend who'd like to talk to you."

I passed the phone to Bob. He listened and then released his grip on my hand. Bob passed the phone back to me, took the five-hundred-dollar tip off the top, and slapped it on the table in front of me.

"We're even," he said to me. Then he turned to Ethan and said, "Don't show your face around here again."

"It has been a pleasure," I said.

On the drive back to the city questions darted back and forth like Ping-Pong balls. Ethan wanted to know who Henry was. Henry wanted to know who Bob was. And all I really wanted to know was why Ethan had a British accent. The only benefit of being the third wheel in the car was that I didn't have to engage in any serious conversation with Henry.

"So you're my brother's consigliere," Ethan said.

I turned to Henry to translate.

"A confidante, usually in the context of organized crime. But it can be used more casually," Henry said.

"I'm his jogging partner," I said. "And I do some other work for him."

"Edward's jogging partner has always been his consigliere," Ethan said.

"Who was his last jogging partner you met?"

"Oh, it was a few years ago. A Glen somebody."

"What happened to him?" I asked.

"Died, I think."

"See," I said, jabbing Henry in the ribs.

138

"Jogging isn't good for you."

Henry pulled the car in front of Slayter's Nob Hill mansion. Maybe it's not quite a mansion, but it's a pretty big house that stands on its own, which is unusual for San Francisco.

"Should I wait for you?" Henry asked.

"Your work here is done," I said.

"Will I see you around?" he asked.

"Until I find a new designated driver," I said.

Slayter was in his pajamas and robe, poring over every last word of *The Wall Street Journal,* when I delivered his brother to him. Before Edward could toss out any kind of admonishment, Ethan said, "I will pay back every penny. I assure you."

"I would prefer it if you didn't lose money in the first place."

"So would I," Ethan lightly replied.

"Why is your brother English?"

"He's not."

"I spent several years abroad," said Ethan.

"Four," said Edward.

"And I simply couldn't shake the accent."

"Like Madonna?" I asked.

Ethan ignored the question, went to the bar, and poured himself a brandy. "I'm knackered," he said. "Off to bed."

When the guest room door shut, Edward

said, "Thank you."

"I think I got him kicked out of that game. But there are always other games."

"Indeed."

"He seems like quite a handful," I said. "Why do you put up with it?"

"I'm sure your parents asked themselves that question more times than they can count," he said.

I boycotted jogging Monday morning and arrived early at the office. On my desk was a photocopy of a sexual harassment complaint referencing a date from 2001. The plaintiff was named Sheila Givens and the defendants were Brad Gillman and Bryan Lincoln. I'd heard the defendants' names before and racked my brain for an answer. D always writes a note when he leaves any documents on my desk. I assumed it could be only one of my two disgruntled employees who'd left this for me. I climbed the stairs and knocked on the door.

"We're sleeping," Mom said, not sounding sleepy at all.

"I'm coming in," I said, counting to five, to give them time to cover up.

I opened the door to find the unit in bed drinking coffee and sharing the newspaper.

"We should get a lock on the door," Mom

said to Dad.

"I'm on it," he said.

"Which one of you left the complaint on my desk?"

"That would be me," Mom said.

"Why do these names sound familiar?" I asked.

"They're two of the executives at Divine Strategies."

"How did D miss this in his research?"

"Notice how the complaint isn't stamped?" Mom said. "It was never filed."

"Then how did you get it?"

"I have my ways."

My mother has amassed a galaxy of sources throughout the years. With an almost prescient understanding that a day like this might come, she has never shared these sources with me. In fact, some of these sources she hasn't even shared with Dad.

"Well, um, thanks. I appreciate it," I said.

"No problem."

"Are you guys coming into work today?"

"I don't know," Dad said, shrugging his shoulders. "There's something at the museum we're thinking about seeing."

There was nothing at the museum they were thinking about seeing. If there were ever two people who cared less about art, I hadn't met them. Still, my mother had given

141

me evidence on a case that I wouldn't otherwise have had. I considered it progress.

"Have a nice day," I said.

I returned to the office and searched for anyone named Sheila Givens who lived in San Francisco, Contra Costa, or Marin County during the time of the complaint. I narrowed the search to women who would now be no older than fifty-five or younger than thirty-two. I had five names left and I ran a credit check on each one, hoping the employment history would go back far enough to reference Divine Strategies. I found the plaintiff Sheila Givens living in Tiburon. I phoned her home line and got her answering machine. Since the complaint was never filed, I had to assume it wasn't a subject she wished to discuss, so I left a message claiming to be from an asset recovery firm and waited for her call.

She called. They always call. And then they are profoundly disappointed when they realize that no assets in their name have been recovered. I apologized profusely, explained the situation, and solicited her help, hoping that she had that common and very human need to share. It's always surprising the things that strangers will tell you. Any woman who has found herself in a public restroom can attest to this fact.

"I'm sorry," Sheila said. "I can't help you."

"You filed a complaint. Something must have happened."

"It was a long time ago," she said.

"That doesn't mean you've forgotten."

"Please don't call me again."

"Has anything like this happened to anyone else?"

"I can't help you," she said again. "And you'd be wise to let this thing go."

And I might have, if she hadn't offered that final reproof.

That afternoon I dropped by Slayter's office to give him the report on Divine Strategies and take Charlie Black sweater shopping. Damien was in Slayter's office doing whatever lawyers do.

"Isabel, you remember Damien, right?"

"No," I said. "Have we met?"

"You do look vaguely familiar," Damien said.

"Don't encourage her juvenile sense of humor," Slayter said.

"If you're going to insult me," I said, "the least you can do is validate my parking."

"Would you please show some manners?" Edward said, nodding his head in the general direction of Damien.

"Nice to see you again," I said.

"A pleasure," Damien said.

"Tonight I think you should show Damien around the city," Slayter said.

"Let me check my calendar, Uncle Ed."

"I checked your calendar. You're free. I'll have Evelyn send you his information."

Sadly, Edward knows I have no social life and can generally be relied on for such things as retrieving indebted gambling addicts, taking navigational consultants sweater shopping, and playing tour guide to satanic lawyers. It wasn't so long ago that I had a life and my availability wasn't a foregone conclusion.

I could see Charlie Black through the glass door staring at his digital watch. He was clearly timing his entrance for the exact moment Edward had told him to arrive.

At exactly one fifteen P.M. Charlie entered the office.

"Timely as usual," Edward said.

"Good afternoon," Charlie said. "I'm ready whenever you are, Isabel."

I turned to Damien and said, "I'll pick you up at eight o'clock. Show you some of the places I like. If you mention Fisherman's Wharf once, I will have you beheaded."

"She won't," Charlie said, as if it were a legitimate threat.

"Got it," Damien said with a smirk.

Damien looked at Charlie and Charlie at

Damien. It soon became evident that avoiding an introduction would appear rude. Edward stammered a bit as he said, "I suppose introductions are required. Damien, this is Charlie. Charlie, Damien."

The two men shook hands, but I could tell that Damien was looking for a job title and, well, giving him the real job title might have been unwise.

"Charlie is Edward's valet."

"Nice to meet you," Damien said, seeming perplexed. Even the lowest-rent valet probably doesn't smell or dress like Charlie. No offense, Charlie.[7]

"I'm his valet," Charlie repeated, which he does whenever he knows I'm lying and I want him to play along. Once he contradicted me in front of an acquaintance and I explained my take on harmless lying to Charlie and how it was at times a necessity, and I asked for his backup when the occasion arose. Charlie agreed so long as he wasn't lying to his boss, Mr. Slayter. I accepted his terms.

"Does anyone want some tea?" Charlie asked, because that's what valets do. They serve tea and take your coat, but no one was wearing the kind of coat you took.

7 "None taken," Charlie would say.

"I'm good," I said.

"No, thank you, Charlie," Slayter said.

"Well," Damien said through a thicket of awkwardness, "I'll get back to work."

After Damien left, I turned to Slayter and said, "Polka, foghorn, shank, and that's shank in the prison-weapon sense, not lamb shank."

"For our purposes, it doesn't make a difference," Edward said. "Polka, foghorn, shank."

"Before we go, I need to talk to you about Divine Strategies. I've got something," I said.

"Have a seat, Charlie," Edward said.

As far as I could tell, Edward's trust in Charlie was implicit. He had not once in the last five months ever asked him to excuse himself, no matter what the context of the conversation. There are few things you can count on in this world. Charlie is one of them.

"My mother found an unfiled sexual harassment complaint against two of the executives at Divine Strategies. The employee is no longer there. I contacted her, but she won't talk."

"One sexual harassment complaint," Edward said. "Is it possible that it was unfounded and the company paid her off to

146

avoid a lawsuit?"

"It's very possible," I said. "In fact, it happens all the time. But I spoke to the complainant and I got the impression she was paid off and signed a gag order."

"And this is the only red flag?"

"Aside from the fact that they make a product called HolyBooks?"

"I repeat, is it the only red flag?"

"It's the only complaint that we found. There could be others who got hushed. There is only so much you can learn about a company through a paper trail."

"Indeed."

Slayter sat behind his desk, rubbing his temples.

"Let me get back to you on this," he said. Then he pulled several bills from his wallet and handed them to me.

"Have fun shopping," he said. "Why don't you buy yourself a dress too while you're at it? When you're showing Damien around tonight it would be nice if you looked like the sort of person who worked with charities and was not in need of one."

"Ouch," I said, not feeling the sting. "Come on, Charlie, we've got a lot of money to blow this afternoon. Do you want to hit the arcade or the burger joint first?"

"I thought we were going sweater shopping," Charlie said.

I turned to Slayter before we departed. "Words?"

Slayter furrowed his brow and tapped his fingers on his desk. "Shank, like the weapon; polka; and banana. No. Something about San Francisco. Foghorn."

The reception desk was empty when Charlie and I departed.

"Where's Evelyn?"

"Her mother broke her hip yesterday. I think she has to find a convalescent home for her. She can't live on her own anymore. She's under a lot of stress," Charlie said. "Try to be nice to her."

"I'm nice to her," I said.

"No, you're not," Charlie said with the flat judgment of an impartial mediator.

"Well, she's not nice to me either."

"That's true."

As Charlie and I strolled the four blocks from Slayter's office to the mall, we briefly touched on Charlie's new job title.

"You need to be really careful, Charlie, especially around people we don't know. It's extremely important that people believe you're his valet, not his navigational consultant. No one can know that Slayter has problems with his memory. That's a secret, okay?"

"So should I be doing things valets do?" Charlie said.

This was a question for Edward, but the comic possibilities were endless and I'm quite fond of the butler persona, so I took the liberty of answering it myself. "I think that would be wise."

We purchased five tasteful new sweaters for Charlie in a variety of colors. To keep my spirits up, I insisted on one fisherman-themed cable-knit with a mock turtleneck and a patched yarn anchor on the front. Charlie reminded me that I was supposed to buy a dress and so I grabbed a navy blue wraparound number that looked good on the mannequin.

The dress didn't look as good on me. But it fit, and so I tossed on a pair of boots since I didn't feel like shaving my legs, emptied the trash from the front seat of my car, and drove to Damien's executive apartment near Van Ness and Washington. The high-rise had a doorman who insisted on getting my name and calling up to the apartment.

"Mr. Thorp isn't ready. He asks that you go upstairs," the doorman said.

I'd never had a chance to visit one of Slayter's executive apartments — I knew he had three, and they were often vacant — so I jumped at the chance.

I knocked on the door.

"It's open," Damien shouted from somewhere, but I was too distracted by my reflection in chrome everywhere to notice.

One bedroom, full bath, a thousand square feet of fresh cherrywood floors, modern stainless steel appliances, and nothing in need of repair. Two entire walls were floor-to-ceiling glass with a real view of the city (i.e., not Mr. Peabody's living room) and had remote-control shades for when the view got old or the glare of a sunny day gave you a headache. And there were probably two more of these vacant right now.

I'll be frank. A flashy new apartment splattered in chrome with a doorman sentinel and suits for neighbors who read *The Wall Street Journal* like the Bible isn't exactly my dream home. However, I live in a musty five-hundred-square-foot illegal apartment with a cattle run above my head from five A.M. until eleven P.M. And I didn't have a bathtub or an oven — not that I'd have used either, but still. I made a mental note to one day invite Slayter to my digs and see if he might take pity on me.

"You clean up well," Damien said, coming out of his bedroom.

"You clean down well," I said, realizing I

was overdressed. Perhaps my casual attire when we had met had guided Thorp's fashion choice for the evening. He wore Levi's and sneakers, with a lightweight button-down shirt that had been washed by a bachelor, no starch, no iron — just removed very quickly from the dryer.

"I'm overdressed," I said.

"I'm underdressed," he said. "I can change."

"It's okay. You have to wear a suit all day. I only have to look nice at funerals."

"And charity functions," Damien added.

"Right. And charity functions."

I scanned the apartment for a second time.

"Nice digs," I said.

"Not bad," he said casually, like he'd seen better, which kind of annoyed me.

"What kind of tour are you in the market for?" I asked.

"What do you like to do on a Monday night?"

Work late, steal some booze and Goldfish from my brother's house, watch television, pass out. Or give rich lawyers with free swanky apartments cheesy San Francisco tours.

"What don't I like to do is a better question," I said.

"Are you hungry?"

151

"I could eat." That was an understatement. "What are you in the mood for?"

"A friend of mine told me to get a famous San Francisco burrito."[8]

"You have a wise friend. But we'll have to go to the Mission for a good one."

"That's what I heard."

"The Mission is less, um, sanitized than what you're accustomed to."

To be frank, no part of the city is all that sanitized. On a hot day much of it smells like urine.

"You're offending me now," Damien said. "I'm from Boston. I'm very familiar with unsanitary conditions."

"Good to know."

Damien hopped into my crappy Buick without comment. As we drove to the Mission, I provided banal commentary on the passing sites.

"There's a church; that's Fell Street. You can take it to the park. There's a restaurant. I think it's okay. If you like opera, the opera house is somewhere around here. Although I couldn't point it out and I won't be taking

8 Seriously, anyone who goes for clam chowder in a bread bowl over a burrito should have his head examined. Tell Dr. Ira I said hi. (Some people will know what that means.)

152

you there. Ever."

We ordered burritos at Pancho Villa, which happens to be just a quick stroll from the Sixteenth-and-Mission BART station, arguably the grimiest corner in the city. What it lacks in prostitution, it makes up for in drugs and public urination.[9] Fortunately, the taqueria is brightly lit, so you can't really see outside. You can, however, see all of my pores, so I suggested we walk the two blocks to the Albion, so that we could eat and drink beer in dim lighting. If you've never eaten a San Francisco burrito, the proper way (no fork or plate) can be a bit unruly. I, of course, have an associates' degree in burrito management and had to school my subject on the appropriate method of consumption.

As Damien began to disrobe his dinner, I said, "That aluminum foil is the only thing between the burrito and your lap. Only remove the aluminum wrapping under that which you plan to consume within the next five seconds."

He tucked his napkin in his shirt, a gesture so lacking in ego, I found it charming. My dad always does it and he really has no ego.

9 I realize I might seem slightly obsessed with this topic, but sometimes I wear sandals.

Like almost none at all.[10] And come to think of it, he generally doesn't care if he has food particles on his clothing. So you kind of wonder why he bothers with the napkin at all.

Once Damien got the hang of eating and drinking, he started talking. Or, more specifically, inquiring.

"Did you grow up in the city?" he asked.

It was a benign question, but one on a personal level I was determined to avoid.

"Yes," I said. "There's a farmers' market downtown on Wednesdays and Sundays. Oh, but you probably don't cook."

"How long have you been Mr. Slayter's niece?" Damien asked.

He was sharper than I thought. The Avoidance Method™ was the only response.

"When you get a car, remember to take Gough or Octavia, not Van Ness, especially if you have any interest in making a left turn."

"Tell me about your charity work," he said.

"It's important to give back. That's what I learned from Uncle Ed. Did you know that

10 No offense, Dad.

Irish coffee was invented in San Francisco?" [11]

"I don't know how you have the time for charity work, what with running your investigative agency and all."

We have a website. Apparently the man knows how to Google. I could have spent the night hanging on to shreds of the charade, but what was the point? He was watching me eat a meal the size of a small cat. Clearly I was no relation to Edward Slayter.

"What else do you know?" I asked.

"Pretty sure you're not his niece."

"But he's kind of like an uncle and a boss and a benefactor all rolled up into one."

"Why did he lie?"

"Maybe he thinks having an investigator on his payroll makes him seem paranoid."

"Is he paranoid?"

"Everyone is paranoid."

"Do you do any charity work?"

"I do some work with kids."

I would pay for that comment. Hell, I'd already paid for that comment.

After I witnessed Damien spill half of his

11 Why are we giving Irish people the credit? They're already taking credit for Irish stew and Irish bread under questionable circumstances.

dinner on his lap and consume two local microbrewed ales, we decided to call it a night. I pulled my car into the loading zone in front of his building.

"That was fun and educational," he said.

"Make sure that's in the report to the boss."

"Well," he said, still sitting in the car.

Since I'd picked him up, was I supposed to get the car door? Does the women's movement involve binary chivalry?

"Well," I said.

I thought maybe a handshake was in order. As I extended my hand, he leaned over to, I suppose, kiss my cheek. I ended up poking him in the gut.

"Sorry," I said. "I'm not clear on how normal people end platonic evenings."

"You were going for a handshake? After all we've been through together?"

"I suppose it was a bit formal."

"I think so," Damien said.

"Stay where you are, so no one gets hurt," I said as I unbuckled my seat belt, leaned over, and kissed him on the cheek.

"Good night, Damien."

"Good night, Isabel."

That Saturday morning, I found myself alone in David and Maggie's house, availing myself of their bountiful breakfast and caffeinated options, reading the paper in my pajamas, and trying to forget that I lived in the dungeon ten feet below. I had no idea where they were, only that they were graciously gone. Since I was alone in their remarkably comfortable home, I reclined on the couch and turned on cartoons. There was an excellent episode of *Phineas and Ferb* playing: "Lawn Gnome Beach Party of Terror." In this episode, Phineas and Ferb decide to build a beach in their backyard and Perry, their pet platypus who is also a secret agent,[12] is on the case of the disappearing lawn gnomes. Having disappeared lawn gnomes in my past, I was particularly engrossed in the drama when the chirpy doorbell interrupted me. I ignored it at first, thinking it was the mailman or some delivery guy. They could have come back tomorrow, but the doorbell rang again and again and I could see someone attempting to peer through the window, even though the blinds were drawn.

I swung open the door to find a man with two children standing on the stoop. One of

12 Also known as Agent P, Perry works for the OWCA. (Organization Without a Cool Acronym). Heh.

the children, I should mention, was Princess Banana. Since no other adult was around and I was already leaping to very bad conclusions, I pretended to not notice this fact.

"Can I help you?"

"Hi, I'm Max," the adult said.

I had a vague recollection that this was a friend of David's, but it was wise to play dumb.

"You selling something, Max?"

Sydney, in her princess dress, now missing a few layers of crinoline, brushed past me and started shouting for her parents.

"Banana," I said. "Mommy and Daddy are out."

"No, Izzy," Princess Banana said, pointing at me.

"This is one thing we agree on," I said to my niece. "No Banana." Then I turned to the only other adult in the vicinity. "Why are you here?"

"I'm returning the kids from their play-date."

"Did you say kids, plural?"

"Yes. We have an understanding."

"You and I don't have an understanding."

"Right. But David and Maggie and I have an understanding."

"You must be early for your understanding," I said.

"No. Eleven A.M. We've been at the park for three hours. That's exactly two hours more than enough."

I couldn't argue with him. That's a lot of park time and Max looked like he needed a break. But that was not my problem. I picked up my phone and called my brother.

"Yello," he answered. I can't remember when he started doing that, but I wished I had some electrical cord attached to him so I could shock him out of the habit.

"Some guy named Max is here. With Princess Banana and some other kid. He's returning both the princess and another kid —"

"Max Klein and Claire," Max clarified.

"Max Klein and Claire from a playdate. Does that make any sense to you?"

"We had to wait an hour for brunch," David said. "We're still eating. Do you mind sticking around?"

"You promised this would never happen again."

"Please, Isabel."

"I can't. I have an appointment," I said. At the moment, I didn't look like the sort of person who had an appointment, but my brother couldn't see that through the telephone.

"Put Max on," David said.

Max just listened. He said *uh-huh* a few times in the form of a question mark and he consulted the ceiling.

Then Max said into the phone, "Who is this person? I'm not comfortable leaving my child with her."

"You shouldn't be," I said, taking the phone from Max. "Listen, David, I fell for this once, it's not going to happen again."

"Izzy, we just got our food. We will eat like Kobayashi.[13] Max has an appointment in a half hour. We promised him we'd take Claire. Two kids for an hour. What's the big deal?"

"Your daughter is totally uncool."

"She's three and a half years old and it's not our fault."[14]

"That was your excuse when she was two."

"Hundred dollars off next month's rent."

"Two hundred."

"One fifty."

"Deal," I said, hanging up the phone. "I'll take the kid," I said to Max. "Does she have

13 Takeru Kobayashi, also known as Tsunami, arguably the most famous competitive eater in the business.
14 If Sydney appears to be aging at an alarmingly fast rate and this is bothering you, see appendix.

any food allergies?"

Sydney was in the middle of the living room barking regal orders at a blond-haired, blue-eyed doll. *Tea, please.* The princess was now trying to affect an English accent. I had a sudden vision of Sydney as an adult, and it wasn't pretty. I turned back to the father-and-daughter duo in the doorway. Claire, judging by the way she was trying to twist out of her father's grasp, clearly wanted to join Sydney, or at least be in the vicinity of the television, but Max held tight.

"You're David's sister?" Max said, as if he didn't believe my brother.

"Yes. I know, the resemblance is uncanny."[15]

"Do you live here?"

"Not here. Downstairs. But I thought it was safe to be upstairs today. Guess I was wrong."

"Are you comfortable taking care of children?"

"Absolutely not."

"How often do you watch Sydney?"

"As little as possible. You've met Sydney, right?"

Max sighed, glanced at his watch nervously, and then looked at his shoes as if

15 It isn't.

161

they would hold the answer to whatever question was on his mind.

"You have an important appointment?" I asked, my manners flicking on like a lazy fluorescent light.

"Yes."

"Don't worry about it," I said. Then I looked at Claire and said, "How's it going? You're Claire?"

Claire just stared at me.

"I'm going to call you Claire until you tell me otherwise. Claire, would you like to go play with Sydney and the blond-haired doll?"

Max loosened his grip on Claire; his daughter brushed past me and found a spot next to Sydney, picking up another doll.

"She'll be fine," I said, sensing Max's epic discomfort. "I'll keep her out of trouble. We'll have juice and Goldfish, and David and Maggie will be back in no time."

"Thank you," Max said. He slowly turned around and walked to his car, the entire journey heavy with contemplation.

The girls eventually fought over the blond doll even though there were three brunettes available. I distracted them from the doll fight with television. I started with a classic *SpongeBob.* Claire was intrigued, but Sydney shouted, "No Izzy," at the television, which makes absolutely no sense. I moved on to *Phineas*. Claire started cheering, but Sydney put the kibosh on that as well with a tear-jerking demand for "Dora!" I asked Claire if she was cool with that and Claire shrugged her shoulders agreeably. I located a *Dora the Explorer* DVD, which did the job. As in, it hypnotized the girls long enough for me to trash (as in, throw in the trash) the conflict-laden shiksa[16] doll.

Within fifteen minutes of snack time, David and Maggie returned home. I didn't bother with a babysitting debriefing or a reminder that forced child care is unacceptable behavior, even among family members. I simply said, "You just paid one hundred and fifty dollars for ninety minutes of babysitting. That's my standard rate from now on. Think twice, next time."

Then I slipped out the back door and returned to the safe haven of my dungeon.

It was past midnight when Slayter phoned. The ringing jarred me from deep sleep and I awoke gasping for breath.

"Hello?"

"I have an idea," Slayter said.

16 For the record, I have no problem with blondes. Just blond dolls.

"Then you should write it down and call in the morning," I said.

I heard a couple of clanking and shuffling noises on the line.

"I'm sorry. I lost track of time. Ethan and I were playing chess all night. He won a few times," Slayter said.

"I've lost every game of chess I've ever played," I said.

"He's never been able to beat me," Slayter said, concern edging into his voice.

"You're distracted. It doesn't mean anything."

"I'm noticing things. Last week I couldn't remember my secretary's name. She's worked for me for seven years and I didn't know what to call her."

"I have a few suggestions."

"It's getting worse."

"I'm sorry," I said.

There was a long silence on the other end of the line. Just Slayter breathing. He'd never done this before, called me in the middle of the night in a panic.

"It's late," he said.

"I know," I said. "But you had something you wanted to tell me."

"Right," Slayter said.

"What is it?"

"I don't remember."

INSIDE JOB

MEMO

To All Spellman employees:
I will be out of the office
Monday, Wednesday, and Friday
mornings for the next few
weeks. Please make sure that
someone is in the office and
available to answer phones.

Signed,
Isabel

Slayter never remembered why he called me, but when we next met, he most definitely had an idea. Without any direct evidence or testimony about the hushed sexual harassment claim at Divine Strategies, Slayter thought it might make sense to get a more personal assessment of the office climate. He'd used some clout at a local temp agency and managed to get me a part-time job as a receptionist. One of the employees was on maternity leave and the company needed a little extra help to pick up the slack.

"It won't take up too much of your time," Slayter said. "Three mornings a week, answering phones, reading magazines, and . . . I think you'll need a new wardrobe."

"I have professional-looking clothes."

"You don't want to be too buttoned up, if you know what I mean."

"I don't."

"You should look more like Evelyn."

"I take it you'll pay for the breast augmentation."

"I don't mean to be indelicate, and if any of this makes you uncomfortable, please let me know and we'll nix the whole idea."

"Oh, I get it. You're sending me in as bait."

"I wouldn't use that word. You're measuring the temperature of the office. See what happens."

"I hate to break it to you, but I'm just not the kind of woman that men sexually harass."

"Maybe if you stopped slouching, you would be," Slayter said in all seriousness.

"I'll work on it," I said as I slouched out of the office.

"Knock it off," Slayter shouted.

When I passed Evelyn's desk, she was chatting with Arthur Bly, Edward's head accountant. He was smiling at some delightful thing she had said, which I found highly suspicious because she's never said anything delightful to me.

"Hi, Arthur," I said cheerily.

His response was a cold nod.

"Hey, Evelyn," I said. "What's a girl got to do to get her parking validated?"

"Park in the garage," Evelyn said.

"Fair enough."[1]

On the way to the elevator bank, I passed Damien's office. I tried to make myself invisible (by walking really fast) but he spotted me.

"Hey there, Isabel the detective."

My fast getaway foiled, I turned back and hovered in his doorway. "Hello, Damien the lawyer," I said. "How are you settling in?"

"Good. I had a nice time the other night."

"I hope you made note of that to the boss," I said.

"Maybe we could do it again sometime."

"Eat burritos? I think you need something

1 There was that *one* time I took the validation when I found street parking and sold it to some guy I met in the elevator bank. A parking attendant ratted me out.

167

more filling."[2]

"What are you doing tomorrow night?"

When people, men specifically, ask me this sort of question I tend to respond to it as polite conversation and don't figure out until much later that it might be something else.

"I haven't thought that far ahead."

"I'll pick you up at eight," Damien said.

"Good afternoon, Spellman Investigations, how can I be of service to you?"

I heard the all-too-familiar cold, staccato voice from the hallway. I almost walked right out the door then and there, but an explanation for her presence was required. I was still clothed in my Divine Strategies uniform. A white silk blouse, buttoned decently; a pencil skirt; and pumps that gave me, I loathe admitting, a newfound respect for Evelyn, or at least her feet.

Wait, I'm jumping ahead of myself.

Just four hours earlier, I'd started my first half day on the job playing receptionist at Divine Strategies. I answered the phone,

2 As I mentioned earlier, Damien had a dreadful time managing the unruly food item and most of it landed on his lap.

"Divine Strategies." Just the name, no other baloney.

Maureen Stevens, the office manager, greeted me and gave me an uneventful tour of the office and made a few introductions to members of the support staff — Amy Cohen, Brad Gillman's executive assistant, and Layla Bryant, Bryan Lincoln's assistant. There was also the bookkeeper, Betty Peters. Objectively speaking, I would have sexually harassed at least three of the four women ahead of me, but there was still a chance I could play confidante.

Whether it was by design or circumstance, I was not introduced to a single male in the office. I gleaned the identities of the two men named in the complaint. Brad Gillman, fifty-two — a carnival guesser would have put him at least five years older — wore expensive suits that strained at his gut and shoulders, as if he wasn't willing to accept that he was never going to lose the most recent ten pounds. Bryan Lincoln, same age, appeared fit and vain and had the uniform hair tone of a man with a mediocre dye job.[3] There were other men in the office

3 Note to men: You will never hear "His hair color looked so natural" unless it actually is natural, and then nobody needs to say it.

whose identity I could only ascertain through the nameplates on their doors: Noah Stark and Steve Grant, head programmers.

The phones rang at an alarming rate, at least compared to the phones at Spellman Investigations, which left less time than expected for office gossip and personal introductions and that magazine reading that Edward promised. I took a bathroom break when I saw Layla head into the ladies' room and attempted girl talk while I pretended to check my face.[4]

"So how long have you worked here?" I asked.

"Six years," Layla said.

"You must like it."

"I do. They're good to their employees here."

"How's your boss?"

"Maureen is great," Layla said. "But I don't think of her as a boss. More like a colleague."

Two thoughts came to mind: It was intriguing that Maureen was considered the boss, and maybe I should stop referring to myself as a boss and go with *colleague*.

"If you need anything, let me know," Layla

4 I'm not sure what I was supposed to find.

said as she returned to her desk.

At lunch I went outside and called my friend Len. He and his partner Christopher had recently moved to New York and promptly moved back to San Francisco. We're not supposed to mention why, but Len is an actor (the kind who auditions but doesn't act that often) who finally decided to test his mettle in the big city. Apparently his mettle was lacking in something. Christopher had never wanted to move and was glad for the return but had been struggling to deal with his partner's deflated ego. I'd recently gone over to their loft for dinner and the primary topic of conversation had been Len's failed acting career. Len eventually got tanked and began lamenting the myriad professional stereotypes that plagued his race and sexual orientation.

"Drug addict, gangbanger, the occasional fashion diva, black lawyer, black judge, black hairstylist, black guy drinking soda."

"Can you play white?" I asked.

The evening ended shortly after that.

When I called, I could hear a soap opera playing in the background. Len quickly muted the TV set.

"What do women talk about?" I asked.

"I don't know, Isabel. I'm a man."

"I'm working a case," I said, "at a mostly female office. I'm trying to get information from my coworkers in the bathroom and I would like to know what women discuss in bathrooms."

"If you had more female friends, you wouldn't have this problem."

"Why, because we'd be spending all of our time talking about our feelings in bathrooms? I don't think so. Maggie and I don't do that, and Petra[5] and I certainly never did that."

"That's because you and Petra were too busy setting explosives off in the toilet."

"Later, Len."

Other than a few friendly exchanges with the female staff involving my complimenting their wardrobe choices, I had one office interaction. Brad Gillman — senior executive with the tight suit — approached the reception desk with a sheaf of papers.

He cleared his throat until I looked up.

"Isabel, right?"

"Yes. Hello. You're Mr. Gillman," I said.

Avoiding eye contact, Gillman said, "Brad is fine."

5 My best friend and partner in crime for many years. We'd lost touch recently.

He put the papers on my desk and stepped back.

"Would you be so kind as to make ten photocopies for me?"

"Of course."

I made the photocopies and put them in the inbox outside his door, as Maureen had instructed me to do.

As soon as I returned to my desk Maureen approached and asked me whether Layla had shown me the filing yet.

"The filing?" I asked.

"Follow me," she said, walking briskly in the direction of an unmarked door next to the copy room. Inside was an eight-by-five-foot area with wall-to-wall filing cabinets.

She pointed to a phone on the wall. "You can answer phones as you file. And feel free to take ten-minute breaks every hour or you'll go crazy in here."

I noticed a small pile of papers on top of the corner filing cabinet.

"Is that it?" I asked.

I followed Maureen's gaze to a three-foot-high stack of loose pages leaning against the wall.

"I'll leave you to it, Isabel. Don't forget to come up for air."

So, some people might call this karma.

There wasn't much reconnaissance I

could do from the prison of the file room, so I took as many breaks as I could and tried to make small talk in the bathroom. I also tried to study the body language of the office staff as I was en route from the file room to the bathroom. It was like watching people driving bumper cars but deliberately avoiding each other. I didn't see so much as a pat on the back. The only conclusion I drew that morning: This would be an excellent place to work during flu season.

After I left Divine Strategies, I dropped by the drugstore and bought a box of Band-Aids for my current and future paper-cut wounds. I entered the Spellman office that afternoon to find Grammy Spellman playing receptionist instead of toddler etiquette coach. I'm not sure which role she was less suited for. Today Grammy was in her best beige polyester. She sat primly, with the posture of someone with a two-by-four strapped to her back, behind my father's desk. In between answering calls, she sanitized the surface area of the desk, the telephone, and the keyboard. She looked as she always does, as if someone had just murdered her cat and she was contemplating modes of revenge. Sure, she's my grandma, but I'd go to the mat against anyone who thought they had a worse grandma. Unless your grandmother is a serial killer. Then you win. Your grandmother is awful, but honestly, she probably has better stories.

My point is, the unit's decision to invite Grammy into the office could only be seen as a direct act of aggression. Clearly no progress had been made in my peacemaking efforts.

Spellman Central was otherwise abandoned. Whether Grammy's presence was responsible for that fact, I did not yet know.

"Grammy, what are you doing here?" I asked immediately upon entry.

"Albert asked me to help out since no one would be in the office this morning."

"Where are Mom and Dad?"

"I believe they're at an appointment."

"What kind of appointment?"

"They didn't say."

"Thank you for your help, Grammy. You can go."

"I have three messages for you. Mr. Demetrius called and he said that he had to do a last-minute interview for one of Maggie's cases. It's near Sacramento. He won't be back in the office today. Vivien was here earlier and said to tell you that she's working on Lightning Fast? Is that some kind of diet?" Grammy asked.

Grammy is diet obsessed, so it would be a natural assumption.

"It's a moving company."

"And your gentleman friend Henry Stone called. He said you weren't answering your cell. He was a very nice man. It was so unfortunate that you couldn't hang on to him."

"Grammy, can I offer you a ride home?"

"Oh no. I'll walk. The exercise is good for me. That's how I keep my trim figure. What's your secret?" Grammy asked, seething with sarcasm.

"I'm on an all-seafood[6]-and-bourbon diet."

"It's doing wonders for your complexion."

"Good-bye," I said encouragingly.

"Always a pleasure," Grammy said, clutching her purse and walking briskly out of the office.

I tried to wake my computer and it responded like a teenager after a night on the town. I pressed restart and the monitor turned black, a bunch of crazy numbers mobbed the screen, and then it froze. I had Robbie Gruber on speed dial, but since I fired him, I couldn't summon the energy

6 Goldfish.

for what would amount to a groveling phone call. I walked over to Vivien's desk and turned on her computer.

Like most companies, we keep our files on a server so that they can be accessed from any computer. I was about to enter a cursory report on my first day at Divine Strategies when I noticed a file folder on Vivien's computer desktop named Lightning. I clicked on the folder. Inside was a collection of JPEG files but not a single text document. Before I looked at the images, I checked the server for a matching file and found a Lightning folder that contained only the scanned information from our intake form. I clicked back on Vivien's desktop, opened the Lightning file, and reviewed the collection of unlabeled JPEGs.

01 The first image was of a male subject, approximately thirty-five years old, medium height and build, with dark brown hair peppered with gray.

02 Second image showed Subject getting into his car.

03 Close-up of his license plate number.

04 Subject standing in foyer of a single-family home being greeted intimately by a strawberry-blond-haired woman with

flotation devices as breasts in a pink silk
robe.
05 Photo through window into bedroom of
home. Subject and same woman undress-
ing in bedroom.
06 The money shot.

There was no other information in the file
and no way to confirm the identities of the
individuals other than checking the license
plate number on the car.

I decided this was a good time to return
Henry Stone's phone call.

He picked up on the second ring. No
hello, just, "Why does it take you three days
to return a phone call, and who hired Ruth[7]
as receptionist?"

"My apologies. I'm running my business
into the ground and having trouble keeping
up with non-work-related phone calls. I
have no comment on the Grammy question.
What's on your mind?" I asked.

"Let's have a drink sometime."

"Don't tell me you knocked somebody
else up."

"No. I just want to have a drink. What are
you doing tomorrow?"

Just when I was entirely convinced that
the universe was conspiring against me, it

7 A.k.a. Grammy Spellman

threw me a bone.

"I have plans," I said.

"No you don't," he said, which wasn't as insulting as it sounds. I rarely do have plans.

"Seriously, I have plans. I'm having drinks or something with Edward's new chief counsel."

Dead silence. Henry might have been more shocked by what might have been construed as me on a date than I was by his pregnancy blindside.

"Why don't you have drinks with your new woman. I'm sure she's thirsty." I said, just to fill the void.

"She doesn't drink."

"You're dating a teetotaler?"

"She's pregnant, Isabel."

"Right. Well, it will have to be another time. Are you sure you can't debrief me over the phone, or via e-mail? I don't mind a telegram now and again."

"Drinks."

"I'll agree to drinks under one condition."

"What?"

"I need you to run a license plate for me."

"Now I know why you returned my call."

After my phone call ended with Henry, I studied the photos on Vivien's computer for a few more minutes before I made the call. I left a standard message.

"Vivien, when you get the chance, call me back."

There was no point in giving her time to conjure an explanation or contact my sister, who at all times has a half dozen very plausible lies waiting in her back pocket.

Meanwhile I discovered yet another deception among my employees. Maggie phoned as I was reluctantly tackling the massive filing heap.

"Hi, Isabel, sorry again about the other day," she said.

"You're not sorry. That's the thing."

"What did you think of Max, Claire's dad? His divorce should be finalized in a few weeks, but they've been separated two years, so he's totally available."

Now I was getting annoyed. "Seriously? Is that why you called?"

"No. I wanted to clear Demetrius's schedule, if that's all right. I need him to handle some prison interviews for me. It'll probably take up about fifteen to twenty hours next week, including drive time. I assume he left you a note. He's at San Quentin right now."

Just then D walked into the office.

"Right," I said. "He said something about that. You sure it's going to take all afternoon?"

"It's a long drive and the interview will take at least an hour."

"No problem," I said. "Let me double-check his calendar."

The inmate interview was clearly written for this afternoon, and yet here D was at the Spellman compound.

I'm no snitch, so I decided to cover.

"I'm sure we can free his schedule whenever you need."

"Thanks, Isabel."

After we disconnected the call, I turned to D. "Aren't you supposed to be at the Big Q this afternoon?"

"The what?" D asked.

"Remember, we're calling San Quentin 'the Big Q.' "

"I had to reschedule," D said, totally ignoring my reminder. "Had a dentist's appointment this morning."

"How'd that go?"

"Great."

The dentist is never great. Everybody knows that. But I like to respect D's privacy, so I let him keep his secret. Besides, that afternoon the office had a lot of foot traffic, so there wasn't much time for fishing.

First Loretta, D's girlfriend, arrived. Everyone loves her. I suppose D loves her most, but she's a favorite among Spellmans.

Loretta is tall, I think taller than D, but he denies it and has refused to engage in a lineup. She's partial to sweater sets and wears glasses and large costume jewelry. That day, she brought a giant Tupperware container of brownies. Loretta and D have been selling D's baked goods at some gourmet shops, restaurants, and specialty stores around the city. And since she was in between jobs and not afraid of an oven, she had been testing out D's recipes.

Loretta slipped off the airtight lid and said, "I think you'll be pleased."

D took a bite of a brownie and chewed. Then he forced a smile and said, "Delicious. Did you make any adjustments to the recipe?"

"Just a dash of cinnamon. Do you like it?"

"Uh-huh," D said. He was lying.

"I got to run. I have a nail appointment in fifteen minutes," Loretta said. "Now, Isabel, don't work my man too hard."

"Haven't you heard? No one works here."

"Nice seeing you, hon."

Loretta kissed D on the forehead and headed out. I picked up the rest of the brownie that D was clearly not going to eat and took a bite. It was excellent.

"This is really good."

"Always with a dash of cinnamon," D

said, shaking his head. "Brownies don't need cinnamon."

"I can't taste it."

Then Vivien and Rae arrived, within minutes of each other, so I couldn't interrogate them separately. I thought about leading the conversation with, "Why do you have pictures of a naked man and woman in the file for a moving company investigation?" but I had hoped they'd offer this information on their own. Besides, Rae was in the middle of crank-calling the moving company, which wasn't exactly part of the "official" investigation, but a memo had gone out requesting that the entire Spellman staff engage in at least one time-consuming fake moving quote with Marcus Lorre.

"Okay, let's go over this one more time," Rae said into a burner cell phone. She proceeded to take five minutes reading off an entire list of household belongings, provided a zip code in the Boston area, and waited for the quote. "Can you bring that number down a little? A little bit more than that? Okay. I can work with that number. One last thing, I'll need the move to happen at midnight and the movers will need to be as quiet as possible. You don't move in the middle of the night? That's going to be a problem. I haven't told my parents that I'm moving them across the country. I wanted it to be a surprise. Huh. You can't work around that? I see. I see. I'm sorry we're not able to do business together. I'll be sure to refer my friends, though."

When Rae disconnected the call, she looked at her watch and did some internal calculations. "That quote took two hours and forty-five minutes off of Lorre's life."

"I got news for you," I said. "It also took two hours and forty-five minutes off of your life."

"But I enjoyed every minute of it."

"How's the legitimate Lightning Fast investigation coming along?" I asked.

I was now working at my dad's computer, since mine was completely offline.

"Good," Vivien said. "My computer has been running slow. Have you called anyone?"

"Still gathering evidence," Rae said.

"And then what is the plan?" I asked.

"Are these for me?" Rae said to D, pointing at the tub of brownies. Apparently Rae is also in on the baked-goods business.

D nodded.

"Excuse me, back to the Lightning update," I said.

"Once we amass more evidence we'll

figure out the best way to proceed," Rae said, taking a bite of brownie.

"Vivien, you haven't had any more contact with Lorre, right?"

"I haven't called him again. I swear. Is there any chance I could get my paycheck a day early?" Vivien asked. "Since I'm not coming in tomorrow."

"Sure," I said, pulling a blank check from the box.

"Blech," Rae said, spitting out her half-masticated brownie in the trash.

"You taste it too?" D said.

"Loretta made these?" Rae asked.

"Yep."

"I hate cinnamon."

"That was obvious," D said.

"I can't promise that I'll get full price for these," Rae said.

"Isabel didn't even notice," D said.

"Lots of things slip by Isabel," Rae said.

"But not voices five feet away from me," I said.

I gave Vivien her check.

"You still don't know how to use the accounting software?" Rae asked.

"I've been busy," I said.

"Are you reconciling the bank statements?"

"What is it with everyone and bank statement reconciliations? Checks are not bouncing. We're good. But if you want to take over this responsibility at any time, please have at it."

Rae started working on Mom's computer and said, "I think we have a virus. I know a guy. Let me call him."

Since the only special relationship I had with a computer consultant was Robbie, I told her to go ahead. Rae made the call, then took her brownies and left.

"How's the case going for Maggie?" I asked.

"Fine. Fine," D said. "I have some tapes to transcribe. Is there anything else?"

"No," I said. Only D hadn't been at the Big Q that day, so what tape was he transcribing? Of course I could have called him out on his lie, but if Spellman Investigations ever splintered into two different camps, I wanted D in mine.

He put on his headphones and began his two-finger typing.

After D left for the day, I paid the bills and then called the bank to double-check that we still had enough cash to cover the amounts. We were still in the black. Mom, Dad, or D must have deposited some checks and not told me. I would have to reconcile the bank statements one of these days. I dropped the bills in the mailbox for the last pickup and returned to the office. I decided to take a quick look at the Washburn interview transcripts that were sitting on top of Demetrius's desk.

It felt like I had the flimsiest grasp on our caseload and I was constantly out of the loop. D was usually forthcoming with all of the work he did for us, but he was being cagey this time around. There wasn't anything out of the ordinary in the interview, except this one section here:

Q: Your mother died three years ago, is that correct?

A: Yes. Bless her soul.

Q: My condolences.

A: Thank you.

Q: And you have a sister, correct?

A: I wouldn't bother her.

Q: Why not?

A: She's a busy woman. Two kids. Maybe three by now.

Q: We'd like to contact her anyway. Do you know where she lives?

A: Lost touch years ago. Think she moved to, uh, Colorado or Arizona.

Q: Is she married?

A: Yes.

Q: What's her married name?

A: I don't remember. Isn't that awful?

Q: Anyone else we should talk to?

A: My cousin Carl.

Q: Carl wouldn't have a last name, would he?

Something about the interview felt itchy, like an old wool sweater on bare skin. I called over to D.

"Sorry to bother you," I said. "I was reviewing the Washburn interview."

"Oh?" D said, sounding itchy too. "The transcripts?"

"Yes. I was just reading them."

"You're reading them," he said. "I'm interviewing his cousin Carl tomorrow."

"Good. When you asked Washburn about his sister, what was his body language like?"

"I don't recall," D said. "He sounded defensive, I think."

"Like he didn't want you talking to his sister?" I asked.

"Yes. I got that impression," D said somewhat hesitantly.

"When you interview Carl, see if he knows where the sister is or can point you in the direction of another family member. Okay?"

"Got it."

"Hey, D? Why didn't you ask him about

his teeth?"

D has this interview quirk. He claims you can judge a man's upbringing by whether his mama made him floss and brush his teeth morning and night. He almost always asks inmates their dental history.

"Forgot, I guess. See you tomorrow."

Mom and Dad came home around dinnertime. Mom checked the office on her way in.

"Where were you all day?" I asked.

"Your father and I went for a drive."

"Why?"

"We're checking out other neighborhoods in the Bay Area. Seeing if there's any other place we might want to live," Dad said.

Their house is worth a fortune and this threat has been hanging over our head for years. The timing seemed particularly cruel.

"Before you make any decisions, will you talk to us first?" I asked.

"I wouldn't consider blindsiding you," Mom said, referring to my corporate takeover.

"You're going to let this go one of these days, right?"

"Sure. What are you doing?" Mom asked.

"I have to enter all the time sheets for the next billing cycle."

"Go home," she said assertively.

"This has to get done."

"I'll do it."

"You'll do it?"

"Yes."

"When?"

She sighed like someone expelling all the air one breathes in a day.

"Tonight. Tomorrow. I can do it in half the time you can. It will get done. Okay?"

"Okay," I said, gathering my files and shoving them into my bag. "Thank you," I said.

"See you later, sweetie," she said in a tone as dull as Grammy's pantsuit.

Still, she called me sweetie. It was the first term of endearment she'd used nonsarcastically in about six months. Was the tide turning, or was something else afoot?

No Snitch Izzy

At home I was minding my own business when David called to beckon me upstairs.

"No way," I said. How stupid did he think I was?

"Max is here. He'd like to talk to you."

"Who is Max?"

"Claire's dad. Remember, the father of the kid you watched the other day?"

"And I need to talk to him for what reason?"

"Izzy, get upstairs. It's not a trap."

I entered their house through the back door, which is only steps away from my front door.

I overheard Maggie say, "Now remember, Claire, be on your worst behavior today."

"I'm not sure you have the right action plan," Max said.

The girls were playing with their disproportionately shaped dolls and the adults were in the kitchen drinking beer. I helped myself to one from the fridge and uncapped it on the corner of the counter.

"Why can't you do that stuff in front of Sydney?" David said.

"What's up?" I asked. It was safe to assume that I was to be reprimanded for something. It's not like I taught Claire the alphabet when she was in my charge.

"My daughter keeps calling me a snitch," Max said.

"Are you?" I asked.

"Izzy," David said, "this isn't an inquisition. Max just wants to understand the origin of Claire's new catchphrase."

"We were eating cookies the other day," Max said, "and I told her she could have two. Then when I wasn't looking she stole a third cookie."

"Smart girl."

"I called her on it and then she starting saying, 'Don't be a snitch, Daddy. Don't be a snitch.' "

From the next room Claire echoed the sentiment.

"My work here is done," I said.

"Did you have the snitch talk with Claire?" David asked.

Meanwhile, Maggie was doubled over, laughing convulsively, trying to keep her beer from expelling through her nose. To

Max's credit, he didn't appear extremely perturbed and I could see him flush at the ridiculousness of the conversation.

Since I was indeed responsible for this nonsense, I decided to come clean.

"I did briefly touch on the topic of snitching, but with Sydney, not Claire. I gave the girls some cookies." I would rather not get into how many.[1] "Apparently Claire took one more than was allowed and Sydney ratted her out. I said to Sydney, 'Don't be a snitch.' For the record, this isn't the first time I've had the snitch talk with Sydney and it's not sticking. Apparently the essence of the lesson was lost on your daughter."

"They're too young, Isabel, to understand the concept of snitching," David said.

"I didn't know that. You're always telling me how smart children are," I said. "I thought I was imparting some valuable wisdom. And I think we should all remember that I was duped into babysitting in the first place."

"Once again," David said, "we apologize. But, you know, most aunties would jump at

---

[1] Four, per child. They had vitamins in them or something. And Sydney only ate one and then asked for Melba toast. She's permanently damaged.

the chance to spend quality time with their niece."

"You can always call Rae."

"We're going to barbecue," David said. "Want to stay for dinner?"

"Are the kids staying?"

"*Yes,* Izzy."

"I think I'll pass," I said.

I have had many meals with Sydney and at almost every one she throws a tantrum so spectacular, you wonder if she's doing permanent damage to your eardrums.

"Nice to see you again, Max," I said. "You have a lovely daughter. She's much nicer than my niece, has no royal aspirations, and doesn't have a peanut allergy.[2]

"Good-bye, snitches," I said to the girls.

Sydney said, "No Izzy."

Claire said, "Izzy stay."

"Anyone want to swap kids? Just an idea."

I decided to drop by Slayter's place while children were running amok overhead. As I left my apartment, an old Dodge pickup truck was idling across the street. Two males sat in the front seat, looking at what ap-

2 Because of this phenomenon David doesn't keep peanut butter in his house anymore, even though *no one* in his house has a peanut allergy.

peared to be David and Maggie's residence.

I stood in the middle of the sidewalk and made eye contact.

"You Maggie? You the lawyer?"

I stepped under the light of the streetlamp so they'd get a better look at my face. I'd rather they identified me than my sister-in-law. The driver had a tattoo on his neck. If he wasn't an ex-con, he would be someday, assuming he got out.

"What can I do for you?"

"Bitch, thought you were a defense attorney."

"What's the problem?" I asked.

"You're talking to too many people."

I pulled my cell phone out of my pocket and the guy with the tattoos peeled out. Never got his license plate number.

I wouldn't say that I make a habit of unannounced visits, but it certainly wasn't unprecedented.

From the front door I could hear jazz playing inside, a male voice holding forth — Edward's — and a woman's laughter adding another layer to the soundtrack. It sounded like a date. Most people would have left then and there, but Edward and I have an understanding.

I rang the doorbell three times. I heard

my boss's clipped footsteps approach. When he swung open the door, he was unpleasantly surprised and visually verified that he was on a date. Edward has a date uniform — a crisp, white shirt unbuttoned to show off his even tan, and he wears loafers instead of the cap-toe oxfords that he prefers for work. Also, he wears cologne. Only on dates; never at work.

"Isabel," he said. "This isn't a good time."

"Entertaining," I said, brushing past him. It wasn't a question.

Inside I found a very attractive and fit woman in her early forties. Her hair was highlighted to give the impression of blondness and her face was three shades paler than her legs. She appeared more than startled to see me and got to her feet defensively when I entered the dining room. To her, I could have been anyone. Edward's daughter, an ex-girlfriend, his minister.

Edward cleared his throat. "Lenore, I'd like you to meet Isabel, my niece. She was in the neighborhood and thought she'd drop by."

"Nice to meet you," I said, shaking Lenore's hand. She had that lady grip, like a dead fish. I always consider it a bad omen. "Uncle Ed, can I talk to you privately?"

Edward took my arm with a tight squeeze

and led me down the hallway into his office. Inside, he shut the door, which is reliably soundproof.

"Please tell me she's a hooker," I said.

"Your timing is atrocious," he said.

"I pride myself on that. Don't high-end hookers usually retire by that age and then become madams?"

"Don't be indecent."

"Where did you meet her?" I asked.

"At the tennis club."

"How convenient. Does she have references?"

"Sheldon introduced us. I believe she's friendly with his ex-wife."

Sheldon Meyers is an old and dear friend of Edward's and one of the three major shareholders of Slayter Industries, along with Edward and Willard Slavinsky. I was sure he wouldn't go out of his way to set Edward up with a gold-digger, but I've noticed that rich old men aren't very good at spotting them.

"And how long has Sheldon known her?"

Slayter avoided eye contact to avoid the question.

"Edward, we discussed this. Any time you date a new woman, you have to let me vet her completely. There's too much at risk."

Slayter's ex-wife was, in essence, a con

artist who had positioned herself to make a lot of money off of her marriage. Slayter's medical condition makes him even more vulnerable, and we have had many discussions about how to proceed should he find himself in any romantic entanglements.

"It's unseemly to pry into the life of someone you've just met."

"What if she finds out?" I said. "She could use it to blackmail you."

"You have such a bleak view of the world," Edward said.

"It's not bleak, it's cautious." It's actually bleak, these days.

Edward played with his collar, as if he were Rodney Dangerfield loosening his red tie.

"Where's Ethan, by the way?"

"I put him up in one of the corporate apartments. My housekeeper threatened to quit if he stayed."

"Does everyone get an apartment?"

"I was having a lovely evening, Isabel."

I took a pad of paper off of his desk. "Give me her name and address and I'll let you close the deal."

"You're so crude."

Edward reluctantly jotted down Lenore Parker's information and passed me the slip of paper.

"We'll talk tomorrow," I said on my way out of the office.

"Was there a purpose to your visit?" Edward asked as an afterthought.

"I was going to debrief you on Divine Strategies. But mostly I was avoiding a play-date."

From the foyer, I shouted my adieu to Lenore.

"Sorry to interrupt your evening. Nice meeting you."

"I hope our next visit isn't so brief," Lenore politely lied.

"Me too," I said.

Thursday afternoon, I returned to the Spellman compound, which was abandoned except for D.

When my parents are in the house, there's an ineffable energy, a vibration. You always know where they are. You'd think snoops would have more stealth, but my parents, especially, seem to have lead feet when they're at home. My point is, within a few minutes of arriving at Spellman Central, I could sense that the unit was out.

"Where is everyone?" I asked D.

"Your parents left around ten and Vivien was here for an hour filling out her time sheets and then she got a call and left."

On my desk was a stack of pleasantly surprising paperwork. My mother had entered all the time sheets and generated the client bills, a chore she hadn't performed in over five months. On top of that was a check from someone named Marshall Greenblatt for two thousand dollars.

"Have you seen Rae?" I asked.

"She was in this morning to drop off the check."

"Do you know anything about this Marshall Greenblatt?"

"She mentioned another case to Vivien, but I don't know anything."

"I think you know something."

"I think the muffins are ready," D said, strolling into the kitchen.

I followed him to see if I could extract any more information or at least get a muffin out of it.

"D, I don't have eyes in the back of my head and I'm not here all of the time. If something is going on that I need to know about, I would appreciate it if you told me."

"Do you know what happens to snitches in prison?" D asked.

"I don't know, but this isn't prison. So those rules don't apply here. Out of curiosity, what does happen to snitches? Do they get their tongues cut out?"

"It was more of a rhetorical question. I don't want to get into it."

"Then you shouldn't have brought it up. Do we understand each other? This is not prison."

"Muffin?"

"See? The opposite of prison. Thank you. Ouch." I probably should have waited for the muffin to cool and Demetrius probably should have waited to offer until the muffin cooled. "Do you know where my parents are?"

"I have no idea where Al and Olivia are," D said assertively, which, in contrast to his lack of assertion about Rae's activities, led me to believe he knew much more than what he was saying. At least about my sister.

Just then the doorbell rang. I opened the door.

"Fred Finkel, computer repairman, at your service," Fred Finkel said.

Fred is Rae's boyfriend. There are many things to recommend Fred. In fact, his only apparent flaw is his affection for my sister.

"Fred, nice to see you. What are you doing here?"

"I'm fixing your computers."

"You can do that sort of thing?"

"I can do a lot of things," he said.

"Be my guest," I said, leading him into

the office.

An hour later, Fred had a diagnosis.

"You've got the Remlu virus. I installed new antivirus software and defragmented all the computers. You should do that every month. Should be fine now."

"What do I owe you?" I asked.

"Fifty for my time, and Rae said I couldn't leave without the oatmeal cookies."

Just then D entered the office and delivered a giant Tupperware container of cookies as if Fred had phoned in a preorder.

I wrote Fred a check and he and his cookies departed. I turned to D and asked the obvious question.

"Does my sister have something on you?"

"We have a mutually beneficial business arrangement," D said.

Once again, the unit had been out all day and returned home sometime in the afternoon. Instead of loitering in the kitchen or dropping by the office to watch other people work, which they sometimes did for fun, and often included some schoolyard mockery, they went straight to their bedroom.

I removed my shoes and tiptoed up the stairs, hoping to catch a few scraps from their private conversation. I knelt down by their bedroom door and caught only a few phrases out of context.

"I didn't like him," Mom said. "I don't think he knows what he's talking about."

"Now you're the expert."

"This is serious. It's not something you take lightly."

As I was shifting weight on my legs, the floorboards creaked.

"Is somebody out there?" my mother asked.

I stood up straight and knocked on their door.

"Come in," said Dad.

"Hi," I said.

"Good afternoon, Isabel. Did you see I left the billing for you?" my mother said.

"Yes. Thank you. I really appreciate it."

"I'll take care of the payroll this evening," Mom said.

"You will?"

"Yes."

"Is there anything wrong with working during the day, like normal people?"

"Are you suggesting that people who work a swing shift aren't normal?"

"Is it that you don't want to be in the office with me?" I asked.

"I think we've earned the right to make our own hours," Mom said.

"Where were you this morning?"

Dad hoisted himself off the bed and escorted me out of their room.

"I need a nap," he said. "Try to keep it down, if you don't mind."

He shut the door before I could make any further inquiries. While I was desperately in need of their help and grateful for it, their motivations didn't sit right with me. It wasn't a complete turnaround, but their sudden agreeability struck me as uncharacteristic. Considering the level our battle had reached, it seemed likely that they had a few more airstrikes to make.

And what the hell were they whispering about?

When I returned to my desk, I found a suspicious business card sitting atop the stack of suspicious paperwork. Despite the company name in our house design, it was not company issued.

Spellman Investigations
Rae Spellman,
Conflict Resolution Specialist

Instead of including the company phone number or address, the card contained Rae's cell number and a PO box address in the Mission District.

As far as I knew, only one person had been

in the office since I left.

I held up the card and said, "D, where did this come from?"

"I have no idea," D said, not turning away from his computer monitor.

"You were the only person in this office since I left."

"Maybe you didn't see it the first time around," D said.

"What is a conflict resolution specialist?"

"That is an interesting question," D said. "Something worth pondering."

I approached Vivien's desk and looked for anything that was in plain view. I certainly wasn't the type of employer who would go through an employee's desk or read her e-mails (which are fair game in the corporate world), but it was absolutely my right to pick up the file folder labeled *Greenblatt, Marshall* (of two-thousand-dollar-check fame) and see what was inside.

I returned to my desk and perused the file, only to find myself more perplexed than when I didn't have the data. The entire case file contained newspaper and magazine clippings of astrological forecasts for the last two weeks. It also included photocopies from books on astrology, summarizing the essential traits of each sign. Several sections were highlighted, with no discernible pattern. There was only one other piece of paper in the file, a page from a legal notepad, handwritten in Rae's distinct script with a date from two weeks ago, the name Yvonne LaPlante, and the word *Aquarius* underlined three times below her name.

I showed the file to D.

"Does this make any sense to you?"

"No," he calmly replied. "But nothing that girl does makes a whole lot of sense to me."

As if on cue, Rae phoned the office.

"Now that I'm back in the fold, so to speak," she said, "the company financials are a little more interesting to me. I'm concerned about your accounting system."

I could hear the finger quotes around the word *system* over the phone line.

"What's your concern?" I asked.

"Mom is under the impression that I have loaned the company money. She thinks we're underwater."

"We're fine. I've been checking the bank balance almost every day."

"Who is GLD Inc.?" Rae asked.

"That was the large deposit about a month ago?" I asked.

"Exactly ten grand. Over three weeks ago."

"I thought it was how Zylor Corporation wired money into the account," I said. "I thought it was a retainer."

"Zylor has always written checks, and in what fantasy world of yours do they pay ten thousand dollars a pop?" Rae said.

There is a particular circle of hell reserved for being shamed by your younger sibling.

"I don't know. I guess I had a lot to do, and since the checks weren't bouncing —"

"Izzy, I got news for you. That ten grand is not ours. We can't touch it. I'm going to deposit a loan from my own funds, so that we don't get in trouble when the bank wants it back. And they are going to want it back. Then I'm going to take over the bookkeeping responsibilities, for which you're going to pay me twenty-five dollars an hour, which is really fair. Okay?"

"Okay. Can you do me a favor and not tell Mom and Dad?"

"Deal. And, one day, I might ask a favor of you . . ."

"Nothing with you is free," I said as I hung up the phone.

Apparently, along with a company apartment, Edward Slayter issues a company car. And a nice one.[3] I tried to arrange a neutral

3 No, I'm not going to tell you what kind, because I'm uninterested in providing any extraneous

207

meeting location or a convenient intersection or bus stop where I was happy to await his carriage, but Damien insisted on an at-home pickup. I was going to use the office, but my mother kicked me out at six, so I texted my brother's address to Damien.

David, Maggie, and Sydney were in the middle of dinner, which calmed my nerves about any flash babysitting scenario. David offered me a glass of wine, which I accepted, but then made it clear he should not make the same offer to Damien.

"Who is this Damien?" Maggie asked.

"He's Mr. Slayter's new chief counsel."

"A lawyer. Is he young? Is he cute?"

"That's a subjective question."

"That's a yes," Maggie said.

"No, it's not like that. I'm showing him around the city and mostly I'm trying to make sure that he's someone Edward can trust."

"I really must compliment you on your ability to lie to yourself," said David.

"Thank you," I said.

David stood up from the table, put his napkin on his chair, and walked over to the

---

advertising for luxury vehicles. If any luxury-vehicle manufacturer would like me to plug their vehicle, I'm open to a quid pro quo situation.

front door. He waited exactly five seconds. The doorbell rang. I raced to the door to intercept my brother, but it was too late. He was already shaking Damien's hand.

"David Spellman, Isabel's brother. A pleasure to meet you. Please come in. Can I offer you a drink? We have everything."

"We have to go," I said.

"Hi, I'm Maggie." You don't need me to tell you who said that, right?

They shook hands and then Sydney was formally introduced.

Then people started stating their professions, as they do, and I realized I was outnumbered. David suggested that Sydney was a likely future lawyer or doctor.

"Or a truck stop waitress," I suggested.

Damien thought he should go to the source and said, "Sydney, what do you want to be when you grow up?"

"A princess," Sydney said.

"Good luck with that," I said (to Sydney).

Sydney perhaps didn't understand the content of my snide remark, but she grasped the tone and responded with her usual two-word retort, "No Izzy."

"Do you want a time-out?" Maggie asked.

"No. We're going to drink elsewhere," I said, tugging on Damien's wrist.

My brother patted Damien on the back as

he walked him to the door, as if they were old college buddies. Then he leaned in conspiratorially and said, "Watch your back."

Damien wanted a tour of the city. I wanted to drive the fancy car. Reluctantly, he handed over the keys. Like any good tour guide, I began with locations associated with our most infamous crimes. We drove past the St. Francis Hotel, where Fatty Arbuckle came to celebrate his one-million-dollar contract and ended up getting accused of rape and murder. Three trials later, he was exonerated and then blacklisted. My dad used to shake his head and gaze disappointedly at the sky and say, "It would never have happened to a thin guy." Then we drove to the Mitchell Brothers O'Farrell Theatre. I'm not sure who runs it now, but not the Mitchell brothers. Their business partnership ended tragically when Jim Mitchell shot Artie Mitchell, although the shooting happened in Marin. There's no point in driving to Marin unless you live there.

"Do you want to see the bank that Patty Hearst and the SLA held up? But it's not a bank anymore. In fact, I don't think there's anything there but an empty building, maybe."

"I think we can skip it."

Since I'd seen Damien drink coffee, I pointed out the civic center location of Blue Bottle Coffee,[4] which is so tucked away you'd think they were giving you a dime bag with your morning brew. I told him where to find hookers and which kind if he was so inclined. Then he suggested we get out of this part of town, which bordered the red-light district, and asked if there was a place with a view. There's always Twin Peaks, but Damien seemed like a museum guy and I'd heard (from Edward Slayter) that the tower at the de Young Museum was open some nights.

First I took a loop through the park and showed Damien where the bison paddock is located, and told him a tragic story of how last year one of the baby bison accidentally killed itself while running away from a little dog that got into the paddock.[5]

"Do you give tours of the city often?" Damien asked.

4 On the coffee side, it's as good as None-of-Your-Business Bakery. Just the lines aren't as outrageous.
5 I became much less judgmental about people carrying little dogs in purses when I heard that story.

211

"Nope."

"That's obvious."

As we drove through the windy stretch of Martin Luther King Junior Drive, I didn't ruin the surprise of the ocean at the end of the road. I'm not one for nature, but I've always found the sudden break of ocean at the end of the woods a fresh surprise.

"Don't swim there," I said. "People die."[6]

"Didn't you mention something about a museum?"

I circled back to JFK Drive and parked near the de Young. We took the elevator to the tower (which is free!) and took in a view of the park after nightfall.

As we tried to decipher the dim landscapes, I reminisced about the old days: "There was a Warhol exhibit here when I was in high school. We went on a class trip and the docent told us that one of the paintings was worth over a million dollars. My best friend, Petra, and I spent six weeks plotting a way we could steal the painting. We decided on a small explosion in the men's bathroom as a diversion and then, of course, we'd need a counterfeit painting to put in its stead. We even commissioned the best artist in our school. But it's not like we

6 Riptides. Seriously, don't swim there.

went to an arts school. His rendering looked nothing like the soup cans. And seriously, how hard is it to paint soup cans, if painting is your thing?"

"I take it the attempted theft never came to be or we wouldn't be having this chat," Damien said.

"The exhibit ended before we could get all our ducks in a row. And that lousy artist demanded payment. Five hundred bucks. We paid him because he knew what we were up to and it would have been hard to explain in small-claims court why two teen-age girls who had no interest in fine arts commissioned a copy of a Warhol when you could buy a poster that looked just like it at the gift shop for twenty-five bucks."

"One final question," Damien said. "Why did you plan the diversion for the men's restroom?"

"Because then the cops would automatically assume the thieves were male."

Damien managed to seem amused, horrified, and confused all at once. Of course, I don't normally confess to strangers crimes or plans to commit crimes from my past, but I was hoping to open a dialogue on past misdeeds and see whether I could get Damien to provide some information I could not acquire through a database search, a surveillance, or interviewing his known associates (strictly off-limits, according to Slayter).

After the tower view, we went to the Plough and Stars for beer and fish and chips. I got the feeling the fish and chips were a rare indulgence for the trim lawyer, because he was enjoying them the way I hear people enjoy a meal at the French Laundry (yeah, I've heard of the place. Never been). Once the lawyer had a beer and a half a pound of fried goods in him, it was time to see what kind of information I could glean from Damien Thorp. I turned on my digital recorder to reference later, if necessary.

The transcript reads as follows:

DAMIEN: These are like the best fish and chips ever.[7]
ISABEL: So your first fish and chips. Congratulations. Have you ever committed a misdemeanor?
DAMIEN: Sure. Who hasn't?[8]
ISABEL: What kind?
DAMIEN: I don't know. Several, I suspect.

7 So not the best fish and chips ever.
8 Answer: no one.

ISABEL: Smoked pot?

DAMIEN: In college.

ISABEL: Hallucinogens?

DAMIEN: Maybe once or twice.

ISABEL: In college?

DAMIEN: Yes.

ISABEL: Have you ever stolen money from petty cash?

DAMIEN: No.

ISABEL: Cheated on a girlfriend?

DAMIEN: I guess I did once. But she was very mean.

ISABEL: Then why didn't you break up with her?

DAMIEN: Because I was afraid of her.

ISABEL: Was she extremely attractive?

DAMIEN: Yes.

ISABEL: Why did you apply for this job?

DAMIEN: Because it was an excellent opportunity and I was looking to move.

ISABEL: You wanted to move from Boston?

DAMIEN: Yes.

ISABEL: Why? I hear good things about Boston.

DAMIEN: I needed a change.

ISABEL: Something go wrong at your last job?

DAMIEN: No.

ISABEL: Leaving someone behind then?

DAMIEN: This is beginning to feel like a deposition.

ISABEL: Okay. I'll stop.

DAMIEN: Just like that?

ISABEL: Sure. A subject on the defensive is useless to me.

I like to think of myself as something of an interrogative savant. However, most lawyers have mastered that skill set as well. Damien returned the interrogation with one of his own.

DAMIEN: Were you a difficult child?

ISABEL: Extremely.

DAMIEN: What's the worst thing you've ever done?

ISABEL: Can I get back to you in a few days?

DAMIEN: How did you and Edward meet?

ISABEL: At the de Young Museum.

DAMIEN: You just ran into him at the museum?

ISABEL: I was surveilling him.

DAMIEN: Why?

ISABEL: His wife hired me to surveil him so she could keep track of his whereabouts while she had an affair with her trainer.

216

DAMIEN: That doesn't explain how you met him.

ISABEL: I found the wife suspicious, so I surveilled her instead, saw what she was up to, and ratted her out to Edward.

DAMIEN: You're a snitch.

ISABEL: Ouch. That hurt. I am *not* a snitch, but I don't work for people who hire me under false pretenses.

DAMIEN: Are your parents speaking to you again?

ISABEL: Edward has been a bit more loose-lipped than I thought.

DAMIEN: We've had a few lunches.

ISABEL: Typical lawyer. Never ask a question if you don't know the answer.

DAMIEN: Ever been arrested?

ISABEL: Yes.

DAMIEN: How many times?

ISABEL: Once or twice.[9]

DAMIEN: Tell me about your last relationship.

ISABEL: It was good. He understood me.

DAMIEN: What went wrong?

9 Actually four to six times. I like to pretend two of them didn't happen.

ISABEL: Me. That's what always goes wrong.

The conversation pretty much died after that. We ordered another round of beers and then attempted small talk, which neither of us had a particular aptitude for.

"How's the new job working out?"

"Have you always wanted to be a PI?"

"The apartment to your satisfaction?"

"You have family in the city?"

"So, how long do you get to use the company car?"

"Is it always this foggy?"

Once we started talking about the weather, we knew it was time to go. Damien insisted on driving because in theory men hold their booze better than women. It had been a long night and I didn't feel like launching into an explanation of my supernatural liquor tolerance. He drove me back to David's house in mostly silence and parked in the driveway.

"Sorry," I said. "That wasn't so great."

"The fish and chips were good, and the beer."

"Both of those things are often good."

"Are you always like this?"

"With strangers? Yes."

"I'm still a stranger?"

"I think so."

"What would make me not a stranger?"

"I'd have to think about it."

While I was thinking about it, Damien leaned over and kissed me. Since I was staring at a streetlamp, thinking about what would make him not a stranger, I didn't see the kiss coming and turned at the last minute toward the door. So, he actually kissed my ear.

"Were you aiming for my ear?"

"No."

"Should we just call it a night?"

"I think that would be best," he said.

"Good night, stranger."

"Night, stranger."

THE VISITOR

MEMO

```
To All Spellman Employees:
Do what you want. I give up.
                    Signed,
                    Isabel
```

The next morning, when I dropped by Edward's office, I found him huddled on his couch next to his accountant, Arthur Bly. Charlie was serving them tea with a formal tea set.

"Hey, Charlie," I said.

"Isabel, would you like some tea?"

"No thanks. Tea reminds me of my grand-mother."

"One lump or two, Mr. Bly?"

"No lumps," Arthur said.

I used to think that Arthur had some kind of social phobia, since he rarely made eye contact and often left the room as soon as I entered. He also mumbled everything he said to me. But after I saw him having an animated chat with Evelyn, who has the personality of a ceramic doll, I realized that Arthur just doesn't like me.

So I overcompensated, by which I mean I gave him a reason not to like me.

"Arthur, it's so great to see you," I said as I entered Slayter's office.

"Isabel," he said, making eye contact for exactly point four seconds.

"You look great. Have you been working out?"

"No."

"Have you been to the beach?"

"No."

"A tanning salon?"

"No. That's all I can tell you now, Edward," Arthur said, getting to his feet. "I'll put in a request with the bank for information on the offshore account."

"Thank you, Arthur," Edward said.

"Great catching up," I said to Arthur as he was scurrying out the door.

He ignored me.

"Leave the poor man alone," said Edward.

"Why does he hate me?"

"Because you're obnoxious. Clearly he hasn't been out in the sun in over a decade. Knock it off."

"Did I hear 'offshore account'?" I asked with maybe a little too much enthusiasm.

Edward flopped into his swanky, yet ergonomic, desk chair.

"Yes, you did."

"What's going on?"

"Over one hundred thousand dollars has been embezzled from the company in the last month."

"How was it done?" I asked.

"Wire transfers. Uneven denominations. Three separate occasions."

"So anyone with access to the company's routing numbers could accomplish this, correct?"

"Yes," Slayter said.

"I hate to say this, but in cases of embezzlement, isn't it always the accountant?"

"It's not Arthur. Why would he bring it to my attention?"

"It's the perfect alibi. Or a perfectly mediocre one."

"I've known Arthur for fifteen years. He's not that kind of man," Edward said.

"About how much money does Arthur make?"

"I'm not comfortable sharing that information."

"Does he have any hobbies, like going to the racetrack? Or expensive stamps. I could see him losing the bank over a stamp collection."

"It's not Arthur," Edward said in that tone that meant he wanted me to stop.

"Who has access to the company financials?"

"There's an entire accounting office, but the information could be accessed by a hacker, another member of the staff. It's hard to say. We need the cooperation of the Cayman Islands bank to identify the owner of the account the funds were transferred into. That information could take up to ten days."

"Maybe you should call the cops."

"We'd have to get the FBI involved and that would make the company look unstable."

"Do you want me to look into the financials of your employees?"

"I have over one hundred employees. Where would you begin?"

It wasn't until I was out the door that the thought crossed my mind. Money had been embezzled from Slayter's account and money had mysteriously arrived in my company's account. At the time I chalked it up to coincidence. Just one more thing on a laundry list of things I got wrong.

■ ■ ■ ■

The assertive approach had done nothing
to improve workplace morale. In fact, when
I gave up on my parents, they finally started
getting work done. I decided to go with it.
My parents continued to keep their baffling
schedule — often absent several hours out
of the day, accomplishing the bare minimum
of office maintenance tasks at some other
mysterious hour — and yet in retrospect
they were becoming my most productive
employees. Vivien and Rae were keeping
their own schedule on a case that was a
personal vendetta and D was devoting most
of his time to the Washburn case. Out of
tradition, I named him employee of the
month yet again. Who else was I going to
pick? Me?

D managed to track down Washburn's
sister, Delia Wayne, through his interview
with Carl. She hadn't moved to Arizona or
Colorado or any other state. She got married, had two kids, worked for Pacific Gas
& Electric, and lived in the Excelsior District of San Francisco. I wanted to keep a
hand in the case, since I knew some element of it wasn't quite right, so I told D
that I'd take care of the interview. I phoned

her and she reluctantly agreed to meet with me at the Greenhouse Café in West Portal. I'll spare you most of the background information and leave you with what ultimately stuck in my mind — and also made me a little grateful for the brother I had.

Q: Does it surprise you to hear that your brother might be innocent of the crime he was convicted of?

A: Wouldn't surprise me.

Q: Why is that?

A: Armed robbery wasn't his thing.

Q: Is there anything you can tell us that would help his case?

A: You mean help you get him out of jail?

Q: Yes.

A: I don't want to help you get him out of jail.

Q: All evidence points to witness misidentification.

A: You do not want Lou out on the streets.

Q: But he's probably innocent.

A: Of that crime, maybe. But he's guilty of a whole lot of others.

Q: When did you and your brother have a falling-out? I noticed you never visited him in prison.

A: That boy has never been right. I keep

my distance. You let me know if he gets out. We might think about moving.

Q: What do you mean he's never been right?

A: In the head. There's something wrong there.

Q: Can you be more specific?

A: When I was ten, he killed my cat. That specific enough for you?

It was a little too specific. I needed a drink to clear the image from my head and since I was in the neighborhood, I dropped by the Philosopher's Club. Gerty, Bernie's girlfriend, my ex-boyfriend's mother, whom I am quite fond of, was minding the bar.

"What'll it be, sweetheart?" Gerty said, leaning over the bar and giving me a kiss on the cheek.

"Depends," I said. "When is Bernie due back?"

"Bank run. About a half hour."

"I think I can finish a beer in that time frame."

"I think you can too."

"So, congratulations," I said as Gerty was pulling a pint.

"Ah, yes," Gerty said. "Thank you."

I could tell she wanted to drop the subject. For my sake, not hers.

"You'll make an awesome grandma."

"Above average, at least. How have you been?"

"I'm okay. Running an empire is exhausting."

Back at the office, Grammy was answering phones while D was, as far as I could tell, planning his next fake move.

"Now, hypothetically speaking," D said, "how much would it cost if I packed my kitchen but not the rest of the house? And if you could work up a quote for packing the kitchen and the office and the bedroom but leaving the living room and dining room, that would be excellent. Let me ask you another question. How much does that bubble wrap go for? You sell it by the yard. A bit pricey, isn't it? My kids love the stuff. Maybe we could work out a deal, if I'm buying in bulk. Another question. Is bubble wrap recyclable? Because if it isn't, I don't want anything to do with the stuff. Okay, I see you have to go. Well have a nice day now. Try to enjoy the sun while it lasts. You know in San Francisco, we just never see the sun. Oh right, you're not in San Francisco. So what's the weather like in San Bruno right now? You don't say? Oh right. You have to go. Get back to me on those quotes and here's to doing some moving business together."

When D disconnected the call, I had to ask once again if my sister was blackmailing him in any capacity.

"Vivien asked me if I'd go to Lightning Fast and have a chat, in quotation marks, with Lorre to see if we could get some of her money back. I told Vivien that even though I did time, shaking people down is not my thing. She was openly disappointed. This was the least I could do."

"Good job. If I worked in customer service that call would make me want a career change."

I typed up the transcript of my interview and gave it to D.

"We should see who we're dealing with here," I said.

"Agreed," D said.

"I think you need to go back to the Big Q and interview some of his cell mates. See if he's confessed to any other crimes."

"The Big Q? You still on that?" D said.

"If you keep saying it, it will become second nature. So, you'll head back to the Big Q?"

"Go back?" D said.

"I'll call Maggie. Let her know it wasn't your idea. Maybe you can go on Monday."

"Monday. I'll see if I'm free," he said.

"Check your calendar," I said.

The phone rang. Grammy picked up the closest phone.

"Good afternoon, Spellman Investigations. Ruth Spellman speaking. How can I be of service? . . . I'm afraid Mr. Spellman isn't in at the moment. Can I take a message? May I have your phone number? He has it? Are you sure? Well, you can't be positive. Let's say he doesn't have it. May I take your number down, please? Yes. Yes. And what is this regarding? He knows? Is Mr. Spellman clairvoyant? Hello? Hello?"

The clients had been complaining about Grammy's message-taking for about a week, but I needed to witness it firsthand before I could take action.

"Who was that?" I asked.

"Mr. Gardner. My, he was in a rush."

D would later tell me he hadn't ever seen me that happy. Firing Grammy Spellman was one of the highlights of my adult life. I couldn't do it just once.

"Grammy, please take a seat."

Grammy was already sitting.

"I'm sorry, but we're going to have to let you go. I think it's best if we replace you with an answering machine. Don't feel bad; it's all part of the industrial revolution or something."

Then I added a pink slip to her final paycheck with the following note:

Dear Mrs. Spellman,
  Thank you for your services. Unfortunately you have been made redundant. We wish you the best in all your future endeavors.

Signed,
The Management

Grammy's only response was, "Now I can go back to my water aerobics class. You might consider getting some exercise. You know how they say men like something to grab on to? It's not true."

Since I was running regularly, I was perhaps more offended than I should have been.

As an afternoon pick-me-up, I wrote a memo.

MEMO

```
To All Spellman Employees:
Grammy Spellman has been
fired!!! We will have a cel-
ebratory cheesecake tomorrow
```

afternoon.

Signed,
Isabel

In retrospect, the firing of Grammy was one of the last stress-free moments we'd have for months. And it never occurred to me that with Grammy gone, there was no one to pawn off the filing to.

Just one week after Arthur broke the news of the corporate embezzlement, I got a visitor at Spellman Investigations. My cloud of fiscal ignorance was finally broken. The doorbell rang. I looked through the peephole and saw a thirty something male in a suit. I opened the door.

"Can I help you?"

The man pulled out a badge. FBI.

"Special Agent Carl Bledsoe. Are you Isabel Spellman?"

"Did I say I was Isabel Spellman?"

"Would it be possible for us to have a chat?"

"Can it wait?"

"No. I don't think so. Mind if I come in?"

I had no idea where anyone was or when they would return, but it seemed wise to keep any FBI business out of the house. I left a note in the office, grabbed my coat, and got into the government-issue sedan.

"I've never been questioned by the FBI before," I said, trying to look on the bright side.

"This must be your lucky day."

■ ■ ■ ■

PART II
ARGUMENTS

■ ■ ■ ■

VOICE MEMO

3:15 A.M.

Can't sleep again. I pulled the recordings today and listened to each one at least ten times. I don't know what to make of it. I know I should just come out and ask. How bad is it? But I learned from David that you should never ask a question unless you already know the answer.

I followed my parents again. I think I know what's going on. I wish I didn't. I'm going to keep it to myself for a while.

There's this ex-con who keeps making house calls. He wants Maggie to quit the Washburn case. I get the feeling his heart isn't in it. He just needs a part-time job. I'm thinking about hiring him. We could use a guy like him around. Everyone here is afraid to get their hands dirty. Maybe that's been our problem from the start.

BLEDSOE

FBI Headquarters

A fluorescent light flickered overhead. My chair wobbled on uneven casters. The office had a kind of blandness so ordinary it was distracting. The man who picked me up from my house and drove me to FBI headquarters at 450 Golden Gate Avenue wore the fed uniform of a navy blue suit and white shirt and tie. There was a time when J. Edgar Hoover demanded that all of his agents wear white shirts. The agent seemed like the kind of man who would follow orders from fifty years ago. I tried to tell myself that I was just talking to an accountant. An accountant with a gun.

"Can I get you anything to drink, Ms. Spellman?"

"Whiskey. Neat. Nothing fancy," I said.

He laughed. Too hard. "We have water, coffee. I can probably rustle up a soda," the accountant said.

"I'm good for now."

He took a seat.

"I just want to ask you a few questions."

"Are you recording this conversation?"

"We're having a chat, that's all."

"I like my chats recorded," I said, pulling a digital recorder from my purse. "If you don't mind?"

The accountant nodded his head in acquiescence. I pressed record.

The transcript reads as follows:

ACCOUNTANT: Ms. Spellman. Can I call you Isabel?

ISABEL: Sure. Can you state your name for the record?

ACCOUNTANT: Agent Carl Bledsoe.

ISABEL: Thank you.

ACCOUNTANT: It is my understanding that you're a private investigator, is that correct?

ISABEL: Yes.

ACCOUNTANT: You are the primary owner of Spellman Investigations, located at 1799 Clay Street, in San Francisco, is that correct?

ISABEL: Yes. Do you want to tell me what this is about?

ACCOUNTANT: Let's get to know each other first.

ISABEL: I'm an Aries. I hate long walks on the beach. I have no hobbies to speak of, but I play a decent game of pool. Had a promising future with darts until I almost took my brother's eye out in the fourth grade. Single.

ACCOUNTANT: Shocking.

ISABEL: What do you want?

ACCOUNTANT: Like I said, I just want to chat.

ISABEL: Do I need a lawyer for this chat?

ACCOUNTANT: Do you think you need a lawyer?

ISABEL: Ask me another question and I'll get back to you on it.

ACCOUNTANT: How long have you known Edward Slayter?

ISABEL: About eight months, give or take.

ACCOUNTANT: What is the nature of your relationship?

ISABEL: I do investigative work for him.

ACCOUNTANT: Is that the extent of the relationship?

ISABEL: We go running together a few times a week, and that's not a euphemism for anything.

ACCOUNTANT: It is my understanding that you've become his confidante.

ISABEL: Why would the FBI be interested in my relationship with Mr. Slayter?

ACCOUNTANT: Do you have access to the Slayter Industries bank accounts?

ISABEL: No.

ACCOUNTANT: In the last two months over one hundred and fifty thousand dollars has been wired from Slayter Industries into an offshore account in the Cayman Islands. In the last month, ten thousand dollars has been wired from that offshore account into your company's checking account.

ISABEL: I have been a bit a lax in keeping up with the books. Can you tell me the name of the offshore account?

ACCOUNTANT: Right now all we know is that it's a corporation called GLD Inc.

ISABEL: I don't know anything about this, Agent Bledsoe.

[Bledsoe silently leaves the interrogation room and returns carrying a thin folder. He spreads several photocopies of bank statements on the dingy table and points to four highlighted transactions.]

ACCOUNTANT: On three separate dates there are transfers from Slayter Industries into an offshore account, under the name GLD Inc., totaling one hundred fifty-two thousand dollars and eighty-one cents. A little over a month ago, ten thousand dollars from GLD Inc. was transferred into your bank account.

ISABEL: Do you really believe that I or anyone would be stupid enough to embezzle money and then leave an arrow pointing directly at the guilty party? Clearly I'm being framed.

ACCOUNTANT: Possibly. Another question comes to mind: How is it that you had ten thousand extra dollars in an account that rarely hovered over three thousand and you didn't notice?

ISABEL: I've been neglecting the books. Look, I'll write a check right now and get the money out of the account.

ACCOUNTANT: These are difficult times. It would be understandable if you took the money. Maybe you didn't do it for yourself. Maybe you did it for your family.

ISABEL: Does Mr. Slayter know I'm here?

ACCOUNTANT: No. He doesn't. This information was brought to us by the board of directors and we have not yet interviewed Mr. Slayter.

ISABEL: The board of directors, you say. So you got the phone call about this, and the person on the other end of the line said, "Hello, this is the board of directors calling from Slayter Industries?"

ACCOUNTANT: It was an individual who called but a decision come to by the group, after careful consideration.

ISABEL: Mr. Slayter will clear everything up. He'll tell you that I'm innocent and that I'm being framed.

ACCOUNTANT: They said he would protect you. Isabel, the money trail just doesn't look good.

ISABEL: It's not a money trail. It's a money pratfall. This is bullshit and you know it. I assume I'm free to go.

ACCOUNTANT: What makes you so sure?

ISABEL: If I went into a bank with a note that said I had a bomb in my bag and got away with ten thousand dollars, I would be arrested and arraigned the moment I was caught, even if I was only carrying a cat. But white-collar criminals — not that I'm admitting to being one — are treated with much more respect. In fact, it's quite possible that a person who embezzles hundreds of thousands of dollars might not do any time at all.

ACCOUNTANT: I wouldn't bank on that, Isabel.

ISABEL: The next time we meet, I'll have a lawyer with me.

I hurried out of the federal building and realized I didn't have a ride. I walked up to Van Ness and hopped on the 42 bus and rode it to Maggie's office across the street from the criminal court building. The bus was packed like a sardine can, but I found an unsavory seat in back and phoned Edward. Since I was seated between two men arguing over which one's girlfriend had the superior hindquarters, I dispensed with the pleasantries and launched straight into the cold facts.

"Edward. I'm on my way to Maggie's office. I need a lawyer. You know that money that's missing from Slayter Industries? Yes. Well, it looks like some of it has ended up in the Spellman Investigations checking account."

At this point the argument got rather heated and I couldn't really hear what Edward had to say.

"I'll call you later," I said.

After I disconnected the call, a man wearing two vests, a yellowed button-down shirt, a fedora that had been through every rainstorm in the last decade, trousers that had never heard of dry cleaning, and an odor of cigarette that blessedly masked the scent beneath turned to me and smiled ever so politely.

"I couldn't help but overhear your conversation. Allow me to introduce myself. I'm Samuel B. Sampson, attorney at law."

He handed me an old bus transfer, which I suppose was his card.

"We have to fight the system," he said. "Call day or night."

It would have helped if the bus transfer had a phone number on it.

Rae arrived at Maggie's office at the same time I did. Since she had found the deposit in the first place and was now handling the Spellman financials, Maggie thought it wise to loop her in.

"Did you talk to him?" Rae asked.

"We talked a little," I said as we entered Maggie's office.

"You don't talk," Rae repeated.

"You talked?" Maggie said, jumping on me the second I walked in the door.

Maggie had two rooms on the second floor above a café on Bryant Street. Since 30 percent of her practice was pro bono and another 30 percent for clients who didn't have a lot of cash to begin with, she didn't have the kind of shiny lawyerly office you see in movies. The shag carpet needed replacing; the paint was a dull ivory that needed a new coat three years ago. However, David had managed to purchase some of the furniture from his old law firm at a steal. Her desk, the reception-area couch, and the chairs were beyond luxurious. The disconnect, once you spotted it, was rather distracting.

"I talked a little," I said.

"Why did you talk?" Maggie said, shaking her head and flopping down in her chrome and leather chair.

"Because I didn't do anything wrong," I said.

"It's the FBI. They have evidence against you. You shut up and you call a lawyer. You don't sit and chat and accidentally incriminate yourself," Maggie said.

Maggie began pacing and then chomping on a cookie from her pocket. Rae, apparently, knows where Maggie keeps her junk food stash. She found a tub of licorice in the closet/kitchen and returned with a fistful.

"Listen to me carefully. Next time, even if all the agent wants to do is play miniature golf, you tell him you need your lawyer with you. Got it?"

"Got it," I said.

"How could you not assert your Fifth Amendment right?" Rae asked.

"I'm going to do that right now."

I took a cab to Slayter's office and debriefed him.

"Ten thousand dollars, that's all?" he said.

"This is serious," I said.

"For one thing, this isn't a significant amount of money," he said.

"Are you referring to the ten grand or the one hundred and fifty grand?"

"Both," he said.

"Rich people."

"I understand that's a lot to you, but when we find the embezzler, he or she won't be a criminal mastermind. Don't worry about this, Isabel. Everything will be fine."

"What next?" I asked.

"Back to work," he said. "Business as usual. This will be over before you know it."

"Easy for you to say. You're not on the FBI's most wanted list."

"You wish."

Just then Lenore entered Edward's office, dressed to the nines in the middle of the day, carrying one of those purses that cost more than my car.

"Isabel, so nice to see you," she said with a perky voice and dead eyes.

"Yes, isn't it," I said with dead everything.

"How are you feeling today, Edward?" Lenore asked.

"Much better, thank you."

"Were you not feeling well?" I asked Slayter.

"I was just a little under the weather last night. Can I have a minute alone, Lenore? Just one minute?" Edward asked.

Lenore reluctantly left the office. Edward folded his arms impatiently and walked over to the window, looking out over bustling Market Street.

"What happened?"

"At dinner two nights ago, I couldn't remember her name and I had a panic attack. I pretended to be sick to cover."

"You think having lunch with her is a good idea?"

"Isabel, I like her. I like the company. The answer to my illness isn't to be alone. It's not the answer to anything. Go home, go back to work. Everything is going to be fine."

I believed him.

NOT-SO-DIVINE STRATEGIES

I had the weekend to recover from my FBI interrogation, and then I returned to work at Divine Strategies. Since I had been imprisoned in the file room for two weeks, it was difficult to gather information, observe unusual behavior, or get sexually harassed. Although I did notice something one doesn't see every day when I surfaced from my fluorescent dungeon one morning and took a brief break to rebandage my paper-cut wounds. Brad, Bryan, and Maureen were in Bryan's office sitting around his desk reading from a thick book that sure resembled the Bible, although I couldn't remember the last time I actually saw one.

When Layla drifted by, I asked her what they were doing.

"Bible meeting. They do that every Monday. Sometimes Thursdays. Or when business is slow."

"Just the three of them?" I asked.

"Every once in a while Betty joins them, but she's not a regular."

"Do you know who started it?"

"No. But Maureen is the one who keeps it going. At least if Brad or Bryan forgets, she reminds them."

I was about to call it quits and tell Edward that the company was so squeaky clean the term *wet blanket* came to mind when I noticed an unusual string of events one morning. Steve Grant, art director, walked into the office of his boss, Brad Gillman. The water cooler was right outside Brad's office, because when he was a child he was struck by lightning (at least that's what Layla Bryant told me in the bathroom) and a phenomenon of that affliction is that the person, should he or she live, tends to be thirsty. It was only natural that the water cooler should take up residence outside Brad's office. I was at the water cooler, drinking more water for those highly uninformative bathroom reconnaissance missions, when I heard Steve ask Brad for a raise, in a polite and reasonable manner. Brad said that he was very pleased with Steve's work and would discuss the raise with Bryan Lincoln, second in command, and Steve returned to his office.

Brad stepped into Bryan's office; I

couldn't hear the conversation, but it was brief. Then he strode over to the office of Maureen Stevens, the office manager, which was located next to the copy room, where I conveniently had copies to make.[1] If you weren't using the copy machine and stood in a particular sweet spot and no one noticed you, you could overhear a solid 48 percent of the conversations in Maureen's office. Fortunately I got the 48 percent worth hearing.

BRAD: [inaudible] Steve has asked for a raise. Six percent. I think he's [inaudible].

MAUREEN: Offer him two percent; if he threatens to [inaudible], you can go up to three.

BRAD: [inaudible] How about five percent?

MAUREEN: I think he'll [inaudible]. You never know when [inaudible] will need a raise.

Then Brad, the boss, said okay to his underling and returned to his office. At least now I knew where to focus my investigation. Maureen Stevens.

1 Of my hand.

■ ■ ■ ■

The Spellman compound had been abandoned by all humans when I arrived that afternoon. On my desk, I found a photocopy of another check from one of Rae's new clients, with a note explaining that she'd already made the deposit. This one was for thirty-two hundred dollars. Rae's cut: twenty-four hundred.[2] The name on the check: Emma Lighthouse. I found the Lighthouse file stuffed in Vivien's desk under a stack of database printouts. A case number had been generated, but inside the folder was only a single piece of paper containing Emma's name and address and scribbled below that, "10–2 P.M." Nothing else. Once again, it might have seemed more sensible to simply ask the question, but on the off chance that Rae was up to something unusual, it was best to catch her in the act.

Meanwhile, I ran a more thorough background check on Maureen Stevens, age forty-seven, divorced, one child, annual income: eighty-five thousand. She paid insurance on a Mercedes E550 coupe. The MSRP on that is just under sixty thousand

2 I write that only to emphasize the amount, not because you're incapable of doing basic math.

dollars. However, her credit check showed no car payments for the vehicle. Her address in SOMA was a luxury high-rise. Since she had a teenage daughter, I had to assume she rented at least a two-bedroom. I phoned the rental office and learned that a two-bedroom in that building started at $4,100 a month. I also knew that three days a week she left the office at six o'clock sharp because she had a six thirty private Pilates appointment. That's about sixty dollars a pop, times three; you do the math. It's a lot to spend on a flat stomach, and she was clearly doing something to her face that also cost money and kept her from frowning. Even her clothes had that I-don't-look-at-the-price-tag feel about them.

Of course, child support and a rich ex-husband could explain that. The ex-husband, as far as I could tell, had been AWOL since the divorce twelve years ago. There was no indication of any alimony or child support payments. Her credit score was extremely high and she was using only 10 percent of the credit on her revolving accounts. Eighty-five thousand a year is a reasonable salary for a seasoned office manager with twenty-plus years under her belt. The thing is, Brad made only one hundred and twenty-five thousand, and

Bryan Lincoln made one hundred and five thousand.

The company financials were sound, and presumably Brad could decide when to give himself a raise. According to his credit report, he was in serious need of one. His mortgage was close to five grand a month. His children went to private school (I saw their uniforms in the picture on his desk) and he was using, on average, over 75 percent of the credit limits on his revolving accounts. Essentially the support staff was living the high life and the partners were scraping by.

I'd never seen this kind of generosity in any company model. There had to be a catch. And I kind of wanted to catch it soon, because the filing was getting to me and my fingers. While I paced the vacant Spellman office trying to foment a tangible explanation for the Divine Strategies infrastructure, I got a text on my phone from D, which was odd since he was sitting right there.

What is a conflict resolution specialist?
I texted him back: **I have no idea. Do you? No. But I'd look into it.**

I turned to D and asked the obvious question: "Do you have laryngitis?"

"No," D said. He turned his attention to his computer and then began shaking his mouse vigorously. "These computers are not fixed."

"Are you more comfortable snitching with your thumbs?" I asked.

"I'm making coffee. Do you want any?" was D's only reply.

"No, thank you."

Whatever D's unorthodox method of communication was, he did remind me that I ought to investigate my sister's activities a bit more thoroughly. I pulled Rae's business card from my wallet and after very brief consideration decided on the best course of action. I decided to drop by Len's place and give him a surprise acting role.

"I have a job for you," I said when I arrived.

A startling expression of hope took residence on Len's face.

"Like the Winslow case?" he asked, backing away from the door and silently inviting me in.

The last time I had offered Len a job, it was as an undercover valet for a rich guy being swindled by his staff. Method acting doesn't even begin to describe Len's devotion to the assignment. We practically needed an intervention to strip him of his valet habits.[3]

"I'm afraid it's only voice work and should take no more than five minutes."

"I see," Len said, flopping on the couch like a punctured balloon.

"You know what they say; there are no small parts, just small actors."

"Bullshit," Len replied.

I sat down in an uncomfortable but very attractive chair adjacent to Len and waited patiently for the haze of disappointment to abate. Len loved to act. I once saw him play a purple-fur-coat-wearing pimp in a non-ironic stage play written by a Christian fundamentalist that was genuinely racist. And he even researched the role.

"Okay," Len sighed. "Who am I?"

"You're a man who has found an intriguing business card and wants to know more."

I gave Rae's "business" card to Len.

"What's my profession?"

"I'm not sure that it matters."

"What's my profession?"

"Let's say you found the card at a café. Maybe you're a student?"

"What's my major?"

Me: sigh.

3 For more information, see document #4 (especially if you like butler action).

"Physics?" Len asked.

"Sure, but unless you know anything about physics I wouldn't bring it up in conversation."

"I'll go with English."

"Great," I said. "Here's the number."

"Where am I from?"

"I don't care."

"Can I be a foreign exchange student?"

"Absolutely not."

"I haven't wrestled with a southern accent in a while."

"Light southern accent. Not Paula Deen." Len and I then went over his lines and I passed him the burner cell phone I'd just picked up.[4] He pressed the speaker button and dialed.

RAE: Spellman Investigations.
LEN: Good afternoon, miss. I found your business card in a café. I'm having some troubles and I'm wondering if you can help. What exactly is a conflict resolution specialist?
RAE: It's a person who specializes in conflict resolution.
LEN: I see. That's rather vague. Can you

---

4 I wouldn't have put it past Rae to do a reverse number check.

describe some of the services you provide?

RAE: That could take all day. Maybe you could tell me the kind of services you're seeking.

LEN: I'm having trouble with a certain individual.

RAE: What kind of trouble?

LEN: The kind of trouble that makes me wish that individual could just kind of vanish, do you know what I mean?

I grabbed a piece of scratch paper and scribbled as quickly as possible, *Too much improvising!!!*

RAE: Let me be clear up front. We do not kill people or have people beaten up or inflict bodily harm in any way; we simply help you deal with another individual or help you constructively deal with your emotions toward that individual.

LEN: Sounds kind of like therapy.

RAE: No. Not at all. We can usually solve your problems in less than two weeks, sometimes two hours. Now, if you would like to tell me about your situation I can make an assessment and see if we can be of service. I should mention, however, that I now have your phone number and I would caution you against doing anything drastic toward this individual who is troubling you so. You won't get away with it.

LEN: Let me think it over and I'll get back to you.

RAE: I look forward to your call.

Len disconnected the call.

"Well, at least we know she's not killing anyone," I said.

The next time I dropped by Edward's office, I caught him having a casual meeting with Sheldon Meyers and Willard Slavinsky. Edward has a 25 percent share of his company and Meyers and Slavinsky each have 15, which means the three men have a lock on any company votes. They've known each other since college, Dartmouth men who eventually found their way to the West Coast. Slavinsky and Meyers came from money, but Edward just married well to a woman who didn't demand a prenup. She probably should have, since she got all of her money from her first husband, who didn't demand a prenup. Edward smartened up with his second marriage, which was wise, since it was pretty much a sham.

Sheldon has always been icy with me. He knows I don't belong in his country club and he can't quite get used to the fact that Edward keeps my company. But Willard is different, maybe because we're cut from the same cloth, although Willard's is cashmere and mine is a cotton blend. According to Edward, Willard was kicked out of five boarding schools before he eventually graduated. Three generations of Slavinskys went to Dartmouth and, despite his weak academic performance, he managed to sneak in. After college, Willard squandered his inheritance on a number of failed business ventures and one bad relationship that resulted in a daughter he had out of wedlock. The family let him go broke until Edward began to look for investors for Slayter Industries. They gave him one final loan, the investment proved a massive success, and Willard was no longer the family shame. Although he did have that one child out of wedlock.

As usual, when I saw the two men, Willard approached with a warm embrace and Sheldon nodded his head politely.

"Where have you been, my girl?" Willard said. "Have you lost weight?"

"He's making me jog," I said.

"Have you reported this to human resources?"

"Technically I'm not a Slayter Industries employee. Willard, Sheldon. You two look like you keep fit. You know what? You should go jogging with Edward sometime. You can multitask. Business and exercise."

"That's what golf is for," Willard said.

"I'm a tennis man," Sheldon said.

"Nice try," Edward said.

"This has been fun. But I have another board meeting in a half hour," Willard said as he made a swift departure.

"Let me walk you out, Sheldon," I said. "I know where to get your parking validated."

Since Sheldon was responsible for the Lenore introduction, I had to see what information I could gather.

"Can I buy you a cup of coffee?" I asked.

It was common knowledge that Sheldon spent a great deal of his free time at Caffe Trieste, especially since his wife had passed. She was an opera fan, and sometimes opera was sung at Caffe Trieste. Fortunately, not that day when Sheldon and I had our awkward cup of coffee.

"Edward thinks the world of you," Sheldon said, adding an unnecessary question mark at the end.

"I think the world of him. I'm sure you're wondering why I asked you here."

"Indeed."

"It's my understanding that you introduced Mr. Slayter to Lenore. Yes?"

"I did."

"How did you meet her?"

"My dear friend Glynnis met her at a book club meeting and invited her to the tennis club."

"Who invited Lenore to the book club?"

"That I do not know."

"Would you mind calling Glynnis and finding out? This may seem overly cautious, but in light of what happened with Edward's last relationship, I just need to be sure."

Sheldon obligingly phoned Glynnis and asked. Glynnis told Sheldon that Lenore was invited by Sheryl's friend Louise. Sheldon didn't know Louise and asked Glynnis to ask Louise how she met Lenore. Glynnis texted him a few minutes later and said that Louise met Lenore at Rodrigo's hair salon in Pacific Heights.

It could certainly have been a coincidence. There are only a certain number of high-end hair salons in the city, but I was struck by the fact that this was also the favorite salon of the ex–Mrs. Slayter, a fact I discovered when I started surveilling her instead of her husband. I made an appointment for a haircut, then changed it to a wash and blow-dry when I heard the prices.

After my meeting with Sheldon, I returned to Edward's office to give him the update on Divine Strategies. When I arrived, Evelyn and Arthur were returning from lunch. Every time Evelyn saw me, I felt like I was crashing a party I was specifically not invited to. Her face would drift from an animated smile to a cold stare, as if I'd sucked all the fun out of the room. While I had no direct recollection of starting this silent battle with Edward's secretary, it seemed time to stop it.

"Hi, Evelyn, how are you?" I said as nicely as I could.

"Fine," she said.

"How's your mom doing?"

Evelyn clearly did not appreciate my interest in her personal life.

"I'll let him know you're here," she said, ignoring the question.

"I like your . . . blouse," I said.

"Thank you," she said suspiciously.

I suppose these things take time.

After I debriefed Edward on Divine Strategies, he said, "Drop it. If it takes this long to vet the company, we can't recommend the client buy them out."

"Give me a little more time."

"No, Isabel. There's no point. I'm sure you're curious. But I'm not interested in the company anymore, and I don't want you wasting our time on that. I think we have more pressing matters to deal with, don't you?"

"Yes. I have news about Lenore."

"What did you find?"

"I think she might have known your ex-wife."

Slayter, properly cautioned, dismissed me. I think he'd had enough bad news for one day. As I was leaving his office, I got a message from D.

What is the CRS[5] doing tonight?

I don't know. Do you?

I passed Damien's office on the way out and it occurred to me that he might be the embezzler. If he was, I should keep an eye on him. If he wasn't, I didn't mind his company so much and I didn't really want to leave things as they were. I knocked on the glass door to his office.

"Isabel, what are you doing here?"

"I came to apologize."

"You came all the way over here to apologize?"

5 Conflict resolution specialist.

"Sure. Sorry about last week. I think I asked about five too many questions."

"Apology accepted."

"Maybe we can hang out again without talking."

That came out wrong.

"I mean," I said, "maybe we could do something that doesn't involve talking."

Wow, still.

"One more time," I said. "Tonight I'm going on a surveillance. Want to come?"

"Like real detective work?" Damien asked.

"Just like Perry the Platypus."

People unfamiliar with the chore of sitting in a car for hours on end watching people do the boring stuff they usually do — watch TV, eat, drive someplace, eat, sit at desk, eat, go to a movie,[6] sleep[7] — have no idea how tedious surveillance really is. But they're always game the first time around.

"I'm in," Damien said.

"Great. I'll pick you up at the office at seven. I think Subject will be on the move by nightfall."

When I returned to the office there was a message slip on my desk from Agent Carl

6 That's a good day. Also when Subject goes to a crowded bar.

7 Sleeping is the worst!

Bledsoe. The message was in D's handwriting.

"Agent Bledsoe called?" I asked.

"Yes," D said.

"What did he say?"

"He said to tell you he called."

"Did he say what it was regarding?"

"No. You in some kind of trouble?" D asked.

"No. I'm helping him with a case."

"Then why did you ask if he said what it was regarding?"

"I wanted to know whether we were keeping the case under wraps or something."

"Okay," D said. D wasn't buying it, but he returned to work.

I stepped outside and phoned Agent Bledsoe against my attorney and my sister's advice.

"Isabel Spellman calling for Agent Bledsoe."

Agent Bledsoe picked up the line. "Ms. Spellman, I'm glad to hear from you."

"How's it going?"

"Good. How are you?"

"Fine. Have you made any progress on the case?"

"I can't really discuss ongoing investigations. Is there anything you'd like to tell me?"

"No. I can't really discuss any ongoing investigations either," I said.

"You shouldn't be investigating any of this."

"It's been good catching up. Talk to you later," I said, and quickly disconnected the call. I should probably work on my pleasantries when talking to government officials.

We have tracking devices on all of the family vehicles. Rae's car is in my dad's name, so her Jetta is not excluded from the tradition. She's tried to remove the device on several occasions, but the unit now has an alarm to alert them to this fact and a new one is always attached to a different location. She still hasn't found the last one.

I met Damien at his office at seven and asked if we could use his car, which is not his car. Rae was less likely to spot an unknown vehicle than my beat-up Buick. We drove to a location two blocks from my sister's residence and parked. From my phone I can access GPS data on Rae's vehicle. Damien had raided the Slayter Industries snack room and so we had a dry happy hour of Perrier and some fancy nut mixes with a sodium content I seriously doubt Edward would have approved of.

Within a half hour, the tracking device

started beeping and the dot on the screen alerted me that my sister was on the move.

"Time to go."

Following a car in nighttime traffic without a tracker can be sticky, but tracker surveillance is kind of like running a foot-race on roller skates. You have the advantage, is my point, unless you're really lousy on roller skates. I drove while Damien held the phone in his hand and provided Rae's current coordinates.

"The dot is on the Bay Bridge," Damien said.

I headed south on Van Ness and entered the freeway at Duboce, following the signs to the East Bay.

As we traveled through the Bay Bridge tunnel, we lost the signal and had to wait until we emerged on the other side. I stayed in the center lane as Damien stared at the device, waiting for the dot to show up again.

"Hit refresh," I said.

After a minute, he said, "Eight Eighty South."

The exit was less than a quarter mile away and I had four lanes to cover. I turned on my blinkers and slipped into a tiny space between a Range Rover and a Honda Civic. Then I cut over two more lanes that were clear, amid horns sounding, and made the exit crossing over the V-shaped white lines where the off-ramp divorces the freeway.

"I don't want to die tonight," Damien said.

"You might have mentioned that earlier."

After we were safely ensconced in the 880 South traffic, Damien said, "We're gaining on the dot."

"Subject," I said. "We're gaining on the subject."

"Why are we tailing the subject?" Damien asked.

"The same reason you surveil anyone. Subject is doing something and you want to know what it is."

Subject exited the freeway in San Leandro, near Oyster Bay. Subject drove to a residential area of single-family homes.

"Subject has stopped," Damien said.

We were on a low-traffic side street, so I extinguished the lights in our car and drove down the block until I could see my sister's Jetta parked outside a residence on Sausalito Road. I pulled out my binoculars and caught Rae casually walking down the sidewalk with a large bag slung over her shoulder.

"What's happening?" Damien asked, certain that an action film was playing through my binoculars.

"A small woman is walking down the street."

"What is she up to?"

"I don't know."

My cell phone rang. Henry. I picked up because I had a nagging sensation that I was forgetting something important.

"Where are you?" he asked.

"On a surveillance."

"So you forgot."

"I guess so," I said. "What did I forget?"

"We were supposed to meet for drinks on Friday, which is today."

"I'm sorry. I forgot."

"That it was Friday or that we were having drinks?"

"Which would you prefer?"

"Where are you?"

"On a surveillance."

"Call me when you're done."

"I'm sorry."

"Talk to you later."

"Wait. I hate to ask. Did you run that license plate?"

I figured with Henry getting a woman knocked up within six months of my moving out, I had a lot of leverage.

"Marcus Lorre," he said.

"I knew it."

"Good-bye."

"Who was that?" Damien asked.

"My police contact."

Through the binoculars I saw Rae scan her immediate surroundings. She swiftly pulled a spray can out of her bag, approached a Porsche Boxster parked in a carport, and began writing something in fluffy white letters on the vehicle. The same car from the photos, owned by none other than Marcus Lorre of Lightning Fast Moving Company. From a distance, I couldn't make out the fluffy graffiti. When Rae was done, she pocketed the can and then jogged back to her car, which she entered on the passenger side. Driver was not visible. The vehicle made a U-turn and drove back in our direction.

"Duck," I said.

Damien went into a tuck like a passenger on an airplane waiting for a crash landing. I peered over his head and saw my sister in the passenger seat, Vivien driving. Once they passed, I turned over the engine.

"You can sit up now," I said.

I angled out of the parking space and pulled up alongside the victimized vehicle. I got out of the car and dipped my finger into the fluffy letters and brought it up to my nose. Three words adorned the car, spelled out in whipped cream. One on the hood, one on the windshield, and one on the back window.

Liar

Cheater

Thief

I quickly snapped photos and returned to my car. As we headed back to the freeway, Damien asked, "Who was that girl?"

"My sister."

"What was she doing?" he asked.

"Working," I said.

So this is what a conflict resolution specialist does.

Damien invited me into his shiny apartment for a drink, since detectives always drink after a long night of surveillance. Our shift was a mere three hours, but I almost never turn down a drink, as you probably have noticed.

Damien mixed whiskey sours, which isn't really my thing. I like my drinks untampered with, out-of-the-bottle, maybe with an ice cube. He opened the blinds to a sparkly view of the city at night.

Damien sat down on the couch next to

me. We drank in silence. Without the running commentary of a surveillance subject as topic, we avoided conversation lest we end up in our previous bouts of mini-interrogatives.

This sped up the drinking.

"Another?" Damien asked.

"Sure," I said. "More whiskey, less sour."

"So you just want a whiskey?"

"On the rocks, please."

"Coming right up."

Drinks were served. Drinks were imbibed. Food was not consumed.

At some point Damien looked at me and said, "What are we doing?"

"We are drinking on empty stomachs. It seems like a good idea now, but we will regret it in the morning."

Damien placed his drink on his glass and chrome coffee table and confiscated my drink as well.

"I wasn't done with that."

"I had to go to a sexual harassment seminar last week. I learned about appropriate and inappropriate touching."

"I see."

Damien extended his hand.

"Nice to meet you," he said.

I played along and shook his hand.

"That is appropriate touching."

"You sure about that?"

Damien then swept his other hand around my waist and kissed me. It was a nice whiskey-sour kiss. I would have preferred just a whiskey kiss, but still it was nice and strange, my first non-Henry kiss; Henry kisses were usually whiskey-free. Sometimes Henry tasted like milk. He was that kind of guy.

I'm not sure who pulled away first, but it wasn't so much a rejection as coming up for air.

"That would be an example of inappropriate touching," Damien said.

"No kidding."

"Here's the thing. I don't believe we are colleagues, technically. Would you agree?"

"I would agree."

"So, we can skip filling out the office-romance paperwork?"

"Yes."

"Good. Because I don't have it."

Damien kissed me again. I could taste the whiskey, no sour, this time. It was strange feeling different hands fumble with my buttons. It's kind of like waking up in a hotel room when you think you're at home. Part of me wanted to go home, part of me wanted to stay with Damien, and part of me wanted to kick Damien out and have the swanky apartment and the bottle of booze to myself.

Damien forgot to close the blinds in the bedroom and I awoke at the crack of dawn the next morning. I slipped out of bed without Damien noticing and dressed piece-meal, gathering my clothes like bread crumbs left on a trail throughout the apartment. Once fully clothed, I began the hunt for my purse. I found it under the couch. My mouth tasted like sour booze and cotton, and I rifled through my purse for a mint but came up empty. I saw a tin of Altoids on Damien's kitchen counter and opened the box. I stole two mints and spotted a collection of mail in an untidy pile nearby.

According to Emily Post's *Etiquette*,[8] you don't go through people's shit,[9] but there was something in the pile of mail, not quite on top, but slipped in there, the corner edged out, just enough to pique my interest. It was a save-the-date card. I slipped it

8 And I know this because Grammy made me study that tome like it was a science textbook as some punishment during my adolescence.
9 If etiquette is your thing, you're in luck. I've shared my wisdom in my own short primer, *Isabel Spellman's Etiquette*.

out of the stack just a smidge and read it.

DAMIEN THORP AND KAREN MURPHY
ARE TYING THE KNOT
NOVEMBER 12TH, 2012
DETAILS TO FOLLOW

I guess my card hadn't arrived yet.

I took the entire tin of mints and slipped out the door without ever waking the bridegroom-to-be. I slept the rest of the weekend.

On Monday morning, I worked another tedious shift at Divine Strategies and then went straight to the office.

"You're getting employee of the month again," I said to D.

"It means nothing to me," he said.

"It means something to me," I said.

Vivien told me her computer was totally frozen and even after an hour of remote tech support from Fred, there were no remedies. Since Finkel had failed, I got a recommendation from Maggie for a high-end computer consultant. I waited to call, since *high-end* translates to *extremely expensive*. My sister sent me an e-mail informing me that she had refunded fifty percent of Greenblatt's check. I phoned her to get the details, but she didn't pick up. She has told me repeatedly that she prefers text messages or e-mails. Since I wanted a quick reply, I texted.

Y R we refunding Greenblatt ck?
Couldn't finish job.
y not?
It happens.

People keep their desks in various forms of disarray, but it has always been company policy to put a case file either a) in the file cabinet or b) on the top right corner of your desk in case another investigator needs to access it. Vivien seemed determined to camouflage all of the files pertaining to Rae's cases. I found Greenblatt tucked away in another drawer under an unruly stash of office supplies and emergency snack food. The file was exactly the same as when I first found it, only on top of the astrological chart the words *subject unresponsive* were written in red ink.

The phone rang. D answered and said to me, "A woman. For you. She sounds angry."

"Hello?"

"Isabel, this is Lenore. If you have questions for me, why don't you ask me?"

"Because you might lie," I said. "I find

outside sources more reliable."

"It would behoove you to treat me with some respect."

"I have never heard anyone use the word *behoove* in conversation. That was awesome. Thank you."

"Keep your distance, Ms. Spellman, or you might find a restraining order in your future."

"Lenore, I am very familiar with restraining orders[10] and I can assure you that by the time you have enough evidence for a TRO, I'll have enough evidence against you to sink a ship. Have a great day."

Lenore Parker was a fool. Before she called, I was suspicious. Now I was sure.

The phones began ringing at an alarming rate. Maggie phoned to remind D that he had an interview in the East Bay. Vivien left shortly after that for class. At this point it seemed reasonable to wrangle at least one of my parents out of bed.

I climbed the steps to their bedroom, knocked twice, said, "Everybody decent?" and then opened the door without waiting for a response. I have been told you're supposed to wait for a response.

My mother was alone in bed, obviously

10 See document #2.

woken by my intrusion. Dad's side of the bed was still partially made, wrinkled a bit by association. Mom looked alarmed when she saw me.

"Where's Dad?"

Mom lifted the covers on Dad's side and made a show of looking for his absent figure.

"He must have gone out," she said.

"Does he usually make the bed when you're still in it?"[11]

"We have more time on our hands these days."

"Mom. Where is Dad?"

"He didn't come home last night," Mom said, avoiding eye contact.

"Where is he?"

"He didn't come home," Mom repeated.

"Did you have a fight?"

Mom got out of bed and gently shoved me out of her room. "Isabel, what happens between me and your father is a private matter."

"Is it? I'm not sure that that's true."

"I need to go back to bed," Mom said, closing the door in my face.

11 My ex Henry Stone used to do that, but I've never heard of that habit otherwise.

■ ■ ■ ■

I grabbed my car keys and was about to drive over to David's house. As I walked down the front steps, Maggie was pulling into the drive.

She got out of her car, slammed the door, and said, "Where is he?"

"He didn't come home last night," I said, sounding extremely alarmed. "I can't get any information from Mom."

"He doesn't live here," Maggie said. "He has his own apartment."

"Who are you talking about?" I asked.

"D," Maggie said. "Who are you talking about?"

"My dad didn't come home last night," I said.

Maggie's expression softened with the new bit of intelligence. She slumped slightly and gripped the railing on the staircase.

"Come in," I said. "I'll make you some coffee."

Maggie demanded a shot of bourbon in her brew, which was entirely out of character. At least her daytime character.

"So where is Albert?" Maggie asked.

"Mom won't say. I was on my way to your house to tell David. Why are you here?"

"I came to see D. I don't know what's gotten into him, but he's pawning off his work onto Rae."

"Why would he do that?"

"That's why I came hunting for him. I was hoping for an explanation. As far as I can tell, all the interviews at San Quentin were conducted by Rae."

"We're calling it the Big Q now," I said. "Like the inmates."

"What?"

"Forget it."

"Do you know where the recordings are?" Maggie asked.

"They're on the server. Let me look for them."

I left Maggie in the kitchen with some crack mix[12] and her spiked coffee. Of course, the second I logged on to my computer, it froze. I returned to the kitchen.

"I'll have to get back to you on that," I said. "Are you sure Rae is doing the interviews?"

Maggie laid out copies of the transcripts in front of me and read some samples aloud.

"D has a certain interview style," she said. " 'Question: "You said that you had an alibi

12 A snack mix that D came up with. You do *not* want the recipe. It's *that* good.

279

for the night of the murder. Ivan Grist was his name." Answer: "Yeah. We called him Snake." Question: "Why did you call him Snake?" Answer: "He had a skin condition." Question: "Why didn't Snake testify on your behalf?" Answer: "Cops had him by the balls. Excuse me. Drug charges. So he testified that he didn't see me." Question: "Sounds like a tool." ' "

Maggie looked up from her reading material. "Convict to ex-con doesn't need to say 'excuse me' for using the phrase *by the balls* and I've never heard Demetrius call anyone a 'tool' in my life. Unless you want to confess to being the substitute interviewer, I'm going to assume it was Rae."

"What is the problem, Maggie? Because Rae is still a good interviewer."

"There are two kinds of people in this world, Isabel. Prosecutors and defense attorneys. Rae is a prosecutor. You don't want a prosecutor working on the defense's side."

"She did free Schmidt."[13]

"That was a mere dalliance. She's just as interested in putting people away as setting them free."

"Are you sure Washburn is innocent?"

13 For details, see document #4. T-shirts are still available.

"He is innocent of the crime he was convicted of. That is all that matters."

"I probably should have mentioned this earlier. There was a pickup truck with a sketchy man outside your house not too long ago. I think he was threatening you regarding the Washburn case."

"And you're mentioning this now?"

"If it makes you feel any better, he thinks I'm you. Do you want me to file a report at the police station?"

"Shaved head, tattoo of a woman on his neck, arms the size of tree trunks?"

"Sounds about right."

"I talked to him the other day," Maggie said. "He dropped by my office. He's harmless. Mostly. People pay him a few bucks and he sends verbal telegrams from prison inmates, but that's it."

My phone rang. It was Charlie Black.

"One minute," I said to Maggie. "Hi, Charlie. What's up?"

"I seem to have lost Mr. Slayter."

I left Maggie in a rush and drove straight to Slayter's office, where Charlie was waiting for me.

As I got out of the car, I got another text from D.

Why does your sister have twelve cans of tear gas in her car?

"He was here," Charlie said, pointing at the couch in Slayter's office. "I went to use the restroom and when I returned he was not here."

"Did you ask anyone if they saw him leave?"

"Evelyn said he left."

"Did you ask her where he went?"

"She didn't know," Charlie said.

It was important that my powwow with Charlie seem ordinary, as if I'd dropped by to visit my boss and he wasn't around. Charlie and I had to sort this out on our own. I looked on Edward's desk to see if he had any appointments in his calendar.

"You called Sam, the driver, right?"

"Yes. He's at the car wash."

"And you've tried Edward's cell?"

"No answer. I think it's turned off."

I picked up Edward's desk phone and looked at his call history. The most recent outgoing call was from Edward to Ethan earlier in the day.

I approached Evelyn and asked for the address where Ethan was staying.

"I'm not sure I can give out this information."

"I think you can," I said. "There's a matter I need to discuss with Mr. Jones."

Evelyn pretended to search her desk for the information and came up short.

"I'm afraid I can't find it right now."

I returned to Edward's office, jotted down Ethan's number, and passed the slip of paper to Charlie.

"Listen to me carefully, Charlie."

"I always do."

"Call Ethan's number and say, 'Put Edward on the phone.' "

"Should I say *please*?"

"Why not?"

Charlie put his cell phone on speaker and called Ethan's number.

"Hello," Ethan said.

"This is Charlie Black, Edward Slayter's valet. Please put Edward on the phone."

"My brother isn't here. Have you tried his cell?"

I didn't give Charlie the rest of the script, so he panicked.

"Okay, good-bye," he said, and hung up.

"You should have asked him if he'd seen him."

I checked Edward's call history again from the company line and saw an incoming call from an unknown number with a San Francisco area code. I called the number and it rang ten times until someone picked up.

"Hello," a deep male voice said.

"Hello," I said. "Someone from this number called recently. Can I ask who I'm speaking to?"

"This is Bill."

"Bill, do you know an Edward Slayter?"

"Yep."

"You do?"

"This is a pay phone, lady."

"They still exist? Where are you?"

"The Nite Cap. You need the address?"

"Nope.[1] I got it. Is he there now?"

"Been here since ten," Bill said.

Charlie and I rushed over to the bar located at O'Farrell and Hyde. Even with the overcast skies, the bar was so dim it took our eyes some time to adjust. We found Edward sitting at the bar with a middle-aged man in a gray turtleneck and sports jacket. The unknown male had slicked black

---

1 It's a local dive bar. Of course I don't need the address.

hair, a gut that could have held a basketball, and fingers adorned with rings that could have doubled as weapons. One might say that he looked connected, but it does seem indecent to accuse every middle-aged man who uses pomade of being in the mob. Plus, I don't want you to get excited thinking this story is going to take some organized-crime angle. That's so 1990s.

I slipped onto the stool next to my boss, who was slumped over a whiskey and mumbling incomprehensibly.

"Hi, I'm Isabel. Edward's niece. This is Charlie, Edward's valet. Who the hell are you?"

"I'm an old friend of your . . . uncle's. Now that he's got someone to take care of him, I'll be on my way," the man said, staggering up from his stool.

"Uncle Ed, is this a friend of yours?"

Slayter turned to me and slurred, "I don't know who my friends are anymore."

"How much has he had to drink?" I asked.

"Just one," the man said. "I think something else is wrong with him."

"Why did you ask to meet him here?"

"We had some private matters to discuss," the man said. Then he made a show of checking his watch. "Would you look at the time? Excuse me, I've got an appointment."

The bartender, an older gentleman in shirtsleeves with thinning gray hair, stole a glance at Edward. I looked at my boss and for a brief moment, his eyes shot to life and he shook his head in the negative. The bartender picked up a glass and began drying it.

"Nice to meet you, Isabel and Charlie," the man said.

"I didn't catch your name," I said.

"I didn't give it," the man replied as he walked out the door.

When the man was out the door, Slayter's back straightened and he turned to me with lucid eyes.

"What's going on?" I asked.

"That man tried to roofie me."

Two Hours Earlier
Slayter received a phone call from a man named Tony who said he had information about Ethan and that they needed to meet privately. Slayter chose the Nite Cap because he knew his friend Bill worked the early shift. He took a cab to the empty bar and met with Tony, the turtlenecked gentleman. They ordered drinks. Tony passed Slayter a slip of paper with a number on it and told him to call a man named Elmer on the pay phone. The phone call was a ruse so

Tony could slip something into Ed's drink. Bill witnessed the attempted drugging and sent Edward a text telling him what transpired. Bill had another drink at the ready, and when Tony got distracted by the entrance of another patron, Bill swapped out the drinks. Edward drank his unadulterated scotch and feigned being under the influence of more than just booze. That's when Charlie and I showed up. According to Slayter, the only thing Tony said about Ethan was that Edward should keep an eye on him.

"This doesn't make any sense," I said. "A guy you don't know invites you to a bar to talk about your brother and all he does is try to drug you. What's going on?"

"It was a trap," Slayter said. "That's all. It wasn't about Ethan or anything. Someone wanted to publicly incapacitate me."

"Why?"

"Someone is trying to prove that I'm incompetent because he knows that very soon I will be. This sheds new light on your embezzlement problem. It's beginning to seem like a well-laid plan."

Bill the bartender poured the tainted scotch into an old Perrier bottle and put the glass Tony used into a plastic baggy.

"Evidence," Bill said.

DOMESTIC DISTURBANCES

By Wednesday morning, I found my father back at the house. He was in the kitchen staring at a bowl of half-eaten oatmeal. He looked like he'd just returned from a two-day bender. I gave him a kiss on the cheek to sniff for booze, but I only detected a slight antiseptic odor. Still, he had dark circles under his eyes, his hands had a slight tremor, and what hair he had left was rebelling against a comb job.

"You look like shit," I said.

"You don't look so great yourself, sweetie," Dad said, messing up my hair. Although I doubt you could have seen a difference in any before-and-after pictures.

"Hey," I said. "You're being nice to me."

Direct communication, nonviolent physical contact, a mild insult. Nice.

Something was up.

"You can't hold on to a grudge forever," Dad said.

"Since when?" I asked.

"I'm going to bed," Dad said, nodding in the vague direction of his bedroom.

"Long night?"

Dad made some noise in his throat that was noncommittal.

"Where's Mom?"

"Out somewhere," Dad said. I don't think he even knew. There was definitely something wrong with their marriage, and it was time to come clean with my siblings. "After my nap," Dad said, "I'll see if I can deal with some of the Zylor background stuff."

"You mean, you're considering doing work?"

"I'm considering it," Dad said.

"That would be great," I said. But this was classic divorced-parent behavior. Divide the children with kindness.

I turned on the answering machine and drove straight to David and Maggie's.

It was only noon, and I found my brother and Max sitting on the couch drinking beer and watching soccer. Their daughters were on the floor re-dressing Barbie dolls in evening gowns — the fresh boxes that once imprisoned the freakish representations of the female form rested guiltily by their sides.

"You two have quite a sweet life," I said to

the men. "It's great that you found each other. Hello, Max."

"Nice to see you, Izzy," Max said.

"Don't you have a job, Max?"

"I do. I just happen to make my own hours."

"Parenting is a full-time job," David said.

"I'm hungry," Sydney said.

"There are Goldfish right in front of you," David said.

"No Izzy food."

"If this phase lasts, you won't have to worry about her raiding the liquor cabinet," I said.

David looked at the clock. "In a half hour, I will make you a sandwich. Keep playing."

I picked up the packaging for Brain Surgeon Barbie (Claire's doll) and Princess Barbie (Sydney's bribe) and waved the incriminating evidence at David.

"Maggie know about this?"

David paused the soccer game, leaving the goalie frozen and contorted in midair. He rushed over to me and tossed the cardboard Barbie coffins in the trash.

"For the life of me, I can't figure out why. But it's the only thing that takes complete hold over them," David said in a pleading voice.

"Some people might say the same thing

about heroin," I said.

"I didn't buy the dolls," Max said, as if he were explaining his presence at a strip club. Clearly the wife and ex-wife had admonished both males against the brain-altering objects.

"I get it," I said. "You just wanted a break. You could have given them each a shot of beer or something."

"Please don't tell Maggie," David said.

"I don't need to tell Maggie anything. Princess Banana will sing like a canary."

"No Izzy," Banana sang on cue.

"Please stop saying that, Sydney. This is your aunt Isabel. She's family. You are supposed to be nice to family."

"Good-bye, Izzy," Banana said. An improvement? You decide.

"I don't care about the Barbie," I said. "Let me just say this. If at some point you notice that Sydney is dismembering her dolls, do not automatically assume she needs a shrink. She might just be looking for a hiding place for her marijuana stash. I am here on an unrelated matter."

"I don't want you holding this over my head," said David.

"Dad didn't come home last night. I saw him this morning. He looked like he'd been on a bender or something. Mom's not talking. Something is going on with the two of them. Since I am currently their least-favorite child, maybe you could sit them down and see what's going on."

"Izzy, I really think you have bigger things to worry about," David said.

"Are you talking about the FBI business? Edward says it's fine. There's no way the embezzlement charges will stick."

"I need to come here more often," Max said.

David shook his head in exasperation and pressed the play button on the remote and continued watching the game. I could have sworn Max took me more seriously than David did. Since I couldn't be sure that my brother would take action, I phoned Rae on my way to my hair appointment.

"Listen, there's something wrong with Mom and Dad. There's this tension between them. Dad didn't come home last night and I've overheard some really strange conversations. I think their marriage is on the rocks. David doesn't believe me, but something isn't right."

"I know," Rae said. "I'm looking into it."

"You see it too?"

"I saw it a long time ago."

"So what's going on?"

"I don't know. I'll tell you when I find out."

I should have considered a wardrobe change before I turned up for my appointment at Rodrigo's salon that Wednesday. I couldn't afford Rodrigo, so I settled for a junior stylist named Rainbow. Even the junior stylist seemed disappointed when her low-rent client arrived. One look at me and she knew that I didn't have a BlackBerry full of Nob Hill referrals in my Birkin bag. It might have been the bike messenger bag with reflective strips that I use that tipped her off. Still, Rainbow was a professional.

"You need highlights and lowlights and layers. And maybe bangs. It will make you look younger. Hide the creases on your forehead."

"Then why am I paying for Botox?"

That stumped Rainbow until she gave me the card of her dermatologist and suggested I switch. Rainbow had to be under twenty-nine and yet she had the set face of a woman at war with time. It seemed particularly tragic to me to be under thirty, already terrified of losing your looks, and yet unable to physically register that emotion.

"So what are we going to do?" Rainbow asked.

"Just a wash and dry," I said. "I have a dinner tonight."

Rainbow circled me, like someone at a used-car lot trying to assess whether the 1972 Oldsmobile could be salvaged.

"Maybe if we put it up," she said.

As Rainbow washed my hair, she told me in excruciating detail about her breakup with her last boyfriend, Gavin. He wasn't a talker, which Rainbow had no beef with since she could pick up the slack, but he also wasn't a listener. He was a head-nodder, which led Rainbow to believe that Gavin was actually listening and had heard her when she said that they needed more milk, or a lightbulb changed, or that she wasn't okay with his having naked pictures of his ex-girlfriend on his cell phone. In fact, even when Rainbow was finally worn down enough to end the relationship, Gavin didn't hear her and continued to show up at the apartment until she sent him a text message and changed the locks.

"Good riddance, girlfriend," I said. "You have to love yourself first or no one can love you back." Yes. I felt totally yucky saying something so cheesy, but the next thing you know Rainbow and I were besties and she was spilling what little dirt she had on Margaret Slayter, the ex–Mrs. Slayter.

I showed her a picture.

"Hey, do you know this woman?"

"Haven't seen her in ages. I heard she got a divorce and the prenup was airtight. Rumor is she's living in a trailer park in San Jose."[1]

I held up both pictures.

"Do you know if these two women were friends?"

"I know I've seen them talking. They were both regulars for a quite a while. Couldn't tell you if they were friends."

"But they were acquaintances."

"Definitely," Rainbow said.

I left the salon before Rainbow could use the flat iron on my hair. I pretended to get an urgent text, paid for the wash and dry, and drove straight to Margaret's apartment, just off Lincoln and Twenty-ninth Avenue.

The ex–Mrs. Slayter got enough in the divorce settlement to live a lower-middle-class lifestyle for a few years. She would use that time wisely and find another wealthy husband. I caught her just as she returned home from what was tantamount to her day job — going to the gym. Since I was single-handedly responsible for the demise of her sham marriage, she couldn't even muster a

1 She was in a one-bedroom in the Outer Sunset.

sluggish hello. She merely opened the door and greeted me with an icy gaze.

"This will be quick. I promise," I said.

No response. I showed her the photo of Lenore. Margaret's eyes clicked in recognition.

"I take it you know her," I said.

Still nothing.

"Did you know she is dating your ex-husband?"

Margaret audibly gasped and her nostrils flared like a dragon's. She most definitely did not know that. My fears that the two women had some play against Slayter were unfounded. Under any other circumstance I couldn't have expected Margaret to be a cooperative informant, but seeing her old friend with her ex-husband might spark some truth-telling jealousy.

"Is she dating him because she likes him or because he has money?" I asked.

"Probably both," Margaret said. "He's not going to find a woman who likes him just for him. His money will always be part of his appeal. If he's hoping to find a woman who doesn't care about it, then he's a fool doomed to spend the rest of his life alone, or maybe he'll just settle for his sloppy PI sidekick."

"Did you love him?" I asked, pretending I

didn't hear the last thing she said.

"Of course," Margaret replied.

"Would you have loved him if he didn't have the money?"

"I don't know, maybe. But I wouldn't have married him."

Despite Edward's direct imperative, I returned to the trenches of the Divine Strategies file room to torture myself some more with grunt work, because something was clawing at the back of my brain telling me that I was missing something. When I arrived I noticed that Steve Grant's office was vacated. I inquired about his absence on a carefully timed bathroom break. Amy Cohen told me that he had quit. Something about needing more money. Whatever hold Maureen Stevens had over the lot, I wasn't going to learn it trapped in that file room. I was at the end of the massive filing pileup, counting the seconds until I could venture out into the cold office and begin my real undercover work, when Brad casually entered the file room with another giant heap of paperwork.

"I was doing some spring cleaning and found this in my office."

I didn't mention that it was close to fall. It's possible that tears were welling up in my eyes because the next thing Brad said was, "Why don't you take a break for today and you can get back to it later."

It wasn't until that moment that I realized how much I loathed being in the confines of Divine Strategies, their weekly Bible study, personal-space office politics, and prison file room. And I had no idea how much I was looking forward to filing away that last sheet of paper. I sat down in the corner of the file room and called D.

"I think your God is punishing me," I said to D.

"For what?" D asked.

"For that filing memo I sent around."

"If we're going to entertain this line of thinking," D said, "let's impose some logic here. You've been arrested, say, half a dozen times in your youth; you did some things we probably don't want to revisit. You were a known vandal, occasional car thief, all-around menace to society, and *my God* decides to punish you for sending out a memo that suggested other employees do the filing, when, I should point out, no one actually followed the directives in the memo."

"All I've done at Divine Strategies is file. I don't think I can work here another day."

"So what are you going to do?" D asked.

298

"I need to get sexually harassed."

I told Maureen I had a family emergency and asked if I could come back later in the afternoon and finish my shift. She didn't have a problem with that. I went home, took a nap, changed into the most Evelyn outfit I had, and grabbed a bottle of midlevel bourbon from David's house before I left.

I arrived at Divine Strategies at four o'clock and hunkered down in the file room, waiting for the support staff to leave, hoping that one or two of the male partners would work late. Maureen left at five to pick up her daughter at school. The rest of the female staff was out of the office by five fifteen. It was down to Brad and Bryan. I'll be honest, I was hoping it would be Bryan who stayed late, because I'd rather be groped by a semiattractive male than an unattractive one. As it was, fate decided. Bryan left before Brad and it was Brad who got the pleasure of my company. I took two buttons down on my blouse and tiptoed over to his office.

"Long day?" I said, leaning against Brad's doorway with a bottle of Knob Creek dangling from my right hand and two shot glasses clutched in the other.

I must have startled Brad because he

yelped and bounced a little in his chair.

"Isabel. What are you doing here?"

"The filing. It never ends, does it?" I said as seductively as one can say those words.

"No. I guess not," Brad said.

"I could use a drink. How about you?"

I put two shot glasses down on Brad's desk and poured.

"Oh, I'm good. I have to drive."

"Really? You're going to make me drink alone, after I did all that nasty filing for you?"

I have never tried to seduce anyone before and instead of taking a nap, maybe I should have Googled it or something.

"I guess one drink wouldn't hurt," Brad said, taking a sip from his shot glass.

I circled his desk and leaned against the edge, trying to nonchalantly hike my skirt up. Then I got an unattractive look at my flattened-out thigh and pulled my skirt down again. I took another shot to erase the memory of my thigh.

"So, Brad, tell me about yourself."

"What do you want to know?"

"I want to know *everything*. What do you like? What don't you like? Any hobbies?"

"I go bowling every Sunday."

"Bowling. Are you any good?"

"I scored a two eighty once."

"Wow. That's amazing. What pound ball do you use?"

"Fourteen."

"You must have some very strong fingers."[2]

"Oh, I don't know."

"Can I top you off?" I asked.

"What?" Brad said, looking frightened. Apparently he was unfamiliar with the phrase and didn't notice the bottle of bourbon hovering above his glass. I added another drop anyway.

I kicked off my heels, thinking that disrobing of some sort would seem suggestive and the only other thing I could imagine taking off was my watch.

I took another shot, crossed one leg over the other, and tapped Brad's thigh suggestively with my toe.

"So, what's a girl got to do to get a raise around here?"

Fifteen minutes later, D was giving me a ride home.

"What happened?" he asked.

"I'm drunk," I said. "And I think I just got fired for sexually harassing my boss."

D pretended he didn't hear that last state-

2 It was the only plausible compliment I could offer.

ment and relayed the day's messages: "Rae called to suggest you take an accounting class or repeat fifth-grade math. Your father is putting in for a three-week vacation and Agent Bledsoe called again. This time he said it was urgent."

I didn't call Bledsoe back. That might have been a mistake.

I granted myself the morning to sleep in after the previous evening's humiliation. I took a cab to Divine Strategies, picked up my car, and drove to the Spellman office, arriving shortly after ten. When I saw that both of my parents' cars were in the driveway, I had a brief moment of clarity and I thought, *why not just ask my parents directly what was going on?* So I climbed the stairs to their bedroom. My fist was poised to knock on the door and then I overheard this snippet of conversation.

MOM: Don't come home tonight.
DAD: Olivia, be reasonable.
MOM: I'm not talking about it anymore. You lied to me.
DAD: It wasn't exactly a lie.
MOM: I'd pack a bag if I were you.

I could hear my mother's footsteps marching toward the door. Instead of facing the conflict head-on, I made a run for it down the stairs and bolted into the Spellman offices, where Rae was working on payroll and billing.

"Mom and Dad are upstairs fighting," I said.

"I know," she said.

"What should we do about it?"

"What do you mean?"

"Should we have an intervention?"

"They're not on meth."

"Clearly something is wrong with their marriage."

"I don't think they're headed for divorce, Izzy."

"How do you know?"

Rae stared distractedly at the computer screen. "Shit. Not again."

"What's wrong?" I asked.

"Looks like we just embezzled another ten grand."

MISSING WORDS

"Another ten grand from GLD Inc. has been transferred into the Spellman Investigations checking account and I deny everything," I said to Edward as we jogged past Spreckels Lake.

"Over a hundred and fifty thousand dollars has been transferred into the Cayman Islands account. And yet, you've only siphoned twenty thousand for yourself," Edward said.

"It makes sense," I said. "I wouldn't want to draw too much attention to myself."

"But if you're smart enough to embezzle over one hundred thousand into an offshore account, why would you then deposit money from that account back into your company's checking account? Wouldn't it make more sense to set up a DBA that wasn't so obviously connected to you?"

"Do you think I should call Agent Bledsoe and point that out to him? This case is a slam dunk. No self-respecting criminal would ever embezzle money in this fashion."

"Yes, why don't you phone the FBI and tell them how you *would* embezzle money. That sounds like a brilliant plan, Isabel. And if for some maddening reason my sarcasm was lost on you, please listen clearly. Do. Not. Call. Agent Bledsoe. Under. Any. Circumstances. Whatsoever. Do you understand me?"

"Yes," I said, catching my breath. "So where did Lenore get that purse? You know they cost as much as your average used car."

Edward slowed to a brisk walk.

"You're walking," I said. "Why are you walking?"

"There are a few matters we need to discuss."

"There is a God," I said as I caught my breath. Running is bad enough. Being expected to run and talk is inhumane.

"I'd like you to quit with your side investigation of Lenore. Got it? I like her and I trust her and I'm not going to disrespect her by allowing you to dig around in her personal life the way you do. Do you understand me?"

"Yes," I said. There was a hint of anger in his voice that I'd never heard before.

"And, Isabel, I heard from the temp office

305

this morning. Even after I told you I wasn't interested in Divine Strategies you returned to work there?" Slayter said.

"I just wanted to know what was going on."

"It doesn't matter, Isabel. It's not our problem. And since we have problems, big problems, don't you think we should be focusing on those?"

"Yes, sir."

"At least now I know you can't return to work there. I won't ask about the incident the other night."

"Thanks."

"Let's focus on this pesky embezzlement business. Who are our obvious suspects?"

"People with access to the routing numbers, so the accounting department and people who don't like me. Arthur and Arthur."

"For a detective, you can be extremely shortsighted."

"Heard it before. I'm sure I'll hear it again."

Charlie rode up on his bike and said, "It's nine fifteen, Mr. Slayter," and then he handed him a towel. The towel thing was new.

"I have a meeting," Edward said.

"Words."

"Let's see. Turtle. Clock. Radiator."

"See you Friday," I said.

Slayter jogged off to his car. Charlie circled me on his bicycle.

"Why didn't you say something?" Charlie asked.

"He got *clock* right," I said.

Tear gas. That's what I was forgetting. D had texted me asking about the twelve cans of tear gas in my sister's trunk and I had failed to investigate. Tear gas isn't something you should forget about, but between embezzling money, watching my parents' marriage deteriorate, trying to keep a failing business afloat, and my part-time job as receptionist, there was little time left to harness my sister's activities.

A few days later I sent D a text.

**Is the tear gas still in the trunk?
don't know.**

There was only one way to find out. I phoned Rae.

"Can we swap cars this evening? I need to surveil someone who is familiar with my vehicle."

"But my car is better than your car," Rae said.

"True, but both cars can take you from point A to point B."

"I believe some compensation for the imbalance would be appropriate."

"Seriously?"

"Your car only has a cassette player," Rae said.

"We're talking six hours tops. It's quite possible that you wouldn't even use your car in that time frame."

"And it's quite possible I would."

"Give me a number."

"Fifty."

"Twenty."

"Thirty."

If there's one thing I've learned about my sister over the years, it's her bottom line.

"Twenty-five. Final offer."

"Deal."

I had been hanging on to the Perrier bottle with the possibly tainted whiskey for a few days, trying to decide whether I should contact my usual source for lab work. Henry. But I knew Rae had a great chemist contact in her sticky blackmail network, so I brought the evidence to her apartment that night when I came to pick up the car.

"Not thirsty, but thank you," she said.

"It's evidence. I need to get it tested and I don't want to go to Henry."

"It'll cost you."

"Of course. Nothing with you is free," I said as I gave her the twenty-five-dollar payment for the car swap.

"Tank is empty," Rae said as she tossed me the keys.

I found the car parked around the corner, her usual spot, and immediately tried to open the trunk, only to realize that my sister had given me the valet key, which makes it impossible to open the trunk. I remembered that my parents, being the pink-slip owners of the vehicle (a calculated point of leverage), had an extra key at the house and drove home. I didn't see either of their cars in the driveway, so it was safe to assume that both of my parents were out. I knocked on the door to be safe, waited a moment, and then used my key.

I called out for my parents and found the house unresponsive. Then I decided to search their bedroom. I won't bother offering an excuse, only an explanation: It was there, and I didn't know when else I'd find the opportunity.

The bed was made with the same fatigue that has informed my own housekeeping. Covers pulled over pillows, but nothing tucked or smoothed. Clothes were strewn on the chair; paperwork sat atop the dresser. I was about to look through the paperwork when I heard the front door slam shut.

"Rae?" my mother called out. Rae's car was in the driveway, blocking the garage. The obvious assumption.

"It's me," I said, hurrying out of the bedroom and down the stairs. "I had some last-minute work."

"The office is that way," Mom said, nodding her head toward the first floor door.

"I was looking for you."

"I'm right here."

"I can see that," I said.

"Why do you have Rae's car?"

"Surveillance. But she gave me the valet key. I need access to the trunk."

My mother plucked the key from its hook and handed it to me. Her face was ruddy from crying.

"Here you go."

Dad lowered himself onto the couch and clicked on the remote. I approached Subject cautiously and sat down in the adjacent chair. I gave him a thorough looking over, which included breathing in the overly co-logned aroma wafting in the vicinity. My direct observations did not go unnoticed and likely unnerved Dad.

"What's that delightful scent you're wearing?"

"It's called Charisma," Dad said.

"I think you've got enough of it," I said. Then I just sat there staring at him, because something looked different.

"Don't you have someplace to be?" Dad asked.

"Sadly, no," I replied. "You've lost weight."

"A little, maybe. I've been watching what I eat."

He was also wearing a new shirt and a bulky cable-knit sweater.

I've seen my parents tired, sick, plain worn out, angry, but at this moment I caught them in a state utterly unfamiliar. They looked stunned. And they wanted me out of there as soon as possible.

"Time to go, Isabel," Mom said, adding, "chop chop," to the end of the sentence. I'm not sure she's ever used *chop chop* before.

She tugged on the back of my sweater, which left me with the option of leaving or allowing my mother to damage my one good sweater.

"See you tomorrow, sweetie," Mom said as she practically shoved me out the door.

I would have to consult with my siblings before we could put a plan in action. Because my parents were not getting a divorce. Ever.

I dealt with the matter in front of me and popped the trunk to Rae's car.

There must have been a special that day. Rae had twelve cans of tear gas in her trunk. I found the receipt in the open box that contained them. There was an address for the store in the South Bay. I'd check it out tomorrow during business hours. I got in the car and headed home. As I was driving, I decided to call Henry. His cell phone voice mail picked up on the first ring. I left a message.

"Hi, it's me. Isabel. I, uh, I'm wondering if it's safe to drive around in a car with, say, a dozen cans of tear gas in the trunk. Not that I have tear gas in the trunk. This is purely hypothetical. Call me back."

I found a parking space three blocks from David's house and decided to leave the contraband in the trunk. I didn't feel like being alone, so I knocked on their front door.

After David served me a drink and a bowl of Goldfish and removed his shoes and socks and put on an indoor T-shirt (Free Schmidt!) to reassure me that he wouldn't ditch me with Princess Banana (Maggie was working late), I voiced my suspicions about Mom and Dad.

"Something is wrong with the unit. I'm not saying that Dad is having an affair, but according to *Me²*[1] — *Me Squared* is how you say it, a women's relationship/fashion magazine — "if he did, he got caught based on their behavior tonight."

"That's impossible," David said. "If either of them were going to have an affair, it would be Mom."

"That's just because the odds are in Mom's favor. More people are likely to want to have an affair with her. But sometimes affairs are about insecurity and so then Dad would be the likely candidate."

"I'm not buying it," David said. "What's your evidence?"

"He's spent at least two nights away from home. He's lost weight and he's wearing cologne."

"He could have been working an overnight job," David said. "He stinks after a night in a car."

"I'm the boss," I said. "I think I'd know if he was working a case."

"Maybe they're taking jobs on the side and pocketing the money."

1 Not a footnote.

"Maybe," I said, realizing that I could hardly theorize about the unit's behavior since they'd barely spoken more than a handful of complete sentences to me in the past six months. "But will you talk to him?" I said.

"Sure," David said. He took a healthy slug of his drink.

"Long day?"

"You have no idea. It's been six months. How long can this go on?"

"At least thirty years. You know about Comic-Con, right?"

"Your mob phase lasted only like three weeks," David said.

"That's because my bookmaking business didn't take off."

David was referring to the time when I was eleven and had managed to watch *The Godfather* parts 1 and 2 without my parents' knowledge. I decided that when I grew up I was going to join the mob. I got a conversational Italian book from the library and began taking bets at school. Some sports-related, but mostly random wagers on statistics of certain faculty members' behavior. For instance, the over/under on how many times Mrs. Weinert would say, "One day you'll thank me." Or whether Mr. Thomas would wear his lucky shirt three or

315

four times that week. My odds-making was on point, but I was only eleven and knew nothing about the vig.[2] I did, however, excel at shaking down preteens delinquent in their payments.

"Maggie and I thought the princess phase would be long gone by now. This is worse than the banana experiment by miles. Six months later, Sydney won't go anywhere without her tiara. The color pink has started to give me a headache. If you try to put a pair of pants on her, she goes ballistic. Except for those pink shorts. It's almost impossible to get a playdate because she orders the other children around as if they're in her court. Max wants Claire to be more assertive, so he's willing to throw her into the lion's den.

"I knew I shouldn't have let Grammy give her the dress. So, after a month of debating, Maggie and I removed the dress and the tiara from Sydney's room late last night. Maggie actually put the dress in the fireplace. A thrilling moment, I will admit, but a joy I have paid for dearly. The wailing started first thing in the morning and didn't let up until about two hours ago when Syd-

2 Sometimes I wonder what might have happened to me if I had actually made a profit.

ney was completely spent. Maggie went straight to work. Notice how she's not home yet? I should feel relieved that my daughter is finally asleep, but I know she's just resting up for another day of battle. You can see a child's personality form at such an early age, and I was so relieved when I saw how different Sydney was from you and Rae. Now I almost wish that she got some of that Montgomery DNA."

"Rae has twelve cans of tear gas in the trunk of her car," I said, "if that makes you feel any better."

I left David an hour later so I could rest up for my own battle the next day. Within moments of putting my head on the pillow, I was out cold. And then I was awake.

There was a steady knock on the back door, slightly slower than the rhythm of a woodpecker. My heart raced from being shocked out of REM sleep. I looked at the clock: 2:13 A.M. I slipped out of bed and tiptoed over to the door. There's no peephole, since it's not a real apartment and most people don't know about this entrance. I put my ear to the door to see if I could recognize the breathing pattern, which sounds silly now that I say it.

"Isabel," a familiar voice whispered. "It's me."

I opened the door.

"What are you doing here, Henry?"

Henry walked into the apartment without an invitation.

"I was in the neighborhood," he said, slurring his words together.

"Are you drunk?"

"A little," he said.

"You didn't drive here, did you?"

"I walked."

"From where?"

"Edinburgh Castle."

"That's a long walk."

"I got your message," he said, taking a seat on my couch. "Tear gas canisters should be safe unless the temperature rises considerably or you get in a car accident. I wouldn't leave them in the trunk for too long. Why do you have tear gas?"

"Did you come here to talk to me about tear gas?" I asked.

"Yes. Why else would I be here?"

"It's past two in the morning."

"Were you asleep?"

"Yes."

"Ah, I'm sorry. Go back to bed."

Henry stood up and weaved through the hallway to the front (well, back) door.

"How will you get home?"

"I'll walk or get a cab."

I followed him to the door.

"Why are you here?"

Henry turned around. He was close enough that I could smell the whiskey coming out of his pores. He pushed me against the wall and kissed me. I let it go on longer than I should have. Then I gently pushed him off.

"What are you doing?"

"I miss you."

"I don't think your baby mama would approve of this behavior."

"You were supposed to meet me last week for a drink."

"I don't recall us ever choosing an exact date."

"We did."

"Then please accept my apologies," I said.

"There's something I wanted to tell you."

"Well, if you've changed your mind and now you don't want to tell me, I'm cool with that. Frankly I'm still wrapping my head around you having a pregnant girlfriend."

"We're engaged."

"Okay. Well, congratulations. I didn't have time to get you a toaster in the last two seconds. But I will start comparison shopping tomorrow. I do think you should go."

"Yes. I should go. I'm sorry about that thing I did."

"No problem. I think it's called cold feet," I said.

"Nope. That's not it," Henry said.

He reached for the door. Before he left he turned back and said one last thing. Maybe the worst thing anyone has ever said to me.

"If only you were a little bit more normal."

And he left.

In the morning, I swapped cars with Rae and left the tear gas where it was. Then I drove my crappy Buick to End Times 'n' Such, the quaint survivalist shop in Millbrae where the items of warfare were purchased.

"Can you help me?" I said pleasantly to the store clerk. Only recently have I learned that being pleasant can often work in your favor.

"What can I do for you?" said the man in the plaid flannel shirt with a seven-blade knife hitched to his belt. He had an unusual collection of scars on his knuckles and forehead, leaving slices of his eyebrows permanently mowed.

"Do you sell tear gas?"

"We do. Although a customer just bought

us out. We've got an order for another case. Should be here on Monday."

"This tear gas you sell. Is it like what the cops use in riots?"

"It's a lacrimator in a canister. Just in a smaller dose," the flannel[3] man said.

"What's a lacrimator?"

"A tear-inducing chemical like chloroacetophenone or orthochlorobenzalmalononitrile, which is generally the compound in tear gas."

"I'm not an expert on the subject."

"When a lacrimator, which is what Mace is — you should have a bottle on you at all times — makes contact with the eyes, the ocular immune system will produce a physiological reaction that will pump out a salty wash of protein, water, mucus, and oil to help rid eyes of the irritant as quickly as possible. If you inhale the fumes, your lungs will have a similar reaction. Now, most reasonable adults and bears will flee from the substance and symptoms will subside within the hour, and there will be no long-term damage."

"What happens if you don't flee?"

3 He was not wearing a name tag, so this is the best way to describe him. I have nothing against flannel or the wearing thereof.

"Depends on the individual. I learned in the army, during drills, that I'm mostly immune to the substance. My eyes water a bit and I sneeze sometimes, but that's about it."

"Some people are just lucky, I guess."

"It's kind of like a superpower," Flannel Shirt Guy said.

"You could say that," I said.[4]

"You looking to buy for your bug-out bag?"

"I'm just getting started on my bug-out bag,[5] so I'm considering my options."

"Well you're definitely going to want tear gas and probably at least a month's worth of freeze-dried meals."

"Can anyone buy tear gas? You don't need a permit or anything?"

"Why would you need a permit?" Flannel Shirt Guy asked, as if I had offended his sense of universal order.

"Are there any other uses for tear gas besides crowd control and evacuation?" I asked.

"Bears don't like it much."

"Bears. Hmm, well, thank you. You've been very helpful."

4 Or, you could not say it.
5 Note to self: Google "bug-out bag" later.

"See you Saturday."

"Saturday?"

"We'll have a fresh case of lacrimators by the afternoon."

"Right. See you then."

I returned to my car and contemplated my next move.

There was an old coffee cup, a plastic water bottle, a newspaper, receipts, and other debris littering the passenger-side floor. I remembered that a few months back Edward had called me for a last-minute ride to the doctor. His driver had taken ill. I had to rush to his house and had no time to clean out my car. Edward found a gum wrapper with a piece of gum in the door handle and a coffee cup on the floor. I actually thought the car was tidy, but he scolded me and told me that I was a grown-up and rubbish should be put in its place. In my family the floor of the car kind of was its place. Anyway, Edward's voice was in my head, so I quickly gathered the obvious trash and threw it in the bin at the edge of the parking lot. I reached into the passenger-side door handle and found a USB device.

I put it in my pocket and drove home. These data storage devices are more common than staplers in a PI office. You can find a couple floating around any of our desks. I stuck this particular device into my computer to see if I could discern who the owner was. Only it wasn't an ordinary file-storage device. It was a voice-activated recorder that had six hours of audio on it. Since it was in my car, I could only assume it was intended to record me. I clicked on a file and heard the strangely unfamiliar tone of my voice.

8.13.12.mp3

Hey, asshole, haven't you heard of turn signals? [sound of horn honking] The light has been green for a year now. Let's move. Are you waiting for a formal invitation to turn left? Satan, learn how to drive. It's not physically possible to drive any slower, moron. [sound of horn honking]

I think you get my drift. The device also recorded a few banal phone conversations, since I don't tend to do too much business in the car. It got this gem between me and Princess Banana.

"Is your daddy home? Hello. This is your aunt Isabel. Can you put your daddy on the phone? I don't understand what you want. Can you put him on the phone? Can you *please* put him on the phone . . . David, do not let Banana answer the phone. I'm not going to be reprimanded by a three-year-old lunatic who is in some kind of Emily Post/Princess Diana cult whose guru is Grammy Spellman. Also, toddlers shouldn't be answering phones. It's inefficient, annoying, and never, ever cute to anyone except the parent or grandparent. And in this case, probably not cute to anyone. Why did I call? You know, I have no fucking clue. Good-bye."

I had no idea who planted the device. I knew it wasn't the FBI (it was too low-rent for them) but likely someone connected to Slayter Industries. Either way, the idea that someone might retrieve the recordings and hear verbal rants without a hint of scandal seemed sad. I know more than anyone how tedious a dull surveillance can get. I decided to give my spy something to bite into.

I returned the device to my car, to match the background audio, and turned it on.

"Len, it's Isabel. There's something I need to get off my chest. I just embezzled twenty thousand dollars from my boss. Pretty cool, huh?"

BLEDSOE: ROUND 2

Back at the office I dove headfirst into the embezzler/boss-drugging investigation and solicited Demetrius's help. I gave D a list of Slayter Industries employees who *might* have access to bank information and had him check their credit reports and insurance coverage. There were two ways to look at the case. Someone was stealing money either to steal money or to poison the perception of Slayter's judgment, and I was simply collateral damage.

D read the list out loud: " 'Evelyn Glade, secretary; Arthur Bly, accountant; guy with beard who works with Arthur; woman with braces in HR; lady who just bought new car.' Isabel, I'm going to need names."

"I'll get to that," I said. "I was just brainstorming."

My next order of business was following up with the members of the Slayter Industries board of directors, any of whom might be voted in as CEO should Slayter be judged incompetent. Aside from Edward, there were three other men and one woman: George Rhinebeck, Reed Farnsworth, Gordon Wells, and Shannon Crane.

I immediately ruled out Reed Farnsworth since he was ninety-two years old, and while I'm in no way an ageist, it seemed highly unlikely that a man who needed a staff of two to even dress for the day would have the energy to stage a corporate takeover. Then I struck Gordon Wells from the list. He spent half the year in Paris and had a net worth of half a billion. I've heard the saying that you can't have too much money, but I've also heard Gordon say otherwise. Apparently, his wife has some kind of condition that will eventually be recognized in the *Diagnostic and Statistical Manual of Mental Disorders* in which she can't stop renovating homes. They own like five, and all are under constant renovation. Eventually Gordon decided to purchase a twelve-hundred-square-foot log cabin in Montana where he goes one week a year to escape the construction that surrounds him the other fifty-one weeks out of the year.

This left George Rhinebeck and Shannon Crane. George was a close friend of Edward's and his time was already stretched

327

in many directions. I think he was on the board of at least three other successful companies. Shannon Crane, objectively, would be the person who would want the job the most. She'd once held a CEO position at another well-established venture capital firm, which she'd abdicated after her second child was born. Her children were now teenagers and I suppose one could argue she had a good reason for wanting to get out of the house. I'd have to look at her more closely. But there was no getting around the fact that there were no obvious suspects on the board of directors, and Edward was close friends with all of them. He never brought anyone into the fold whom he didn't trust implicitly.

I logged on to my computer to connect to a credit-check database; my computer began to run in slow motion. I shook the mouse and then it was as if a poltergeist had control of my computer. The cursor clicked onto the web browser and then a ghost in the machine typed in the URL for Her Li'l Majesty, a shopping site for all things involving dressing young girls like princesses or prostitutes. The monster in my computer began adding various items into the shopping cart. Mini prom dresses, mini beaded evening gowns, sashes, pumps in size three, toddler makeup, body glitter. I unplugged the computer and dialed the number that Maggie had given me for Craig Finch, computer consultant.

Craig is a shut-in. Even if your hard drive actually needs to have physical repairs, no contact is made. Instead, you're given a drop-off location. No one has ever seen Craig, according to Maggie. However, the invisible repairman comes highly recommended.

"Mr. Finch," I said. "This is Isabel Spellman; I'm Maggie Mason's sister-in-law. She gave me your number. I have some strange things going on with my computer."

"Can you be more specific?"

"Yes. Sometimes it freezes. Once a lot of crazy numbers started showing up on the screen, mostly zeros and ones."

"Binary code," Finch said.

"Sometimes it's slow. Sometimes it's not. Also, sometimes our old computer repairman is inside our computer playing mind games with us. Me specifically. We gave him remote access once and I think he still has it."

"Are you sure about that?"

"I know it sounds paranoid, but you're going to have to take my word for it."

"You're going to have to give me remote

access to poke around," Finch said.

"And then what happens? You have a bad day, you don't like the way I talk to you or something, and the next thing I know you're making me watch you buy toddler ball gowns on my computer?"

"Think about it and get back to me."

As soon as I disconnected the call, Mom entered the office and said that she needed her paycheck early.

"What's happening to all your money?"

"We have only a few more days to put money in our IRA.[1] Your father and I would like to retire one day."

"Talk to Rae. She's writing the checks these days."

Mom returned to the kitchen, where she proceeded to make toast, her signature dish.

"Is there something I should know?" I asked.

"Yes," Mom said. "Navy blue and black are *not* the same color."

"We're going to have to agree to disagree."

If you have to line up a shirt and sweater next to each other because you can barely tell the difference, the difference becomes

1 Later I learned that IRA deadline is April. When it comes to fiscal matters, it's really easy to pull the wool over my eyes, it seems.

irrelevant. I've argued this point many times before, and would gladly have argued it again, but at that juncture I needed to stay on point.

"Are you and Dad okay?"

"Yes, dear. We're fine."

"Are you still thinking about selling the house?"

"You've always known this, Isabel. We've never made much with the business. The house is the only thing we have of value."

"Should I be more worried than usual?"

"Yes, Isabel." Mom said. "You're thirty-five, single, you live in a dump, your hair looks like shit, and your little sister knows more about running the business you own than you do. You should most definitely worry."

"That was a little harsh, Mom."

Mom kissed me on the cheek.

"You're right. I'm sorry. It's just been a long day."

"It's eleven A.M."

The doorbell rang.

"I'll get it," Mom said.

Mom returned to the kitchen with Agent Bledsoe.

"This gentleman, Carl, says he's here to see you."

I didn't overhear what introductions were

331

made at the door, so I fished for a cue.

"Carl, I knew I was forgetting something. Lunch, right?"

"We'll take my car, if that's all right?" Carl said.

"Yes. Your car is fine. Bye, Mom. See you later."

"Carl, can you give me a moment?" my mom said, holding me back.

"I'll wait outside," Carl said.

"I'm glad you're making new friends," Mom said. "It would be so much nicer if they weren't married."

I'd learned my lesson. The second I got into Agent Bledsoe's car, I lawyered up and called Maggie; she got an extension on her armed robbery case and met us at the federal building.

"Did you say anything?" Maggie sternly asked when she arrived.

"She wouldn't even chat about the weather," Agent Bledsoe interjected.

"Good. If you look at the evidence, it's obvious that Isabel is being framed. Until you find out who owns GLD Inc. and where the bulk of that money is going, you have no idea who the real embezzler is. My client is happy to write a check now and put it in a trust. Or freeze the account to prevent any more wire transfers. You have our full cooperation as long as I understand that this isn't a witch hunt on my client."

"Thank you," Agent Bledsoe said. "May I ask your client a question unrelated to the financial issues?"

"Ask and I'll let her know if she can answer."

"What do you think happened to your boss last night?"

"What are you talking about?" I asked.

"You didn't hear?"

"Hear what?"

"Edward Slayter was found wandering around Lake Merced at three A.M. last night in his pajamas. He's being held on a 5150 at the county hospital."

I got to my feet and turned to Maggie. "I have to go. Now."

As we left, Agent Bledsoe said, "Don't take any vacations, Isabel."

"I never do."

Maggie dropped me at the house, so I could get my car. I phoned Ethan on our way because, as Edward's closest living relative, he would be able to get information from the hospital. He returned my phone call ten minutes later.

"The only way we can get Edward out of

the psych hold," said Ethan, "is with the support of his physician. No one seems to have this information. Can you help?"

"I have it."

"Call him and then if you would be so kind as to pick me up at my apartment."

Ethan and I arrived at the hospital and were referred to the row of plastic chairs in bondage against the wall. I poured a cup of coffee that had no business calling itself that and waited impatiently for Dr. Lorberg, Slayter's personal physician, to arrive.

Ethan played the role of concerned brother with aplomb. He ranted at the nurse at the front desk. He threatened legal recourse. He made a phone call to an attorney friend. He demanded to see the supervising physician. Then Ethan turned to me.

"You know something," he said.

"I know as much as you know."

"What is it between the two of you?"

"He trusts me."

"Why?"

"I got that kind of face, I guess."

"I don't know if I trust you," Ethan said.

"I don't know if I trust you either."

Dr. Lorberg arrived and spoke to the woman at the front desk. The door to the psych ward buzzed and Dr. Lorberg disappeared behind it. Two long hours later, he returned with Slayter, who was wearing a torn oxford shirt and wrinkled trousers in a wool-silk blend. He had a twelve o'clock shadow and his eyes had the hollow look of someone who'd just seen a ghost.

Ethan rushed to his brother's side and gave him a warm embrace. It was a believable gesture if you were in the mood to believe things. Ethan then turned to Dr. Lorberg and asked for medical instructions.

"Make sure he drinks plenty of fluids, has a good meal, and gets some rest."

While Lorberg was debriefing Ethan, Edward pulled me aside.

"Who is doing this to me?" he asked.

"I promise I'll find out."

"It's not the disease."

"I know," I said.

"How do I look?" Edward then asked. Slayter's vanity can take hold at the oddest moments. He looks good for his age. Although I've learned to leave out the last three words.

"You look okay," I said. "More like a painter than a wealthy business mogul."

"I can live with that."

"But you smell awful."

Slayter shook his physician's hand and

thanked him profusely. Lorberg said he would drop by Slayter's house in the morning to check on him.

Ethan, Edward, and I drove to Slayter's house. I knew I couldn't leave my boss alone with his brother, so I texted Charlie from the hospital and told him to be at Edward's place when we arrived.

Charlie had a pot of tea and a plate of cookies on the coffee table when we came inside.

"Can I offer you some tea, Edward?" Charlie asked.

"No, thank you," Edward said.

Charlie looked disappointed.

"I'll take some," I said.

"Milk and sugar?"

"Why not?"

"One lump or two?"

"Three."

"Excuse me," Edward said. "I've been told I need a shower."

I followed my boss down the hallway and broke the news.

"While you were in a padded cell, I was picked up by Agent Bledsoe again. Someone is trying to make you look bad by trying to make me look bad."

"Maybe it is time to retire."

"I think I'm too young to retire."

I guess that wasn't a time for bad jokes.[2] Edward stared blankly at me.

"You are not giving up," I said. "Just get some rest. I'll get Ethan out of here and we'll come up with a plan in the morning."

While Edward was in the shower I checked Edward's bar and collected every bottle of brown liquor (Edward doesn't drink gin or vodka) in a box.

"What are you doing?" Ethan asked.

"I'm having a party," I said. When Ethan continued to gawk at me, I continued. "He was drugged. I don't know how, but any open bottle is suspect."

"I think I should stay," Ethan said.

I couldn't leave Ethan alone with his brother, but I also knew that I was not the one to persuade Ethan to go home.

We drank tea and waited for Edward to come out of the shower.

"Ethan wants to stay," I said.

"Ethan, go home. Charlie and I will be fine. I need some quiet after my evening in the cuckoo's nest. Let Isabel drive you home. I insist," Edward said.

He then took his brother by the shoulder

2 When is a good time is the question, because I've got a lot stored up.

and marched him to the front door.

"Call if you need anything," Ethan said.

"I will," Edward replied.

Before I left I whispered in Charlie's ear, "Order Chinese food. I think he'll eat the soup, and don't answer the door for anyone."

"Except the Chinese food delivery guy, right?"

"Right."

It had been an exhausting morning; Ethan and I didn't speak on the drive home. The USB voice-activated recorder was still under a wadded-up tissue in the change pocket of the door. If it was Ethan who planted it there, he'd have to swipe it at some point. I kept checking him out of the corner of my eye.

That's when I noticed Ethan checking his side-view mirror, and then I noticed the tail. We were being followed by a silver Toyota Prius. It's a good choice for surveillance in San Francisco and whoever was driving knew what he or she was doing.

I changed lanes on Gough and made a right turn on Geary. I stayed in the center lane and then swung over to the left lane, cutting off a sluggish pickup truck, and made a left turn onto Van Ness. The Prius got stuck at the light.

"What the hell was that?" Ethan asked.

"We were being followed."

"That maneuver was unnecessary."

"I lost the guy, didn't I?"

"You could have caused an accident. Drive like that on your own time."

"Yes, sir."

I followed the basic laws of traffic the rest of the way to Ethan's apartment. In the distance I could see the Prius resuming the tail. Ethan noted this fact and calmly watched the car through the mirror. I pulled up in front of his apartment.

"As always," Ethan said, "a pleasure."

Ethan got out of the car and entered the building. I pulled around the corner and checked for the USB device. Still there. It was then that I spotted the Prius again. The driver parked the car in an illegal parking spot that also had a visual on the building. Thirty minutes later, neither Ethan nor his tail had budged. I circled the block to be sure that the car wasn't following me and returned to the same spot to see the Prius in place. I parked at a meter and casually walked over to the compact fuel-efficient vehicle.

A large man in a short-sleeved button-down shirt and sunglasses, with the gut of a man who sits in a car all day, was at the wheel. He didn't notice me until I knocked on his window.

"Well hello there, pretty lady. I don't believe we've been introduced."

"Who are you?"

"My friends call me Jimmy."

"What do you want me to call you?"

"You can call me Jimmy too. And you're Isabel."

"How do you know my name?"

"I have friends."

"You got it from my license plate?"

"Yep."

"Ex-cop?"

"You're a sharp one."

"Why are you following Ethan?"

"I want to make sure he doesn't do anything stupid. Men in his situation get desperate."

"What do you think he's going to do?"

"I don't know," Jimmy said, "leave the country, maybe."

"Would that be so bad?"

"Uh, yeah," Jimmy said. "That would be really bad. I'd be out ninety thousand bucks."

"This is what I don't understand. Why do you boneheads keep playing poker with somebody if you know they don't have the money to pay you back?"

"Lady, I'm a bail bondsman. Jonesy here

has three more weeks to get his affairs in order. After that he's doing a ten-year stint in Lompoc."

Ten minutes later I knocked on Ethan's door.

"I was about to draw a bath," he said impatiently.

"That sounds like a good idea. You should take as many baths as possible while you have the chance."

"Excuse me?"

"Invite me in for a minute."

Ethan backed away from the door. I entered the tastefully gender-specific apartment. I've discovered there's an exact measurement of television size that can inform you whether the dwelling is inhabited by a man or a woman without any other evidence. Unfortunately, as flat-screen televisions become more economically friendly, that number grows, and I must admit to being lax in updating my graph.[1]

I sat down on Ethan's couch across from a forty-six-inch flat-screen LCD that was mounted to the wall.

"What can I do you for, Isabel?"

"What is the nature of this San Francisco

1 I was bored and made a graph one day.

visit? Are you really thinking about buying a bar?"

"It can be a good investment."

"Don't you think several dozen cartons of cigarettes would be a better one?"

"Cigarettes," Ethan said as if he were repeating a word in a spelling bee.

"I'm not suggesting you take up smoking, but they are the best currency in prison."

Ethan flopped down in a leather chair that was probably worth more than my car.

"When did you find out?" he asked.

"Like ten minutes ago."

"Don't tell Edward."

"If you're not here to shake down your brother, why are you here?"

"To say good-bye."

"That's all?"

With everything that had transpired in the last few days, it was a good story, but I wasn't 100 percent sure I believed him. How trustworthy is a gambling-addicted American with a fake British accent who has done seven years for a Ponzi scheme and is getting ready to go down for ten more? I took his confession with a grain of salt.

"It was my second conviction. I got ten to fifteen. My earliest chance of parole is eight years."

"Were you just going to disappear and not tell Edward?"

"I'm already an embarrassment to him. I wanted him to remember me fondly."

"Too late. Get some rest, Ethan. Then you and Edward need to have a serious talk. Okay?"

"I'm not telling him."

"Then I will," I said. "But I think you can put a better spin on it." Before I left, I held up the USB device. "Is this yours?"

"No. What is it?"

Was it my imagination, or was I getting *everything* wrong?

I returned to the Spellman compound and found D sitting behind his desk, running diagnostics on his computer. It was long past quitting time.

"D, what are you doing here?"

"Waiting for you."

"Why?"

"Things are slipping through the cracks."

"I'm trying, D."

"I know that Mr. Slayter is important to you, but you have family. They should be more important."

"They are," I said.

"Then start paying attention. You're missing things."

D got to his feet, nodding in the general direction of my desk, and left for the day.

The first thing I saw atop the mass of paperwork was Rae's flimsy case files, which Vivien had assembled. After perusing them briefly I decided it was time to get some answers.

I drove to my sister's apartment in the Inner Sunset and found a parking space a few blocks away. I knocked on her door. Fred Finkel answered.

"Fred."

"Isabel."

"Invite me in."

"Please come in."

I took a seat on their thrift-store couch. It had to be twenty years old, but during its previous occupancy it had likely been shrouded in plastic. Faded by the sun, but vigorously spotless. Rae has probably ten times as much money in her bank account now than I ever have, but she'd never blow it on luxuries like a previously unowned couch, a contradiction I've always found admirable to a certain extent.

"Where is she?"

"She should be back in about an hour. I'll leave you two alone."

"Fred, what is a conflict resolution specialist?"

"I don't get involved in her business," Fred said. "If you get hungry, there's some leftover pizza in the fridge. It might be good for one more day. But I'd nuke it first. Don't take any chances."

As I waited for my sister to come home, I searched the apartment for booze. I found an open half bottle of Manischewitz wine. I poured myself a glass and returned to the couch. I sipped the saccharine beverage, slowly adjusting to its cloying aftertaste, finding that I almost liked it one hour later when I poured my third glass.

I heard my sister's light steps on the stairwell, approaching her apartment. I flicked off the lights and waited until she entered.

I turned on the reading lamp by the couch as my sister dropped her book bag in the foyer.

"What are you doing here?" she asked, slowly turning around.

If I had startled her, she hid it well.

"We need to have a talk," I said.

"You should have made an appointment," Rae said.

"What kind of twenty-two-year-old doesn't have any real booze in her house?"

"Is that what you want to talk about?"

Rae took a seat in another second- or

third-generation chair across from me. This one they'd found on the street, so they'd covered it with a light blue sheet. I tossed Rae's case files on top of several milk crates that doubled as a coffee table.

"What is a conflict resolution specialist?"

"It's exactly what it sounds like."

"Marcus Lorre. The man from the moving company. You whip-creamed slurs on his car. Is that what a conflict resolution specialist does?"

"He needed to understand that actions have consequences."

"What else have you done?" I asked.

"Aside from at least twenty crank calls?"

"Yes."

"I let out the air in his tires."

"And what about those compromising photos of him with a woman who was not his wife?"

"I'm hanging on to those. I'm still hoping that I can reason with him."

"So a conflict resolution specialist is a revenge artist, am I correct?"

"You've got the wrong idea," Rae said. "Lorre was a special case. Mostly I help solve people's problems."

"With twelve cans of tear gas?"

"I never used the tear gas. I went with a stink bomb instead."

Maybe it was the Manischewitz, or the afternoon waiting for my boss to be released from the psych ward, or the sudden realization that more and more questions were piling up as I remained completely in the dark, but I felt like I could have fallen asleep for days on their twenty-year-old couch. However, I managed to get to my feet and somehow reached the front door.

"For now, even though it doesn't seem like it, I'm still the boss and I need to know exactly what my employees are up to. In twenty-four hours I want an exhaustive report on all of your recent activities as a *conflict resolution specialist.* I shouldn't have to remind you of this, Rae. We're private investigators. We report. We don't mediate with whipped cream and stink bombs."

"You know what a private investigator is?" Rae asked. "It's a glorified snitch."

Rae Spellman, Conflict Resolution Specialist

Mission Statement

Private investigators, for the most part, observe and inform. There are times when clients need more than data. I, Rae Spellman (hereafter referred to as the CRS), want to offer clients an alternative beyond the reaches of your average private investigator, a full-service operation, if you will.

As an investigator, I grew tired of passive observation. I wanted to take a more active role in achieving full resolution of my clients' problems.

Advertisement

Do you have a problem that cannot be solved through traditional avenues of conflict resolution?

Have you tried . . .

The police
A lawyer

A mediator
A minister
A rabbi
A veterinarian
A clown
A landlord
An arborist
A psychologist
A psychiatrist
A gardener
A private investigator

Have all of these individuals failed to help you with your problem?

That's when you call a conflict resolution specialist.

If a problem can be solved within reasonable ethical boundaries, we can solve it.

Call now for a free consultation. 415-xxx-xxxx

Report on activities from August 2012 to September 2012
Client #0000001[1]

Vivien Blake, college student and part-time employee of Spellman Investigations, hired Lightning Fast Moving Company, located in San Bruno, California, to store her

---

1 The zeroes seemed unusually ambitious.

belongings for one month and then move them into her new apartment in Berkeley, California, at the beginning of July of this year. When the movers arrived, they added two surplus charges to the bill (one charge was for items going above the two-thousand-pound weight limit and the other charge for a short flight of stairs). The movers refused to deliver or release her property until she paid two thousand seven hundred fifty dollars and twenty-five cents. Vivien paid the fee, and her property was delivered. But several items were damaged, destroyed, or missing. Vivien left several unanswered messages for the representative at the company whom she first made contact with in spring, Marcus Lorre (a.k.a. Owen Lukas). After fifteen calls, he eventually answered the phone and firmly suggested that Vivien review the contract.

Vivien showed the contract to the CRS, who reviewed it for inconsistencies. The issue of the property's being over the weight limit would now be impossible to prove without the items being removed from the apartment and put on a scale, and no one would be able to confirm which items had originally been in the van. As for the flight of stairs, the language in the contract is extremely vague (*a surplus might be added for any additional stairs*).

Ultimately, extraneous and unjust charges can be added at the discretion of the company. An investigation into LFMC revealed that many clients had similar complaints without avenues of remuneration. There were twelve small-claims court filings against the company. It's worth noting that women were the plaintiffs in ten out of twelve of the cases. It is believed that LFMC targets females who are alone when the movers arrive.

The CRS paid a visit to Marcus Lorre at his place of business with Vivien's contract in hand. CRS went over in detail every issue that client had, pointed out the gender bias in the way clients were handled, and firmly suggested that company reimburse client for the surplus charge paid under duress.

Lorre repeated after every comment or request, "Please review the contract."

A letter to the company and to Lorre on the letterhead of David Spellman, attorney at law,[2] received no response.

After reviewing the results of previous

2 Rae apparently has a stack of his letterhead, which she uses, she claims, only in extenuating circumstances.

legal claims against the company, matter was discussed with client, who did not wish to pursue the case in court. Vivien was mostly concerned with sending a message to Marcus Lorre. The money did not concern her; she wanted the *morally bankrupt slimeball* to understand the sense of being violated and powerless.

On 8/2 CRS freed the air in the tires of Lorre's BMW.

On 8/4 CRS took compromising photos of Lorre and unknown not-his-wife female.

On 8/25 CRS painted in whipped cream character-identifying words on Lorre's vehicle.

CRS has also maintained a consistent tail on Lorre to assemble any more intelligence on compromising behavior and to remind him that he is under constant supervision. Lorre has confronted CRS, who has denied any wrongdoing. He has also threatened CRS with legal recourse, but CRS knows that he has no evidence.

Case Status: Pending.

Dissemination of the compromising photos will be last resort. Vivien and CRS are willing to give Lorre one more chance at redemption.

Marshall Greenblatt contacted CRS through an advertising campaign. He had an unusual problem. His girlfriend, Yvonne LaPlante (Aquarius), an intelligent woman in many ways, had become increasingly obsessed with her astrological forecast. She would pay for subscriptions to daily newsletters, read the forecasts in every circulation available, and adjust her day accordingly.

If her favorite astrologer suggested that she needed a day to recharge her batteries and remain thoughtful, Yvonne would call in sick to work and spend the day at home making a dream collage and watching television. Should her forecast suggest that a business opportunity might be coming her way, she would actively consider every spam mail opportunity presented to her. Should her forecast suggest that she needed to create more lines of communication in her relationship, she and Marshall would have a marathon session discussing their future.

When Marshall confronted his girlfriend about his discomfort with her obsession, she cited several esteemed men in history who strongly believed in astrology, including Sir Isaac Newton. Marshall, an educated man, reminded her that Newton also devoted an extraordinary amount of time to trying to discover the elusive and impossible philosopher's stone, a fabled substance that could turn base materials into gold. Yvonne's response was that just because the philosopher's stone hadn't *yet* been discovered didn't mean it wouldn't eventually be.

At his wits' end, Marshall contacted the CRS at Spellman Investigations and worked up a plan to deal with his situation. CRS, with the aid of a graphic designer, jumbled the forecasts in the astrological newsletter *Stardance,* to which Yvonne was most devoted. Marshall would print out the newsletter for Yvonne every morning in an act of conciliation, he explained (their fights on the subject had put an extraordinary stress on their relationship). For a full week Yvonne strictly adhered to the guidelines for a Taurus (Monday), a Libra (Tuesday), a Pisces (Wednesday), a Leo (Thursday), a Capricorn (Friday), a Gemini (Saturday), and a Virgo (Sunday).

Once Subject's experimental week was complete, Marshall informed his girlfriend of the educational ruse. Yvonne became outraged at the deception and claimed that she had felt discombobulated the entire week and now she knew why. Marshall insisted that Yvonne never mentioned feeling discombobulated and an astrological war of words ensued. Marshall brought in CRS to mediate and CRS attempted to reason with Subject. CRS came prepared with astrological quizzes at the ready to try to persuade Subject that astrology is the mild-mannered equivalent of witchcraft, the guidance for each sign merely the whims of astrologers who have no accreditation beyond a talent for their conviction.

Subject remained unresponsive. Marshall informed CRS that they broke up two days later.

Status: Unresolved (50 percent refund offered)

Job #0000003

Client, Emma Lighthouse, contacted the CRS branch of Spellman Investigations via referral. She had recently broken up with her live-in boyfriend, Cameron Berg. Emma had taken over a rent-controlled apartment in Berkeley, one mile from campus, from her friend Tanya Grey a year before. The lease remained in Tanya's name. Three months after Emma and Cameron began dating, Cameron moved in. Five months later, when Emma decided to break up with Cameron, she asked him to move out. Two weeks later, Emma noticed that Cameron was making no effort to find a new apartment. She repeated her request and gave him a timeline, which he verbally agreed to but then did nothing to facilitate. When client realized that her ex-boyfriend had no plans to move out of residence, she threatened Cameron and explained that the next time he went out, she would have the locks changed.

Cameron responded by refusing to leave the apartment. His friends brought him class notes and food and since there was a washer-dryer in the apartment, he was able to remain self-sufficient. Finals were still two months away and Emma did not wish to continue this farce until Cameron had no choice but to leave. She appealed to Cameron's friends and family and found no assistance in this matter. Finally she contacted CRS.

CRS took possession of the apartment keys and suggested Emma find another place to stay for a few days. The CRS first attempted to reason with Subject. Subject was beyond reason. CRS realized that the situation called for extreme measures. She considered how military and police might handle a similar situation and considered (briefly!) tear gas.

CRS then considered that there might be a compound similar to tear gas, without the extreme side effects, that would encourage Subject to vacate premises. CRS went to a survivalist shop and asked for such an item. The store clerk insisted that real tear gas was a better option. CRS then discovered how easy it was to buy tear gas and decided to purchase the entire stock for no other reason than the simple fact that she could. And it seemed wise to take it off the market.

[This is only to explain why there was tear gas in the trunk of the CRS's vehicle. Please note it was never used. It is now located in David Spellman's garage. Next to a box of disposable diapers.]

CRS continued to contemplate the client's predicament and eventually came upon an idea. She recalled a book she'd read some years ago, *War Is Smell*,[3] about the use of stench warfare in combat zones. CRS went to Misdirections, a novelty gift shop on Fillmore Street, and purchased five stink bombs.

3 Everyone in the Spellman family has read this book. There was a brief Spellman family book club that my father initiated about eight years ago. Arguments over book choices became so heated that they negated any family bonding that might have been accomplished from reading and discussing same tome.

CRS phoned Subject one last time, requested that he vacate premises, and attempted one final negotiation. Subject hung up on CRS.

CRS entered apartment with leaseholder's approval and set off five stink bombs throughout. CRS waited outside front door. Subject lasted fifteen minutes and finally departed with a small bag of clothing. CRS, an adept locksmith, then changed the locks and gave a copy of the new key to the client. After the apartment was aerated for three days, Client returned to her apartment, where she currently resides alone. Smell hasn't entirely dissipated.

Status: Resolved.

Misdiagnosis

When I arrived at the office the next morning, my brain felt as foggy as a San Francisco summer. As I waited for the second pot of coffee to brew in the kitchen, I replayed the conversation with Agent Bledsoe in my head. I needed to figure out who'd tipped him off. I had been so sure it was Ethan, but in light of his impending incarceration, he didn't have a great deal of motive or time to set in motion the series of events.

And then I let my imagination run loose like a large boulder down a hill and began to wonder what would happen if I couldn't beat these charges and the FBI decided to set an example with me. Innocent people go to prison all the time. How well would I survive in a federal prison? Martha Stewart set the standard pretty high, and you know you can't live up to that. And you wonder what kind of ridiculous hobbies you might take up. Ceramics? Gardening? Creative writing? That shit is not for me. So, if I would need to flee the country, I had to get my affairs in order.

My dad got to the coffee first and kindly poured me a cup, and sat down at the table next to me.

"How are you doing, Isabel?"

"Honestly? I've been better. You?" I asked.

"Things can only go up from here."

"Dad, your nose is bleeding."

I grabbed a paper towel and squeezed Dad's nostrils together, but it wasn't quite doing the trick. Blood began pooling on top of the kitchen table. Dad picked up a dishrag and leaned his head back.

"Damn, that's a lot of blood," I said.

Rae came out of the office and into the kitchen about then.

"Shit," she said. "Izzy, call nine-one-one."

"Rae, it's just a nosebleed. I think ice helps."

"Call nine-one-one," she repeated assertively.

I picked up the phone and dialed, while my sister pulled another towel from the drawer and clamped my father's nostrils shut. She must have been pinching really hard, because he was moaning in pain.

"Where's Mom?" Rae asked.

"I think she went to the store."

"Call her," Rae said. Her hands were busy trying to stanch the bleeding.

Ten minutes and what looked like a crime scene of blood later, the paramedics arrived. They put my father on a gurney and checked his vitals while my sister provided the relevant details.

"His name is Albert Spellman, he's sixty-nine years old. He's just been diagnosed with acute myeloid leukemia."

PART III
LAST WORDS

Voice Memo

We don't have any secrets anymore. Everyone knows that Dad's sick, that Isabel is in serious trouble, and that the bottom could drop out of the business any day. "The truth will set you free" is bullshit. I still can't sleep.

I know I can't cure Dad. But the other stuff, I know I can do more. I'm not sure I can sit back and watch it all fall apart. This is mine as much as it's hers. At least it used to be. I let a piece of it go and watched her run it into the ground.

I don't want to take anything away from my sister. I just want to take back what's mine.

SICK

Dad was immediately admitted to UCSF Medical Center at Mount Zion on Divisadero Street. While Mom was filling out the paperwork, Rae debriefed me on the trajectory of events.

The unit was fighting because Dad was ill and refused to see a doctor. Dad eventually relented, had a checkup with his family doctor, and played down his symptoms, and Dr. Smiley dismissed Dad with a clean bill of health. Mom insisted that Dad get a second opinion. When he refused, she told him that he couldn't come home until he went to a specialist. After two nights without Mom, Dad capitulated and went to another general practitioner on his HMO plan, who ran some tests and sent him to an oncologist, Dr. Chang, who ran a few more tests and diagnosed Dad with acute myeloid leukemia and strongly encouraged my father to check into the hospital and begin treatment immediately.

Dad said he needed a few days to absorb this life-altering information, and that's when I found him in the kitchen with the nosebleed.

"And how do you know all this?" I asked Rae.

"I put a listening device in their car."

"And my car?"

"Yes."

And I found that bit of information soothing. So goddamn wrong.

"This way I knew what was going on, and if I needed to intervene it wouldn't be too late."

"In the future, I would like us to cut back on interfamily audio surveillance," I said.

"I think we can see Dad now," Rae said.

Once Dad was stabilized and his nose was no longer a fountain of blood, we were allowed to visit. The three Spellman spawn converged on room 857.

"You have some explaining to do," David said.

"How could you keep this from us?" I asked my parents.

"Let's not get into this now," Mom said.

"When were you planning on telling us?" I asked.

"After I beat this thing," Dad said.

I studied Mom's guarded reaction while Dad held court, boasting of the great nursing staff and bemoaning the limited cable TV options. Dad said he'd give the hospital an overall three-star rating on Yelp. I suggested David and Rae stay with Dad while Mom and I got coffee across the street at Peet's.

"How long has this been going on?" I asked after we found a table.

"I've been trying to get him to go to a doctor for over a month."

"When were you planning on telling us?"

"I'd never seen your father so terrified. The last time anyone went into the hospital, it was when Uncle Ray got sick."

"But he can be cured, right?"

"With leukemia you hope for remission," Mom said. "And he can go into remission for years. They don't use the word *cure*."

Dr. Chloe Chang, Dad's oncologist, came by his room later that day and debriefed the family about Dad's treatment. With AML, the first phase is induction chemotherapy, in which the patient remains in the hospital for up to four weeks: intensive chemotherapy for about a week and then palliative therapy, including antibiotics, antifungals, whatever is required to offset the damage done by the chemo. After the induction phase, 70 to 80 percent of patients are expected to enter complete remission. If complete remission is achieved, then the patient is allowed to go home and rest, usually for about a week, before starting the second phase, which includes consolidated chemotherapy and possibly an autologous (using the patient's own bone marrow) or allogeneic (donor) bone marrow transplant.

When Dr. Chang was done explaining Dad's treatment plan, Rae said, "If he needs bone marrow, he should take mine. It's definitely the best."

"Why would you have the best bone marrow?" I asked.

"Because I'm the youngest and healthiest."

"Youngest, maybe. Healthiest, that's debatable. Your bone marrow might actually be made of marshmallows," David said.

"I'll do it," I said.

"Any one of us will do it," David said.

Dr. Chang said, "We need to make sure we have a match first."

"What if more than one of us is a match?" Rae asked.

Mom cradled her head in her hands. "Kids, that's enough."

"That would be good news," Dr. Chang

said. "But, once again, we'll continue with chemotherapy and see how that plays out. I'll see you tomorrow, Mr. Spellman."

"Don't forget your boyfriend's Social Security number," Dad said, winking at his doctor.

Chang departed and Rae stayed her course.

"So, Dad. Let's say all three of us are a donor match, which one would you choose?"

"I'd have a talent competition first. And then I'd decide," said Dad.

Dad's the kind of person who makes friends fast, and since Mount Zion was going to be his home for the next month, he made the best of it. His Jamaican day nurse, Tralina, and he hit it off like gangbusters. Especially after he had Mom locate the whereabouts of an ex-boyfriend she'd never quite gotten over. Mom managed to find a current photograph on a website from a tech company where he was working. And then, just as quickly, Tralina was over him. Dad, after discovering *Hayley's Fortune*, Tralina's favorite soap opera, would leave it on his television every afternoon, so she could watch when a patient didn't require her tending or he could at the very least debrief her when she was away. Occasionally Tralina would bend the rules and let more than two Spellmans in the room at a time, until Dad told her that he really couldn't handle more than two of us at once.

"You haf a lovely family, Mr. Spellman," I overheard her say as I was lingering by the door for a visit. "Da little blond one, is she yours?"

"My youngest," Dad said.

"I'd keep an eye on dat one," Tralina said without a hint of humor.

I really liked Tralina.

David created a daytime schedule to make sure that at no time was Dad alone and bored in his hospital room. Even with Tralina, we knew there would be moments when he might start thinking about his illness and mortality, and David knew that there were few people on the planet more distracting than a Spellman. At the end of David's first shift, he debriefed me.

"His pillows seem to drive him crazy. He's going to make you adjust them every ten to fifteen minutes. And he really likes reminiscing, so sit back and get used to it."

"Did you leave a flask?"

"No, Isabel, we're in a hospital."

"Right. They have drugs."

"They give him a container of Jell-O with

every meal," David said. "He's partial to cherry, but sometimes he likes to mix it up with strawberry, blackberry, and lemon when he wants a palate cleanser. He hates lime. If they give him lime, he'll tell you a very long story about a bad margarita he had."

"Are *you* going anywhere with this story?"

"If you see lime Jell-O, try to swap it with another patient's meal. They leave the trays in the hallway when they're serving."

When my shift with Dad began, he asked me if I had made peace with Robbie Gruber, our computer repairman, who'd been playing a cyber-game of cat-and-mouse with me. I told him I was working on it and Dad offered this gem of advice: "I think a magazine subscription would be nice. You might think he's a *Penthouse* kind of guy, but Robbie is a romantic, deep down. Go with *Playboy.*"

Dad asked me to fetch a Popsicle. I grabbed a cherry-flavored one from the stash. When I returned to his room, Tralina was on her cell phone.

"Allo, Mr. Lorre. I been tinking about moving. I would like a quote. How much ta move one bedroom from San Francisco to New York? Let's say tree tousand pounds. Okay, okay. How much t' move two bedroom from San Antonio, Texas, to Dayton, Ohio? I am not wasting your time. I am calling for different people who want to move two different places. Also, can you give me a quote for a move from Seattle t' Montego Bay, Jamaica, a tree-bedroom house? You don' do any moving to Jamaica? That's crazy. Do you have a problem with Jamaica? You need an airplane. You should get an airplane. *Is there anything else you can help me with?* I don' tink you've helped me at all. Good day, Mr. Lorre."

Tralina disconnected the call and smiled at my father. "So I can tell my daughter that today I was a detective?"

"Today you were a detective," my dad said.

"She'll like that," Tralina said, breezing out of the room.

I gave Dad his Popsicle.

"Is this cherry?" Dad asked when I returned.

"Yes. It's your favorite Jell-O flavor; I could only assume it was your favorite Popsicle flavor."

"I like strawberry Popsicles."

I kept the cherry Popsicle for myself and fetched Dad a strawberry one.

"Thanks, dear," Dad said with a sweet smile. "You were always my favorite."

"I overheard you say that to David just three hours ago."

"I think my pillow is slipping."

Edward sent a health basket filled with green drinks and macrobiotic energy bars that no one in my family would consume, except maybe David out of nostalgia. Still, I called Edward and thanked him.

"It's nice of you to send a gift basket to a man you've never met."

"Maybe we could remedy that soon."

"At least these days if you met him in bed clothes, it would be appropriate."

"How is the patient?"

"He's great. He's being waited on hand and foot. He doesn't even have to pour his own water if he doesn't feel like it. This has never happened before and will never happen again."

"How are you doing?" Edward asked.

"Other than those pesky embezzlement charges?"

"Isabel, just take care of your father. I'll deal with that."

"How's Ethan?"

"He's Ethan."

"Anything new with him? Is he planning to go away any time soon?"

"You mean like a vacation?"

"Something like that."

"Not that I know of. He did mention that his visit here would eventually come to an end."

"I see."

When my shift ended and Rae took over, I phoned Ethan from the parking lot.

"Why haven't you told him yet?" I said as soon as he picked up.

"I was thinking it might be better not to tell him."

"Wrong answer."

"I want him to remember me fondly."

"Too late. You're a gambling-addicted con man who has already done seven years in the slammer."

"This is a family matter, Isabel. You should stay out of it."

"You have an hour to tell him or I'll do it. Don't make the mistake of calling my bluff."

I love my father. Most people who meet my father eventually grow to love him, but spending six-hour shifts with him as he reminisced, brought me up to speed on *Hayley's Fortune,* and demanded his pillows be adjusted repeatedly could be trying. And then when he ran out of his usual material, Dad took to tossing out a series of random personal and impersonal questions:

"So, when's the last time you went out on a date?"

"Are you thinking about finding an apartment that's not in your brother's basement any time soon?"

"What the hell are these bath salts everybody is talking about?"

"Have you ever listened to Justin Bieber's music? I mean *really* listened?"

My point is, I was glad to keep Dad company, but it was exhausting, and some days I came to dread my shift. Then, one day, I arrived and Rae had somehow managed to induce a soporific state in my father.

"What did you do to him?"

"I asked him to read my term papers for the last three years. I wanted his honest opinion about whether higher education was worth the cost. I think they'd like another lawyer in the family; it makes up for having one child with only a high school diploma."

Dad's illness had derailed, well, everything, and I'd never had a chance to voice my concerns about my sister's "report."

"When I'm done here," I said, "we need to talk about your caseload."

"Looking forward to it," Rae said. "One more thing: If Dad needs a bone marrow transplant, he agreed that I get to be the donor."

"Really? How'd you swing that?"

"First I had to rule out David. Being the primary caretaker of Sydney, he really couldn't afford to be out of commission for any time at all, and every operation has its risk. And then we discussed the impact of your alcohol consumption on your general health, and we both agreed my bone marrow was less contaminated."

"There is no scientific evidence that beer contaminates bone marrow."

"And there's no evidence that it doesn't. My point is, I win."

"Don't you always?"

THE SPECIALIST

I scheduled an official meeting with the conflict resolution specialist. Straight after my shift with Dad at the hospital, Vivien and Rae met me at the office. Rae was working on one of the computers, and Vivien, after many attempts, was carving a tiny little derringer out of a bar of handmade lye soap — apparently much sturdier than any store-bought brand.

"Sit down. Both of you."

They were already sitting, so my directive lost some dramatic effect.

"Let's talk about your side project, Rae."

"Before you say anything, Izzy, you need to know something. This is the future of private investigation. Although we've got to lose that tired moniker."

"What you're doing isn't PI work, Rae. It's preschool vigilantism."

"I've already had one positive outcome, and if you met Greenblatt's girlfriend, you'd know she was a lost cause. I did him a favor. Once I complete the Lightning case, I'll be two and a draw, which is like two-point-five out of three. If I can stay at those numbers and advertise anything over an eighty percent success rate, we can grow this business and finally start making some money. But don't take my word for it. Let's ask the client. Vivien, have you been satisfied with the work we've done?"

"Very satisfied so far. All we need to do is finish the job," Vivien said, still playing with her soap-bar sculpture.

"What does 'finish the job' mean?"

"I think it's time to give the photos of Lorre and his girlfriend to his wife," said Rae.

"Agreed," said Vivien.

"Why don't you just show the photos to him and firmly suggest he pay Vivien what he owes her?"

"That's blackmail, Isabel. *Hello.* You could go to jail for that. Since we already have embezzlement charges hanging over our head, doesn't seem like the wisest idea."

"So what is your brilliant plan?" I asked.

"That man is dead inside," Rae said. "The only way to get through to him is to speak his language. The only way to make him stop extorting money from people is for him to realize there are consequences. We've completely unsettled him. But it's not enough."

"No," I said. "The Lorre case is over. If you want to file a small-claims suit, I'll get behind that. Otherwise, we're done here."

"I'm not going to threaten you and say that I won't handle the billing or the payroll; I'm just going to ask a favor of you," Rae said.[1] "Pay one visit to Marcus Lorre and try to reason with him. After that, if you still want me to shut it down, I will."

We sealed the deal with a handshake.

"Take me with you," Vivien said. "I'll stay in the car and listen on my cell phone. Please?"

I agreed to their terms, since I was only agreeing to having a talk with Marcus Lorre.

Rae gathered her belongings and reminded me to call Robbie.

"Robbie and you are in a cyber-war and he's winning. You need to throw in the towel. Do you know how to do that?"

"Apologize?"

---

1 Notice how she was, in fact, threatening me by mentioning the threat she could make.

"With a porn gift basket," Rae plainly explained.

Vivien and I made the thirty-minute drive to the bland stucco headquarters of Lighting Fast Moving Company in San Bruno. The shingle of the company hung just over a single door up a short flight of steps (surplus charge, I think). Aside from three moving trucks, a cluster of practical cars were parked in the lot. Lorre's impractical Porsche Boxster stood out like a debutante in a biker bar.

"Don't key his car or write any words on it, even with a harmless whipped-cream substitute, got it?"

"Got it," Vivien said.

"Keep your phone on."

I opened the door to the pungent fragrance of burned coffee and old rug. The receptionist was smoking, I suspect to cover the unpleasant odor.

"I have an appointment with Marcus Lorre," I said.

"An appointment?" asked the receptionist. I got the feeling that Lorre didn't have many appointments.

The telephone rang. She picked up. "Lightning Fast Moving. How can I help you?"

"I'll find him myself," I said.

The receptionist looked like she was about to protest but gave up, as she probably had on most things in life.

I walked down the hallway, which was most likely decorated by a bachelor who still wore wide-lapelled polyester shirts. Lorre's office was at the end of the hall, his name on a marker by his door.

I heard a lone male voice inside, presumably on a telephone call.

"You sound like a nice girl," he said. "Listen, I don't do this for everyone, but I'll take five hundred off the quote. Great. I'll e-mail the documents and all you have to do is sign them virtually. Yes, you can do that now."

I knocked.

"You're in good hands. I promise," the male voice said.

I knocked again.

"Come in."

I opened the door. A dark-haired man with a sharp widow's peak slicked back with Brylcreem sat behind his desk. He wore a crisp white shirt open at the collar, stained by the spray tan on his neck. He had one wormy eyebrow and teeth so white, they were probably veneers.

"Hi, are you Marcus Lorre?"

"Who are you? And who let you back here?"

Lorre had clearly been served papers before. He was looking for an escape route and trying to figure out where I was hiding the documents.

"My name is Isabel. I'm a private investigator. I was hoping we could have a little chat."

"I'm very busy right now. Maybe you can make an appointment."

"This won't take long. I want to talk to you about Vivien Blake."

"I can't recall the name at the moment."

"You handled the contract for her move. And then, on the day all of her worldly possessions were to be delivered to her new home, three large men held them ransom and made unsubstantiated claims about the total weight of her belongings and added other ridiculous charges and refused to move a single item until she ponied up over two grand. Where I come from, that's called extortion."

"I believe if she read the contract she we would see that there's a surcharge when the items go above the estimated weight. The young woman provided the best estimate she could and we went with the numbers she gave us. The contract is clear."

"You had her belongings for only a month and never informed her that they were over the estimated weight."

"I believe if she read the contract —"

"You've had twelve small-claims suits against you."

"Seven of the cases were dismissed for lack of evidence."

"The plaintiffs in ten of the twelve cases were women. Why is that?"

"I don't know," Lorre said. "The men can move their stuff on their own?"

"No, that's not it," I said. "Try again."

"Women don't read contacts?"

"Is this really how you want to play it?" I asked.

"Oh, you're one of those tough girls."

"Mr. Lorre, I would watch how you talk to me. There are things I can do to you."

"I'd love to hear them over a drink sometime."

"A woman actually married you?"

I had a visual, beyond the photos, and then a physical reaction to the visual.

"I have a beautiful wife and two beautiful children."

"I take it you'd like to hang on to her and the kids?"

"We're doing just fine."

"We'll see," I said.

"Anything else I can help you with?" Lorre asked.

"Have a nice day."

As I passed his car in the parking lot, I pulled my knife out of my purse, walked over to his car, and stabbed the front left tire. When I got into my car, Vivien glared at me.

"I wanted to do that," she said.

I reluctantly handed over the knife.

"One tire only. Then get back in the car immediately."

Vivien looked like I'd told her she won the lottery. While Viv vandalized Lorre's car, I made the call I had hoped to avoid at all costs.

"Rae, it's Isabel. I just met with Lorre."

"What's your ruling?" Rae asked.

"Take him out."

Status: Resolved.

UNRESOLVED

Slayter returned to work a week after being released from the psych ward. Charlie Black phoned to keep me abreast of his employer's activities.

I drove to his office to have a word with Edward, since he was refusing to return my calls.

Evelyn was returning from a coffee run at Caffe Trieste. Apparently, the run was just for her and Arthur Bly. Arthur came to the front desk to retrieve his brew and Evelyn said in the sweetest voice, "Decaf, double mocha. I know you said no whip, but you've been working so hard lately, I made an executive decision."

"You're going to kill me, Evelyn," Arthur said, boyishly accepting his beverage.

"That might be her plan," I said.

Evelyn responded with an icy stare. "I'll let Edward know you're here."

"He'll figure it out when I walk into his office."

When I was presumably out of earshot (I'm rarely actually out of earshot when people presume I am), I heard Arthur inquire about Evelyn's mother. She had found a temporary home for her, but it was state-run and Evelyn couldn't bear the thought of leaving her mother there permanently. Arthur sympathized and said he'd gone through the same thing with his own ailing father. I swear, those two acted like human beings with each other and androids in my company. I refused to accept all the blame.

Charlie was keeping vigil outside of Edward's office, reading a business magazine from the waiting room.

"How is he?" I asked quietly.

"He looks fine. The doctor said there was no long-term damage. Won't get the drug tests back for a few days, but it was probably out of his system by the time they drew blood."

"Has Ethan been by to see Edward?"

"Yes. He's been over a few times."

"Did they talk?"

"Yes. And I don't think Edward liked what they talked about."

"Good."

"Why is that good?"

"Because it means that Ethan told his brother the truth."

"Then I guess that's good," Charlie agreed.

Through the glass walls of Slayter's office, I could see his telephone call come to an end.

I entered without invitation.

"What are you doing here?" I asked.

"I work here," said Edward. "Guess who I was just talking to?"

"Without any other information, I'm going to go with Morgan Freeman."

"No. Agent Bledsoe with the FBI."

"I'm familiar with his work. I think Morgan Freeman[1] makes a better FBI agent."

"Agent Bledsoe has suggested I keep my distance from you," Slayter said.

"I think that's good advice for anyone."

"Nonsense," Edward said, pulling me into a warm embrace. "How are you doing?"

"I'm fine," I said, shrugging him off. I wasn't used to affection from my boss. "Tell me what Bledsoe had to say, other than disparaging my character."

"The account that was compromised has

---

1 If you like Morgan Freeman references, please see previous document.

been frozen," said Edward. "But the receiving account is now closed. All we know about that account is that it was a Delaware corporation, GLD Inc., and the bank finally gave us a name associated with the account. Clayton Knight. Apparently they have a passport number for him, but it appears he might be deceased."

"So someone used a dead guy's identity to open up a Delaware corporation, used that corporation to open an offshore account and transferred funds from your company into the offshore account, transferred that money into another offshore account, and then closed it out. So now you follow the money into the next offshore account. Right?"

"That's the gist."

I wanted to ask if Lenore was smart enough to open and close a bunch of offshore accounts, but I heeded his warning about Lenore and kept the question to myself.

"I'll keep looking into it," I said.

"How's your father doing?"

"He's making the best of a difficult situation. Translation: He's not squandering the opportunity to have his entire family at his beck and call. Who knows when he'll get this sick again?"

"It must be nice to have family. On the outside," Edward said wistfully.

"Ethan finally talked to you, I take it."

"Yes. Some people never change," Edward said.

"He wanted to see you before he went away. That's a good thing," I said.

We left the other part unsaid. Ethan's second Ponzi scheme, like his first, was a desperate attempt to emulate his brother's success. He could have avoided the plea deal if he had gone to his brother for help. But, after years of turning to Edward only for cash, Ethan couldn't bear to repeat the same mistake. And this mistake would likely keep the brothers apart for the rest of their lives.

All I said was, "I'm sorry. I hear Lompoc is nice in spring."

"Thanks, Isabel. Now go home and take care of your father."

"See you Wednesday, at nine?" I asked.

"You can take the morning off. I think Lenore will join me."

I was startled by being dismissed so suddenly. It couldn't have been that I actually wanted to go jogging.

I passed Damien's office on the way out. It was empty, and in light of the fact that I'd caught him in one significant lie I didn't think another would be entirely off base, so I thought I'd give his office a cursory search.

I opened desk drawers and file cabinets and found office supplies and files, nothing that would help me incriminate him. Not that I was convinced Damien was the person behind the funds transfers, but until he started working for Slayter, no one had embezzled money from the man and tried to frame me.

"What are you looking for?" Damien asked from the doorway.

"A mint."

"In my file cabinet?"

"That's where I keep them. I was also looking for paper. I was going to write you a note."

"What was the note going to say?"

" 'Where do you keep your mints?' "

"Hey, I had a good time the other night," Damien said.

"The other night?" I said, gazing upward and to my left, which is where you look when you're recalling a visual memory. "Oh yeah. Now I remember."

"You didn't return my call."

"I didn't, did I?"

"Maybe we can hang out again sometime."

"Oh no, I'm late," I said, looking at my wrist. "I'll catch you later."

The exit would have been better had I been wearing a watch.

As I was heading out of the office, Charlie sent me a text and told me to meet him at the elevator bank.

"I have this app on my phone so that I can track Mr. Slayter. Well, it can track Mr. Slayter's phone. It doesn't work if he doesn't have his phone on him, as we discovered that one time. Remember?"

"Yes, Charlie."

"Then I was thinking it would probably be good for me to have his friends' numbers in my phone so I could track them too, in case Mr. Slayter forgot his phone but I knew he was with his brother or Lenore or Willard."

"That's a good idea, Charlie."

"I asked Mr. Slayter if that was all right, and he jotted down a few numbers for me and I put them into my phone," Charlie said.

"Are you going somewhere with this, Charlie?"

"Are Willard and Lenore really good friends?"

"I'm not sure they've even met."

"They've definitely met."

"How do you know that?"

"Her phone has been at his house all morning."

I camped out in front of Willard's three-story house on Jones Street in Russian Hill. It was the family home that he inherited by virtue of being the only living Slavinsky. He once told me that his parents considered donating their entire estate to charity but thought again when he found his success with Slayter Industries. They had hoped that someone would carry on the family name, never believing that their son would remain a devout bachelor well into his sixties.

I had to wait two hours for the evidence against Lenore that I knew I would find, but there it was. She and Willard, locking lips outside his front door. I took the photo, waited until she got into her car and left, and knocked on Willard's door. He was still in his bathrobe and had to make some decency adjustments when he saw me.

"Isabel, what a lovely surprise. I would have at least worn boxer shorts had I known you were coming."

"I think this is a conversation that requires at least boxers, maybe even pants."

Willard told me to make myself at home and made a quick change in his bedroom. When he returned, he was wearing a velour sweat suit.

"Tony Soprano wants his wardrobe back."

"It's very comfortable. And you should be the last person to mock anyone's fashion sense."

"Fair enough."

"To what do I owe the pleasure?" Willard asked amiably.

"Are you seeing someone new?"

"Why, are you jealous? I've always told you, Isabel —"

"I'm being serious, Willard. It's about Lenore."

"Who is Lenore?"

"The woman who just left your house."

"You mean Nora."

"Well, Edward calls her Lenore. Has he spoken to you about her?"

"The woman he's been seeing?" Willard asked, the gist of our conversation finally sinking in.

"Yes. Lenore and Nora are the same woman."

"Impossible," Willard said, outraged.

"It's the same woman. She drives a navy blue 2002 BMW. She gets spray-tanned every two weeks. French manicure once a week on Polk Street. She doesn't eat carbs at all. *At all.* Not even fruit. Does that sound familiar?"

"Yes."

"How do you not eat fruit?"

"I don't know," Willard said, slumping into his chair.

I guess he liked her. I should have been more sympathetic.

"I'm sorry. It's true. And you need to tell Edward, because he made me promise that I wouldn't investigate his girlfriend, and here I am. Can you take care of this for me?"

"Yes, yes. Of course, Isabel."

Willard walked me to the door. "Oh, and I'm very sorry about your father. Edward told me. If there's anything I can do — that's a silly thing to say, isn't it? I can't cure cancer, can I?"

"Thank you, Willard. You're a good man. Now dump that bitch. You weren't in love with her, were you?"

"Of course not, Isabel. I can't afford love."

Edward phoned me later that night from a bar. He and Willard were drowning their sorrows together.

"I'm sorry I doubted you," he said, slurring his words.

"I'm sorry I was right," I said.

"No, you're not."

"I'm sorry you have bad taste in women."

"If it's any consolation, I think Willard is taking it worse than I am."

"Really?" I said. "The man does have a good poker face."

"Always has."

"You know, Edward, there are women out there who are not grifters."

"I'm sorry, Isabel. I just don't think we're compatible."

"Good night, Edward."

"Good night, Isabel."

INTERMEZZO

A few days later as I was trying to work from home, I was interrupted again by an overhead playdate. I use the term "playdate" loosely. David was swilling beer while trying to reason with his daughter, who had become hysterical after watching the animated Disney version of *Cinderella*. She immediately wanted to watch it again and David was trying to explain to his daughter that one should have some breathing time after watching a film, to let it settle into one's subconscious and to have some time to sort through the experience.

Max[1] and Claire gawked at the moronic father-daughter duo with the appropriate shade of concern and alarm. I stayed in the foyer because children become downright terrifying when it comes to anything on a

1 Claire wasn't the kind of child who drove you to drink.

flatscreen TV, and parents do irrational things like leaving said children with irresponsible aunts when their wits are at their end.

"Hey, Max," I shouted over the guttural wailing and my brother's stern appeals.

Max turned to me.

"Can you get me a beer?" I asked.

Max appeared happy to have any reason to leave the room. He grabbed a beer and two juice boxes for himself and Claire.

"Step into my office," I said, leading Max and Claire onto the front stoop. I closed the door, which quieted the chaos inside, and took a long swig of the pale ale.

"Did you like the movie?" I asked Claire.

Claire nodded noncommittally as she tried to stab the straw into the juice box. Max took the box and handled the fine motor skill while he coaxed a more expansive answer out of her.

"What do you think of the mice?" Max asked.

"I love the mice."

"What do you think of the stepsisters?"

"They're like Sydney."

"You're an insightful young girl, Claire," I said.

"So," Max said, "your brother has been

telling me about some of your legal problems."

"I'm innocent. What legal problems are
you referring to?"[2]

"He said someone was embezzling money
from your employer's account and framing
you."

"David's got a big mouth."

"I think he's just happy to discuss anything
other than your father's illness and the
princess's kingdom."

"Fair enough. I should have this thing
sorted out soon. I think I've got the suspects
narrowed down. There are only a couple
dozen people who would be able to access
the account information."

"You are assuming that this is someone
who works for the company?"

"Or is closely connected to my boss."

"It could also be a cybercrime. Have you
thought of that?"

"A hacker?" I said, mulling it over. And
then I stopped mulling when I realized what
a complete imbecile I'd been. Gruber could
have been behind all of this.

"Excuse me," I said, placing my beer on
the stoop. "There's someone I need to see."

2 "Deny everything" is my policy.

■ ■ ■ ■

The old me would have gone in with my metaphorical guns drawn. But I knew who I was dealing with, and nothing short of an Oscar-worthy performance of submissive contrition and conciliation would do. First I had to purchase provisions. Aside from the mix-and-match pack of varietal savory snack foods, a stolen stash of crack mix, and a cheesecake with a personal message (*I'm sorry, I'm an awful person*) written in red letters on top, there were the more embarrassing purchases. These acquisitions required some limited educational surveys, which included me asking strange men questions like, *Is there some kind of new fetish I should know about? Is* Jugs *magazine passé or retro-hip?* I assembled all of the items in a large basket that I found in my parents' garage, left over from the Frank Scharfenberger[3] days, and wrapped it all up in a giant ribbon, which had faux cutouts of a pin-up girl in the style of truck mudguards. The basket was topped off with a glitter-coated Hallmark card adorned with flowers and carrying a rhyming message of friendship.

3 To date, our worst client ever. His relatives would often send us apologetic gift baskets.

I got into my car and was about to have a face-to-face meeting with the man responsible for many of my recent troubles when I got the phone call.

"Isabel, it's Edward."

"What's up? I have a really important meeting that might be the answer to most of our problems."

"That's great. Um, I need you to bail me out of jail."

"I'm sorry, I don't think I heard you correctly."

"I was arrested. You need to post bail."

"Arrested for what?"

"Indecent exposure."

EXPOSED

I've never posted bail for anyone before; it's always been the other way around. I will freely admit I relished this opportunity to walk into a police station without a bull's-eye on my back. My inappropriately perky mood shifted into deep concern when I caught a glimpse of Edward as he was escorted out of the holding area. They had given him a pair of light gray sweats in size extra-large. His face was pale and drawn and his eyelids so hooded, he appeared to be sleepwalking. When I found him at the mental hospital, he had been on guard, in fight mode. His expression and composure now hinted at helplessness, and I suddenly felt the same way.

Someone was doing this to him, but I had no idea who and I couldn't help but feel I had been remiss in my duties since learning about my dad's illness. It was starting to seem like everything I came in contact with was contaminated. I couldn't recall a time when I'd had less of a grasp of what was going on around me.

"What's the last thing you remember?" I said when we got in my car.

"I was working late."

"Did you get any phone calls?"

"I don't remember."

"Who was in the office with you?"

"I don't recall. The next thing I knew, I was asleep, naked in front of a grammar school, being woken by two patrol officers. I think someone knows."

"Are you sure?"

"I was *naked* in front of children. The only way to defend that would be to admit I had Alzheimer's and the incident was a product of the disease. But I know it wasn't. I get lost. I lose nouns. I don't strip in front of schoolyards."

"Do you remember what you had to eat or drink before this happened?"

"I was in the office. I drank water. Maybe some green tea. That's the last thing I remember. I could have been somewhere else when it happened. Who is doing this to me, Isabel?"

"I don't know. I'm sorry. I have been —"

"You've had other things on your mind," Edward said. "And someone took advantage of that."

"Where the hell is Charlie?" I asked.

As it turned out, Charlie had drunk the Kool-Aid, too. Or whatever concoction knocked out his boss. Evelyn found him passed out on the floor. Instead of waking him and sending him home, she called an ambulance, since Charlie was slow to respond. The paramedics arrived and carted Charlie off to the hospital, where they ran a slew of tests. Charlie had left several messages on Slayter's cell phone, but that phone was sitting in Slayter's office. Charlie gave the nurse my information, but she only called me when he was ready to be discharged.

Charlie had almost no new information to provide. He couldn't remember that Willard had had the Lenore/Nora talk with Edward or if there had been any visitors the night before.

While I was picking up Charlie from the hospital, I got a phone call from David.

"Where are you?" he asked.

"I was bailing Edward out of jail and picking Charlie up from the hospital."

"Did you forget your shift?"

I checked my watch. I was two hours late.

"I'll be there as soon as I can," I said.

"Try to remember who your real family is," David said.

After Dad got sick, the hospital became the Spellmans' center of operations. You could arrive at any time and find two Spellmans in Dad's room, one or more in the cafeteria, and another in the main waiting area, drinking coffee and using the Wi-Fi. When I finally did arrive at the hospital, my father was hardly alone. Tralina had waived the two-person limit and David, Rae, Maggie, Demetrius, and his crack mix were all crowded into the ten-by-twelve-foot room. Everyone was wearing masks.

"How's the patient?"

"I can't complain," Dad said.

Maggie sat on the edge of the bed and held Albert's hand.

"So how many times has Ruth come to visit? This must be hard on her."

Everyone in the room looked at their feet, except Dad, whose feet were blocked by Maggie. He looked at the ceiling. That was an excellent question.

"Oh my God. Are you insane? Your mother doesn't know you're sick?" Maggie asked in disbelief.

Rae chimed in. "She totally thinks Dad's sick."

Dad cleared his throat. "We told her I have the flu. Since she's deathly afraid of communicable illnesses, we knew it would keep her away."

"As a mother, I can tell you that's really fucked up," Maggie said.

"Can I offer you some lime Jell-O?" Dad said. "I'm partial to lime."[1]

"I'm good," Maggie said, pulling a half-eaten oatmeal cookie out of her pocket.

Once Maggie was done speaking her mind to Dad, she turned her attention to the trio of slapdash investigators undermining her Washburn case.

"You people," she said, looking at Rae, D, and me. "What the hell are you up to?"

My phone rang, just as the drama was starting. Damien. I thought there was a slight chance I could escape Maggie's wrath if I answered the phone.

"Do not answer that phone," Maggie said.

"Business," I said.

Then Maggie snatched the phone out of my hand and answered. "Isabel's phone. Oh hello. Hi, Damien. We met once. Isabel is going to have to call you back. She is busy answering questions. How long? She might be answering questions for a very, very long

1 Dad hates to see it go to waste.

406

time. Hope you're enjoying the city. Bye."

Maggie ended the call and tossed the phone at me.

"You can call him later," she said.

"Nah, that was perfect," I said.

Rae mistakenly thought she could derail the conversation by mentioning Mom's disappearing acts.

"What does Mom do when she's not here?" Rae asked. "Because I know she's not at home."

"Maybe a new hobby," D suggested.

"She hates hobbies," I said.

"Let's take this outside," Maggie said.

"Let's keep this inside," Dad said. "There's nothing good on TV right now."

Maggie dramatically tossed a report on Dad's bed. It was an odd gesture, since the report was obviously related to the Washburn case and would require a lengthy debriefing to bring him up to date.

Since I had helped assemble the report, I knew it contained an impressive collection of witness testimonies on the wrongful-conviction case for Louis Washburn, only decidedly skewed in favor of the prosecution.

"I don't even know what question to ask first," Maggie said. "D, you are aware that we are trying to exonerate Louis, not launch a personal attack against his character or provide fodder for the prosecution team?"

"Yes," D said. He was totally ready to take the fall for me and Rae.

Rae remained silent; however, you could tell she really had something to say.

"Let's start with an easy question. Why was Rae doing all the prison interviews?"

"I was busy," D said, "so I asked Rae to step in."

"Busy doing what, baking cookies?"

Rae and D had one of those silent eyeball conversations. Eventually D spoke.

"I had a panic attack," he said.

"When?"

"The first time I got to San Quentin."

"The Big Q," I said.

D ignored me and continued. "I made it past security and then I started sweating. I couldn't breathe. I tried one more time, but I couldn't get out of the car. I can't do it. I can't go back there. You were so busy, I didn't want to bother you. Isabel was gone. Everyone was out of the office, so I asked Rae. We swapped cars, since I figured you'd check the mileage."

"So that's how you knew about the tear gas," I said.

"Tear gas? What tear gas?" Maggie asked.

"Yes. What tear gas?" Dad asked.

"Relax, I went with a stink bomb," Rae said, tired of the conversation.

"Do we need to talk about tear gas?" Maggie asked.

"No. It's done. Continue, D," I said.

"Rae is good at getting information. I thought she'd do a good job."

"I did a good job," Rae said defensively.

"Until you decided you just didn't like him," Maggie said. "Washburn did not rob that liquor store. The witness has already recanted. What have you got against getting an innocent man out of prison?"

"Nothing," Rae said, "only I'd bet dollars to donuts that he's guilty of way more crimes than that."

"Me too," I said, raising my hand.

"Be quiet," Maggie said to me like a schoolteacher. Then she said to D, "Do you agree?"

Dad seemed to be really enjoying this reality TV show.

"I do. He doesn't want to use DNA evidence. He wants his case to rely solely on witness misidentification," D said.

"But that's what applies in his case."

"Still, there was DNA at the crime scene," Rae said. "It could help substantiate his claim and he won't get tested."

"That's why you started interviewing

other inmates and known associates not on my witness list?"

"Yes," Rae said.

Dad handed Maggie the lime Jell-O and a spoon.

"D, what do you think?" Maggie asked.

"I think you need to make him do the test," D said.

Maggie sat down on the bed and opened the seal on the Jell-O.

"You should have told me. I would have never made you go there if I thought it reminded you of — this is disgusting," Maggie said after taking a spoonful of the lime Jell-O.

Mom found all of us in the hospital room.

"Tralina let everyone stay?" Mom asked.

The next thing we knew, Tralina was kicking everyone out.

"Okay, this isn't the ferry terminal. Everybody out. Now. Immediately. Albert needs to rest."

It was my shift, so I stayed put.

Dad showed Tralina the barely consumed lime Jell-O and asked for a cherry.

"Dear, do you have any idea what you're eating?" Mom asked.

"Water, sugar, and gelatin, which is an animal product rendered from hides and bones. Not cow hooves, like Rae originally said. I looked it up."

Mom put on her mask and crawled into the narrow bed next to Dad and nestled her head on Dad's shoulder.

"You can go home, Isabel. We're good."

They were good, and it was a sign of how unclearly I was looking at the world that I could have doubted their marriage for even a moment.

Throwing in the Towel

Late that night as I was getting ready for bed, wearing my usual evening attire, a threadbare JUSTICE 4 MERRI-WEATHER T-shirt and flannel pajama bottoms, there was a knock at my back door. Since my last uninvited guest was Henry, I assumed the worst. Or, maybe, in the back of my mind, I was hoping for the worst. Either way, my nerves were as raw as sushi until I opened the door.

"Edward, what are you doing here?"

"I wanted to talk to you."

"Did your phone battery die?"

"Did your manners die?"

"Please come in," I said, taking the hint.

As Edward entered my "apartment"[1] his eyes darted about the room, studying every detail with disappointment and pity.

1 I could imagine him using finger quotes to describe it that way.

"You live here?" he said.

"It's temporary."

"This isn't how a grown woman lives," he said, opening the refrigerator.

"I'd offer you something to eat, but —"

"Then I'd have to have my stomach pumped."

"Did I sign up for a home inspection and forget about it?"

"Is there a place to sit?"

"Yes! Sort of."

There was one old La-Z-Boy, a Bernie leftover,[2] in the corner. I pointed at the chair. Edward hesitated but sat down. I took a seat on my bed.

"What's up?"

"I'm going to step down as head of Slayter Industries," Edward said. "I'll make the announcement tomorrow morning. I will remain on the board and we'll vote for a new CEO."

"Don't do this," I said. "You are not there yet. You can still run the company."

"Not if someone has me in the crosshairs every minute. I can't live like that. I was charged with *indecent exposure*. In my entire life I never thought I'd have to utter

_____

2 I guess if I'm taking scraps from Bernie, it is time to rethink my entire existence.

that last sentence."

"You fight them," I said. "We have the lab tests from the guy in the bar. That whiskey contained Rohypnol, and the bartender will testify."

Even as I was saying it, Edward and I knew it all sounded too preposterous.

"Isabel, I was held on a 5150 without any explanation. Then I was discovered naked in front of a schoolyard. It's much more dignified to say I have Alzheimer's than some mystery man is forcing me into compromising positions. No one will believe it. If I back down, maybe whoever is trying to set you up on the embezzlement scam will stop."

"What about the indecent exposure charges?" I asked.

"My physician explained my condition to the DA and he's willing to drop all charges. No record, no probation. Nothing."

"You already talked to the DA?"

"Yes. Today."

"So, it's done?" I asked.

"It's done."

"I think you're making a mistake."

"We knew this couldn't go on forever. Maybe I'll take up golf. I bet Charlie would make an excellent caddie."

"You hate golf," I said. "That was always

one of my favorite things about you."

"You'll find another favorite thing."

"I don't think so," I said. "So I guess this means we won't be going jogging anymore."

"Nonsense. Now we'll have more time. Five days a week, minimum. And afterward we can go apartment hunting. Although I don't know how we'll find a place as charming as this."

"Okay, time for you to go."

Edward got to his feet. He put his arm around me and I walked him the ten steps to my back door. He gave me a reassuring squeeze and said, "I never had any children. The few moments when I entertained the idea, what I envisioned was something so very different from you."

"Thank you."

"Let me finish. If I did have a daughter, now I think someone like you would do just fine."

"When I was fifteen, I had this math teacher who hated me. He had exactly five pairs of shoes he wore on rotation every day of the week. My best friend and I broke into his house, bought or stole another pair of each shoe, wore them down to a match, and swapped out the left for the right, so that one morning he would wake up and have only shoes for his right foot."

"And you're telling me this so I know how difficult a child you would have been?" Edward asked, smirking.

"No, I was just bragging."

"Did you get away with it?"

"Not exactly. Mr. Blind — seriously, that was his name — suspected me all along, but he couldn't prove anything. So every time I got a math test back after that, whenever I wrote the number three, he'd correct the test as if it were the number nine. If the correct answer was thirty-three, I'd get marked incorrectly since he read it as ninety-nine. The number was clear and I debated him on this until finally Mr. Blind called the principal into the room to make the final call. Mr. Blind pointed to what was clearly the number thirty-three and said, 'What number is that?' What do you think Mr. Lang, the principal, said?"

"Ninety-nine."

"Yep."

"That was a lovely story, Isabel. I must say, no one can distract me from my troubles quite like you. Well, I better go. I'll need my rest for whatever is coming next."

He said, "Turtle, radiator, zoo."

"Right," I said as I watched Edward walk away.

I hadn't given him any words that day.

After Slayter left I thought about what else I could have done and came up blank. From the moment I set foot in Slayter Industries, I'd had a sense that I was out of my element, that this new world I was suddenly ensconced in was one I couldn't ever truly comprehend. I understand individuals and their personal motivations, but when those same individuals become a part of something bigger, some amorphous corporate ball of greed, I can't anticipate the logical next move, because it has long ago stopped being human. Your average human being has a conscience and the world is structured with checks and balances to shed light on that individual should he or she become something ugly and cruel. But a company can hide its corruption; the individuals responsible can sit innocently and united behind their desks for years before they are discovered. They are as guilty as the guy robbing the liquor store in the ski mask, only they're free to show their faces. I had no idea whether I should be looking for the worker bee or the nest, or both, and my nearsightedness cost my boss his job.

Life and other matters[3] had postponed my

3 The crack mix had melted in the gift basket

Gruber visit. And, deep down, I had always hoped that there was another option besides a groveling apology. But it was possible that Robbie could do more for me than just fix my work computers and so the next morning, I planned my visit.

D made a fresh batch of his signature junk food; I put on a vintage *Star Wars* T-shirt that was way too tight, retied the bow around the basket, applied a thick coat of black eyeliner, and made the drive of shame to Gruber's cheap basement apartment in the Mission-Duboce triangle. While dogs and owners frolicked day and night in Duboce Park, Robbie was just steps away in his cave, figuring out ways to keep his virtual hands on my cyber-throat.

I rang his doorbell and waited. I could hear his heavy Cheeto breath on the other side of the door.

"Who is it?" he asked.

Robbie is not the kind of man who can open the door in the middle of the day to a face obscured by a gift basket bow.

"It's Isabel," I said.

Robbie's also not the kind of man who can open the door in the middle of the day

---

when I became distracted by the Slayter disappearance.

to someone named Isabel.

"What do you want?" he said through wood.

"I want to talk."

"What are you holding?"

"A gift basket."

"What's in it?"

"Lots of things. If you open the door, you can find out."

"Leave the basket and return to your car. Keep your cell phone on."

I followed Robbie's instructions. I could see him peer through the curtains to be certain I was not lying in wait outside his door. I waved from the driveway. Robbie swiftly retrieved the basket and closed his front door.

He phoned me ten minutes later.

"Is this sincere?"

"Yes. I'm very, very sorry," I said. "The power got to my head. We need you. And, also, we need you to stop messing with our system."

"I'm not confirming or denying," he mumbled.

"I understand."

"How do I know the crack mix isn't laced with a laxative?" he asked.

"I'll eat some in front of you," I said. I was feeling snackish.

"That means inviting you inside."

"There is this other matter I'd like to discuss."

"Take off your jacket," Robbie said.

"Robbie, have you ever known me to wear a gun?"

"Remove your jacket."

I did as I was told, but I had no doubt that the jacket removal was Robbie's lascivious ploy to get a better look at my boobs in the snug shirt. I comforted myself in knowing that one day there would be payback. There's always payback when it comes to Robbie. It's just a matter of patience.

In Robbie's piece o' shit apartment I ate three mouthfuls of the crack mix in front of him until he told me to stop. Obviously he wanted to have some for later. I sat by his desk as he freed up the Spellman computer system.

"I have to know. How'd you do it?" I asked.

"I set up an alert on my phone to monitor when the computers were active in your office. Based on the keystrokes, I could tell when you were at work, regardless of what monitor you were working on. Mostly I just messed with you, but occasionally I'd mix it up and slow another computer down."

"Impressive," I said.

"I thought so," Robbie said. "Once I coded a logarithm that made your computer run at the pace of the J train. Wasn't as satisfying as I had hoped. It was on schedule that day."

"Nice work," I said. "I hope we can put the past behind us."

"I never forget anything," Robbie said. "You might want to watch that Donald Trump shit in the future."

Then Robbie did his best Donald Trump impression. *You're fired. You're fired.* The only way to get him to stop was to dangle the equivalent of a shiny bag of Cheetos in front of him.

"Would you be able to hack into my boss's computer system and figure out who is embezzling money from him?"

"Hacking is a crime."

"You'd be solving a crime."

"I'd need your boss's permission. And probably in-house access."

"But, then, could you do it?"

"Sure."

"Do you own any clothes that don't look like you just came from a Unabomber convention?"

AGGRESSIVE TREATMENT

Dad had been in the hospital for over a week now. He had already received his induction chemo, of idarubicin and cytarabine. Now he was given antibiotics and anti-nausea medication, not that it always did the trick. What was left of Dad's hair was falling out in clumps. I've always thought it was fortunate that Dad was tall, so the top of his head was out of most people's line of vision, but the thing about chemo is that it gets rid of *all* of your hair. I worried that he would appear like a Muppet without a brow.

Tralina began cracking the whip on the number of visitors she allowed in the room, and the visitors always had to wash their hands first and wear face masks. When I arrived in the afternoon, Dad was asleep. I couldn't concentrate on anything, so I just watched the droplets of rain on the window drip like clear paint.

Dad woke up and promptly vomited in a

plastic receptacle. What was left of his hair was matted down to his sweaty pate, and his eyes were bloodshot and glassy. I felt nauseated looking at him, but I knew if I showed him how scared I was, he'd feel it.

"Do you want me to get Tralina?" I asked.

"Why? So she can hold my hair?"

"Are you okay?"

"Imagine the worst hangover you've had," Dad said.

"That sounds awful."

"It's worse."

"Can I get you anything?"

"Ice chips."

I was glad for a chore and took a moment to breathe in the fresh air of the antiseptic hallway. It hadn't really occurred to me before that there was a real possibility my father could die. Then I did everything humanly possible to beat that thought out of my head. I even imagined Robbie Gruber naked.

"One order of ice chips, sir," I said when I reentered the room.

Tralina was back fluffing Dad's pillows.

"Maybe I should start smoking the ganja," Dad said. "What do you think, Tralina?"

"I tink you haf enough drugs in ya body as it is."

"But I hear it makes you feel better. Do

423

you know where I can get some?"

Dad winked.

"You tink because I'm Jamaican, I'm da hospital ganja dealer."

"I thought you might know someone," Dad said.

"I have Popsicles. Cherry, strawberry."

"Cherry."

Tralina left and I gave my dad a cup of ice.

"I bet you know where to score me some weed," Dad said.

"Just because I had a steady supply fifteen years ago doesn't mean I know where to get you quality product now. Maybe you should discuss this with your doctor."

"I don't want the prescribed stuff. The word on the ward is that it's bullshit. I want some quality grass. Maybe Rae has some connections."

"The only thing Rae smokes is those candy cigarettes with the single puff of powdered sugar that floats into the air."

"I'll ask Maggie," Dad said. "All those convicts she hangs out with, surely one of them knows somebody who knows somebody."

"You do that," I said.

"So," Dad said. "How's your embezzlement investigation going?"

424

"I've got Gruber on it."

"You made peace with Gruber."

"I wouldn't go that far."

"Still, I'm proud of you."

"Don't be. I haven't done a single bit of solid investigative work in the last six months. Does deductive reasoning go with age?"

Dad never answered the question. Tralina interrupted with a cherry Popsicle and then David arrived in a state of complete panic.

"Dad, have you told Grammy Spellman yet?"

Dad pretended like this was a fact he had to think about. He looked upward and to his right.

"I don't recall."

"You didn't, Dad."

Tralina was checking Dad's vitals and shaking her head. "Ya poor mama. Ya need ta let her know immediately."

"At least before you lose all of your hair," I said.

When Mom showed up, Tralina insisted one Spellman exit. I had been there all morning, so I took off.

Gruber had sent me three text messages in the last hour. I headed over to Slayter Industries to see what the Cheeto-chomping hacker had to show me.

I dropped by Evelyn's desk. She appeared more buttoned up and less styled than usual. Her hair was in a bun and her lips had faded, like maybe she had left her lipstick at home. Two discarded cups of Caffe Trieste sat on her desk. She had the coffee jitters. I wanted to ask her if she was all right. It was obvious she wasn't. But I also knew that my asking, knowing that she was in a weakened state, would hurt her more than pretending I didn't notice. So I pretended I didn't notice.

I asked her where Gruber was stationed. She stared back at me blankly. I provided a generous description of him: "A larger gentleman in a suit with sporadic facial hair."

"Pamela Desmond's office. She's on maternity leave," Evelyn briskly replied.

"Thank you," I said.

She trained her gaze on her computer screen.

As I roamed the cylindrical hallway, I knew I had to pass Damien's office, but I thought I had a good shot of slipping by unnoticed. Until, of course, I came upon Damien and an unknown woman with a blond pageboy haircut, walking straight in my direction. I put on my best cheery face.

"Damien," I said in a perky voice very few

get to hear. I used to think only animals and small children could hear it.

"Isabel," Damien said, his eyes shifting with massive nervous energy.

"How's it going?" I said, looking directly at his female companion.

She was studying me with calculated jealousy. I decided to put her out of her misery. It wasn't her fault her fiancé was a cad. Well, actually, it was. Frankly, I think you know when you're dating that kind of guy, and you should probably cut your losses the second you figure it out. But this wasn't any of my concern. The only thing of value I could accomplish would be to give Damien a few more uncomfortable moments. I think he deserved at least that.

"You must be Karen," I said. "I suppose congratulations are in order."

I extended my hand. Karen shook it limply.

"Thank you," Karen said. "So how do you and Damien know each other?"

"We go to the same barbershop," I said.

"Oh," Karen said.

"Just kidding. I work here sometimes. I'm the boss's private investigator. I know everybody's secrets. Even Damien's."

There was some delightful uncomfortable laughter.

"I hope you're not lactose intolerant," I said.

"Excuse me?" said Karen.

"I never buy gifts from the registry. I always send cheese. The stinkier the better, if you ask me."

"It's been great running into you, Isabel," Damien said. His eyes were swimming with gratitude and confusion.

I could have hung around a bit longer and let Damien stew in his questionable betrothed ethics, but there are far, far better uses of my time.

"Nice meeting you. I got to run. I have a consultation with a computer hacker."

I like to think that was a dignified exit. Sure, there was some tiny ache in my gut, maybe my spleen or gallbladder (an organ you don't need), that felt like I just should have known better. No man or woman likes to be a fool, but here's the thing my mother taught me long ago, and it is a lesson that stuck.[1] You can spend hours speculating on a man's motivations, trying to pinpoint what clue you missed, what missteps you made, when the relationship turned, or why he didn't like you as much as you thought he

1 Unlike the one about how you should wear clean socks every day.

did. And you could sit around like a fool letting someone else hold court in your mind when you were hardly a blip on his radar. Or you can just let it go and look at the person in the rearview mirror and keep driving.

To be honest, my mother never had to have this talk with me. I was too private to share my youthful heartbreak publicly. But I remember once as a teenager watching my mother nurse Aunt Martie after a particularly brutal breakup. For two months Martie barely left her house; she cried constantly and obsessed relentlessly about the women her ex was likely dating. (In the current climate of social media, she would have been on Facebook all day long.) My mother, finally, at her wits' end, grabbed Aunt Martie by the shoulders, shook her violently, and said, "The sexual revolution didn't happen so you could sit by the phone sobbing like some stupid little girl. Enough. Fucking pull yourself together. He's just one guy."

Maybe that was the part that always stuck. I never wanted my mother to look at me with such horrified disrespect. Then again, she has on many occasions, most notably when I was caught trying to steal half the liquor cabinet from Lieutenant McClane's widow at her husband's wake. In my defense, I was only fifteen and I heard she was a teetotaler.

I was so accustomed to seeing Robbie out of his element that it was shocking to see him suited up in a corporate environment looking almost in place. Apparently Robbie is the black sheep of his family, which really is good news for Robbie's family, but even better news for our undercover operation. When Robbie's only brother got married last summer, the groomsman suit (alas, he did not make the cut for best man) was dictated from on high (his mom) and micromanaged from the measurements to the impeccable design. My point is, Robbie's suit fit, and a really good suit can make shoulders appear on the most amoeba-shaped individuals. In short Robbie looked normal, which meant that when he roamed the corporate offices, people saw an IT consultant, not a computer geek[2] who lived in a blacked-out room surrounded by sci-fi movie memorabilia figurines and posters of

[2] To any maybe computer geeks out there: My representation of Robbie is in no way meant to disparage your entire demographic. And just you wait. Robbie really pulls through. But he could still work on his table manners.

Megan Fox and Yoda.

"The system doesn't look compromised," Robbie said. "My guess is that whoever made the transfers did so from a computer inside Slayter Industries."

"Can you tell who is making the transfers?"

"No. I'm trying to narrow down maybe which IP address it came from, but that wouldn't tell me who did it. Your embezzler could be logging in as someone else. If you want to give me a list of suspects, I can probably hack into their personal computers, especially if they're using Wi-Fi, and maybe check their financial data, see if there are any suspicious deposits."

"Isn't that illegal?"

"I got news for you, Spellman. What I just did was illegal."

"What do I care? You're talking to an accused embezzler."

As I walked Gruber to the elevator bank, we passed Evelyn's desk, where she and Arthur were having yet another hilarious conversation about something.

"Who is that guy?" Gruber asked.

"Arthur, the accountant."

"Is he funny?" Robbie asked.

"Not in the slightest."

"Is he rich?"

431

"Not really."

"How long has she worked here?"

"Seven years."

Robbie studied the duo carefully as he waited for the elevator to arrive.

"That's your girl," he mumbled.

The elevator doors parted and Robbie stepped inside. I slipped in after him.

"What are you talking about?" I asked as the elevator doors closed.

"An accountant has all the routing numbers. But that guy is too stiff to break the rules. He orders his shirts on full starch. Nobody does that anymore. That lady wouldn't give that guy the time of day unless she was getting something from him."

"I can't believe that Evelyn could be the mastermind behind a giant conspiracy against my boss. She'd have to do a lot more than sweet-talk a lonely accountant."

"I'm not saying the chick is the mastermind, but she's got something going on with the accountant. You want me to look into it?"

I whispered, "You mean hack into her personal computer and check her finances?"

"What, are you wearing a wire?"[3] Robbie

---

3 Actually, yes, I was. Robbie had me on the ropes once before. It would never happen again.

asked sarcastically. "Yea or nay, and it'll cost you."

I gave him the thumbs-up signal. The elevator doors parted and Robbie waved good-bye.

"I got to bolt," Robbie said. "Have a date with my lady friend tonight. She loves me in this suit."

I contracted the five-minute flu from Robbie's last words to me and remained paralyzed in the elevator until I could get my gag reflex under control. When the silver blades shut in front of me, I saw my reflection split in two. I'm sure I could draw some kind of boring metaphor out of that, but I was too tired and sick to think of one.

CONSPIRACY OF SILENCE

Imagine a rotating door on Dad's hospital room. When one Spellman went in, another went out. You never knew who you'd find at one time or another. Funny thing about Mom, though. She was at the hospital plenty, don't get me wrong. But when she wasn't there, she was incredibly hard to track down.

I found the room empty when I arrived the next morning. It was rare to get a moment alone with Dad.

"You just missed your mom," Dad said. I had a funny feeling he was lying.

I sat down in the chair next to his bed.

"How are you doing?" I asked, using that soft, sympathetic hospital voice.

"What?! I can't hear you!" Dad shouted to mock me.

"How are you doing?" I bellowed back at him to be sure he understood I got the message.

Tralina dipped her head in and said, "If you need me, use the button."

"That was the television," Dad said.

"I don' tink so. Be back in a half hour for our program, okay?" she said.

"Bring the electric razor," Dad said.

"Okay," Tralina said.

"I'm going Telly Savalas. Do you think your mom will dig that look on me?"

"I think if Mom likes your current look, she's going to be cool with almost any look."

"Was that an insult? Because, you should know, you're my only child who actually resembles me."

"Please stop reminding me of that. How are you feeling?"

"Today wasn't as bad as yesterday."

"If you have the slightest premonition that you might puke, please let me know," I said, waving the plastic receptacle in his eye line.

"I promise I won't puke on you unless it's absolutely necessary."

"Thanks, Dad. You're the best."

We sat silently watching a terrifying talk show involving a woman who had cheated on her boyfriend with his son and then his son's best friend. Oddly, the most enraged party to this scandal was the son's best friend. When the dire state of humanity or fake television got to be too much for Dad, he turned off the TV.

"I'm not going to die, you know."

"Ever?" I asked.

"I am not going to die from this."

"I didn't think so. I always figured it would be Colonel Mustard with the candlestick in the library."

"I'm trying to have a moment."

"So am I. And my moment seems way better than your moment."

Dad then pinched my cheek.

"You were always my favorite," he said.

"Stop saying that. It doesn't mean anything when you tell your other children the exact same thing."

"Right now. You're my favorite."

Since Maggie had scolded all of us about not informing Grammy of Dad's illness, the family convened to come up with a plan. Rae suggested we draw straws to determine who would tell her. Mom drew the short straw and demanded a redraw, in which she would not participate. Rae suggested we send Grammy a text message and offered to do it herself.

"A text message?" David asked incredulously.

Rae, thinking David was balking because Grammy was a Luddite, said, "I showed her how to text ages ago. I thought the less we had to hear her voice, the better."

And that was coming from Grammy's favorite.

Even Mom admitted that a text message seemed cruelly impersonal. Yet I heard her mumble something about a telegram under her breath. David, the most dignified, humane, and responsible of us all, made the phone call. And then he even sacrificed himself to pick her up and bring her to the hospital. He timed it so she would arrive just a half hour before the end of visiting hours and made sure that no doctor visit was planned during that time frame.

"How do I look?" Dad said, rubbing his hand over his newly bald head.

"Like a cancer patient," Rae replied.

To her credit, when Grammy S. entered the hospital room and saw her son in bed with needles in his hand and monitors tracking every beat of his heart and his blood pressure, and with almost no hair except the shadow of his stubborn brows, she had that universal maternal look of concern. She approached his bed, straightened his sheets, gently touched his brow, and kissed him on the forehead. Then she stepped back and looked him over carefully.

"Look on the bright side," she said.

"You've lost weight."

I squeezed my mother's shoulders. To a stranger it would have looked like a massage, but I was actually holding her down. Meanwhile, David managed to usher Grammy out of the hospital at breakneck speed.

"You can come visit tomorrow or maybe the next day," he said. "We're not supposed to have too many people in the room at once."

Grammy made protests, which David knocked down, and when they were eventually out of earshot, I released my mom, kind of the way you let go of a dog that's stopped barking at a threat. Mom slumped in her chair.

"Bitch," she said.

Dad laughed. "When I get out of this place, you are buying me the best steak dinner in town."

The next day, while David and Mom were keeping Dad company in his room, I was stuck with Grammy and Rae in the waiting room. Rae purchased every health and diet magazine at the gift shop to occupy Grammy while we both worked on our laptops. Gruber phoned me after he completed his investigation on Evelyn Glade.

"We need to meet," Gruber said.

"Are you sure?" I said. "Because neither of us actually enjoys being in the other person's company."

"I'm sure."

Gruber had always maintained a distantly friendly relationship with my father, so he agreed to meet me at the hospital. He even brought my dad a bag of salt-and-vinegar chips from the gift shop with a *Get Well Soon* card attached.

Robbie and I spoke in the hospital corridor.

"Evelyn has the IQ of a prom dress."

"Finally, we agree on something," I said.

"She keeps all of her passwords on her computer in a spreadsheet called 'Passwords.' The spreadsheet isn't even password protected. Anyway, her PayPal account information was right there, so I took a look-see."

Robbie then took a long drag on his caffeinated smoothie, either because he was thirsty or for dramatic effect.

"And?"

Robbie passed me a spreadsheet with highlighted transfers and arrows pointing to the money trail.

"She has had five transfers in denominations of ten thousand dollars from PayPal over the last month. The same time frame as your suspicious funds."

"Did they come from an account in the Cayman Islands?"

"No. They came from another PayPal account, with the screen name loyalservant47."

"And who is that?"

"Rufus Harding, Evelyn's boyfriend. Through their communications I got access to Harding's computer and then access to his PayPal account. His spreadsheet was password protected, but there's a back door, because what are you going to do if someone has forgotten the password to a document that holds the formula for the polio vaccine?"

"Surely someone has memorized it by now."

"Shall I go on?"

"Please."

"Harding's PayPal account had much more action. There were transfers coming in from a Cayman Islands account, and some of the funds were transferred to his personal account and some to his girlfriend's account."

Robbie pointed out the flow of transfers. They also occurred during the same time frame, but the transferring account was different from the original one that incriminated me. However, I would have bet Robbie's entire *Star Wars* memorabilia collection on the trail of transfers leading back to that one offshore account under GLD Inc.

"How is it that the FBI can't figure this shit out, but one computer nerd can?" I asked.

"For one thing," Robbie said, "the FBI still has to work within the confines of the law. Me, I work around it. I haven't found a system I couldn't hack. Although I haven't yet tried the FBI."

"I owe you, Robbie, even with all that crap you pulled with our computers."

"Speaking of that, here's your bill."

Robbie handed me an envelope. I cracked the seal, just to see what I was in for.

Balance due: $0.00

"This one's on the house," Robbie said.

Later that night, I drove to Evelyn Glade's apartment. She lived only a mile or so from the Spellman compound, in a three-unit building in Russian Hill. I rang her doorbell and heard footsteps approach. I could sense an aerobic organism on the other side of the door, probably looking through the peephole. I smiled cheerily.

441

"Just open up, Evelyn. We can hash this out here or at the office."

Evelyn opened the door. It was past eight. She was in a nightgown and a silk robe fit for a gentleman caller.

"Are you expecting company?" I asked.

"No," she said. "Why are you asking?"

So, some women dress like that when no one's looking?

"No reason."

"Have a seat," Evelyn said with less enthusiasm than anyone has ever used in offering me a place to plant my ass.

"Nice couch," I said as I took a seat. This wouldn't take long, but I wanted her to think it would.

"What can I do for you, Isabel?" Ms. Glade said as she reclined on an antique fainting couch.

"Thanks for the cash. What's the occasion? It wasn't my birthday."

I gave Evelyn 50 percent credit for her poker face; the other 50 percent went to Botox.

"I can only assume," I said, "that your boyfriend helped mastermind the plan. But the jig is up. I have the trail of funds leading from Slayter Industries to GLD Inc. in the Cayman Islands to another offshore account in the name of HRD Inc., then Rufus

Harding's PayPal account and then your bank account. You guys got really creative with your corporate names."

I dropped the file folder on her coffee table.

"Another copy is on its way to the FBI right now."

Evelyn went to her bar and poured herself a drink out of a crystal decanter. She looked to me and silently asked if I wanted one.

"How do I know you won't roofie me?"

This time the poker face was even better.

"You don't," she said.

"Whatever. Yeah, I'll have a drink."

What? I was thirsty.

Evelyn poured us both a drink from the same bottle and sat back down.

"Why did you do it?" I asked.

"Because I'm forty-five years old and I answer phones for a living and now I have a mother with a broken hip, and one day I will be sixty-five years old and answering phones for a living and maybe then I'll fall down and break a hip, but there won't be anyone to take care of me and I'll be counting cans of tuna fish until the next Social Security check and spending my Sundays cutting coupons and scraping by while I fantasize about the life I never had. I've already disappointed myself enough. I don't want to compound that by being desperate. It's just enough to make the rest of my life bearable. It's not like they'd even miss it."

That was true, in the scheme of things, in this greedy world we live in. It wasn't that much money, and I would have genuinely felt something for Evelyn if she hadn't tried to frame me and my boss.

"And what was the point of transferring funds into my account?"

"My boyfriend said we needed a fall guy. He asked me to pick someone. You pissed me off that day with your stupid parking-validation scam. And you always had Edward in the palm of your hand."

"Did it ever occur to you that using a private investigator as your patsy wasn't the smartest move?"

"Later, it did."

"Edward trusted you. If you had talked to him, asked for a raise, maybe he would have helped."

"And maybe he wouldn't have. There's always someone younger and prettier who knows more."

"Twenty years ago this plan might have worked," I said.

"Twenty years ago, I would have married the boring engineer I was dating."

"Worth millions now, I take it?"

"What happens next?" Evelyn asked.

"First you need to tell me who you're working with, aside from that genius boyfriend of yours. Arthur, I assume. And how you arranged Edward's public indignities."

Evelyn finished her drink and gazed at me like a cat in repose.

"What are you talking about?"

"You are one of the best liars I've ever met."

"All I did was trick Arthur into giving me the bank routing numbers. And steal a little money. I had nothing to do with Edward's recent difficulties."

"Now would be the time to come clean," I said as a warning.

"I swear, Isabel. I thought Edward had a drinking problem."

I pressed Evelyn again, but she held firm. Knowing that she'd have the full weight of an FBI investigation on her, it seemed unlikely she'd hang on to this final lie. I left her apartment with the heavy knowledge that my work wasn't done.

I remember a time when my mind wouldn't have been able to shut down, the cases churning so relentlessly that I could barely see the person standing right in front of me. I remember when it had to be me who solved the case, who figured out the riddle. Now I didn't care who did it, how it came about, just as long as it was over. I'm tired of seeing all the rotten things one person does to another person. Don't get me wrong, I'm not going to open a flower shop. But this is my dream: One day, I leave my job at the office and it doesn't follow me home and haunt in me in my sleep. Another dream: I don't live in my brother's basement apartment. After everything I've seen and done and mused about endlessly, I'm convinced of one thing: There's more to life than this, and sometimes when I picture more, it looks like something so simple, like so much less.

After my meeting with Evelyn, I drove home to my basement apartment and called the hospital to check on Dad. The nurse said he was asleep. Mom was camped out on the chair by his bed. I took two aspirins and went straight to bed. And I didn't care if I woke up the next morning with any of the answers.

Well, maybe I cared a little.

ONE ANSWER

I didn't have the answers, but other people did, and for once, I didn't mind. I dropped by the hospital first thing in the morning. My father looked like someone who'd had his guts turned inside out and then just tucked them back in. He was out cold. Mom, however, had clearly been up all night. When she wasn't tending to Dad, she was working. Her laptop, a messy stack of folders, and several Styrofoam cups sat on the windowsill.

"You've been busy," I said.

"Couldn't sleep," said Mom.

"Coffee probably didn't help."

"There was nothing to read so I started looking over some of the open cases. Are you still working on Divine Strategies for Mr. Slayter?" Mom asked.

"Not exactly," I said. "He advised his clients not to invest and told me to let the case go. I kept looking into it, but I'm going to stop now."

"Good idea," Mom said, rubbing sleep out of her eyes.

"But you know something, don't you?" Dropping the case is one thing, but if the answer is sitting right in front of me, I'm going to ask.

"I don't *know* anything. I have a hunch. I gave you the wrong lead with the sexual harassment suit. There's a one-year statute of limitations on sexual harassment. There's no way a single woman could hold that kind of leverage for more than ten years."

"What are you thinking?"

"One-year statute of limitations on sexual harassment. No statute of limitations on rape."

Maureen Stevens's maiden name was Maureen Clyde. She had one sister. Naomi Clyde. Naomi hadn't held a full-time job since 2004, when she worked at Divine Strategies in its infancy, with Brad Gillman and Bryan Lincoln. She had a few employment markers on her report up until 2005, when she virtually dropped off the face of the credit world. There's one credit card to her name and the address listed for her is Maureen's.

Something happened in 2004, and it probably involved the police. What people don't know is that police files are not public record; only court files are. For the sake of argument, let's say you know a police officer intimately, one who might feel guilty about getting a certain woman pregnant and planning a wedding not six months after you broke up. You'd have a good shot at looking at a case file.

I called to make sure Henry was in and drove to his office at 850 Bryant Street. They know me there, so I didn't have to sweet-talk anyone at the front desk. I was buzzed into the back room and worked my way through the maze of desks until I found Henry's. I probably should have called him first, because he looked like I was a thug in a ski mask accosting him with a knife in a back alley.

"Hi," I said to ease the tension. Surely there are better ways to ease the tension.

"You are the last person I expected to see," he said.

"Not Morgan Freeman?"

I took a seat on the edge of his desk.

"How are you?" he asked.

"Okay."

Henry gave me a suspect's study. "You're not okay. You're lying."

"I need a favor. I think there might be an old police file under the name Clyde. Either

Naomi or Maureen. Sexual assault, I think. Can you find it for me?"

"Is someone sick?" Henry asked.

I have no idea when Henry turned into Carnac the Magnificent. I attempted the Avoidance Method™.

"I wouldn't be here unless I had no other option."

"Write down the name and any other information you might have. I'll look into it."

"Thank you," I said.

Finally the Avoidance Method™ was working. Clearly a training video and book deal were the next order of business.

"I'm sorry about the other night," Henry said.

"You remember that?"

"Vaguely."

"How's . . . ?"

"She's good."

"You're still . . . ?"

"Yes."

"Let me know when you have the file."

"I remember what I said."

"Yeah?" I said, trying to figure out if I could leave right then. There was an unobstructed path to the exit. I could just make a run for it.

"I didn't mean it."

"People say all kinds of things when they're drunk."[1]

Dad had now been in the hospital two weeks out of what would be close to a monthlong stretch. He had lost twenty pounds; his eyebrows were all but gone; he required regular blood transfusions, antibiotics, and antifungals; and only Mom was allowed to touch him, after she scrubbed her arms like she was going into surgery. The chemo had hopefully killed all the bad stuff, but it had killed his immune system as well. This was all part of the induction chemotherapy and everything was going according to plan, but he looked like he was dying.

Dad smiled for show, but he didn't like to talk that much since he had sores in his mouth and a pounding headache most of the time. I had this uneasy feeling that he was never going to completely bounce back. Tralina was good at reading body language and managed to know when Dad was or wasn't in the mood for visitors. The Spellmans were so ubiquitous in the hospital, you could tell we were kind of wearing on the staff. Maggie brought cookies to win

1 For a long but nonexhaustive list, see appendix.

them over; Rae brought bags of candy; I gave Tralina the spa gift certificate that I'd gotten from Edward last Christmas. Clearly it was a good move, based on the force behind the hug she gave me and the way she got all teary-eyed afterward.

Mostly we were trying to compensate for Grammy Spellman's presence. Being Grammy, she didn't seem to grasp the difference between a nurse and a diner waitress.

"Dear, could I trouble you for a glass of water? And maybe some carrot sticks."

Thing was, the water and the carrot sticks were for Grammy.

Mom slipped the rest of the nursing staff gift cards and all the complicated coffee beverages they could drink and other bribes to keep Grammy Spellman under containment. Since Grammy Spellman's likability quotient was on par with Rush Limbaugh's, the bribes may have been extraneous.

One morning when my mom and I were in the room with Dad, Mr. Slayter dropped by unannounced. Tralina let the two-visitors-at-a-time rule slide for Slayter. He's the kind of man people make exceptions for. I had no idea he was planning to visit. He arrived bearing a small gift, the size of a thick magazine, wrapped tastefully in red wrapping paper.

"I thought it was time we finally met, Mr. Spellman. I'm Ed."

"Hi, Ed. I'm Al and this is my wife, Olivia."

The two men nodded at each other in lieu of a handshake and Edward looked at my mother and father and said, "I can see the resemblance."

"Unfortunately," I said, because it's Dad's side that dominates.

"Have a seat," my mother said, clearing off a chair. The one I was sitting on.

Edward took a seat and I hopped on the window ledge.

"You raised a very unusual daughter."

"Tell me about it," Dad said.

"We didn't read any of those parenting books," Mom said, as if she had to explain herself.

"Obviously," Edward lightly replied.

On cue, Maggie arrived, lugging a car seat and Sydney, who was in a sparkling new pink taffeta dress with not only a tiara as an accessory but also a chopstick doubling as a wand.

She was ranting something about how she was princess of all the kingdoms. Sydney was, not Maggie.

Maggie scooped up her daughter so she

couldn't stab anyone with the chopstick and tried to contain that *Diary of a Mad Housewife* look that I'd only seen a handful of times.

"Hello," Maggie said to the room. Then she saw Edward and said hello again.

Edward turned to Sydney and said, "Are you a princess?"

"Yes," Sydney said. "A magic princess."

"No, she's not," Maggie said. "She's a little girl without any special powers."

"Do you need a cookie, Maggie?" my mom asked.

Mom gave Maggie a couple of cookies from one of Dad's gift baskets, which Maggie stuffed in her pocket.

"I want a cookie," Sydney said.

Sydney scanned the room, not sure who to turn to. Eventually it became obvious that no one was going to give her a cookie or their kingdom.

"You need to take her," Maggie said directly to me. It wasn't a request. It was a direct order. Still, I needed more data to acquiesce.

"Step into my office," I said as we slipped into the hallway. "What's going on?"

"Louis Washburn's DNA tests came back," Maggie said.

"Good news?"

"I've got good news, bad news, good news. What do you want first?" Maggie said.

"Surprise me."

"His DNA was *not* found at the scene of the crime for which he was charged."

"Awesome. Between that and the witness recanting her statement —"

"However, his DNA is a match to a rape/murder that happened two years before he went in."

"Shit. What's the second good news?"

"The victim's boyfriend was convicted of that crime. Since Washburn has some history of sexual assault and was not a known associate of the vic, we assume he's the killer."

"So the boyfriend will go free?"

"Yes. David is in court today with his one case. He's helping our elderly neighbor stay in her apartment. I have to get to work."

I picked Sydney up and the car seat and said, "Sydney, let's go find you some serfs you can abuse."

"No Izzy," Sydney said.

Maggie lowered the chopstick wand in her daughter's hand, looked Sydney dead in the eye, and said, "That is your aunt Izzy and you are stuck with her whether you like it or not."

"Thanks," I said. "She's going to need like

455

five therapy sessions for that."

Sydney and I walked Maggie down the hospital corridor. We caught Grammy on her way in.

"Ruth," Maggie said, like some cowboy in a western about to challenge another cowboy to a duel. "A word, please."

The corridor was narrow, which added to the whole duel element.

"If you ever try to give my daughter a princess dress again, I'll rip it into shreds before it's even out of the box. And if you ever use the word *diet* in front of her, I'll sew those shreds together and strangle you with them."

Grammy's body clenched into a sinewy statue, and she clutched her purse to her chest in her veiny claws.

"How dare you talk to me like that. She's my great-granddaughter."

"*And my daughter.* I win. Back off, old lady. You do not want to mess with me."

If Maggie had stormed off right then and there, it would have been an exquisite exit. Instead, she pulled a cookie out of her pocket, took a giant bite, chomped away, and said with a mouthful, "Izzy, I'll see you at home."

Then she stormed off.

Alas, the perfect moment came just seconds later, a moment that would have made Maggie so very proud.

Sydney waved her chopstick wand in front of Grammy Spellman and said, "Time out, Grammy."

Sydney and I returned to the hospital room, where my father and Slayter were catching up on the last several months, having not met.

"I need to take Banana home. Is everybody good here?"

Dad seemed to be having a good few hours, and he and Slayter said they had many things to discuss. I wanted particulars, but Sydney started whispering, "No Izzy," in my ear, which was incredibly distracting, so I left the two men to their devices and hoped that not too much note-sharing would take place.

There aren't many places you can take a thirty-pound dictator carrying a sharp stick. I decided to bring my niece home so she could rule her kingdom of stuffed animals and leave the rest of the universe alone. As Princess Banana banished her bunny to the gallows, I phoned Agent Bledsoe, asked if he'd received my paperwork, and pled my case. Then I e-mailed him my supporting documentation and told him how to contact Evelyn Glade and Rufus Harding. Bledsoe sounded skeptical, but evidence doesn't lie. With the threat of a felony conviction off my shoulders, I celebrated with a glass of fancy bourbon and a bowl of Goldfish and watched several episodes of *Phineas and Ferb* in a row.

There was a knock at the door. I looked through the peephole and saw Max Klein. Since I'd never seen Max without Claire, my gut told me not to take any chances. I peered through the window and, as predicted, Claire was standing to the right of her father. There wasn't a chance in hell I was falling for this scam again.

Max knocked more vigorously on the door. He shouted hello. It's very likely he saw me look through the window. In fact, it's more than likely; we made eye contact.

Princess Banana then went to the window and waved at her friend. She tried to open the door, but the dead bolt foiled her.

"No one is home," I said through the door. Yes, it's a ridiculous thing to say, but the essence of the message is generally heard.

"Isabel, open the door," Max said.

"Time out," the little tyrant said.

"You can't tell me what to do," I said, to

both Sydney and Max.

There was a lot of noise coming out of the children. Eventually the home line rang. I picked up.

"Hello," I said, trying to disguise my voice.

"Isabel, it's Max. Is there a problem?"

Clearly I didn't disguise it well enough.

"Listen, I didn't want the one kid today; there's no way in hell that I'm taking two. If you want to swap, I might go for *that,* but I'm not getting suckered into watching two children for the price of zero."

"Take a deep breath," Max said.

Apparently Max couldn't hear the deep breath on the other end of the line, so he repeated his imperative.

"I want to hear you take a deep breath."

I inhaled deeply and exhaled slowly. "Done."

"Listen to me carefully. I've come to take a child away, not add one. If you do the math, that leaves you with *zero* children."

"I like that math, but how do I know I can trust you?"

"Frankly, I don't want to leave my child alone with you."

He made an excellent point. I opened the door.

"Nice to see you, Max."

459

"No snitch," Claire said when she saw me, and then she did the oddest thing. She gave me a hug, or, more specifically, she gave my thighs a hug, because of our height differential, not because my thighs deserve a hug. They most certainly do not.

"Who wants a juice box and Goldfish?" I asked, trying to be hospitable.

Princess Banana in her fancy new gown asked Claire if she wanted to play a game. Claire agreed, not realizing that the game in no way resembled a game and involved doing whatever Sydney wanted Claire to do. They sat at the tea table and Sydney told Claire she had to sip tea exactly like she did. Claire ignored her and began playing with one of the dolls. Sydney told Claire that she was being rude. Claire said, "Shhh," which was a lovely sound. Sydney clanked some silverware angrily and told Claire that a guest was supposed to be polite.

Claire found a spot on the floor and began playing with the doll she came in with.

When Banana realized that Claire was not going to rejoin her for tea, she crawled onto the floor and took the doll away from Claire.

"That's my doll," Sydney said.

Claire snatched it right back and said, "No, it's *mine.*"

Max pumped his fist into the air in victory; even I have to admit Claire was pretty badass in that moment.

"Congratulations," I said.

Princess Sydney then said, "Time out."

I stormed over to the bossy pink fluffball and said, "No. Time out for you."

To David and Maggie's credit, time-outs were in rotation enough that Sydney regally walked over to the pink chair in the corner of the room, took a dignified seat, and sat in silence. I turned to Max.

"Can Claire watch TV?"

"Age appropriate," Max said.

"So, *Breaking Bad* is out?"

Max rolled his eyes. Since Claire and I have similar tastes in animated entertainment, I turned on the *Phineas* episode I had been watching earlier.

After dethroning the princess, I decided I deserved another drink. I poured a glass and offered one to my guest. Max, not Claire.

"Drink, Max?"

"Too early for bourbon."

"Juice box?"

"Beer," he said. "I'll get it."

We sat at the kitchen table, keeping an eye on the quiet kingdom.

"How's your dad?" Max asked.

"I really don't know. He finishes this

461

course of chemo, takes a break, then another course of chemo followed by a bone marrow transplant or another adjunct therapy."

"How are you?"

I must have been tired, because an unfiltered answer just slipped out.

"I'm not ready for my dad to die."

"No one is ever ready for that."

"The problem is, I'm not sure I'm ready for anything. Everything you're supposed to do when you grow up. Move away from home, buy your own food and groceries, get married, have children. Sometimes even the easy part of all that seems impossible to me. And then I wonder what will happen ten, twenty years from now. Will I be a fifty-year-old adolescent, completely alone, still sponging off whatever family I've got left?"

"People grow up at their own pace. And there are no rules for how you're supposed to live your life. Why don't you cut yourself some slack? If I had such a well-stocked pantry within spitting distance, I don't know that I would do any grocery shopping either —"

Max's cell rang.

"Excuse me," he said. "I have to take this. It's a patient."

He then stepped outside and had a brief conversation. When he returned, I realized I had no idea what Max did for a living.

"Patient?" I asked. "Are you a doctor?"

"Yes. A psychiatrist."

"I just spilled my guts to a shrink?" I shouted.

"Inside voice," Claire said politely.

"We were having a conversation," Max said.

"You tricked me."

"It's not like I charged you."

I gathered my jacket, paperwork, and bag and marched over to the front door.

"I'm out of here. If you run out of Goldfish, there's more in the pantry. Any questions, call David or Maggie. Banana, play nice. Adios, Claire."

Claire rushed to the door to hug my thighs good-bye. It kind of ruined my outraged exit.

"See you around," Max the shrink said cheerily.

WORKING BACKWARD

Three hours later, when I returned to the hospital, Edward was still in Dad's room. The gift that Edward had given my father was an iPad, the perfect portable device for stakeouts and extended hospital stays. While Edward showed my father a variety of useful office apps, Dad showed Edward his favorite computer game, the one involving some plants and some zombies. Edward quickly became an addict and played for the next four hours. In between bouts with zombies, Dad and Edward bonded over a variety of topics, including my bad sense of humor, cherry Jell-O, the overrated pastime of golf, and my mother's various charms. Apparently bygones happened quickly regarding the whole small corporate takeover that Edward assisted me with.

My father shared his medical problems with Edward and Edward shared his professional and medical problems with Dad, and by the time I arrived the two men had come up with an ironclad plan to smoke out Edward's crafty adversary.

Dad's model for the plan was how he solved cases as a cop. "You start with the dead body," he said, "and work backward."

"I don't mean to rush to judgment, but that plan sucks," I said.

"She must have been an impossible teenager," Edward said.

"You have no idea," Dad said.

"Starsky and Hutch, do you want to tell me what your master plan is?"

"We wait," Edward said, as if he'd just revealed the blueprint to break into the vault at the San Francisco Mint (back when the vault contained stuff worth breaking in for).

"Wait for what?"

Both men looked at me as if I were wearing a dunce cap.

"Too much booze," my dad said.

"Not enough exercise," Edward said.

I believe they were commenting on why I was slow to wrap my head around their brilliant plan. I was too worn out from, well, the past thirty-five years, really, to endure any more abuse. I departed without a word and went to the hospital cafeteria and ordered French fries and cake (they didn't have a liquor license).

I picked up a discarded newspaper and began reading two-day-old headlines. After I devoured my entrée and began to deconstruct my dessert, a shadow blocked a rather upbeat headline about a lone gunman whose plan to take out his direct superior in the mailroom at a talent agency office (so he'd be next in line for the head of the mailroom job) was foiled by his gun jamming.

"I thought I'd find you here," the shadow said.

I had a mouthful of cake, so I didn't respond. The shadow, otherwise known as Henry, took that as an invitation to sit down. The cake was extremely dense and so my chewing created an awkward silence that Henry thought needed filling. What it needed was milk.

"How've you been?" he asked.

Still working on that cake, my eyes said, *How did you find me here?*

"Your father suggested you'd be in the cafeteria."

My eyes then said, *How did you know my father was in the hospital?* My eyes were doing all the talking because I was still chewing.

"I ran into Maggie at the courthouse. She told me."

I finally stopped chewing and asked about the file.

"Oh, here's the file you asked for," Henry said. "The names have been redacted, but it's pretty clear what happened. There was an office party at Bryan Lincoln's house. People were drunk. Some illegal drugs were involved. Two days after the party, Naomi Clyde came into the Northern Station on Fillmore with her sister Maureen and filed rape charges against Brad Gillman and Bryan Lincoln. There were no witnesses. According to the victim, it happened in Bryan's bedroom. They couldn't do a rape kit because she came forward after forty-eight hours. However, the DA believed her and, after questioning both men, was ready to press charges, but Naomi recanted when the prosecutor started to discuss with her what would happen if they went to trial. Gillman and Lincoln lawyered up immediately and they were not going down without a fight. That's all I know," Henry said. "I'm sure you'll fill in the blanks."

"Thank you," I said.

I didn't have any other safe topics of conversation, so I pretended to be reviewing the file. Henry had already relayed the relevant information and yet he stayed put until he got my attention.

467

I closed the file and said, "How have you been?"

"Okay. How have you been?" he asked again with a little more weight.

I was in no mood for a meaningful conversation.

"I'm in the best restaurant in town. How do you think I am? Sorry I didn't save any fries for you. But you didn't tell me you were coming. Unannounced visits. This is a relatively new habit of yours, no?"

"Yes. Because you stink at prearranged visits."

"That's debatable."

"How's your mom doing?"

"Not bad. Dad in here means a lot less cooking. The woman knows how to look on the bright side. How's, uh, your pregnant fiancée? I forgot her name. I'm sorry."

"Annie. Annie Bloom. She's good."

There was a hiccup between the last two words, but it was none of my business and Henry offered no further information. I'm pretty sure the best way to move on is not to dig around in your ex-boyfriend's personal life. I saved the metaphorical shovel for other matters.

"Glad to hear it," I said in a tone that suggested, *Let's wrap this up.*

"What's your dad's prognosis?" Henry

asked. Sometimes I mix up the *let's wrap this up* tone with the *I've got all day* tone.

"He's going to live," I said. *"One way or another."*

It wasn't Dad's official prognosis; it was mine. And I was shocked how angry the words sounded as I said them.

"If you ever need anything . . . ," Henry said, trailing off.

"Thanks," I said.

The days of my asking Henry for anything other than running license plate numbers or looking up ancient police files were over. We knew that. It was a saying left over from another time. Those days were gone.

"I'll see you around," Henry said. "Take care of yourself."

"You too," I said.

I didn't say good-bye, because we'd already said good-bye. And I knew I'd see him again. It's always good to have a cop in your back pocket.

I was alone but five minutes, reviewing the file, when Charlie's shadow ruined my reading light. A much more welcome shadow.

"I thought I'd find you here," Charlie said.

"Why is that?" I said a bit snappishly.

"You seem to like the French fries."[1]

"I take it Edward's still chewing the fat with my dad."

"They're really hitting it off."

"Do you know anything about this genius plan they've come up with? Dad said something about waiting for the dead body, working backward?"

"Habit number two: Begin with the end in mind, from Stephen Covey's *The Seven Habits of Highly Effective People.*"

"What?"

"Didn't you read anything in those business books Mr. Slayter gave you?"

"No. They were incredibly dull. No guns, no murders. You read those books?"

"When Mr. Slayter gave them to you, I figured there might be something valuable in them."

"I still don't understand how this is going to smoke out Edward's adversary."

"Edward was explaining his problem to your dad and I reminded them of habit number two: Begin with the end in mind. See, once the board of directors gets together and votes, it will become obvious who benefits from having Edward out of

[1] Note to self: Cut back on French fries. Especially hospital French fries. That's just sad.

the picture. Then you know who set him up and it will be easier to assemble evidence if you only have one suspect. Once you have the evidence, you can go back to the board and have Edward reinstated."

"That was your idea?"

"Yes."

"Those two goons are taking credit for it."

"Who cares, if it works?" Charlie said.

"Good point. Only there's one problem with your plan. If the board knows about Edward's illness, they won't give him his old job back."

"Your dad came up with the solution to that. The deal with the prosecutor is hush-hush. All they know is that an arrest and deal were made. As far as the board is concerned, Edward was charged with inde-cent exposure, which can be defended once you find out who was drugging him. If, of course, you find out who drugged him."

"And if we don't," I said, "Edward's career ends behind a curtain of scandal and shame."

"Nobody said it was a perfect plan."

After my father's long day with his new BFF, he needed some rest. And I needed to close a case that had been nagging at me

471

for the last two months. I decided to pay a visit to Maureen Stevens. Whatever was going on at Divine Strategies was not any of my concern, and the company had long ago ceased to be of interest to Slayter Industries. The simple truth is I wanted to understand.

I knew we couldn't meet in the office and I didn't want to trouble her at home. I caught Maureen at seven thirty outside of her Pilates studio. She did a double take when she saw me.

"Isabel, what are you doing here?"

"I was hoping I could buy you a cup of coffee."

"I don't drink coffee."

"Whatever you want. I would like to go someplace and sit."

"What's this about?"

"I have a few questions. About Naomi."

Maureen could have walked away on the spot, but some secrets are so bottomless, you're always treading water. There's a danger in keeping those kinds of secrets and they always have to be tended, like a domesticated rose garden.

We went to a café that served just about every beverage known to man. Maureen ordered a hot water with lemon. I've noticed that people who drink that beverage regularly have a disturbing level of restraint. If I fished for information, she wouldn't bite. I had to bluff.

"How long has this been going on?" I asked.

"What are you talking about?" Maureen asked as she warmed her hands on the mug.

"This arrangement you have with Brad and Bryan."

"Who are you?"

"I'm a private investigator. I was hired by a venture capital firm to look into the fiscal health of your company. Some things were a bit off, like your peculiar position of power."

"It's peculiar when a woman is in a position of power?"

"Why didn't she press charges?"

Maureen took a sip of her hot water and decided how to play it.

"Those files are not public record."

"And I'm not interested in making anything public. I just want to understand personally why you wouldn't want to put two rapists in jail."

"Because my sister refused to testify. She couldn't bear the humiliation. She knew the defense attorney would eviscerate her on the stand. Naomi had quite the reputation in college and the idea of twelve strangers watching the video . . . it was too much.

She was on so many meds she was practically catatonic."

"What video?"

"They taped it. You didn't know that?" Maureen asked.

"No. Where is the tape?"

"I have it. One of the secretaries back then told me they were showing it to their friends during lunch hour. I paid her a thousand dollars to make a copy. Then I applied for a job. Different last name. I was married then. They didn't know who I was. The rest is history."

"What do you get out of this?" I asked.

"The satisfaction of knowing that they'll never forget what they did. And the money to cover my sister's expenses."

"And your expenses," I said.

"Yes. If they went to prison, they'd have been out ages ago and maybe they would have done something like this again."

"So this is justice? Don't you trust God to mete out justice on the other side?"

"I have full faith in the Lord," Maureen said. "But just in case he doesn't . . ."

"I'm not sure I understand the point. You couldn't send Brad and Bryan to prison, so you made sure all of you got stuck in one. No one survived this. How can you stand to go into an office every day and look at your sister's rapists?"

"Because I know it hurts them more than it hurts me. Any more questions?"

"No," I said. "I'm done."

I could have asked a thousand more questions, because her motivations were so beyond the scope of my comprehension. But then I realized I simply didn't want to understand her.

THE DEFECTIVE DETECTIVE

Maybe now would be a good time to call attention to the elephant on the page. Let's review the cases, official and unofficial, that have been on my roster since becoming CEO of Spellman Investigations.

- Lightning Fast Moving Company, the corruptest movers in the west
- Ethan Jones, suspicious brother
- Rae Spellman, conflict resolution specialist
- Evelyn Glade, embezzler and framer
- Divine Strategies, the company with the dirty little secret
- Unknown, Edward's corporate enemy
- Louis Myron Washburn, the guiltiest innocent prisoner at the Big Q

Of all the cases that can be filed away, it's impossible not to notice that I didn't solve a single one of them. Ethan was just suspicious and hardly capable of the many crimes I'd considered he committed. I didn't solve anything. I walked up to a bail bondsman and asked him why he was following us, and he told me. And then Ethan filled in the blanks.

Maggie figured out that Rae was running the prison interviews instead of Demetrius, even though I was the first to read the transcripts and could have easily deduced the language patterns. And if the strange interviews hadn't come to light, eventually a guy with tattoos making vague threats from the Big Q would have tipped us off.

Robbie Gruber turned my virtual binoculars in the direction of Evelyn Glade.

Mom practically solved Divine Strategies in her sleep. And if the end of Edward's story revealed his true adversary, I'd be there to file the paperwork, but let there be no mistake: Charlie Black, navigational consultant, was the brains behind the operation.

If I'd failed at my job this profoundly a year ago, I'd have considered a career change and then quickly realized that I had no job skills. My only defense was that I was management now, and everyone knows that managers need to delegate. And, as far as I could tell, there was really only one problem with this setup: I wasn't a manager; I was a detective. No, I was a burned-out detective on the precipice of calling it quits. I know, I sound like a broken record. You might hang on to the scratched-up vinyl for a while, but eventually you'll just throw it away, because it doesn't sound like it used to.

The board of directors met on Monday. Their first order of business was to relieve Edward of his duties as CEO. Shannon Crane was named temporary CEO, but she made it clear that her duties were transient and she was not interested in a full-time position. Edward, however, still owned 25 percent of the company, which made him the majority shareholder. When it came time to vote in a new member of the board, and the likely candidate for CEO, the shareholders had a meeting and two names were submitted: Connor Glenn and Lowell Frank.

When Edward returned from the meeting, he gave me the names and I went to work. Vivien surveilled Connor, and Demetrius made a rare exception to his rule against following white people and tailed Lowell, since the rest of the family was busy keeping Dad company and in Jell-O and

Popsicles at the hospital. One of the nurses, in an attempt to pay Dad a compliment, said that she had never seen a person going through chemo who did such a good job of maintaining his weight. Dad was not flattered.

Mom, as expected, was holding it together extremely well. Too well, I noticed. When Dad dived too deeply into the helpless-patient mode, she snapped him out of it with a well-timed verbal jab. She stroked his brow when he needed it and made sure that nothing lime flavored passed the threshold of his room. If he pressed the nurse call button more than one time every two hours, she disconnected the switch, so Dad just thought the nurses were busy. Then when visitors or family took over the room and Mom was given a respite, she would disappear for a few hours and presumably go home to shower and change.

Eventually my siblings and I compared notes and we realized that no one had seen Mom at home when she wasn't at the hospital.

So where did she go?

Not for the first time in my life, I followed my mother. The next day, Rae, then David, then Grammy, then several of Dad's old cop buddies were stopping by the hospital to keep him company and Dad told Mom to go home and get some rest. Fortunately I was there to witness the exchange. Mom reluctantly said good-bye and went home, as she claimed she would. I had to keep a close tail because she had conveniently disabled the tracker on her car.

Mom was at home for no more than an hour, where she clearly showered and changed, and swiftly departed. I followed her along the barren stretch of highway that begins the journey to Sacramento. She stopped in Vallejo. There's not a lot to recommend Vallejo, but my mother had found a place to her liking: Jimmy's Casino Card Club. My mother is not a card player; my mother is no gambler. And yet, when I followed her into this lowest-rent casino, she was playing blackjack as if her life depended on it.

The place didn't serve booze. They had a lousy restaurant with a dry roast beef advertised on a chalkboard sign by the front door. Cocktail waitresses who had seen better days in 1972 wore polyester miniskirts and served carbonated beverages to the clientele. The club advertised being open twenty-four hours a day, seven days a week, three hundred and sixty-four days a year, which would explain why there was no time to vacuum or give the joint a rest from the odor of life.

My mother is an attractive woman for her age. In this joint she practically had to beat them off with a stick. I don't think some of these men had seen a woman this striking in real life in years. Some official-looking guy who apparently knew my mother by name had to stand guard around her as she played. She was clearly winning, which they don't like. But she kept the men at her table, which they like, so they treated her well and made sure she had a bottomless glass of club soda. Mom must have set her phone on a timer, because exactly two hours later, when the dealer stood on seventeen and Mom took her chances and broke twenty-one, she didn't try to end on a win; she let the timer decide and she promptly cashed out. Maybe she made five bucks for two hours.

I let her see me as I waited outside in the blazing sun.[1] She was putting on her sunglasses and it took her eyes some time to adjust.

"Annie Duke," I said. "Fancy meeting you here."

1 Vallejo is a lot hotter than San Francisco.

"She plays poker, Isabel. Learn your card games."

"I know my card games," I said. "I just don't know any famous female blackjack players. What are you going to do with all that cash? Pay Dad's hospital bills?"

"Izzy. My husband, your father, is gravely ill. Are you really giving me shit right now?"

There were so many things wrong with this moment. The first thing wrong with it was me. I was, obviously, incredibly insensitive and hadn't paid enough attention to Mom.

"He's going to be fine," I said. I'm not sure if I added a question mark at the end of the sentence.

"He is going to be fine." She said it like a mantra, to convince herself it was true.

"Are you going to be fine?" I asked, putting my arm around her and walking her to her car.

"I'm going to be fine," she said. I was not convinced.

"Can I ask why? The hospital is a pretty depressing place, and yet Jimmy's Casino Card Club makes the hospital look like Alcatraz."[2]

2 In our family, Alcatraz is the equivalent of Disneyland.

"His odds were kind of like blackjack by the time we caught it. But the thing about blackjack that most people don't know is that you can win. The odds, if you play it right and don't take any unnecessary risks, are on your side."

"Is that why you play?"

"No. Honestly. Those two hours I'm playing cards, I'm not thinking of anything else. It's kind of like your dad with that dumb-ass video game with bobbing plants."

"I'm sorry," I said.

"For what, sweetie?" Mom asked.

I was sorry for so many things it didn't seem like a good idea to list them, in case some had slipped her mind. I was sorry that I didn't communicate more when I took over the business. I was sorry that I was such a monster when I had them on the ropes. I was sorry I had stopped asking my parents simple questions, like *How are you doing? Have you been to a doctor recently? Can I see the results of your latest blood work?* Mostly I was sorry because when all of this went down I never just stopped and looked my mother in the eye and asked her if she was okay. She would have lied to me, but at least I'd have asked. At least I would have known the truth.

SMOKED OUT

Vivien surveilled Lowell Frank for two days. It seemed like four to me, because she called me every hour on the hour to tell me that he was still at work and that she needed to pee. Sometimes I, or Rae, or the Spellman of the hour who needed a break from the hospital, would meet Vivien outside of her stakeout location on Battery Street and relieve her of her duties so she could relieve herself, but more times than not, we'd just tell her to risk it and find a bar or café. Vivien made more money those two days than she ever had in a two-week period, but sadly, I think it permanently cured her of any notion of becoming a PI.

Most of our conversations went something like this:

VIVIEN: Do you know what's more boring than surveillance?
ME: What?

VIVIEN: Nothing. Absolutely nothing.

Demetrius had better luck with his subject. Or worse, depending on how you look at it.

Connor Glenn had a life. And Demetrius followed him as he went about it. Connor became paranoid and began doing things to evade the black man who he assumed was following him to steal his wallet. Connor got into a car accident and Demetrius promptly quit the assignment. I made the greatest executive decision of my life and asked Demetrius and Vivien to switch subjects.

Demetrius had a delightful time sitting on a stoop catching up on his reading and coffee (and didn't even bother calling in to request bathroom breaks, since he understood that Lowell Frank was not going anywhere).

Vivien stopped consuming beverages when she discovered that she had a subject who was at least marginally entertaining. Connor Glenn never noticed the cute, twentysomething coed who was on his heels sixteen hours a day. He didn't notice her when he dropped by his fiancée's apartment and he didn't notice her as she was snapping shots of him at Boulevard with his future father-in-law, Willard Slavinsky. The father-in-law status had to be confirmed with a few pretext calls, but that was ridiculously easy.

Vivien had no idea when we were flipping through her camera phone that she had the money shot. I immediately called D and relieved him of his responsibilities. I sent Viv straight home and told her to take a shower, a twelve-hour nap, and the next day off. And then I went straight to Edward's house, where I found him engrossed in a perfectly tedious game of chess with Charlie.

"I've got the who and the why, but not the what, otherwise known as evidence," I said.

I showed Edward the photos. This was the kind of news that probably required a bit of delicacy, but I was all out. While I should have been consoling Edward, I was kicking myself for being so taken in by Willard. I should have known the moment I caught him with Lenore.

"I'm sorry," I said. "It's Willard and he's angling for Connor Glenn."

Edward stared at the photo of his friend, the recognition of the betrayal showing itself in a look of anger I'd never seen in my boss. The universe had disappointed him lately. I think he believed that a friend wouldn't. Slavinsky had sold out a man he'd known for forty years for a son-in-law with bad job prospects.

"What do you know about Glenn?"

"I guess he needs a job," Edward said.

"Now we need proof."

"How are you going to do that?" Edward asked.

"Relax, I'm a detective," I said with the enthusiasm of the first runner-up for Miss America.

I had no idea how I was going to get that proof.

Linking Willard to his son-in-law was easy, but convincing the shareholders or the board of directors that something untoward was happening required proving that Willard was behind Edward's scrapes with sanity. I had no brilliant ideas beyond twenty-four-hour surveillance of our primary suspect, and the damage was already done. And surveillance is expensive.

I had delivered the Slayter Industries funds from my bank account back to Slayter Industries and not only was I broke, but my parents were broke and my company was broke. I could postpone paychecks to anyone with a last name starting with S, but once I paid Vivien and D and the vendors that our livelihood depended on, we had less than a thousand in the bank.

The only good thing about a life-threatening illness in the family is that it puts your dire financial situation in perspective. I simply managed to put it out of my mind.

Monday was a nail-biter for Mom; she knew Dad's latest tests would be in, which would determine the course of treatment and whether Dad could go home. He had been in the hospital four weeks now.

Dr. Chang allowed the immediate family into the room while she debriefed us.

"The hope with the four-week induction chemo is to induce remission. I'm happy to report that Albert's tests look good."

The room exploded in celebration.

"Wait," Dr. Chang said. "It's too soon for that. Now you need to go home and rest for a week, and then consolidated chemotherapy is the protocol for this type of leukemia. Often we do chemotherapy with a bone marrow transplant or stem cell transplant. I'd like everyone to get tested and then we can decide what to do next. But I'm releasing Albert tomorrow. He should remain on bed rest. His immune

488

system is still compromised. Please limit visitors and I'll see you in a week."

"I started drinking the green stuff in David's kitchen last week," Rae said. "So my bone marrow would be at its best."

"Rae, that algae shake mix is like two years old. You should stop," said Dad.

"Should I take up exercise now?" Rae asked. "Or will that just weaken my immune system since I'm not accustomed to it?"

Tralina walked into the room to say goodbye. "I heard you were leavin' me. I'll miss ya, Albert." She turned to all of us and said, "Behave yourselves. I saw you all stealing other people's food. I let it slide. Next time, I'll turn you in. You have a beautiful family, Albert. I tink they could use more discipline."

Dad came home. Other than Dad not looking like Dad and spending most of his time in bed, you could almost pretend he wasn't sick. My father had always been a popular man, and news traveled fast. Gift baskets arrived at an alarming rate. Most were sent through a delivery service since we had asked for no visitors, but there were always exceptions to the rule.

Max dropped by to pick up Princess Banana. It's a general rule that grandparents cannot get enough of their grandchildren, but Banana is an iconoclast. Anyway, when Max visited he had Claire with him, of course. I had forgiven him for trying to shrink me.

"Claire wants you to take her to the Big Q," Max said. "What is it? She couldn't explain that to me."

"Wow, children really are sponges."

I pulled Claire aside and said, "We don't want to go to the Big Q. It's not a nice place."

Max looked at me suspiciously and then said, "Claire asked if she could have a play-date with you."

"What is that?" I asked. "Free babysitting?"

"No. I would be there. You think I'd leave you alone with my child again?"

"Have fun with the princess," I said, ushering the trio out the door.

Speaking of the Big Q, I caught a glimpse of Rae chatting amiably with that ex-con, the one with the neck tattoos, who sent prison telegrams. He was sitting in his truck; she passed him a Tupperware container full of baked goods. When they were done chatting, they shook hands and Rae returned to the house.

"What was that all about?" I asked.

"Skip looked hungry and we're swimming in stale gift basket crap."

"Skip? When did you two get on a first-name basis?"

"It's always good to have some muscle on your side and since D doesn't like getting his hands dirty . . ."

"Should you really be consorting with a known felon, Rae?"

"One of us has to," Rae said as she breezed out of the room.

Agent Bledsoe dropped by after Dad came home. Bledsoe made the house call to bring me the good news that the case was closed, our name was cleared, and he had come to a settlement[1] with Evelyn Glade.

"She's not going to do any time, is she?" I asked.

"No," he said. "It was her boyfriend's idea, anyway."

I didn't condone what Evelyn did, and I couldn't for the moment pretend I understood her, but the last thing I'd wanted was to see her go to prison.

Before Bledsoe left, he said the strangest thing to me.

1 Like I was saying, white-collar criminals can get away with murder. Well, not exactly.

"I should have given you more credit," he said. "If you were going to pull something, it wouldn't have been *that* stupid."

"Thanks," I said. "I like to think I could've come up with a decent embezzlement scheme."

There was only one other visitor to speak of. We weren't expecting anyone. The doorbell rang in the middle of the afternoon. I looked through the peephole and saw a woman standing with a large gift basket blocking her face. She didn't seem dangerous, so I opened the door.

"Petra, what are you doing here?"

Perhaps you recall the name. It's come up a few times, mostly in reference to crimes from my past. I don't think I'd seen her in more than two years. We had been inseparable for years. Then she married my brother, cheated on him, and they divorced. I suppose that was the beginning of the end. If you think about it, that was also a good thing. If they hadn't divorced, he wouldn't have met Maggie and they wouldn't have had . . . Well, let's just leave it at *he wouldn't have met Maggie.* Since I'd last seen Petra, she'd had a child, grown out her hair, and started wearing clothes that served more to conceal than reveal her collection of tattoos.

She still had her nose piercing, though. I always knew she'd be that kind of mom.

"I heard," Petra said as she stood nervously in the doorway. "Len and Chris told me and I thought about calling, but then they told me that he was home and I thought on a hunch I'd bring this by. You can just throw it out, if he doesn't want it."

Petra offered up a homemade gift box with brownies and lollipops and other confectionary items infused with the cannabis crop.

"I got it from High Heals,[2] that medical marijuana dispensary in the Castro. There's lollipops and cookies and I made the brownies myself, so you know they're good. Also, I left a little bit of the weed in the canister, if your dad wants to smoke. I hear it helps. But if you think this is a bad idea . . ."

"No, it's a great idea," I said. In truth, I had no idea if Dad genuinely wanted the ganja or if he just wanted to know he could have it. Either way, I knew he'd appreciate the gift. "That was really nice of you," I said.

"It was nothing," she said. "Your dad meant a lot to me for a long time, and he bailed me out of jail once. I miss him. I miss

2 It's closed now. So don't Google it.

all of you. It's been strange not being around the Spellmans, you know?"

"I do. I haven't even met your son."

"Let me show you a picture."

Petra dug through her overstuffed bag and eventually found her wallet. She plucked a snapshot of a two-year-old boy in skateboarding gear with dark hair, devilish eyes, and a Mohawk. I desperately wanted him to meet and torment Princess Banana.

"He looks just like I thought he would," I said. "Hey, do you want to come in? Have some coffee?"

"I have to run," Petra said. "But maybe I can call you sometime and we can do something. I don't know what. Break into the school cafeteria. Or just get a drink somewhere."

"That sounds great," I said.

We hugged awkwardly and Petra left, but I knew that a shift had happened, and I wasn't saying good-bye to her for another year or two. I'd see her again, sometime soon.

I brought the gift basket upstairs to Dad, who looked like, well, a kid in a candy store. He immediately asked for a lollipop, which Mom immediately confiscated.

"This is not for recreational use, Al. When

494

you're sick as a dog, we'll revisit this conversation."

Dad turned to me for sympathy and said, "Your mother is such a square."

Reversal of Fortune

Dad returned to the hospital for the consolidation chemo and Dr. Chang had the results of the antigen test.

"Good news," Dr. Chang said. "We have a match."

Rae pumped her fist into the air.

"It's Isabel," Dr. Chang said. "She's a six-out-of-six antigen match."

"What was I?" Rae asked.

"A half match," Dr. Chang said.

"Is it possible they accidentally got the samples crossed?"

"No," Dr. Chang said.

Rae was visibly disappointed. My mother sank into the chair next to Dad, breathing a sigh of relief. Dad winked at me.

"The next step," said Dr. Chang, "is DNA cross-matching, to test for the antigen compatibility."

"I'm sure our antigens are compatible," Dad said, as if all we needed to do was have a friendly chat with them.

"We take white blood cells from Isabel and mix them with your blood, Albert. Hopefully there's a negative cross-match, which is a good thing."

"Assuming Dad's blood doesn't attack Isabel's white blood cells, when would this happen?" David asked.

"In about a week, after we finish the consolidation chemo," Dr. Chang said. "Isabel, here's some literature about what to expect. If you have any questions or concerns, let me know."

Rae followed Dr. Chang out of the hospital room with a question or concern. Mom and David went across the street to get coffee, leaving me and Dad alone.

"I knew it would be you," Dad said.

Late that night, when I had just fallen asleep, Rae knocked at my back door. She was carrying that ridiculous briefcase she'd brought to the job interview she did for Mom. Although, this time, her attire was decidedly less professional. I believe she had pajamas on under her raincoat.

"Isn't it past your bedtime? I know you like to rise with the stock market," I said.

"I have a proposition for you. Where can we discuss it?"

"Wherever you can find a place to plant your ass."

"This needs to be a professional conversation," Rae said.

"Then maybe you shouldn't have worn pants with anthropomorphized peanut butter sandwiches on them."

Rae sat down on my easy chair; I took the bed.

"What's up?" I asked.

"As you know, the business continues to have some financial difficulties."

"Yes, Rae. I am aware of that."

"You haven't paid me the money you owe me. We currently have over five grand in outstanding bills and we need more clients. I believe I've come to a sound conclusion."

"Things could be better," I conceded.

"What you need is a legal cash infusion," Rae said.

"I am aware of that. Can I go to bed now? You're not telling me anything I don't know."

Rae opened her briefcase and withdrew several formal-looking documents along with a bank check for a sizable amount.

"I want to buy back in," she said. "Right now you own sixty percent of the company and Mom and Dad own forty percent. I want to buy fifty percent of your shares. You can take that money and then give the business a low-interest loan until we're back on our feet."

"If I give you thirty percent, then Mom and Dad are back to having the majority share."

"True," Rae said. "But if we promise to have each other's back, we can work together and no one can steer the ship off course."

"I thought you were done with this business," I said. "What's changed?"

"Have you seen a newspaper lately? The economy is sunk. The job prospects for someone with just an undergraduate degree are dismal. I'm not sure about graduate school yet and I don't want some crappy entry-level job working for the man when I can be the boss of me. I think this new business venture of mine has some traction."

"Are you referring to the business that involves you spraying whipped cream on cars?"

"I'm referring to the business that has fifteen potential clients ready to hand over retainer checks. In fact, right now we don't have the personnel to handle all these cases, so I'm going to have to cherry-pick my favorites. Can you say that about your caseload?"

"I'm concerned about your loose ethics. Is there a line you won't cross?"

"Of course," Rae said.

"What is it?"

"The line shifts on a case-by-case basis."

"That's the part I don't like."

"Let me remind you of something. I let the air out of Marcus Lorre's tires. You slashed them and then let Vivien have at it. Can I be blunt?" Rae asked.

"Please," I said.

"You and I both know that I have more restraint than you. So if you're worried about ethical boundaries, maybe you should just keep an eye on yourself."

"I need to know what you're doing," I said. "All cases should be run by me."

"I will you keep informed, but I work autonomously."

"Shit," I said.

"That's a yes?" Rae said.

I didn't have a choice and we both knew it. I couldn't run this business alone anymore, and I didn't want to. I didn't just need Rae's money; I needed her help. Whether I was signing a deal with the devil only time would tell, but I signed it on the spot and immediately lost my status as boss.

Before Rae left, she turned on my computer

and had me watch a video of a bone marrow donation procedure, providing her own narration.

"You'll be anesthetized, so you won't feel a thing. They'll stick a long needle into your pelvic bone and take some marrow you won't need. As you can see, you'll be lying on your stomach with part of your ass exposed. It's probably too late to tell you that you should have been cutting back on the Goldfish and maybe doing some squats. Anyway, my point is, the procedure is no big deal. I could have done it without the anesthetic."

"Good night," I said.

Sometimes my sister doesn't understand that bidding adieu actually means *leave,* so I picked up her backpack and threw it outside. Then she got the hint.

I had hoped to tie up any loose ends before the procedure, but I remained stalled in my investigation, or more specifically, my incrimination of Willard Slavinsky. We knew he framed Edward, but I had no way of proving it. I felt as if I had failed my boss.

"I had a good run," Edward said. "I would gladly step down. I just don't want to do it under a cloud of shame."

As Edward and I lamented his current

predicament, the oddest thought crossed my mind.

What would a conflict resolution specialist do under the same set of circumstances? I'm not in the business of revenge, but sometimes people need to be schooled. Those are two entirely different concepts.

"Call Willard," I said to Edward. "Invite him over to your office. See if maybe you can come to an understanding."

"He's not a fool, Isabel. He won't confess on tape."

"Then seduce him."

"I'm not in the mood for your jokes."

"I have a plan. Call him and make sure he comes alone."

Three hours later, Willard reluctantly dropped by Edward's office. He had the pinched expression of a man concealing every scrap of emotion. Before Edward said a word, Charlie showed up and offered to get Willard's parking ticket validated. Charlie passed the ticket to me and I breezed past Evelyn's vacated desk and stamped the ticket. Then I headed down to the garage and waited for the parking attendant to deliver Willard's car.

Meanwhile, Edward struck up as benign a conversation as he could.

502

"I'm not sure what I'll do with all of my free time," he said.

"You'll figure out something," Willard said.

"There's always golf."

"Keeps me out of trouble."

"Maybe I should play more tennis," Edward said.

"Tennis is good. Was there a particular reason you wanted to see me?"

Edward's phone rang.

"Excuse me," he said, picking up the phone.

"It's me," I said as my sister met me in an alley behind a dim sum restaurant in Chinatown. "Can you hold him for fifteen minutes? I'm still waiting for your brother to arrive."

"I'll do my best," Edward said.

"I'm going to hang up," I said. "But you might want to continue this phone call."

Edward chatted with a dead line for another five minutes, until Slavinsky started checking his watch and shifting impatiently in his chair. Edward ended his fake conversation and killed the next three minutes complimenting Slavinsky's casual wear and asking him about his shopping habits. When Willard's patience had all but dried up, Edward then looked him dead in the eye and said, "Can you sleep at night?"

"I sleep just fine."

"I know you didn't do this alone. Who helped you?" Edward asked.

"Where is that boy of yours? I'm going to be late for my tee time."

"We wouldn't want that."

Charlie was huffing and puffing when he rushed into Edward's office and returned Slavinsky's ticket.

"Good catching up," Willard said as he swiftly got to his feet.

"Let's do this again sometime," Edward said.

Fifteen minutes later, a plainclothes police officer flashed his lights and motioned for Slavinsky to pull his Mercedes to the curb.

"Is there a problem, officer?" Slavinsky impatiently asked.

The officer said, "We received an anonymous call about a man driving erratically matching your description. The caller suggested you were carrying explosives."

"Do I look like the sort of man who carries explosives around with him?"

"I don't know," the officer said. "I don't work in the bomb squad. Do you mind if I check your vehicle?"

"Fine. Whatever. Just make it fast."

"Please pop your trunk and put your hands on the steering wheel."

The officer checked the trunk of the car, called in for backup, and asked Slavinsky to step out of his car.

"Is there a problem?"

"Where were you planning on going with twelve cans of tear gas and three dozen sticks of dynamite?"

One hour later, Henry Stone served up his most disapproving gaze as he directed me to Slavinsky's interview room.

"Don't look at me like that. You agreed to this plan," I said.

"You owe me," he said.

"I recently came into a bit of money. Will forty bucks do it?"

"I want to be friends. I don't want you to completely vanish from my life. Those are my terms."

"Seriously?" I said, eyeing the fidgety Slavinsky through the one-way mirror.

"I'm not letting you into the room," Henry said, "until you agree."

"I'm not going to your wedding," I said, clarifying the terms. "And don't invite me to any baby showers."

"Fine."

I held out my hand. "So we're friends," I said.

"We're friends," he said.

"It's really over, isn't it?" I asked.

"Yes," he said.

I looked him in the eye. I couldn't remember the last time I did that. He had the kindest eyes, eyes you knew were never lying to you. You cannot say that about most eyes. Henry refused to take my hand. He kissed me on the cheek and left. As endings go, this one was unsatisfying. It was like a leaky faucet that finally got fixed, only you had gotten so used to the leak, you almost didn't care. Also, you had some guy in an interview room waiting for you, so you really had no way to segue out of that metaphor.

It didn't take Willard long to sort out his predicament, especially after I walked in.

"Isabel," he said. "I believe I called an attorney."

"I don't know anything about that. I just happened to be in the station and saw you here in *the box,* as they call it on some TV shows from the early nineties.[1] Thought I'd say hi. Hi. Can I get you anything? Water? Soda? I know where they keep the water

1 *Homicide: Life on the Street.*

and the soda."

"What do you want?"

"I want you to fix Edward's problem. You and Edward own enough shares of the company that you can dictate any decisions made by the board of directors. If you wanted, you could get them all to forget about his little indecent-exposure incident, which has already been settled in court, and reinstate him as CEO."

"Why would I do that?"

"So they'll drop the terrorism and hate crime charges against you," I said. "Where have you been?"

"What on earth are you talking about?"

"The tear gas and explosives in the trunk of your car when you were obviously en route to your country club."

"You put them there."

"No, I didn't. You were going to blow up the place."

"Why would I do that?"

"Because you were really mad that they recently let in a Jew and a black. And not one of those Sammy Davis Jr. twofers."

"As usual, I have no idea what you're talking about, Isabel."

"I think that's an excellent defense. It's certainly my go-to defense, but what about the e-mails?"

"What e-mails?" Slavinsky asked. He was turning the shade of a Campbell's soup can. The red part, of course.

So, I showed him the e-mails, which contained very brief threats to his country club from the e-mail address statusquo@ [redacted].com. The tone was a bit off for a rich/angry/elitist racist, but it did the trick.

"I didn't write these e-mails, I don't know who this statusquo person is, and I most certainly do not share this sentiment."

"That might very well be true, but as you know, sometimes the truth is irrelevant."

"You still need proof," Willard said smugly. His tomato-soup face was returning to its usual shade of princess pink.

"But we can prove that the e-mails were sent from your computer," I said.

"That's impossible," Willard shouted, slamming his fist on the screwed-down table.

I whispered, "It's actually not impossible. Our computer expert checked the headers and can trace the e-mails through the IP address back to your home computer."[2]

"You won't get away with this."

2 Robbie Gruber was going to get another porn gift basket.

"No. You won't get away with it. Trust me, these e-mails were written on your computer. I had no idea you had so much anger in you."

Willard studied the e-mails, his face white as a sheet, his hands trembling like a drunk with DTs. Mostly he was furious, trying to keep it under containment. His eyes darted around the room as he tried to figure out his next chess move. As has been established, I suck at chess, so I can't really draw a proper analogy. I can only tell you that Willard was cornered and he had no way out. I made sure of that.

"How do I make this go away?" he eventually asked.

"When Edward is CEO again, I'll make sure all the evidence disappears. Do we have a deal?"

"This is outrageous."

"Do we have a deal?"

"Yes."

"One more thing," I said. "I know you didn't do this alone. What is your relationship with Lenore or Nora?"

"We're involved."

"How much did she help?"

"She helped."

"Did she drug Edward?"

"Yes."

"I want to know how."

"The first time, his bourbon. Once he was knocked out, we drove him to Oakland and dropped him off. The second time, in the teapot in his office. Once he and Charlie were unconscious, we got him out of the building."

"Then stripped him naked and dropped him in front of the elementary school?"

Willard cleared his throat.

"Why, Willard? You have enough money. I've seen where you live."

"He got lucky. He married a rich woman who was stupid enough to not have a prenup and then all of this is his. I didn't think he deserved it. I helped him make decisions every step of the way. It was as much mine as his."

"What about Damien? You recommended him. Was he in on any of it?"

"He was just a recommendation," Willard said. "Are we done here?"

"You are most definitely done. Obviously, I don't think you and Edward should work together anymore."

I left Slavinsky in the box and phoned Edward as I left the police station.

"I'm on my way."

"Want me to see if I can find any uranium on the black market?" he asked.

"Nope," I said. "I think we're good."

I returned to Edward's office. I suppose I had a spring in my step for the first time in months, so Edward knew our plan had succeeded.

"It worked, I take it?"

"It worked. It couldn't have been easy to get your hands on that much dynamite in ninety minutes."

"I know people," Edward said.

"Please don't say anything that I would have to deny in a court of law."

"I'm sure you say that to all the boys."

"I wish I could have video-recorded it for you. It was so satisfying."

"I'm sure."

"So what happens next?" Edward asked.

"Willard will recommend to the board that you be reinstated as CEO and you buy him out. I think this partnership has run its course."

"And that's that. He gets away with everything he's done?" Edward asked.

"There's still a police record, and we have the interviews if he gets any wild ideas in the future."

"It doesn't seem like enough, does it?"

"No," I said. "That's why I got him a

subscription to *American Renaissance*[3] magazine and had a KKK hood put in his locker at the country club."

"Isabel!" Edward exclaimed, somewhere between mortification and amusement. "Do you have any sense of decency?"

"A little."

Edward sat there, contemplating what we had done and what we would be doing to Willard over the next few weeks. His amused smile turned into a slight chuckle. Then he began laughing convulsively, I think more out of relief than anything else.

3 A white supremacist magazine. Please don't look it up. Even out of curiosity.

THE LAST FOOTNOTE

Honestly, I don't think I have anything more to say. I could keep documenting my life until I find that perfect moment to end these reports. Maybe it would be a transient instant of bliss that would fool you into believing in happily ever after, but it wouldn't fool me. I have no idea what's in store for me, but there will be no walking off into the sunset. I could kill a few more decades waiting for a goddamn epiphany and then reflect back on my youth and say something so wise, you'd want to quote it back to your friends again and again, but it would take me months to come up with that wise saying and I probably wouldn't even mean it. Or I could just keep writing about my misadventures into my twilight years: "My walker is on the fritz again; even the tennis balls need replacing. My neighbor Ellie wants me to look into who is stealing her newspaper. I'm getting too old for this shit. One day, maybe, I'll retire and . . ."

Sometimes people die mid–narrative sentence. Rather than leave you with a half-baked ending thirty, forty years from now, I'm going to take my final bow. This is no easy feat, since I'm lying on a gurney.

The anesthesiologist just gave me some really awesome sedatives.

Before I go, or before I go under, there's a lot of information to disburse and I don't want to leave you hanging, so I better get started.

Edward Slayter was offered his old CEO position back, but he declined. He said he was going to try to live his life while he could still remember it. The first thing on his agenda was firing Damien, just to be safe. Then he took a road trip with Ethan, like the one they planned when they were teenagers, only they didn't drive across the country, they went to Reno and gambled and saw some shows that I decided I wouldn't ask them about. Charlie then drove Ethan and Edward to Lompoc, so Ethan could turn himself in. The brothers said good-bye and Edward promised to visit whenever he could.

Edward, no longer CEO but still the key decision-maker in his company, encouraged the board of directors to look for a CEO who was not a white male. You'd be surprised how many people fall into that category.

Evelyn Glade returned 90 percent of the money she embezzled, got probation, dumped her boyfriend, and got engaged to Arthur Bly. I'm not sure why or how he forgave her involvement with the company embezzlement, but I suspect their relationship always ran deeper than I thought. Do I think it's a perfect match? No. But I think they're both getting what they want.

Grammy is on a yearlong seniors' cruise. She corresponds by postcard and the occasional text message. All she writes is, *I'm alive. Hope UR 2.*

Princess Banana has given up her tiara. She now wears a blue mechanic's jumpsuit and wields a wrench. She talks about working at an auto repair shop. It's amazing how quickly children grow up.

Rae and Vivien set out to completely massacre the reputation of Lightning Fast Moving Company. Right now their Yelp rating average is a two, and last we checked they were filing for bankruptcy.

Vivien is on academic probation. Apparently she spent more time writing those Yelp reviews than working on her papers. Her parents have insisted that she take a short break from Spellman Investigations.

Morgan Freeman[1] has at least three films coming out this year.

Charlie Black, navigational consultant, apparently never forgot about Sweatergate. Perhaps overestimating the risk of my going under general anesthesia, he decided to absolve me of my sins. How he figured out this particular sin, I never learned.

"I forgive you for stealing my sweater," Charlie said magnanimously. "You must have really liked it."

"I *loved* it," I said.

And I meant it.

Now on to the more important stuff, before they wheel me away. I broke the news to my parents about the deal I brokered with Rae. They seemed pleased until Rae started running prospective cases by the company.

"I've got a possible client who would like us to make his girlfriend stop sneezing. And another potentially lucrative case involving a custody dispute over a boa constrictor."

"What were you thinking?" my mother asked me when we finally had a moment alone.

1 This is not only my last footnote, but also my last Morgan Freeman reference.

"I was thinking what everyone is thinking all of the time: *How can I make this last just a little bit longer?*"

Although I don't think anyone is thinking that at the opera.

As they steered my father's gurney down the hallway, I shouted, "You owe me."

"Don't I know it," he replied.

Mom looked at me all gooey-eyed and held my hand.

"Mom, relax. He's going to be fine."

"I know," Mom said. "It's you I'm worried about."

"Why?"

Mom never answered the question, but days later I understood what she couldn't say. If it didn't work, I'd blame myself. Fortunately, there was little time for melancholy with Rae still grumbling over the fact that she wasn't a match.

I didn't even feel it when they put the needle in my hand. I'm that tough.

I'm starting to get tired, so I better wrap this up.

Dr. Blank Blank asked me if I was okay. Sure, I was fine. Have you had these drugs before? There's a really good reason people try to steal them. I was fine. I think the hospital could have used better lighting and a pair of sunglasses would have been nice.

But it's not the Ritz.

I like to think I'm a good person, but I don't think I've ever claimed to be a magnanimous one. I could blame the drugs, but this next part was 100 percent me.

As I was being whisked away, I called my sister to my side.

"Good luck in there," she said.

"There's something I have to tell you," I whispered.

Rae leaned in close.

"What?" she asked.

"I win."

Afterword

We all won. Dad's alive. The doctors say he's in remission for now, but I think he's cured. They hate it when I use that word, so now I just use it in private or behind the doctors' backs.

A lot has gone down in the last six months. I'm not sure where to begin. I'll start with the easy stuff.

Dad gained ten pounds. That was really hard on Grammy.

Mom repainted the bedroom a color she calls spring. I call it one she will regret in two years. It kind of looks like the lime Jell-O Dad was always trying to offload on everyone.

Demetrius asked Loretta to marry him. She said yes, of course. Based on the size of the rock he gave her, I think he made more in his settlement than he's letting on.

Sydney can count to ten, although she skips four and seven, so no one has alerted the ten o'clock news. When Sydney learned that there was royalty more powerful than a princess, the princess phase passed. Now she wants to be queen (forget about that mechanic's-suit business you heard earlier — that was the drugs talking).

Grammy is Grammy. She will always be Grammy even when she dies and then we'll be left with the memory of Grammy, which is more of the same. Grammy. And she's not on a yearlong seniors' cruise. That was also the drugs talking.

I should tell you about Isabel, since this is mostly her story. I asked her if she had any last words and she said, "Leave me alone; I'm in the shower."

Kind of a waste of last words if you ask me, but I gave her a chance.

There's other stuff I should tell you about. Mr. Slayter's condition got worse. Isabel suggested that Charlie move in with him and everyone thought that was a great idea. Edward started tying up loose ends in his business and personal life. Then one day he gave Isabel one of those swanky corporate apartments. He said something about how if she lived like a grown-up, she might start acting like one. Has he met her? She's not allowed to sell the place for ten years, even if our company tanks. But it won't.

Henry got married. I saw the license; it's totally legal. When I heard he had a pregnant fiancée, I tried to talk some sense into him.

"Clint Eastwood has seven children from *five* different women; Jack Nicholson has three from four. No, the other way around. Sorry. I just memorized these facts in the car. Bob Marley had *eleven* children from eight different women."

"What is your point, Rae?" Henry asked.

"My point is that society no longer dictates that you settle down with your first baby mama. Wait. See what happens. You know?"

"For forty-eight years I've watched civilization unravel around me. I have no need to join in the mayhem."

Clearly my slapdash statistics did little to bolster my argument. If you're going to marry a woman, the number of children P. Diddy has sired should certainly not talk you out of it.

I saw Annie Bloom, Henry's betrothed, just once in the halls of 850 Bryant Street. She was the kind of belly-only pregnant where you could get away with congratulating her and not risk an unrecoverable insult. She had dark eyebrows and wavy brown hair, and skin the color of Demetrius's favorite overpriced coffee beverage. Henry was meeting her outside security. He kissed her on the lips and patted her belly and they looked so goddamn happy I could have puked. I left him alone after that. I don't know why, but my sister never made him that happy.

Claire, the daughter of Max the shrink, took a shine to Izzy. David says it's because they have so much in common — Goldfish snack food, *Phineas and Ferb,* and a general ambivalence toward Sydney. Claire and Isabel have had several supervised playdates, which everyone understands is code for dates with Max and Izzy. David thinks it's a perfect match. Dad thinks it's a great match, but that's just because Max has a job and no tattoos. Mom was still hoping for an attorney, but I think that's more so Izzy can save money on legal representation. Frankly, I think she might save just as much money with a shrink. So far Izzy hasn't messed up whatever she's got going on with Max. I give her another six months.

Three months ago, Edward went out for a solo morning run, ran all the way to the Golden Gate Bridge, and jumped off. Isabel didn't see it coming. She looked like she'd been kicked in the gut day after day. Edward bequeathed his house and a large chunk of his estate to Charlie, which was a blessing because the suicide rendered him useless. For at least a month, Charlie couldn't leave the house. For the first few days he didn't speak. He thought Edward had gotten lost and jumped out of despair. Instead of leaving a suicide note, Edward left a carefully constructed will that took care of everyone who was important in his life. Isabel thinks that Edward had it planned for months, but he never knew that precise moment he'd have the courage to do it. She tried explaining this to Charlie, but Charlie lost his entire life when Edward died. He was inconsolable.

Isabel moved into the big house with Charlie until Charlie's grief softened and Edward's plan came into sharp relief. Charlie's sister, Sarah Norton, and her three kids lived in Minneapolis. She had been in the middle of a nasty divorce. Isabel suggested the family come for a visit. Once the Nortons arrived, it became obvious that the family should move in with Charlie in Edward's giant house. Isabel sealed the deal by reminding Sarah that the last time it snowed in San Francisco was 1976.

All the noise and bustle in the five-bedroom home eventually shook Charlie out of his depression. Now he's almost back to his old self. Once a month he and Isabel go sweater shopping and buy the most ridiculous pullover they can find. They'll spend hours hunting for that perfect sweater, a specimen so hideous that Edward would have visibly cringed at the sight of it. *That's* how they honor his memory.

It's business as usual at Spellman Investigations. My parents wear normal clothes to work these days. Vivien still takes an occasional job and Isabel is back. She doesn't work the cases with the same drive that she used to, but I figure one day soon, another will get under her skin. Business has improved with the new branch of Spellman Investigations. Sometimes my colleagues want to hear about my cases, sometimes they politely ask me not to speak of them.

There have been more than a few occasions where we've had a weekly summit and I've been encouraged to drop a case. Like the one where the girlfriend wanted her boyfriend to wax his unibrow, even though he had flat-out refused for the last five years. My parents insisted that infringing on someone's personal being crossed not only a physical but also some kind of imaginary boundary. I understand electric fences and property lines, but when you mention theoretical frontiers, you lose me. If the fence isn't real, why can't you move it a few fake feet? Sure there's a line I won't cross. But every morning when I wake up, it's in a different spot.

This thing I'm doing is new. If I don't believe in it, how I can I expect my clients to put their trust in me? I'm a conflict resolution specialist; the challenge is to see the resolution no matter how unorthodox it is. As Oscar Wilde said, "An idea that is not dangerous is unworthy of being called an idea at all."

Today, I was approached by a potential client. She wants her dignity back.

I'm not sure if I can get it, but the least I can do is try.

Rae Spellman
2013

APPENDIX

Dossiers

Isabel Spellman

Age: 35

Occupation: Private investigator

Physical characteristics: Tall; not skinny, not fat; long brown hair; nose; lips; eyes; ears. All the usual features. Fingers, legs, that sort of thing. A few more wrinkles than last time I described myself.

History: Recovering delinquent; been working for Spellman Investigations since the age of twelve.

Bad Habits: None.

Albert Spellman

Age: 69

Occupation: Private investigator

Physical characteristics: Six foot three; large (used to be larger, but doctor put him on a diet); oafish; mis-matched features; thinning brown/gray hair; gives off the general air of a slob, but the kind that showers regularly.

History: Onetime SFPD forced into early retirement by a back injury. Went to work for another retired-cop-turned-private-investigator, Jimmy O'Malley. Met his future wife, Olivia Montgomery, while on the job. Bought the PI business from O'Malley and has kept it in the family for the last thirty-five years.

Bad habits: Has lengthy conversations with the television; snacking; can't accept defeat.

Olivia Spellman

Age: 60

Occupation: Private investigator

Physical characteristics: extremely petite, appears young for her age, quite attractive, shoulder-length auburn hair (from a bottle), well groomed.

History: Met her husband while performing an amateur surveillance on her future brother-in-law (who ended up not being her future brother-in-law). Started Spellman Investigations with her husband. Excels at pretext calls and other friendly forms of deceit.

Bad habits: Willing to break laws to meddle in children's lives; likes to record other peoples' conversations; can't accept defeat.

New David Spellman (For Old David Spellman, See Documents #1–4)

Age: 37

Occupation: Stay-at-home dad

Physical characteristics: That kind of weird good-looking-without-trying-at-all kind of thing, even dressed in stained T-shirts and ratty pajamas. Like a movie star playing a person who is not supposed to be down-and-out. You don't buy it.

History: Honor student, class valedictorian, Berkeley undergrad, Stanford law. You know the sort. Then he throws it all away to raise a child who might not amount to anything.

Bad habits: Parenting skills could use some work. Or his daughter could use some work.

Rae Spellman

Age: 22

Occupation: Part-time Spellman Investigations employee

Physical characteristics: Petite like her mother; appears a few years younger than her age; long, unkempt sandy blond hair; freckles; tends to wear sneakers so she can always make a run for it.

History: Blackmail, coercion, junk food obsession, bribery.

Bad habits: Too many to list.

Henry Stone

Age: 48

Occupation: San Francisco Police Inspector

Physical characteristics: Average height, thin, short brown hair, serious brown eyes, extremely clean-cut.

History: Was the detective on the Rae Spellman missing-person case over six years ago. Before that, I guess he went to the police academy, passed some test, married some annoying woman, and did a lot of tidying up. Was Ex-boyfriend #13 for a while, but now he's just Henry Stone.

Bad habits: Won't just go away.

Demetrius Merriweather

Age: 44

Occupation: Employee at Spellman Investigations

Physical characteristics: Tall, athletic, a few prison scars.

History: Wrongly incarcerated for murder; spent fifteen years in prison for a crime he didn't commit. Was released, moved into the Spellman household, and currently works for Spellman Investigations.

Bad habits: Must have back to wall at all times; jumpy; good at keeping secrets.

To learn more about wrongful convictions, please visit www.innocence project.org, and if you're interested in a Free Schmidt! T-shirt (mentioned in document #4), they're still available at www.free schmidt.com.

Maggie Mason

Age: 37

Occupation: Defense attorney

Physical characteristics: Tall; slender; long, unkempt brown hair.

History: Dated Henry Stone; they broke up. Rae introduced her to David, and they began dating. Then they married.

Bad habits: Keeping baked goods in pockets; camping.

Bernie Peterson

Age: Old

Occupation: Drinking, gambling, smoking cigars, being there. And bar owner now, I guess.

Physical characteristics: A giant mass of human (sorry, I try not to look too closely).

History: Was a cop in San Francisco and friends with Uncle Ray. Moved to Vegas, took up with a showgirl. Moved back to San Francisco. Took up with Henry Stone's mother. They're still together for reasons that defy all logic.

Bad habits: Imagine every bad habit you've ever recognized. Bernie probably has it.

Sydney Spellman

Age: 3.5

Occupation: Child

Physical characteristics: Extremely short, brown hair, brown eyes, the heart of a tyrant.

History: See chapter titled "Princess Banana and Her Wicked Great-Grandmother."

Bad Habits: Too many to list.

A Note on Sydney's Age: W.C. Fields once said, "Never work with animals or children." This might be why Grammy Spellman's dog is glaringly absent from this document and why Sydney has aged exactly one year faster than the rest of the characters. This might not trouble some people, but unless I wanted to repeat the Banana gag from document #5, I had to increase her vocabulary skills, and apparently two-year-olds can be really difficult, but they can't say a whole lot. Don't worry, I expect her to age from now on in real time.

"Crime and No Punishment: Misdemeanor Rates Skyrocket as Criminals Realize Prison Time Is Shorter for Nonfelonies" (2011), p. 11

This is a fake study, based on a logical premise. If there are any criminology students out there who would like to take this research on, I'd support your research any way I can, except financially. And I wouldn't want to do any actual research. But I could provide emotional support, from a distance.

Things People Say When They're Drunk

I love you, man.
Lemme tell you what your problem is.

Why didn't we ever hook up?

Is this room spinning?

High Five! Fist Bump! Hug it out!

What happened to your nose?

I really, really love you man.

Why do you hate me?

I'll have another.

I'm not drunk. I'm fine.

Oh my god, who are you? Who is this guy?

Here, take this. Seriously, take this.[1]

You have a great face.

I don't think we need to have police.

You are the best.

I can't find my phone. Do you have my phone?

Where am I?

You know why I fucking love you, man? Because you speak the truth.

I'm not gay or nothing, but *Magic Mike* was awesome.

I could eat the shit out of some chili fries right now.

That's the thing people don't get about me.

A Note on the Medical Research

I did consult an oncologist regarding Albert's diagnosis of acute myeloid leukemia and all errors deliberate and accidental are

1 This can be anything.

mine and mine alone. I believe that most of the medical protocol is close to accurate; however, I did take one major fictional detour when I had Isabel undergo a bone marrow donation because I needed her, for storyline purposes, under anesthesia. I believe that the common procedure these days for this diagnosis is a PBSC donation, which is an outpatient procedure involving drug injections and blood work, which requires no hospital stay. This means that the donation process is actually much simpler. However, that is the procedure just for this diagnosis.

There are many different ways to donate and I recommend you go to www.marrow .org (www.bethematch.com), if you're interested in learning more. It's easy to register, and for a healthy individual, it's a relatively benign process. It seems to me that a minor inconvenience and a little bit of discomfort is a small price to pay to save a life, even a stranger's. At least think about it.

ACKNOWLEDGMENTS

The book ended a page or two ago. If you had the patience to get through the appendix, bravo. But this is the acknowledgments. No need to continue reading unless you know me. Really, stop now. I think this might be a long one, because it was one long goddamn year.

I'm going to begin with my agent since this whole book-writing business began with her seven and a half years ago. Stephanie Kip Rostan, you're the best. I don't know what'd I do without you. Well, I have a few ideas and they're not pretty. The rest of the Levine Greenberg Literary Agency team is pretty awesome as well. Thank you, Melissa Rowland, Elizabeth Fisher, Monika Verma, Miek Coccia, Daniel Greenberg, Jim Levine, Lindsay Edgecombe, Tim Wojcik, and Kerry Sparks.

At Simon & Schuster: I'm going to switch things up and thank Jonathan Karp first.

Thank you for bringing my editor back. Although that was a fun six months or so when I was telling people *you* were my editor. That brings me to my editor, Marysue Rucci. You were very wise to suggest the book switcheroo,[1] but at the time I was researching mental health facilities in up-state New York. Now I realize we would be doomed if we'd stuck with the original plan. So, thank you. And thank you for your wise guidance, insight, and friendship.

I am incredibly grateful for all the other outstanding people at Simon & Schuster. As always, I am indebted to Carolyn Reidy for her unwavering support for the Spellman series. Also, thank you to Richard Rhorer, a huge thanks to Emily Graff, Wendy Sheanin, Andrea DeWerd, Tracey Guest, Jessica Zimmerman, Jackie Seow, Irene Kheradi, Gina DiMascia, Davina Mock, and everyone else who has worked on the Spellman books over the years.

A special thank you (always) to Jonathan Evans, my production editor, and Aja Pollock, my copyeditor. I'll be honest: This time around I couldn't even wrap my head around the timeline. It hurt my head so bad. And frankly, I just thought, *well, Jonathan*

1 See, this won't make sense if you're a stranger.

will fix it. It's wrong, I know, and one day you won't be there for me. But thank you. My next book is going to take place over a one-week timespan. Every chapter will be a day of the week, and I'll dedicate it to you.

As I mentioned before, this year kind of kicked the shit out of me. I couldn't have survived without Julie Ulmer, Morgan Dox, and Steve Kim. I don't think I could have survived the last twenty years without you. And Rae Dox Kim, I'm going to be borrowing your name just a bit longer. Dude, thanks for making the year more interesting and reminding me that I'm not that far from civilization.

Next up, David Hayward and his clan. Dave, thanks for years of covering up my crimes against the English language and being my joke conscience and listening to me as I sobbed repeatedly on the phone during my many nervous breakdowns this year. I would also like to thank you for lending me your nephews for my author video. I'm pleased to hear about their steady recovery and I will continue to abide the restraining order. Thank you, Alex, Charlie, and Willie Rounaghi. As always, thank you Linda and Jerry Hayward for your hospitality.

Julie Shiroishi, thank you for finding me my beautiful home and being a good friend.

And I'm going to thank you in advance for lending me at least one of your children for book promotional purposes. He'll be just fine. He's tough. I can tell.

My family: Dan Fienberg, you really saved the day (well, the year) last year. Damn, I don't know what I would have done without you. Maybe tried to eat that fish in my creek? Started living off the land? Become way more country than I've already become, which I'm starting to think already is too country. Jay and Anastasia, thank you again for your website genius, Robbie Gruber for consulting and gardening advice. Thanks, Uncle Jeff, Aunt Eve, Uncle Mark, Aunt Bev. Thanks, Kate, for the gardening labor.

And to all the people who help me survive book tours or book promotion: Diana Faust, Jaime Temairik, Jon and Ruth Jordan, and Judy Bobalik. Bill Young, I'll always smoke a cigar with you, even though I don't smoke cigars. And thank you to all the awesome booksellers who refuse to give up on a world where *Fifty Shades of Grey* can top the bestseller list for what seems like a decade.

I am grateful to the many writers I've met along the way whom I can now count as friends. This year a number of you have shown me a great deal of kindness and I will be eternally grateful. I'm not going to name names, because then it sounds like I'm name-dropping.[2]

I *know* I'm forgetting many people. Thank you _____.[3]

If you're thinking of moving this year, I've given you some valuable information about what to look for or look out for in a moving company and basically given you a thinly disguised name of a moving company you should *not* use. Please heed my advice. They really are the new mob.

Finally, I'd like to thank my readers for staying with me all these years. I especially want to thank the ones who understand that the world isn't made up of happy endings, but messy, complicated, and untidy ones.

2 It's already common knowledge that I have a standing poker game with Lee Child every Thursday.

3 Please write your name here.